SILENT

AUCTION

OTHER JOSIE PRESCOTT ANTIQUES MYSTERIES BY JANE K. CLELAND

Killer Keepsakes

Antiques to Die For

Deadly Appraisal

Consigned to Death

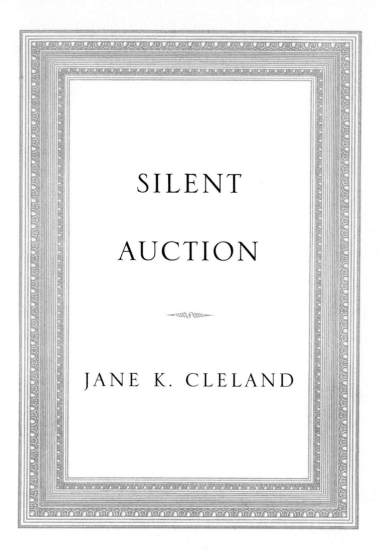

SILENT

AUCTION

JANE K. CLELAND

MINOTAUR BOOKS

NEW YORK

SILENT AUCTION. Copyright © 2010 by Jane K. Cleland. All rights reserved. Printed in the United States of America. For information, address St. Martin's Press, 175 Fifth Avenue, New York, N.Y. 10010.

www.minotaurbooks.com

Library of Congress Cataloging-in-Publication Data

Cleland, Jane K.
    Silent auction / Jane K. Cleland.—1st ed.
        p. cm.
    ISBN 978-0-312-58655-3
    1. Prescott, Josie (Fictitious character)—Fiction.   2. Antique dealers—Fiction.
3. Antiques—Expertising—Fiction.   4. Murder—Investigation—Fiction.
5. New Hampshire—Fiction.   I. Title.
    PS3603.L4555s56 2010
    813'.6—dc22

                                                                2009041518

First Edition: April 2010

10 9 8 7 6 5 4 3 2 1

This is for my mother, Ruth Chessman.
And, of course, for Joe.

AUTHOR'S NOTE

This is a work of fiction. While there is a Seacoast Region in New Hampshire, there is no town called Rocky Point, and many other geographic liberties have been taken.

SILENT

AUCTION

CHAPTER ONE

I growled into the mirror. Sadly, I didn't look the least bit ferocious.

Glancing back and forth from my face to a photo of a Bengal tiger I'd printed out, I saw the problem—my coloration was off. I needed to darken the stripes, make the base more orange, and add a starker line of white around my eyes. I nodded, pleased that, if nothing else, I knew what needed to be done.

I'd volunteered to include a face-painting activity in my company's booth at next month's Rocky Point Harvest Festival, and I was practicing. When persuading me to agree, the festival's organizers had assured me that enthusiasm mattered more than skill, but looking at my jaundiced face, I wasn't so sure they were right.

Before I could begin the repair job, Cara, my company's receptionist, IM'd that Guy Whitestone's assistant was on the phone, wanting to schedule a time for her boss to talk to me about appraising his maritime art and artifacts collection.

"Great!" I typed, grinning at the thought. "Soon?"

Seconds later, her reply appeared: "10:15."

According to the display on my computer, it was just before ten. I shook my head. I'd been fussing with my face for twenty minutes, too long if we had a queue of kids waiting their turn. I needed to get the time down—by a lot. I sighed and picked up a paintbrush.

Seconds later, a *rat-a-tat* sounded. Eric, my back room supervisor, stood on the threshold, frowning and waiting for an invitation to enter my office.

Eric was tall and twig-thin, with sandy-colored hair that straggled over his collar. He was only twenty-three, but he held an important managerial position at my company, Prescott's Antiques and Auctions. He'd been one of my first hires—he'd started as a part-time general helper back when he was in high school. Now he was charged with everything from merchandising to facilities management. He took his responsibilities seriously, sometimes too seriously, allowing his insecurity and inexperience to undermine his confidence.

"Come on in," I said.

"We have a problem," he said, walking toward me. "The gutters are pretty full, and the weatherman says it's going to rain on Thursday. I budgeted having the gutters cleaned in October, but I don't think we should wait. Is it okay if I call Frankie and ask him to come over today or tomorrow, before the rain?"

I was thrilled to see him showing initiative, and said so. "Absolutely. This is really smart thinking, Eric—and a good example of what I was talking about when I said a budget was a guide, not a straitjacket."

He thanked me, his discomfort and pleasure at receiving a compliment evident as his cheeks turned bright red and he looked down, shoulders hunched forward.

"What do you think of my face?" I asked, showing teeth and pawing the air.

"Good," he replied, obviously glad for the change of subject. "You look really funny."

"Funny? I'm supposed to look fierce."

I snarled at him, then did it again into the mirror. I didn't look fierce; I looked silly.

"You're supposed to be a tiger, right?"

"I guess it's good news that at least you got the animal right."

He grinned, nodded, and left, and I got busy with the orange paint. When I was done, I growled again. *Much better,* I thought, realizing how much I'd needed the photo as a reference. I decided that we'd bring a laptop and printer to the festival so we could print out images to refer to as we painted. I was adding a final dab of dark brown to a stripe when Cara buzzed up to tell me that Guy was on line one.

Half an hour later, I hurried down the spiral stairs that led from my private office on the mezzanine level to the main office on the ground floor to share the good news—we'd been hired for a plum appraisal job.

I crossed the cavernous warehouse and entered the front office, leaping in as if I were pouncing from behind a rock or bush. "Grrrr!" I roared.

Sasha, my chief appraiser, laughed, then stopped and looked away, tucking her fine brown hair behind her ear, embarrassed. Sasha was shy and self-effacing except when talking about art or antiques—then she became an assertive intellectual powerhouse.

"Oh, Josie, you look great!" Gretchen said. Gretchen, my newly promoted administrative manager, had just turned thirty. She was radiant, with titian hair that fell in soft waves to below her shoulders and eyes that sparkled like emeralds.

My other appraiser, Fred, leaned back with his hallmark ultracool suavity. He pushed up his small, square-framed glasses, then made a V-for-Victory sign with his fingers. "Go, Tigers!" he said.

I laughed and flashed a return V.

Cara, grandmotherly in appearance and demeanor, with silvery hair cut short and a complexion my mother would have called peaches and cream, smiled. "The children are going to love it!"

"Thanks," I said. "I hope you're right. All I can say is that it's way harder painting on a three-dimensional surface like a face than I thought it would be. Anyway, I have good news. We've been hired to do a really interesting appraisal."

I filled them in, explaining that because Guy wanted us to begin right away, I needed an update on everyone's schedule during the next several days. Sasha reported she was deep in analyzing whether a collection of Chinese dinnerware that had once been owned by a Revolutionary War hero, General James McCubbin Lingan, would benefit from that association. Fred said he was looking at some nice, but unsigned, botanical prints. Gretchen was scheduled to meet with our database management company about a possible upgrade, and Cara was helping Eric create inventory reports. A busy day, a typical day, at Prescott's.

Frankie Winterelli, the Whitestones' live-in caretaker and our part-time helper, stepped into the front office, setting the wind chimes Gretchen had hung there years earlier jangling. Frankie was short, maybe five-six or so, and wiry, with curly black hair and an olive complexion. His eyes were almost black, and he sported a diamond stud in his left ear.

"Don't come near me," he said to me, feigning fear, raising his hands, palms out, as if he were warding off an attack. "I'm afraid."

"I take that as a compliment," I said, smiling, "to my face-painting skills."

"You should. I've never seen a better leopard."

"I'm not a leopard!" I protested.

His eyes crinkled, and he smiled like he'd just won the jackpot at bingo. "Gotcha good that time! I know you're a lion!"

I grinned.

"You're right, Frankie," Fred said, his tone earnest. "I didn't see it at first, but it's definitely lionlike. Good call."

"I think she looks more like an ocelot," Gretchen said, giggling.

"An ocelot?" I replied, faux-shocked. "I'm only five-one—don't you mean an oce-little?"

Everyone started laughing, me included.

"I'm surprised you don't know the correct term, Josie," Cara said, joining in. "It's oce-petite!"

"Are you sure it's not just oce-short?" Fred asked.

"Or oce-small?" Sasha suggested, still laughing.

"At least you're not calling me an oce-runt," I said, sending everyone off into fresh gales of hilarity.

As our laughter quieted, Frankie said, "Good-looking tiger, Josie."

"Thanks. I was just getting set to call you," I said.

"About the appraisal? I just heard. Mr. Whitestone wants me to show you the alarm system and give you a key. I was on my way over here anyway—Eric called about the gutters—so I thought I'd stop in the office and coordinate directly with you. I don't have a spare key with me, but I can meet you there later, whenever you want."

"Great." I paused, thinking about my schedule. Today, the Tuesday after Labor Day, was, for me, a light day—I didn't have any appointments scheduled. "How's three o'clock?"

He nodded. "Works for me. Meet me at my place, okay? I've got some gardening things to do out back." He waved a general goodbye and headed out, striding toward the rear of the building to hook up with Eric.

When I'd first met Frankie two years ago, he'd acted like a real punk, filled with anger and resentment. Now he was cheerful and confident, a testimony to the truth of the old adage that success breeds success. Once Frankie got himself started on the right track, there'd been no stopping him.

Frankie's aunt Zoë—my friend, neighbor, and landlady—had never, not for a minute, doubted his inner goodness, and she'd been right. I'd been the skeptic, and I was thrilled to have been proven wrong. From his epic work ethic to his whispered inquiry at Zoë's barbecue this past weekend about whether he could bring the cake to the birthday dinner I was planning for her later in the month, Frankie was a poster boy for second chances, and it made me proud to know him.

Something was wrong. I could smell it. I dug my phone out of my tote bag to check the time. It was ten past three—Frankie was ten minutes late, which sounds like nothing, but not with Frankie. He was 100 percent reliable. Last spring, he'd been scheduled to help Eric with some plantings when his tire blew out on the interstate and he'd ended up in a ditch. He'd called us before he'd called for a tow. If he'd known he was going to be late, I would have heard by now.

I circled his cottage, looking for signs that he'd been working outside. Rhododendron, forsythia, and mountain laurel marked the property's edge. Near the back door, a charcoal grill and two white plastic lawn chairs sat on a small flagstone patio. Everything was still. I saw nothing that indicated that Frankie had been working in the area—no freshly laid mulch, no bags of leaves waiting for disposal, no debris from pruning or trimming plants.

I wondered if our wires had crossed. Maybe he thought we were supposed to meet at the lighthouse. *No.* I shook my head. We'd been clear—I was to come to his cottage at three. I frowned. This wasn't a casual meeting. This was his job.

"Frankie," I said softly, speaking to the cottage, "where are you? Are you okay?"

Back at the front, I pushed the doorbell again, and again chimes sounded. After a few seconds, I used the ship-shaped brass knocker, clapping it several times, waited fifteen seconds, then pressed the doorbell one more time. The chimes echoed, then faded away.

Frankie lived in one of two identical fieldstone cottages on the Whitestones' property. Their housekeeper, Ashley Morse, lived in the other unit. One cottage was original to the property, but the Whitestones had built a duplicate when they'd decided they needed both a live-in housekeeper and a live-in caretaker. Both had Colonial blue trim on the doors, window frames, and shutters. Each had a chimney to the right of the center entrance and an attached garage to the left. Even though one dated from the early nineteenth century and the other was new, they were, to me, indistinguishable; both appeared equally well-tended and charming.

As a crow flies, the two cottages were only a few hundred yards from Rocky Point Light—the decommissioned 1817 lighthouse the Whitestones had purchased as a weekend retreat a year earlier—but thick stands of evergreens, maples, oaks, pine, and birch made them seem a world apart. In the time they'd owned it, they'd refurbished it inside and out, maintaining its historically accurate appearance down to the unusual widow's walk at the top—except for the walls of windows that replaced the wood—while adding every imaginable modern convenience and luxury. From where I stood, I couldn't see the lighthouse at all. Looking in the other direction, I caught a glimpse of the heliport the Whitestones had added during their two-million-dollar renovation.

I knocked and rang again. Still no answer.

All around me, towering hardwoods grew in uncultivated abandon. Deep in the woods I saw dots of neon-bright yellow and coral pink that shone as if they were backlit. In two weeks, maybe three, the canopy of leaves would resemble a quilt of fire.

I approached the window to the right of Frankie's front door and cupped my hands to see in. Nothing. I looked inside through three other windows as I walked around the cottage again. I could see into the kitchen, bathroom, and bedroom. Frankie wasn't home. His car wasn't in the garage. My amorphous uneasiness grew stronger. I checked the time again. Ten more minutes had passed.

I drove up the paved road that led to the lighthouse. Frankie's Jeep was parked at one end of the circular drive. I walked around it, peeking in windows. Nothing inside offered any hint to his whereabouts.

The lighthouse was situated at the far end of the island, and from its position on a rocky jut-out a hundred feet above the water, it offered an unobstructed 180-degree view of blue-black ocean that stretched endlessly to the horizon. I walked across the groomed lawn, past the pool, and stepped over a row of flower-filled ancient Chinese troughs that I'd sold to the Whitestones last June. They stretched across the lawn, dividing it into two sections, the close-in patio area and the outer grassy area. As I stood at the water's edge, a soft breeze teased me. I bet it was close to seventy, a halcyon day. Looking south, I could see most of New Hampshire's eighteen-mile shoreline. From somewhere close by, I heard a bird calling, *whoop, whoop, whoop.*

"Frankie!" I shouted toward the manicured property. "Frankie!" I called again, facing the lighthouse this time. "Frankie!"

No response.

Walking along the side, I passed the tall grasses, lavender, and rambling roses that had been artfully planted along the brick pathway to create a naturalized border, then a line of red maples, their leaves crimson, the color of blood.

The front door was painted glossy red. The doorbell was fitted with old ship's bells, and when I pushed the button, they clanged and reverberated for several seconds. No one answered the door. I looked through the tall windows that flanked the door. Nothing appeared disturbed, but the place felt empty. I checked the time again. It was three thirty-five.

I called Frankie's cell phone. Voice mail picked up after six rings. "Hi, Frankie," I said. "It's Josie. I went to your place, and now I'm at the lighthouse. I see your Jeep is here—I'm a little concerned. Are you all right? Call me, okay?"

I walked to the back again. Standing close to the precipice, I looked down and watched as thunderous waves crashed into the boulders a hundred feet below. There was no stairway to the shore because there was no beach or dock. I turned around. To my right was a swimming pool and spa under a latticework pergola laced with ancient wisteria vines. In May, clusters of purplish blue flowers would hang heavily over the water. A small cabana sat near the tree line. To the left was a fire pit. Great blue lobelias and wild bergamots sat in huge terra-cotta pots by the rear entrance. All the shades were up. A window was open on the ground floor to the left of the back door. *Ashley must be airing the place out,* I thought, *now that the Whitestones have returned to New York City.* There was no sign of Frankie.

I approached the back door and knocked. The latch hadn't quite caught, and the door swung wide. I stepped into the mudroom. In front of me, the inner door was ajar. Little hairs on the back of my neck rose as disquiet grew into fear.

"Frankie?" I called, expecting no reply and getting none. My voice cracked as alarm closed my throat. I stood for a moment taking deep breaths. "Frankie?" I repeated, and I was pleased to hear that despite the sharp barbs of anxiety that stabbed at me, I sounded calm and in control.

I took a small step forward and entered the kitchen. I was standing on ceramic tiles the Whitestones had imported from Italy. It was cold, too cold, much colder than outside. It was quiet, too, the thick solitary sound of emptiness. I took another step, then stopped short.

There, sprawled on the floor, partially hidden by the central island, lay a body.

My heart stopped, then began beating too fast. My mouth went dry. One blue-jean-clad leg was bent, the other straight. Whoever it was wore dirty and scuffed work boots. Streaks of sunlight crisscrossed pools of blood that had streamed like rivulets toward the cabinets. A wooden rolling pin streaked with mahogany-colored stains and a white dish towel smeared with dark red lay near the body's thighs.

I wanted to run away, but I couldn't. I needed to see if the person was alive, to see if I could do something to help, CPR maybe, or by applying pressure to a wound to stop the bleeding. I stepped forward and saw a hand, its fingers curled like talons, clutching something pale and wispy. The skin was flour white. I squatted and touched a finger—it was cold. I stood, took another deep breath, and forced myself to walk around the island and view the face, knowing before I looked what I would see.

Frankie.

"Oh, God," I whispered.

His eyes were open and staring at the ceiling.

I couldn't move. I could barely breathe. My first thought was that just this morning Frankie had stood in my office, joking, and now he was dead, and from the ghastly dent in his skull, I could tell that he'd been murdered. My second thought was for Zoë. She'd be shattered, just crushed. As far as I knew, besides her kids, Frankie was her only family.

The soft hum of a car engine broke the silence. A vehicle was approaching. The sound grew louder, then stopped. *The killer,* I thought. My eyes lit on the rolling pin and towel. *He's come back to clean up.* I'd read that killers were often drawn to the scenes of their crimes. I heard a car door slam; then, seconds later, the ship's bells sounded. Still I couldn't move. Someone jiggled the front doorknob, and as if the sound released me from a trance, I flew across the room and fled.

CHAPTER TWO

I sprinted across the clearing. As I approached the Chinese troughs, I lengthened my stride; I cleared them by two feet, landing hard, jarring my right ankle. I scrambled up and kept running until the cliff's edge loomed in front of me, then braked and whipped around to face the lighthouse. I leaned over, pressing my hands into my thighs to catch my breath, while trying to look everywhere at once.

Stop. Think. Breathe. Stop. Think. Breathe. Stop. Think. Breathe. Repeating my father's advice on how to maintain my cool during a crisis worked now as it always had in the past, and I felt myself regain my equilibrium. *Stop. Think. Breathe.*

I had to get out of the open. I had to assume that if I was seen, I'd be killed, and I couldn't depend on my ears to warn me of an approach—I couldn't hear anything but the booming ocean waves far below. I didn't know where to go. The cabana by the trees could be a sanctuary—or, since there was only one door, it could be a trap. Then I saw the answer. A boxwood hedge fronted the woods to the left. It would conceal me, but it wouldn't pen me in. I ran for it.

Reaching the protection of the hedge, I sank to the ground and forced myself to be still, to breathe evenly. After several seconds, I pried apart the dense growth, trying to see through to the other side. Twigs and prickly bits poked at me, nicking my fingers and cheek. I didn't care—I was out of sight but able to see the rear of the lighthouse and part of the front drive. For the moment, I was safe. Keeping my eyes on the clearing, I rooted through my tote bag for my phone, and when I found it, I dialed 911.

I gave the operator my name and described the nature of the

emergency. She told me she was notifying the police, then began asking me questions I couldn't answer. I didn't know if the killer was still in the lighthouse. I didn't know if there were additional victims. I didn't know who'd driven up. I didn't know anything beyond what I'd told her.

For six minutes that seemed like six hours, I sat on dirt and fallen leaves. I was cocooned by a mantle of sound as the unrelenting waves thrashed the barnacle-covered rocks. I clutched the phone to my chest, stricken and disbelieving. Gulls swooped over and around me, spiking into the water, then soaring up and away. *How could Frankie be dead?* I kept asking myself.

Frankie was more than just another part-timer to me, more than Zoë's nephew. When he'd first arrived in New Hampshire, just out of jail, with a chip on his shoulder the size of Montana, Ty Alverez, my boyfriend, and I had helped him, and I'd been proud of his success.

From far away, I heard a buzz. Within seconds, I recognized it as a siren. Peeking through my eyehole, I watched a black Rocky Point police SUV pull up, its lights flashing. The siren stopped abruptly, and without giving myself time to think, I ran like a deer toward the front. Two men stood on the circular drive. I recognized one of them—Officer Griffin.

"Griff," I shouted.

"You okay?" he asked, jogging to meet me.

I nodded, breathing hard from the run and the relief. "I'm sure glad to see you," I said.

The other man was a stranger. He was tall and broad and older than me by a decade or so, in his midforties, I guessed. His hair was dark brown and cut short. His nose was crooked, as if it had been broken a long time ago and never properly realigned. He had a small jagged scar near his right eye. He wore a brown wool blazer, a blue shirt, a blue and brown striped tie, and khakis. He looked like a nice guy.

"I'm Chief Ellis Hunter. Rocky Point police," he said as he approached. He flipped open a leather case to display his badge and ID card.

Until a couple of years ago, my boyfriend, Ty, had been the police chief. Now he was a Homeland Security regional director, and evidently the town had finally hired his replacement. "I didn't know they'd hired a new chief."

"Today's my first day. And you are?" he asked.

"Oh, sorry. Josie Prescott. I called in the emergency."

"Where's the corpse?" he asked.

"Inside. In the kitchen. The back door's open."

"You said you heard a car drive up. One of these?" he asked, looking from my sedan to Frankie's Jeep.

I shook my head. "No. That's Frankie's—the victim's," I said, pointing. I paused to take in a deep breath. "This one's mine. I didn't see the car that drove up; I just heard it. I was in the back, in the kitchen."

"Was there anything unusual about it? Did it sound like a truck, maybe making a delivery?"

I shrugged helplessly. "It was just an ordinary engine sound, followed by a door slamming. Then the bell rang and someone tried the doorknob. That's when I ran out the back."

"Did you see or hear the car leave?"

"No . . . but I doubt I would have—I was behind a hedge close to the ocean within a minute or so. From back there, the lighthouse blocked most of the driveway, and all I heard was waves crashing."

"No one came around back?"

"Not that I saw, and I think I would have."

He nodded. "Okay . . . I'll just be a sec."

He turned his back and took a couple of steps away from me to make a phone call. *It's too late to set up a roadblock,* I thought. From the lighthouse to the mainland took no longer than five minutes flat. He flipped his phone closed, told me to wait where I was, signaled Griff to follow him, and set off at a trot.

I leaned against my car and closed my eyes. A slide show of gruesome images played in my mind's eye, each picture more disturbing and bloodier than the last, a repeating loop of horror. There'd been so much blood. I opened my eyes, and still the images came flooding back. I hugged myself and rubbed my arms for comfort.

Chief Hunter appeared from the far side of the lighthouse, a notebook in hand.

"I know you've had a shock," he said as he walked toward me, "but I'm hoping you can answer some questions. The quicker I can get information, the better. I gather you knew the victim?"

"Yes. His name is Frankie Winterelli."

He wrote the name in his notebook. "How do you know him?"

"His aunt Zoë is my friend. He works for my company sometimes. He's the caretaker here."

"When did you see him last?"

"Today."

"Tell me about it."

Standing in the dappled sunlight filtering through the trees, my hands deep in my pockets, I closed my eyes for a moment. I repeated Frankie's jests about my tiger face, my arrangement to meet him at his cottage, and my hunt for him that culminated in discovering his body.

He nodded. "Can you give me a quick character sketch about him? What's his background? What's he like? Is he married?"

"Frankie's great—he *was* great. He was friendly and funny. He's single."

"And his background?"

I looked out over the endless ocean. I didn't want to tell.

"I'll find out soon enough," Chief Hunter said. "You can help speed the investigation along by telling me now."

I nodded. "Frankie served time in prison."

"For what?"

"Drugs, mostly," I said.

"More than once?"

"Maybe half a dozen times all told. He was a stupid kid—I think he was twelve the first time. I'm telling you, though, he'd really straightened himself out."

Chief Hunter kept his eyes on my face. "Any arrests for something besides drugs?"

I hated telling tales out of school, and this one was especially shocking. "Yeah. It's bad." I looked away, out over the ocean, then back. Chief Hunter's eyes were fixed on mine, but I sensed no impatience or condemnation. He just wanted to know the truth. "Frankie mugged an eighty-year-old woman walking with a cane, can you believe it? He ripped her purse from her hand and flung her aside like she weighed nothing. She broke her leg. He served eighteen months of what I think was a three-year sentence, and still has—had—about six months left on his parole." I shrugged. "When Zoë told me she'd agreed to let him move in—this was about two years ago—I was worried. She has two young kids, and he had a violent past. But Zoë said she had to let him in—he was family and he had nowhere else to go."

"It worked out all right?"

"At first, Frankie was surly as all get-out, but he got over it."

"How?" he asked.

I shrugged again. "I don't know. I mean, I'm no expert. I guess he was ready to change. For sure, Zoë never gave up on him. My boyfriend, Ty Alverez—he used to have your job, by the way—he helped him in a man-to-man sort of way. I deal in antiques, and I gave him a job. He helped us with outdoor work. That was all I could offer, since with his record, he couldn't hope to pass my insurance company's background check, and no one is allowed past the warehouse door who hasn't. From that he got a position with Jackson's Landscaping. He worked there for over a year until he got this job."

"Any bumps in the road?"

"No. We were all pretty surprised, to tell you the truth, but Frankie was a model employee from the start. He never missed a day's work for me, not one, and I think he had the same great record with Jackson's. He was diligent. He showed initiative in suggesting shortcuts, like blowing fallen leaves aside rather than sweeping them from the parking lot, which is what we had been doing."

Chief Hunter nodded and surveyed the grounds. "How did he land this job, do you know?"

"He got it on my recommendation. When the Whitestones mentioned they were looking for a live-in caretaker, I suggested him. It was a perfect fit. Frankie got to do work he liked and was good at; he had his own cottage on the property, loads of scheduling flexibility, including the ability to help us out, a good salary and benefits, and most of the time, he was his own boss." I gestured, palms up. "I'm not exaggerating if I tell you he was in heaven. He loved his work. He was really happy."

"So you don't think he was back doing drugs."

"No way. Part of his deal with the Whitestones included random drug testing."

"What can you tell me about them? All I know is what I've seen in the papers."

I wondered which ones he read. It could be anything from a daily newspaper or monthly business magazine to a tabloid gossip sheet. Guy Whitestone, the legendary New York City financier, and his wife, Maddie, the European beauty, were media favorites. While Guy's Midas touch was fodder for business sections in major newspapers and serious finance journals, Maddie's style and charitable good works received nearly constant coverage from lifestyle publications worldwide.

"I met them when they attended one of my company's auctions last June," I explained. "They're clients—and they're really super people. They were the successful bidders for a scrimshaw tooth showing the ship *Susan*. It had been carved by a famous nineteenth-century scrimshander named Frederick Myrick. They also bought an anonymously crafted nineteenth-century boat-in-a-bottle."

"Scrimshaw . . . ivory, right?"

"Usually. Scrimshaw refers to objects with designs etched onto ivory or bone, then stained with dark coloration. The antiques were mostly scrimmed by sailors at sea."

"Valuable?"

I shrugged. "Everything is relative, right?"

"Give me context," he said.

"The Whitestones paid $82,500 for the tooth and $4,800 for the boat-in-a-bottle."

Chief Hunter's eyes opened wide. "That qualifies as valuable," he said, jotting something in his notebook. He looked up at me, and I could almost see the wheels turning. "If they're both nineteenth century, why the price variance?"

"The scrimshaw came with a meticulously researched provenance. The boat, while an excellent example of American folk art, did not."

He nodded. "Gotcha. So Mr. Whitestone called today and asked you to appraise his collection?"

"Yes."

"Why?"

"Two reasons. He wanted to learn whether the objects he and

Maddie had bought on their own were good buys or not, and he wanted to update his insurance coverage."

He glanced at his watch. "A detective will be here soon. Then you and I can go to the station."

"The station?" I asked. "How come?"

"Just routine," he said.

His response sent a shiver down my spine. Maybe it was routine to him, but even though I'd been interviewed about murders in the past, it wasn't routine to me. I didn't want to go.

"I want to go to Zoë's, to tell her what happened," I said. "I know her—she's going to be beside herself."

Chief Hunter nodded. "We're checking with his employer now about his next of kin. Is she it?"

"Yes. I mean, I don't know, but I think so."

"Is her last name Winterelli, too?"

"Yes. Zoë's divorced. Winterelli is her maiden name. Frankie is—*was*"—I corrected myself again, swallowing hard—"her sister's son." I took a breath. "Her sister and brother-in-law, Frankie's parents, died in a car crash about ten years ago, a drunk driver. After the accident, Frankie moved in with his grandmother, Zoë's mom. She had a heart attack and died while Frankie was in prison. That was when he was nineteen or twenty." I paused again. "Can I be the one to tell Zoë? Or at least, can I be there when you tell her?"

"Yes," he said.

"Thank you. I can come to the station later."

"We'll figure it out," he said, which didn't reassure me at all.

A patrol car drove up. A young police officer I didn't know sat behind the wheel. Detective Claire Brownley was in the passenger seat. She was about my age and striking. She was also smart and methodical and nobody's fool. Her skin was creamy white and her eyes were sapphire blue. She had a new hairdo since the last time I'd seen her, about a year earlier. Her luxurious black locks had been cropped short. It suited her.

I stood by my car, watching as Chief Hunter spoke to her, gesturing first toward the lighthouse, then to me, then listening to her for a minute. Detective Brownley mouthed hello to me as she walked by heading toward the rear, and I nodded back.

"Detective Brownley will take charge of the crime scene," Chief Hunter told me. "I need to look at Mr. Winterelli's house for a minute and talk to anyone else who might have been on-site. Does anyone else live on the property?"

"Ashley Morse, the housekeeper. She lives in the cottage next to Frankie."

"Anyone else?"

"No."

"I'll ask you to show me the way. We can pick up your car as we're leaving."

"Okay," I agreed, and we climbed into the SUV. "The road's just past that big tree over there," I said, pointing. He started the engine and headed in that direction.

The wind had picked up, and the ocean was dotted with whitecaps. A large brown bird with a white belly glided across the water and up over the clearing, disappearing on the far side of the forest. A squirrel darted into the woods and scampered up a tree.

"Was he killed with the rolling pin?" I asked.

"The medical examiner will ascertain the cause of death," he replied, sharing nothing.

I directed him down the side road that led to the two cottages, and he stopped in front of Frankie's. He left me in the car and approached the front door. He rang the bell, then knocked, then tried the door. He stepped to the right and peered into the window, the same one I'd looked through earlier, then circled the house. When he reappeared, he was on his cell phone. He stood with his back to me and finished his call. I shivered. The temperature had dropped. I looked up. Clouds were thickening as I watched, and I wondered if we were in for a storm.

"I saw another house through the trees," he said as he climbed back into his vehicle. "Is that Ms. Morse's?"

"Yes."

We drove the short distance. Gray-white smoke poured from Ashley's chimney. Lights were on in the front room. She answered the door wearing a long white smock smeared with brown and black stains—her scrimshander's uniform. Ashley worked as the Whitestones' housekeeper to pay her bills, but her passion was designing and producing scrimshaw objects. I lowered my window, thinking that I might be able to hear what they said.

"What?" Ashley asked, the word floating on the breeze.

Chief Hunter said something I couldn't hear.

Ashley looked as if she didn't think she could have heard him right. She was older than me by at least a few years, and she was plain and tall, maybe five-eight or -nine, with a stocky build, limp blond hair, and washed-out blue eyes.

"I can't," she said. "Not right now."

Chief Hunter stepped forward, an aggressive move. Ashley backed up.

The wind swung to the north and whistled through the open window, and suddenly I could hear both sides of their conversation.

"I can't leave my materials out," she said.

"I'll wait while you secure them."

The wind shifted again, and their voices evanesced. Ashley mouthed words and gestured over her shoulder. It was as if she were a mime. Chief Hunter took another step forward.

It began to rain. *So much for the weather forecast of no rain until Thursday,* I thought.

The sun was still visible to the west, but looking east, the sky was battleship gray. I raised the window halfway. Chief Hunter flipped up his jacket's collar. The rain slanted in, pelting me, and I closed the window. Ashley backed out of sight. Chief Hunter followed her in and shut the door. Five minutes later, Ashley reappeared wearing a yellow rain slicker with matching boots. She stomped down the pathway, her irritation evident in her gait. She stopped for a second when she spotted me, then continued on. Chief Hunter opened the SUV's rear door, and she climbed in.

"Thank you both," he said as he started the engine. "We appreciate your cooperation."

"I'm glad to help," I said, staring through the water-streaked windshield into the distant woods.

Ashley didn't reply. "I didn't know you were here," she said to me. "Were you at the lighthouse?"

"Yes, to start an appraisal."

"Oh, right, right. Mr. Whitestone called to tell me you'd be in and out."

When we passed Frankie's cottage, I saw the uniformed officer who'd driven Detective Brownley to the lighthouse standing on the front stoop. His cap offered little protection against the rain. He looked miserable.

Chief Hunter came to a stop and lowered his window. "We'll get a car down here for you," he called.

"Thank you, sir," the young officer said, shouting to be heard in the rain.

Back up at the lighthouse, Griff was standing by Frankie's Jeep watching as a tow truck operator attached his hook.

I transferred to my car, Ashley took my place in the SUV's passenger seat, and we set off for the Rocky Point police station, a necessary first stop, Chief Hunter told me, before proceeding to Zoë's. We passed a patrol car idling at the gated entryway, then another at the mouth of Lighthouse Lane. Chief Hunter told the second patrol to join the young man guarding Frankie's cottage.

Once we crossed over onto the mainland, I found myself driving on autopilot. The rain continued unabated. The storm clouds were spreading; the sky to the west was now mottled gray.

Maybe Frankie surprised a thief, I thought, then shook my head. *No way.* It had to be someone he knew. I'd seen no sign of forced entry, and a burglar would never wander up to the lighthouse casually or find himself there by accident; it was too isolated. Except . . . maybe, given that it was general knowledge that the Whitestones only came up for weekends, a robber might have known—or thought—that he'd have clear access. I wondered if anything was missing.

Having killed someone, would the thief stay to ransack the place? Probably not. Then again, if he'd packed up some objects—or everything, for that matter—before Frankie had interrupted him, I might be able to help the police track him down. I nodded. *If* anything was stolen, and *if* we could locate it, we'd catch more than a thief. We'd catch a killer.

CHAPTER THREE

I slipped my earpiece in and called Ty. It was four thirty-five. He was in an all-day planning session in Boston, one he expected would run until six, or even later. Most likely, he wouldn't be available, and he wasn't. His cell phone went directly to voice mail.

"Ty," I said, "I have bad news. It's Frankie. Oh, Ty . . . he's dead. He was murdered. I was there to start an appraisal and . . . oh, God, Ty . . . I found the body—" I choked, then continued. "I'm going to the police station now. Did you know they'd finally hired someone to replace you? Ellis Hunter. Anyway, I'm just so upset . . . I wanted to talk to you. I'll keep you posted."

Two seconds later, my phone rang, and I flinched, startled. I answered it without looking at the display, assuming—hoping—it was Ty calling me back. It wasn't. It was Wes Smith, a reporter for the local newspaper, the *Seacoast Star*.

"Josie," Wes said, jumping in. "I picked up the news on my police scanner. Didn't you get my message?"

"No," I said. "I haven't checked messages."

"A murder in a lighthouse—great imagery! Fill me in."

I didn't take his crassness personally. Wes would always rather hear bad news than good. It wasn't that he was sordid or malevolent; it was that bad news sold newspapers.

"It's awful," I said.

"Yeah. So what do you know?"

"Nothing."

"You must know something. You called it in. Were you there when he was killed?"

"No," I replied. "I'm upset, though. It was a bad scene, Wes—very bloody—and Frankie was a good guy."

"Not from his record."

"Old news."

"Come on, Josie. Do you really think he changed? You know the stats. Recidivism is the norm, not the exception."

"Not in his case!" I protested, stung. "He was doing well, Wes. Really. He'd turned his life around."

"How do you know he didn't go back to drugs?"

"He got tested all the time. It was part of his employment agreement," I replied, realizing that as usual, Wes was drawing more information out of me than I wanted to give. He was one heck of a good reporter.

I was tempted to hang up but didn't. I knew myself—between Zoë's certain need to know what happened to her nephew and my innate curiosity, I didn't want to prematurely shut a door to information that I might later wish were open. Talking to Wes now would create credit for questions I might have later. Our arrangement was fair, but risking the glare of public exposure always made the muscles in my shoulders and neck throb with tension.

"We're off the record, right, Wes?" I asked, having learned the hard way to confirm our terms before I spoke and not to assume anything.

"Josie, the details about his murder are public info—or they will be soon," he said patiently, as if he were justifying an unwanted rule to a recalcitrant child.

"His arrangements with his employer aren't part of the public record. You know our deal, Wes. You can't quote me, not ever, about anything, unless I explicitly say you can."

He sighed, Wesian for begrudging acceptance. "Okay, okay. Off the record. Shoot. What do you know?"

"Frankie had to get weekly drug tests, plus unannounced, random ones. He passed with no problem."

"When was his last one?"

"I don't know."

"What about drinking? Maybe he boozed it up with the wrong guy."

I shook my head. "Not Frankie. He wouldn't even have a beer."

"So he goes on a bender. It's been known to happen."

"No way, Wes. A couple of hours before he died he was at Prescott's, and he was stone-cold sober."

"So maybe he got started right after you saw him. A drunk can down a lot of booze in a couple of hours."

My heart leapt into my throat. Wes was right—of course it was possible. "I don't believe it."

"I guess they'll find out during the autopsy," Wes said. "So . . . give me some background. How long has he been working at the lighthouse?"

"Since July. Ever since construction was done and the Whitestones starting coming up for weekends."

"You know them, too, right?"

"Yes. I've sold them some antiques and helped them buy others."

"What are they like? I mean really—the story behind the story, you know?"

"Did you read the article about them in the current *Antiques Insights* magazine? It might be good background for you."

"I'll check it out. In the meantime, tell me."

As I paused to think how to explain the Whitestones' fairy-tale lives, Chief Hunter exited the interstate and headed toward the shore.

"Guy Whitestone is, if I'm remembering right, forty-eight," I said. "His is a real Horatio Alger success story. He's the son of a fourth- or maybe fifth-generation Nantucket fisherman, but he broke away. He won a full scholarship to Yale, then another to Harvard Business School. I'm telling you, Wes, he's really something. He made his first million on Wall Street before he turned twenty-five—the old-fashioned way, by becoming a trusted adviser to individuals and families. All on the up and up—no Ponzi scheme for him. When he was twenty-seven, he was named one of *Kaylin Business Review*'s 'Thirty Under Thirty.' You know that journal, right?"

"Haven't run across it. Is it a biggie?"

"Absolutely. It's a business weekly, really prestigious, and in that world, their annual listing of the most powerful Wall Street up-and-comers is the equivalent of knighthood. You're not a top dog until *Kaylin* says you are, and they said he was."

"Good stuff, Josie. What about Maddie?"

"Maddie—which, by the way, is short for Magdalina—came to America to study business at NYU. She's from Slovenia."

"How old is she?"

"Twenty-nine, I think. She met Guy when she went to work for his hedge fund as an intern, and boom, that was it. Bells rang. Birds sang. The whole nine yards. You must have heard about their wedding— that was six years ago. They got married in one of the mansions up in Newport. You know the places I mean—fifty rooms on the beach. They call them cottages. They invited something like seven hundred people. It was called the wedding of the decade."

Their world was filled with opulence and pomp, but their relation- ship also had a magical flavor to it, as if they lived in the moonlit realm of Fairyland in Shakespeare's *A Midsummer Night's Dream.* Seemingly they were protected by fairy dust.

"Did she marry him for his money?" Wes asked, shattering the romantic aura I was trying to convey.

"I don't know. I assume she married him for his brains and per- sonality and demeanor—all of which contributed to his ability to acquire great wealth."

"Fair enough," Wes said. "They sure don't look like they fit to- gether."

I knew what he meant. Guy and Maddie were a study in contrasts. Guy was short and portly. Maddie was tall and ethereal. Everything about Guy was quick. He spoke in a rush, his words tumbling out as if he only had seconds before his time would expire. To him a re- laxing walk was an eight-minute mile. Maddie exuded a traditional European sensibility, relaxed and refined. I could picture her stroll- ing through Parisian gardens. "You know what they say: Opposites attract."

"Do you believe that?" he asked, momentarily distracted.

I thought of Ty. We were more alike than different. "Sometimes, I guess. I don't think there's ever only one answer in questions about love. I can tell you this, though, Wes—from what I've observed, they adore one another."

"How did you meet them?"

"They attended one of our auctions last spring. When they decided to spend some time up here, Guy thought it would be fun to build a collection of maritime art and artifacts. It's part of his personality. He's not the kind of guy who relaxes by sitting around, if you know what I mean."

"He's too competitive," Wes said, and from his tone, I could tell that he was half-asking if he got it right.

"I wouldn't say 'too' competitive. He's competitive, of course, but he's also curious and research-oriented. He doesn't do anything halfway. He doesn't just want to buy an antique or two—he wants to know everything about everything, and he wants to build the finest collection in the world."

"Why maritime stuff? Because he was a fisherman's son who made good?"

"Probably."

"What did they buy?"

I told Wes about the Myrick tooth and the ship-in-a-bottle that they'd won at the auction.

"So your relationship is all business?" he asked.

I thought how to put it. "Not really. I mean, yes, but it's a little more than that. When Maddie came to pick up the objects that first time, she and I just clicked. She's a wonderful woman, Wes—kind and smart. I like her a lot. Anyway, one thing led to another, and we had lunch. A couple of weeks later, Ty and I went to a cocktail party at the lighthouse. We're not friends, but we're more than mere acquaintances or business associates."

"Gotcha. How good is his collection?"

"Stellar. I don't know everything he's bought, but the objects I know about are pretty incredible."

"Like what?"

"In addition to what he won during that first auction, he's also bought several nineteenth-century maritime paintings including a rare Fitz Hugh Lane luminescent ocean scene, a pie crimper, several baskets, some ship's bells, and a ship's log. I went with them to Sea View Gallery once and helped them by some modern objects, too."

"Repros?"

"No, contemporary original art. He bought an Eric Holch silk-screen, a Michael Liebhaber oil, and a Lenny Wilton scrimmed tooth."

"Gotcha. How much is everything worth?"

"I don't know yet. I haven't even started the appraisal."

"Ballpark it for me."

I did a quick calculation. "Four million, maybe more."

Wes whistled. "Maybe Frankie interrupted a heist. I mean, the police say he had his wallet on him with forty-three dollars in it, so it wasn't a mugging for ready cash, but four million dollars for a few paintings and a handful of other stuff—that sounds like a motive to me."

I caught my breath. "I had the same thought," I said, aware that he'd already garnered inside information from one of his many anonymous sources.

"Do you know if anything's missing?" he asked.

"Not yet, no."

"When you do your appraisal, keep me posted, okay? Both about the collection's value and whether there are any missing objects. And take some photos for me. Of the good stuff."

I paused, considering his request. While I wanted to provide Wes with something of value, I didn't want to risk compromising the police investigation. I couldn't see any downside in doing as he asked. "I can do that," I said.

"Good. Tell me what you saw when you found the body."

At his question, my heart began to beat wildly. The imagery was too fresh and too horrific to be casually discussed. "I can't," I whispered.

"Come on, Josie. Just a quick-and-dirty so I can get it clear in my head. I promise I won't ask for all the gory details."

I took a deep breath and did as he asked, rushing through a description of the wound, the rolling pin and towel, Frankie's clawlike grip holding strands of something, and the ocean of blood covering his head and much of the floor.

"When you saw that he was dead, what was your first thought?"

"I didn't think—I felt. I was terrified. It was the most awful thing I've ever seen, Wes."

"Was the place messed up? Did it look as if there'd been a struggle?"

"No."

"The police put out a BOLO for a car leaving the lighthouse right after the murder was reported. What do you know about it?"

"Did they find it?" I asked, translating Wes's jargon, BOLO, to words—be on the lookout—and using a trick I'd learned from him years ago. If you don't want to answer a question, ask one instead.

"No. They think they were too late. What do you know about it?" he asked again.

I told him what little I knew.

"If you didn't even see it, no wonder they couldn't find it," he said. "How about relationships? Was Frankie involved with anyone? Did he have a girlfriend? A boyfriend?"

"Not that I know of, and I think I would have. If Zoë knew, I'm sure she would have mentioned it."

"If the Whitestones were gone, maybe he invited someone in to show off the place. It's possible they got into a fight and Frankie lost. Who does he hang out with?"

"The only guy I know of is Curt Grimes. He works for us sometimes."

"What's he like?"

I shrugged, thinking that I'd never warmed up to Curt. He had slicked-back hair, a permanent sneer twisting his lips, and eyes that were always on the move, on the lookout for an angle to make a quick buck. He was filled with nervous energy, as if he couldn't stand still. I couldn't recall ever seeing him without an exercise ball in his hand, squeezing it as if he wanted to force it into submission. He'd once joked that if he couldn't get enough work doing odd jobs, he'd hire himself out to single women as a jar opener—he'd never met a jar of spaghetti sauce or pickles that he couldn't open on the first try. I didn't want to express any of those thoughts to Wes, though. I'd learned over a lot of years not to judge a book by its cover.

"He's one of half a dozen local men we call on when Eric needs help loading or unloading a truck or moving heavy furniture," I said. "I've never worked with him myself."

"Still . . . what's your gut tell you? Could he be a killer?"

Chief Hunter signaled the turn into the Rocky Point police station parking lot.

"I've got to go, Wes."

"Answer my question first."

My father once warned me that the only people to really worry about were the people you trusted the most—no one else could get close enough to do much damage. I took a deep breath. "What does my gut tell me?" I repeated. "My gut says sure . . . it's possible."

CHAPTER FOUR

T he Rocky Point police station had been designed to fit into the upscale beach community. It looked like a traditional ocean bungalow. Its wooden shingles had weathered to a soft dove gray. The front door and shutters were painted ice white.

I ran through pounding rain that pricked my skin like shards of glass until I reached the gabled overhang. I was drenched and shaking by the time I got inside.

Chief Hunter called to someone behind the counter named Daryl. "Please escort Ms. Morse to Room One," he said.

Ashley shook wetness from her slicker, then followed Daryl down a long corridor that led, I knew from past experience, to a small interrogation room with a human-sized cage in the corner.

"You're shaking," he said to me. "You might be in shock. I'm going to have you looked over."

"No—please," I said. "I'm fine. There's nothing wrong with me that a hot shower and dry clothes won't cure. First I need to talk to Zoë, though."

He stared at me searchingly for several moments, then nodded and asked me to wait for just a minute. "I won't be long," he said.

He followed Daryl and Ashley down the hallway.

I looked around. Cathy, a big blonde, a civilian admin for the department, was behind the counter typing something. I sat on a wooden bench. Across from me was a bulletin board labeled COMMUNITY NOTICES. I got up and stood in front of it. A poster for the upcoming Harvest Festival was tacked up next to an announcement from the Rocky Point Community Center about winter hours at the pool.

"How are you holding up?" Chief Hunter asked when he returned.

"I'm okay. Sort of." I shrugged and added, "You're having quite a first day."

"Yeah . . . I thought I was moving to a quiet community—tourist-based, you know?"

I laughed, and it felt good. "Where are you from?"

"New York. I'm retired NYPD."

"Me, too. From New York, I mean. I moved up here about five years ago to start my own business."

"And? What do you think?"

"I like it. I like it a lot, actually. Of course, it's way different from New York."

He gestured toward the bench. "Let's sit down for a minute." He skewed around to face me. "We checked with the Whitestones. You were right—Mr. Winterelli listed his aunt, Zoë Winterelli, as his next of kin. Are you certain you want to come with me to talk to her?"

"Yes, absolutely. My being there may make it a bit easier for her."

"Okay, then. I'm hoping we'll get to her before she sees it on the news."

"We don't have much to worry about on that front," I said, smiling. "Zoë will tell you that as a single mom with two small children, she doesn't see the news—all she sees is directions on packages of mac and cheese."

Chief Hunter smiled, stood up, and said, "Got it." Before he pushed open the heavy front door, he added, "Let's ride together. You need to come back here and give a statement anyway."

"Can't I do it tomorrow? I'm going to want to stay with Zoë."

"You could, but it would be best if it were tonight. I want to get as much information as possible as quickly as I can."

His unspoken message came through loud and clear: A killer was on the loose.

"What did you think of Mr. Winterelli? Were you close?" he asked as we drove.

I took in a bushel of air. "Sort of. Not really. But I liked him. He lived next door to me for a while. He was doing so well."

"He was at your office when, exactly?"

I pursed my lips, thinking. "About quarter to eleven. Maybe ten fifty. Something like that. Eric saw him after that. They cleaned the gutters."

"I'd like to talk to him directly. Can you reach him?"

"Sure." It was five fifteen. Eric would have left for the day. Chief Hunter turned on the speaker function of the hands-free phone built into his vehicle, and I dialed Eric's cell phone from memory.

"Eric," I said when I had him on the line, "I'm putting you on the phone with Chief Hunter, the new Rocky Point police chief. It's about Frankie."

Chief Hunter inserted his earpiece and pushed the button to take Eric off speaker.

"I'm afraid I have some bad news," Chief Hunter said after introducing himself. "Frankie Winterelli is dead, and I'm investigating the circumstances of his death. I'm hoping you might answer a few questions . . . Yes, that's right . . . No, not yet . . . Thank you. What time did Mr. Winterelli leave Prescott's today?" He listened for several seconds. "Are you sure it was right at noon? . . . During the time you were working together, what did you talk about? . . . What else? . . . Anything personal? . . . No mentions of music, sports, girls, or what you did over the weekend, nothing like that?" He glanced in the rearview mirror, listening some more, then thanked him and ended with a brisk "Okay, then. I'll be in touch."

"Was he able to give you any useful information?" I asked.

"Hard to say."

"What do you do now?"

He glanced at me. "We look for inconsistencies."

"What kind of inconsistencies?"

"Timing, relationships, details, anything."

Inconsistencies in facts regarding means, opportunity, or motive, I thought. It was a safe bet that the rolling pin was the murder weapon—I recalled the blood-colored stains. If so, the means was known. Opportunity was apparent: Someone could have crawled in the open window, walked in the unlocked back door, or been invited in by Frankie.

"Who opened the window?" I asked.

"It's one of the things we're looking into."

"How about the door? Do you think it was left open by the killer? Or do you think the killer entered that way?"

"We're checking with everyone involved," he replied, giving yet another vague answer.

Regardless of how the killer got in, opportunity was, evidently, no problem. Motive, on the other hand, was less apparent. I'd thought of one possible reason why Frankie was killed: He'd interrupted a burglary. It was possible, I supposed, yet it didn't seem real to me. Then again, nothing would. I couldn't imagine anyone killing Frankie.

Ty called. "I got your message," he said. "How are you doing?"

"I'm in the car with Chief Hunter. We're on our way to tell Zoë what happened."

"Then I'm betting you're going back to the station to give a statement."

"Right."

"How about if I go to your place? That way, in case you're stuck there and Zoë wants some company, I'll be handy."

What a guy, I thought. "That's great, Ty. I know she'll appreciate it." I glanced at the dashboard clock. It was just after five thirty. "Do you know when you'll be back?"

"By eight, I should think."

"Okay. I'll tell her."

"I know you can't talk openly. Here's a yes or no question. Do they have a suspect?"

"No, not that I'm aware of."

"You sound upset."

"I am. Incredibly."

"Yeah," he said, and from the way he spoke that one word, I understood that he wished he could be with me to hug and comfort me. "Soon. I'll see you soon."

We ended that way, and I closed my eyes for a moment. Simply hearing his voice was reassuring beyond measure.

I called my office, and Fred answered. He filled me in on the news of the afternoon, and I was relieved to be thinking about something other than murder.

Eric and Gretchen had analyzed sales of the Lenny Wilton's Leon brand scrimmed barrettes we sold for five dollars from a basket near the cash register at the weekly tag sale. The barrettes were one of only a few items we offered that weren't either antiques or collectibles. They were selling so well, Gretchen had ordered more for the holidays.

I wasn't surprised at the strong sales numbers. Lenny was more than just an award-winning scrimshander. He was also an astute businessman and a genius at production. He'd patented a scrimming machine that both etched designs into resin and applied permanent ink. It allowed him to price the barrettes low enough so we could position them as an easy impulse buy; five dollars was a perfect price point for an affordable luxury, a little treat, or a stocking stuffer.

"Lenny said he'll bring over a gross of mixed designs in a day or two," Fred said. "He has some new seasonal ones."

"Terrific," I said, somehow succeeding in hiding my grief and sadness.

We discussed the essay he was writing for our cobalt glassware auction catalogue, and I found the conversation soothing and distracting. In times of strife, work has always seen me through.

"Should we stay on Ocean or turn onto Main Street?" Chief Hunter asked after I was off the phone.

"Turn onto Main, then take Route 95 north for one exit."

"It's dropped six degrees in an hour," he remarked, nodding toward the temperature display on the dashboard. "Fifty-nine. Is it always this cold in September?"

"Pretty much. There's a saying that there are two seasons in New Hampshire—winter and July."

"Yikes."

I looked out over the ocean. Through the steady rain I could see that most of the green-blue surface was white with windswept froth. "It looks like it's going to storm for hours."

"How can you tell?" he asked.

"There are whitecaps as far as I can see." I squinted. "Not that I can see all that far in this downpour."

He took a look and nodded. "The wind is strong."

"Very much so." After a moment, I added, "You said you were with NYPD. Were you a detective?"

"Captain. Homicide."

"Why'd you move up here?"

"I like Norman Rockwell, and I thought I'd check out whether I'd like small-town living, too."

"Really?"

"Why are you surprised?" he asked.

"You don't look like a Norman Rockwell sort of guy."

"What's a Norman Rockwell sort of guy look like?"

"Good question. I don't know."

"Well, then, what kind of guy do I look like?"

"Not someone who's much into nuance."

"Norman Rockwell is nuanced?"

"Very."

"You've piqued my interest . . . but it's a conversation for another time. Right now, tell me about Zoë Winterelli."

I held my hands up to the vent while I considered how to communicate her special qualities. Zoë was a pistol, an Italian firecracker with a heart of gold and smarts up the kazoo. I felt completely at ease in her company. "She's a really good friend—considerate, I mean—and fun to be around. She's informal and loose about most things, and not at all loose about the important things. Even though she grew up in New Hampshire, she's a nut about the Yankees—watches as many games as possible and takes her kids to see them whenever they're in Boston over a weekend to play the Red Sox. She's a good cook and a better baker." I shrugged. "What specifically do you want to know?"

"How did she and Mr. Winterelli interact?"

"After that rocky start I told you about, they got along well. Better every day."

"Who did he hang out with?"

I repeated what I'd told Wes about Curt.

"What about Eric?" he asked.

"I think Frankie really admired him. After he started at the Whitestones', I overheard him telling Eric that now they *both* had great jobs. Frankie thanked him for putting up with him when he first started working for Prescott's. That was Frankie's phrase, 'putting up with me.' I thought it was kind of sweet . . . humble, I mean."

"Any romances that you know of?"

I shrugged again. "He never brought anyone over to Zoë's."

"How did he and Ashley Morse get along? They're co-workers and neighbors. Were they also friends?"

I thought about Ashley. She was an artist to her toenails. Her drive to create defined her very essence. She hated it that she had to sell or even promote her work herself, believing that it should stand on its own, and that somehow marketing or promotion was beneath her. I didn't understand it, but I'd observed that attitude over and over again in all sorts of creative people at college, during my years in New York, and here in New Hampshire—they despised and condemned the business imperatives of their work. Ashley lived, breathed, and slept scrimshaw. Most of the time she was aloof and brusque, seemingly unengaged and uninterested in anything going on around her. Only when she talked about scrimshaw or fossil materials or artisan techniques did she show any animation. I couldn't imagine Frankie caring enough about scrimshaw to have become friends with her.

"I don't think so. They got along fine, I guess. I mean, I don't think they hung out or anything. They're pretty different sorts of people."

"How so?"

I directed him off the interstate, then said, "Part of it is age. To a twenty-three-year-old man, a woman of Ashley's age—I'm guessing she's in her mid- to late thirties—she's got to seem more like an older sister than a peer, you know? And vice versa. Also, they just didn't have a lot in common. They worked for the Whitestones, but for different reasons. For Ashley, it was a means to an end. She took the job because she needed the money to fund her scrimshanding passion. For Frankie, it was a career. I don't think he ever would have left the lighthouse. He loved his work. He loved living by the ocean. He loved having his own house. Landing this job fulfilled every dream he'd ever had—and some he hadn't even aspired to."

Chief Hunter nodded, a thoughtful expression on his face. "What can you tell me about his friends?"

"Curt Grimes seems to be a happy-go-lucky handyman type, doing a little of this and a little of that. If he has a regular job, I don't know it, but if he wants one, I don't know that either. My impression is that he's content doing pickup work. I mean, he's not a transient or anything. He's worked for my company for a couple of years. I know he works on installations at Sea View Gallery—that's where I met him—and he helps . . . helped . . . Frankie at the lighthouse on two-man jobs."

"Can you give me his address and phone number?"

"Sure. They're in our personnel files." I pointed to the left. "That's our driveway—Zoë and I share it. Her house is on the left. The little one on the right is mine."

"They look alike, except yours is smaller."

"Yeah, it's kind of cute, isn't it? Mine was built as an in-law residence. It's like a dower house in England."

"Look up. You left a light on."

"Always," I said, smiling as I saw the soft golden light that glowed behind sheer curtains in my bedroom. "I hate walking into dark houses, so I leave a lamp on."

"You're a practical woman. You don't try to overcome a minor fear—you do a work-around."

"'Tis true, 'tis true," I said, thinking that Chief Hunter was definitely more astute than the average bear.

Chief Hunter pulled into the driveway, parking behind Zoë's car. "Before we go in, I just want to take a minute and jot down that name." I watched as he flipped to a fresh page in his notebook and wrote down Curt's name. "What's Sea View Gallery?"

"An art gallery owned by Greg Donovan."

"High-end?"

"Not so much. He targets tourists. He has some nice stuff, modern crafts, but he also has some, well . . . less nice stuff. More in the category of souvenirs than art, if you know what I mean."

"He sells a lot of schlock."

"That's too harsh. I wouldn't say he sells any schlock. Rather, he sells art that's easy to understand and pleasing to the eye. Nothing wrong with it."

"Like Norman Rockwell."

"Not a bit! Norman Rockwell's illustrations are layered with social commentary. That they're pleasing to the eye is a bonus."

"Someday you're going to have to explain some of them to me so I can see what I've been missing, not being a nuance sort of guy."

I smiled again and punched the button to unlatch my seat belt. "Chief, I hope you won't think I'm sassy to contradict you, but I have a feeling there's very little that you miss."

He grinned. "Glad you noticed."

CHAPTER FIVE

U h-oh," Zoë said as soon as I introduced her to Chief Hunter. "This can't be good news."

We stood by the couch in her living room. I could hear Jake, age seven, and Emma, age five, squabbling somewhere out of sight, in the kitchen probably.

Zoë was thirty-one, tall, a hair over five-ten, and slender. She'd clipped her long black hair into a loose French twist. Her eyes were caramel, flecked with gold. She wore a fitted, olive green V-neck sweater that barely reached the top of her low-rider jeans. She looked like a model. When Zoë had inherited her uncle's estate three years earlier, she'd decided to jettison a bad marriage out west and return home to New Hampshire, and we'd been friends ever since.

"Don't try to break it to me gently," she said.

"It's about your nephew, Frankie Winterelli."

"What did he do now?" she asked, her eyes shooting sparks. "He's been arrested, right?"

"Why would you think that?" he asked.

She put her hand on her hip and met his eyes. "Because I'm a natural-born cynic, and as much as I love him, I know the score—bad apples usually rot."

He shook his head. "He hasn't been arrested. I'm sorry to inform you that he's dead. His body was found this afternoon in the kitchen of his employer's residence, Rocky Point Light. An investigation is ongoing."

Zoë stared at him for a few seconds, then covered her face with her hands.

"Oh, Zoë," I whispered, drawing her toward the sofa. "I'm so sorry."

She sat next to me, thigh to thigh. Her shoulders rose up a half inch, then dropped down—up and down, up and down—but she didn't make a sound. Silent crying, the loneliest kind. She stayed like that for several minutes, then raised her head. Her cheeks were streaked with mascara-stained wetness.

I reached for a box of Kleenex and slid it toward her.

"Thank you, Josie." She wiped her face with a tissue, then took a deep breath. "Please—sit. What happened?" she asked Chief Hunter.

He sat on a nearby club chair. "We don't know yet. It looks like he died from a head injury, but that's pure speculation on my part. The medical examiner hasn't even officially ruled it a homicide."

Lightning bolts shot from her expressive eyes, and in that instant, the atmosphere in the room shifted from slowly mounting grief to sparking outrage.

"A homicide?" she asked. "You mean he was hit on the head? Someone beat Frankie over the head?"

"It looks that way."

"I'll bet you my kids' college fund that I know who killed him— *and* why." Her chest heaved. "The son of a bitch."

Before Chief Hunter could speak, the phone rang. Zoë jumped up and grabbed the portable handset from the coffee table.

"Hello?" Her back tensed. "Are you kidding me?" she shrieked. "What's your name? Jesus!" She punched the OFF button and slammed the phone down. "It's that reporter, Wes Smith. Can you effing believe it?"

"That's the first of what is likely to be many reporters' inquiries, Ms. Winterelli," Chief Hunter said. "A murder on the Whitestones' property is national news—probably international news, given the scope of Mr. Whitestone's business dealings and the universal interest in his marriage."

"Oh, joy," she said. sinking into the sofa next to me. She held up a palm to stop him from replying. "Sorry, I hate sarcasm. Let me start over . . . Chief Hunter, I appreciate the warning." A corner of her mouth went up. "I guess you can tell that I won't have any trouble telling reporters to take a hike."

"Yeah," he said, smiling. "I get the impression you can probably take care of business."

Zoë seemed to focus on him for the first time. Her eyes scanned his face. "Thanks," she said.

"So . . . you say you know who killed your nephew. Tell me."

"Mel Erly."

Who? I wondered. I'd never heard the name.

Zoë's eyes filled again, and she impatiently brushed away tears. "I'm sorry . . . I hate crying almost as much as I hate sarcasm." She inhaled deeply. "I got a call last night from a lowlife drug dealer named Melvin Erly. He said he was in jail in Portsmouth—no surprise. He needed bail money, so he called his good old pal Frankie. I told him in no uncertain terms that Frankie didn't want to hear from him, that Frankie was doing great and that as far as I was concerned, Mel could do his time. He said to shut the eff up and put Frankie on the line."

Zoë took a deep breath. "I told Mel that Frankie didn't live here anymore and there was no way I was going to tell pond scum like him where he'd gone. Mel called me a . . . well . . . let's just say that he cursed a blue streak and it got pretty personal." She sighed and shook her head. "All in all, it was ugly. Mel said that Frankie owed him big, and it was time to pay up. I didn't know what he was referring to, and I didn't want to know. I hung up on him. But I can add two and two. Mel gets out of jail, tracks Frankie down, and kills him."

"*If* he's out of jail, and *if* he could track him down," I said. "Those are two big ifs."

"All ideas are helpful at this point," Chief Hunter said to me. He looked back to Zoë and asked, "Have you ever met Mr. Erly?"

"No, but Frankie talked about him some. He once told me—" She broke off as tears welled in her eyes and ran down her cheeks. Her fingers curled into tight fists for a moment; then she pulled another tissue from the box and wiped the wetness away. "Sorry . . . Frankie once said that when people talk about getting in with the wrong crowd, they're talking about Mel." She shook her head and turned to me. "You know how Frankie got a cell phone with a new number when he landed the Whitestone job?"

"Right, so no one from his past could reach him."

Jake came running full tilt into the room with unconscious glee. "Shhh!" he said to us and began scouting hiding places. He zipped behind the club chair, then changed his mind and scooted behind the entertainment center, then changed his mind again and ran upstairs.

Emma's voice came from the kitchen. "... eight ... nine ... ten." She burst through the doorway, saw Chief Hunter, and stopped. "Hello."

"Emma," Zoë said, "this is a new friend, Mr. Hunter."

"Hi, Emma," Chief Hunter said. "Are you playing hide-and-seek?"

"Yes. Do you know which way Jake went?"

"I saw, but I can't tell. That wouldn't be fair."

"Yes, it would, 'cause I'm littler, so I need help."

"I bet you're clever enough to find him on your own."

"You think?" Emma began a systematic canvass of the room, and when she didn't find him said, "Maybe he went upstairs." She dashed to the staircase and headed up.

"She's a doll," Chief Hunter told Zoë.

"Thanks. She really is—they both are."

He nodded, then said, "I'll check out Mel Erly. Who else might have had a grudge against your nephew?"

"No one. Frankie was a nice kid. I mean, he was becoming a good guy, you know?" She turned her face aside and bit her lip to stop herself from crying.

I rubbed her back lightly.

Chief Hunter extracted a business card from a leather case and laid it on the coffee table. "I'm terribly sorry for your loss. I'll be talking to you again, but if you think of anything else in the meantime, even something small, or seemingly insignificant, please call me, okay?"

She nodded.

"I've asked Ms. Prescott to come back to the station with me so I can get her statement," Chief Hunter said. "Is there anyone you'd like us to call for you before we go?"

"No, thanks," she said, gulping, then waving her hand. "I'll be fine. I always am."

"Found you!" Emma shrieked from the second floor. "Found you!"

Chief Hunter smiled. "I told her she could do it."

"Even if she's littler," Zoë said with a small sad smile. "Thank you for telling her that."

"I'll be back as soon as I can," I said, "and Ty will be at my place by eight. He said to call if you want him to come over."

"I'll be okay," she said, her expression softening as she spoke. "I have to. It's almost bathtime."

"If you need anything," Chief Hunter told her, "you call me, okay?"

She looked up at him, their eyes meeting for a moment. "Thanks," she said.

I hugged her, fighting my own tears, then hugged her again, wishing I could will her grief away, knowing there was nothing I could do to dull her pain.

When my mom died, I'd been a kid, only thirteen, and I'd had my dad. When my dad was killed, I'd been a grown-up, in my late twenties, living in New York City on my own, and I'd had no one; my boyfriend at the time, Rick, thought I wasn't bouncing back fast enough from the shock of his murder, and he'd broken up with me within weeks. I shook my head, dispelling the dreadful memories. Zoë wouldn't be alone—she'd have me, and she'd have Ty.

I borrowed an umbrella, then dashed through the heavy rain to Chief Hunter's SUV.

I felt impatient and itchy to do something, to act, not merely to observe or answer questions. I wanted to call Wes. Discovering whether Mel was out on bail when Frankie had been killed was exactly the kind of inquiry Wes excelled at.

I turned to look out the window. The rain continued its constant drone.

I couldn't call Wes while sitting next to a police official, but I sure as shootin' could text him.

I got my phone from my bag, and without commenting to Chief Hunter, I typed: "Melvin Erly. Portsmouth jail. Alibi?" After I hit SEND, I kept my phone in my hand, willing it to vibrate. Knowing Wes, there was a good chance he'd have the info I wanted within minutes.

CHAPTER SIX

e drove through the center of Rocky Point's small village, and as we passed the gazebo where bands played on summer evenings, Chief Hunter asked, "Where's Sea View Gallery?"

"Over there." I pointed to a double-wide storefront.

"It's open," he said, sounding surprised.

"They want to catch the dinner crowd."

"Would you be okay with stopping by to introduce me to the owner . . . Mr. Donovan, right? And Mr. Grimes, if he's there?"

"Sure."

He drove around the block and parked in front. Five people, two couples and Greg, stood in the gallery. Dave Brubeck's "In Your Own Sweet Way" played softly in the background. Spotlights mounted on tracks illuminated specific paintings and objects. One man was whispering into his companion's ear as they looked at a watercolor of a harbor. The other couple stood in front of a hand-carved replica of a tall ship in a Plexiglas case, chatting with Greg Donovan, the owner. He noticed us as soon as we entered, smiled broadly, and held up a finger, indicating he'd be with us in a minute.

I smiled and mouthed, "Take your time." Chief Hunter and I gravitated toward a display case in the center of the room filled with scrimshaw objects.

"I hail from Down East . . . Maine," Greg said to the couple with an exaggerated a-yup Maine twang. "I moved to the big city—Rocky Point."

I'd heard him use that sally countless times, and it always worked. This pair, like most tourists visiting from genuinely large cities like

Boston or New York, were charmed at the thought that someone from Down East considered Rocky Point a big city. His jocularity wouldn't have worked with me—at all. Greg's hearty, hail-fellow-well-met demeanor always set my teeth on edge. I'd never known Greg to be serious, and I wondered whether hearing about Frankie's murder would make a dent in his unremitting affability.

Greg Donovan was gregarious and astute. About fifty, he was big and broad, and his Norse heritage was evident in his coloring and countenance. He loved art and coastal living, and had found a way to combine the two. He was one of the lucky ones—his talent matched his ambition, and he knew it. When I'd first moved to New Hampshire, I'd visited every gallery, antiques store, and auction house within a hundred miles, introducing myself and feeling out the competition. In that first conversation, Greg had told me that he liked running the little gallery he'd opened twenty years earlier and had no plans to expand. He said he was content to leave high-powered deals to gals like me.

"That's scrimshaw, right?" Chief Hunter asked in an undertone, pointing to a display case containing scrimmed teeth, belt buckles, earrings, and bookmarks.

"Yes." I pointed to a tooth featuring a traditional whaling scene. "That's an Ashley Morse."

"Really." He leaned over to study it. "She's good, huh?"

"She's a talented technician."

He squinted at me. "That sounds like damning with faint praise if I ever heard it, as Pope would have said."

"You like Alexander Pope?" I asked, thinking that a man who liked Norman Rockwell and quoted Alexander Pope bore watching.

"Doesn't everyone?"

I smiled. "There's a lot of subjectivity in art," I said.

"Now you're avoiding the issue."

I glanced around. I wasn't going to say anything to Chief Hunter that I wouldn't say to a client, but I didn't want anyone overhearing my commentary to think that I was merely gossiping. No one was paying any attention to us.

"If I were advising a client," I said, lowering my voice, "I would comment on both the subject matter and the etching process." I pointed to the tooth. "The maritime theme is typical and appropriate, but the choice of subject—the whaling boat *Susan*—is derivative. In fact, this specific design might be an actual copy. If I were appraising it, that's something I'd check. Regarding the technique, do you see that drop shadow etched behind the sail? It's out of place. It doesn't enhance the illusion of billowing wind; it diminishes it by calling attention to the etching technique itself. The line is well drawn but fails in its purpose. But I want to stress, I'm giving you the kind of opinion I'd render if called on to value the tooth. That has nothing to do with individual preference—and as I said, there's a lot of subjectivity in art."

"So you're saying it's not great, but it merits being sold in the gallery?"

"I wouldn't put it that way. I'm an antiques appraiser, not an arbiter of taste. I'd say that it's probably not going to increase in value over time, so I wouldn't recommend buying it as an investment, but if you love it—go for it."

He nodded. "Does she sell many?"

"I don't know. She sells some. The Whitestones bought one over the summer."

"How much do they sell for?"

"Around eight thousand."

He whistled. "That sounds like a hefty chunk of change for something you don't think is investment grade."

"That one goes for fifty thousand plus," I said, pointing to a Lenny Wilton scrimmed tooth showing a young woman in traditional nineteenth-century garb tending a garden. "I've talked to Guy about buying it. It's a remarkable piece."

He looked from one to the other, then back again, comparing them. "The Wilton features a land-based subject," he said. "Is that why it sells for more?"

"Not exactly, but the fact that he chose such unusual subject matter certainly adds value. The text, which you can't see from this side, reads: 'My beautiful Maribella in our garden at home.' It's as if a sailor missing his wife created a romantic image to sustain himself. It's sweet, it's quaint, and it's beautifully executed. Look at the workmanship—

Lenny is one heck of a craftsman. Note the detail in the lace trim on the woman's gown and in the vines. Remarkable."

"Which is why it sells for so much more than Ms. Morse's."

"That and the fact that despite his relative youth, his work has already been included in several important private collections and a couple of museums." I thought again of Frankie. Lenny's experience was another example of success begetting success.

Chief Hunter nodded. "Interesting. Will Mr. Whitestone buy it, do you think?"

"Yes."

Greg waved a final good-bye as the two couples called out their thanks and left. Then he came over to us and kissed my cheek.

"Josie! Sorry to keep you waiting. What a delightful surprise!"

"Hi, Greg. No problem. Have you met Chief Hunter?"

"No. Good to meet you," he said, offering his hand, ebullient as ever. "I read in today's paper that we had a new chief. Welcome to Rocky Point. So what can I do you for?"

"Glad to be here. I'm hoping you can help me with an investigation—Frankie Winterelli. Have you heard about his death?"

Greg's mood changed on a dime. "Just now on the news. Terrible."

"Did you know him?"

"I don't think so." He looked at me. "Did I ever meet him, Josie?"

"Maybe at the lighthouse," I said. "He was the Whitestones' caretaker."

He shook his head. "The name doesn't ring a bell."

"You know the Whitestones, though, right?" Chief Hunter asked.

"Certainly. They're good customers, and I hope they wouldn't think I was overreaching if I said they were good friends as well."

I cringed inwardly at his unctuous tone.

"How about Curt Grimes?" Chief Hunter asked. "Is he here now?"

"No, sorry. I could get you his number if you'd like."

"I'd appreciate it," Chief Hunter said.

We followed Greg to his desk, which was angled outward from the rear corner of the gallery. I watched as he tapped into his computer, then wrote the phone number and address on a sheet he tore from a memo pad.

"Thanks," Chief Hunter said, accepting the paper. "Is there any-thing you can tell me that might help with my investigation?"

"Like what?" Greg asked.

"When you heard the news, did anything come into your head? Something related to the victim, perhaps, or to Rocky Point Light? It doesn't have to be logical—any thoughts at all might prove useful."

"Sorry. Nothing came to mind," he said, answering quickly, "except how shocking it was."

"What's Mr. Grimes like?" Chief Hunter asked.

Greg laughed. "Like lots of young men who live nearby. He hunts. He fishes. He's a hard worker, but not much interested in a full-time gig. He lives with his sister and her family, I believe. He drives an old car. He's been a reliable helper." He paused, then raised his hands, showing us his palms. "If there's any dirt, I don't know it."

"Thanks for your time," Chief Hunter said, proffering a business card. "If something does occur to you, please get in touch."

"Of course, of course," Greg replied, dropping the card into a drawer, his oh-so-jovial manner returning as quickly as it had van-ished. "Anything I can do to help the police—consider it done."

Back in the chief's vehicle, I remarked, "I'm tired of the rain."

"At least it's slowed up some. What would you call this?" Chief Hunter asked, squinting to see through the windshield.

"Mizzle. That's New Hampshire for misty drizzle."

He smiled and said, "Mizzle. Got it."

My phone vibrated, and I grabbed it. "Erly still in jail. Why?" Wes texted.

"Pal of F. Just ckg," I typed in reply.

Mel Erly was in jail—a perfect alibi, I thought. But that didn't mean he couldn't have deputized a cohort to teach Frankie a lesson about loyalty to old friends. Maybe the guy was only supposed to push Frankie around a little and things got out of hand. If Frankie fought back, it was possible that the attacker grabbed the rolling pin and what had started as a fistfight ended as a murder.

This scenario assumed that Mel had succeeded in learning about Frankie's whereabouts and arranging for the beating while he was incarcerated, and in only a few hours, which seemed pretty unlikely. *Just because something is conceivable doesn't mean it's credible,* I reminded myself, dismissing him, for the time being at least, as a suspect.

I recalled the material I'd seen in Frankie's grip and wondered if Wes had learned what it was. "Have police ID'd what was in F's hand?" I texted.

Wes's response was immediate. "Leather," he wrote.

Leather? Everyone, or almost everyone, wore leather. Belts. Shoes. Jackets. It could be anything.

I felt my frustration grow. I didn't even know enough to ask additional questions.

CHAPTER SEVEN

I sat in Interview Room Two answering Chief Hunter's repetitive questions, the video camera recording my every word. I felt nail-bitingly on edge. I wanted to be with Zoë, not doing what felt like busywork, answering the same questions that had been asked and answered earlier in the day.

Toward the end of the interview, just before nine, Detective Brownley stepped into the room and handed Chief Hunter a note. While he read it, she turned her intelligent blue eyes on me and watched me watch him. He placed the paper facedown on the table and thanked her, and she left.

He laced his fingers behind his head and leaned back. As he did so, I felt his mood change. What had been conversational became solemn. Seconds ticked by. Under his scrutiny, my pulse began to throb and the muscles in my neck and across my shoulders tightened. I glanced at the note, white-hot curious. Finally, he reached over and turned off the video camera. I watched as the red light faded to black.

"I understand from Detective Brownley that you sometimes talk to a reporter named Wes Smith," Chief Hunter said.

"Sometimes," I acknowledged, instantly on guard.

Chief Hunter touched Officer Brownley's note. "This is the medical examiner's preliminary report. Based on what it says, I think Mr. Winterelli knew his killer. For some reason, the murderer went ballistic, grabbed the nearest weapon, and killed him—which means the murder probably wasn't premeditated."

"Why are you telling me this?" I asked.

He shrugged. "In case you talk to Mr. Smith."

"You want me to repeat it?" I asked, incredulous. Up until now, the police had always warned me *not* to talk to reporters. "Why? Why not tell him yourself?"

"That would make it official."

"Isn't it?"

"No. It's my current theory of the crime, but that's all it is—a theory."

"Why not explain that to Wes, too? He's smart. He'll get it."

He flipped a palm. "I don't want the comment to carry the weight of the office. If you say it, it's an uncorroborated quote from a person close to the investigation."

I stared at him, unable to decide what to say or do. I didn't want to admit talking to Wes, but I was intrigued by Chief Hunter's idea.

He leaned forward. "You can help me—if you will. You know about the antiques. You know everyone who's involved or who may be involved. You're on good terms with a reporter."

I had the discombobulating sensation of having strayed onto unsafe ice. When I was a girl in Welton, Massachusetts, a tractor would drive across Bullough's Pond to test whether the ice was thick enough for skating. Sometimes the driver would reach the middle and turn back, saying that he'd felt the ice begin to crack. My friends would groan with disappointment, then run off to make snow angels on the flat area near the boathouse, mostly unaffected by his revelation. Not me. I stayed close to my mother, holding her hand, as terrified as if I were the one about to plummet through the ice into the murky, frozen depths, not him. He never did, and usually the ice was deemed safe, but I never understood why that man risked dying just so kids could play. Wasn't he scared?

Chief Hunter again touched the paper Detective Brownley had handed him. "The report contains no surprises. The medical examiner has ruled the death of Mr. Winterelli a homicide, and the rolling pin is definitely the weapon. So we know that, but I don't know enough about the victim. I need people to tell me things, to repeat rumors. I want anecdotes. I want facts. Someone knows something—and I want it."

"Maybe his murder has nothing to do with people he knows. Maybe it's a robbery gone bad."

"We're checking into that."

"But you don't think so," I said.

"No. I think he was killed by someone who hated him. You saw his body."

I shuddered.

"Please talk to Wes Smith for me," he said.

I didn't like it. I was being maneuvered into the middle, always a risky place to be. I shook my head, but before I could begin to explain my hesitation, he leaned toward me and said, "I want you to gossip, not be an envoy. I'm counting on human nature to do the rest. People will start gabbing the way people do. They'll whisper to their friends and co-workers and family, and with any luck, those whispers will be repeated as insider news and I'll get wind of it. That's what I want—the tittle-tattle, as my mother used to say."

"Tittle-tattle?" I repeated, amused.

"So you'll do it?"

"Wes has police sources who feed him information—and misinformation—from time to time," I said, thinking fast, trying to get out from under the burden of the chief's expectations. "Let one of them drop a hint in his ear and keep me out of it."

He frowned. "Who are his police sources?"

"I have no idea," I said, kicking myself for having let anything slip. As I thought of it, I realized I'd only assumed Wes had a police source. I didn't actually know whether he did or not. It occurred to me that I was proving Chief Hunter's point—people talk. "I don't know for sure whether he has police sources. I'm speculating."

"Speculate some more. Speculate about the police investigation to him. It can do no harm, and it might do good."

"How can my talking to Wes possibly help more than allowing him to quote an anonymous 'high-ranking police source'?"

"A story reporting an official police theory reads differently than an article reporting a rumor from some unnamed person who's 'close to the investigation.' That has the sound of in-the-know to it. An official police theory makes people complacent—the police are on the job. Inferences and guesses make people remember tidbits that support or contradict them, and that's what they talk about over the water-cooler." He leaned back, his eyes fixed on my face, gauging my reaction. "All you have to do is let it drop that you got the impression that the police think Mr. Winterelli's killer was known to him and that the murder was probably unpremeditated."

"And when he asks what gave me that impression?"

"You can say that I asked you if the victim had any beefs with people . . . if he had a reputation for fighting . . . if he was involved with a married woman . . . or if you'd heard anything about any of his relationships that might suggest that someone was out to get him— and when you said that you didn't, I revealed that my working theory was that someone was enraged when they killed him."

"Except that you didn't ask me any of those things."

"Sure I did, just not in so many words."

"I hate this," I said. "You're asking me to lie."

He switched on the video camera. The red light glowed.

"As far as you know, did Mr. Winterelli have any beefs with people?" Chief Hunter asked.

"No," I replied.

"How about fighting? Did he have a reputation as quick on the draw?"

"No."

"How about when he was high? Was he an angry drunk?"

"I don't know."

"You've never seen him drink?"

"Not lately. Not in years."

"How about his love life? Had he gotten himself into any kind of romantic jam?"

"Not that I know of."

"Would you know?"

I shrugged. "Probably not."

"Thank you very much for your assistance," he said, turning off the camera again. "Now I've asked you the questions. So, what do you say? Will you help?"

I nodded. "You'd make a heck of a negotiator, Chief. You're relentless. I'll call Wes on my way home."

"You were going to anyway, right?"

"Wes is a good reporter. I'm curious what he might have learned."

"Ask me what you're planning to ask him."

I blinked at him. He looked wise and knowing.

"I mean it," he said. "Maybe I won't be able to answer you, but you'll never know if you don't ask."

I took a deep breath. I understood what he was doing. From my questions, he hoped to gain leads or ideas about avenues he should investigate. "Curt Grimes," I said. "What's his alibi?"

"Don't know yet."

"Is it true that you found no evidence suggesting that Frankie interrupted a robbery?"

"Yes."

"Have you excluded an interrupted robbery as a possible motive?"

"No."

"So in other words . . . you don't know anything," I said.

"Pretty much, that's true."

"Inviting me to ask you questions is a heck of a deal. You find out what I'm thinking, and I learn nothing at all."

"Seems fair. So what else do you want to know?"

I smiled. "What do you think happened?"

"Someone was out-of-their-mind angry."

I shivered, recalling the blood-streaked scene. "Yeah."

"How long will it take you to appraise the Whitestone collection?" he asked.

"I don't know. I never know until we're into it. There are too many variables both in the authentication and the valuation processes."

He tapped his pen on the edge of the desk, thinking. "What if all I want to know is if something is missing? How long would that take?"

"Not too long. The first thing we do is video-record everything to create a permanent record. From that, I generate an inventory. Guy told me where the receipts are, so I should be able to confirm that everything is accounted for within a few hours or a few days, depending on how organized the paperwork is and whether some objects are hidden away."

"Let's hope for a few hours, not a few days."

"There's no way to predict." I smiled. "Sort of like detective work."

He nodded. "What happens after you have your inventory listing and match the receipts to the goods?"

"I have the Whitestones check the list to be sure nothing is missing."

"How come? If you have the objects matched to the receipts, can't you assume it's complete?"

"Not necessarily. Unless I helped them acquire an object, I might never have seen it, so I'd have no way of knowing that it had ever been part of their collection and was now missing." I shrugged. "For instance, maybe someone stole an item that they picked up at a flea market or a craft fair, something they didn't get a receipt for. Or maybe someone stole both the object *and* the receipt."

"Does that ever happen?"

"Sure. Professional thieves do it all the time." I paused. "The Whitestones own some real treasures. In fact, an article about the collection just appeared in *Antiques Insights* magazine. The lighthouse was uninhabited. It's possible that a professional took advantage of the opportunity."

"And Mr. Winterelli interrupted him."

"I had that thought."

"We need to know if the collection is intact, and we need to know it as soon as possible. Mr. Whitestone is in London—he was in the air when the corpse was discovered. He'll be back in a couple of days. Mrs. Whitestone will be here in the morning, so she'll be able to help you nail down the inventory. I'm hoping you can get started on the appraisal right away. The crime scene guys tell me they should be done by midday tomorrow."

"I can do that," I said. "Should I meet you there?"

"I'll call you as soon as I get the all-clear, and we can decide then. About Wes Smith . . . call me after you connect with him, okay?"

"Okay," I agreed.

"Thank you," he said, sounding like he meant it. He stood up and extended his hand, and we shook. "I appreciate your help."

I smiled, disliking my assignment but gratified that Chief Hunter trusted me enough to let me take it on. As I walked down the long corridor, across the reception area, and out into the parking lot through the soft rain to my car, I realized that I was exhausted. My feet felt leaden. I couldn't think. I wanted to confirm that Zoë was all right, and then I wanted a hug from Ty, a martini, food, a hot bath, and bed, in that order.

CHAPTER EIGHT

I was just about all done in, too tired to talk to anyone where holding up my side of the conversation required either concentration or quick wit. Talking to Wes required both, but I'd promised Chief Hunter that I'd make the call. I took a moment to think through what I wanted to say and how to best express it.

I waited until I was on the interstate, then slipped in my earpiece and dialed.

"Josie, whatcha got?" he said, skipping hello, recognizing my number.

"You don't sound surprised to hear from me."

"I'm not. I knew you'd call. So, talk. You're just leaving the police station, right?"

"Right. I gave a statement."

"Did you tell them anything you haven't already told me?"

"No—I don't know anything else."

"What did you learn? Do they have any leads?"

There's my opening, I thought. "Their questions were pretty routine. One thing . . . I got the impression the police think Frankie knew his killer and are hoping that someone will come forward with information about who might have been angry enough to kill him."

"What gave you that idea?"

"The questions they asked focused on his relationships with people."

"Good one, Josie. I like it. What else?"

"Nothing."

"Why did you text me about that Mel Erly guy?"

When I explained Zoë's theory, he asked, "You're thinking Erly hired a hit man? Is he connected like that?" It sounded as if he were salivating at the thought.

"No," I said. "Mel's a lowlife druggie, Wes, not a Mafia don."

"Yeah, I guess you're right," he said, disappointed.

"How about you? What have you learned?" I asked.

"The Whitestones' security company reports that the alarm was turned off at six thirty-eight this morning. According to Mrs. Whitestone, that's when they left the lighthouse for their helicopter. They left the alarm off because they knew both Frankie and Ashley would be coming in that morning. Frankie had arranged for that guy you mentioned, Curt Grimes, to come at eight thirty to help him hang a door. They were having Frankie convert a display cabinet in the upstairs sitting room into a closed-in storage unit. Ashley was supposed to clean the place top to bottom starting first thing."

"Did she?"

"No. She said she got involved scrimming. She told the police that since the Whitestones weren't expected back anytime soon, there was no urgency."

I wondered whether he learned that tidbit from Ashley herself or from the police, but I knew better than to ask. Wes kept his sources confidential, which is why I felt safe talking to him.

"Do the police know who opened the kitchen window?" I asked.

"No. Do you?"

"It's possible that Frankie was planning on using chemicals for some project and wanted plenty of fresh air."

"What kind of project?"

"I don't know. Polyethylening a table or something like that." I signaled my exit. "Or the killer was trying to confuse the time-of-death calculation."

"Yeah . . . I thought of that. There's no word yet from the medical examiner about when he was killed."

"Did Curt show up on time?" I asked.

"Yup, and the door got hung."

"So when Frankie came to my place after he and Curt finished with the door, the alarm system was still off?"

"Right."

"Amazing," I said. "It's hard to prevent a break-in if you don't even set the alarm."

"So you're still thinking it was burglary?" he asked.

"I don't know what to think. Has there been a confirmation as to whether the rolling pin and dish towel belonged to the Whitestones?"

"Nothing official, but they found a drawer full of matching towels, so it's a pretty good bet that it's theirs. The rolling pin, I haven't heard anything yet."

"What about Curt's alibi?" I asked.

"I'm checking. I don't have anything yet—but I will. You got more?"

"No."

"Keep me posted," he said and hung up.

I drove slowly. The rain had stopped, but the roads were still slick. As I turned north onto the secondary road, I realized that I was so tense I was grasping the steering wheel as if it were a life preserver. I couldn't stop thinking about the murder. A faceless someone had stood across from Frankie, arguing with him, fury blazing in his eyes, blinding him to reason. Yet even as the killer's rage exploded, cold calculation drove his actions. Heat and ice. Heat grabbed the rolling pin. Ice covered his tracks. The killer had been simultaneously furious and shrewd. Who, I wondered, fit that profile? No one I knew.

I raised and lowered my shoulders and rolled my head, trying to ease the knots in my neck and upper back. It didn't work.

What, I wondered, had happened to make the killer lose control? One man's cutting insult or cataclysmic betrayal or monumental rejection was another man's yawn. Some emotions simmered, sometimes for years, only to explode for a seemingly absurd or insignificant reason. I'd read an article about a fifty-year-old accountant, a man known in his community as a stand-up guy. He'd killed his seventy-five-year-old mother. When he turned himself in to the police after butchering her, he'd explained, "She burned the lamb chops." Burning the lamb chops was, to him, the last straw.

Had Frankie been killed because he had metaphorically burned someone's lamb chops? According to Zoë, Mel hated him. Hate, left unchecked, grew more toxic over time, fermenting into what could become deadly menace. Maybe the killer had felt cornered, figuratively or literally, and panicked, his hate erupting into murderous rage.

My phone vibrated, and I checked the display. It was Ty. I slipped my earpiece in and said hello. In his greeting, I heard the sound of strength.

"Are you still at the station?" he asked.

"No. I'm almost home."

"How are you holding up?"

"I'm beat. And I'm starving."

"I'll take a sandwich with me to Zoë's for you. She called a minute ago—the kids are asleep and she doesn't want to be alone."

I told him I'd be back in about ten minutes, and when I got there, I sat in my car for a moment and listened to the quiet. The night was still and darker than dark. I looked up toward the sky. The rain had stopped, but the cloud cover remained absolute. Outside, I heard a rustle in the woods on the far side of the stone wall that marked the border of the undeveloped property across the road and the *who, who, who* of an owl from somewhere in back of the house. The temperature had dropped steadily throughout the evening, and as I walked to Zoë's door, I could feel winter closing in.

"Zoë told me about Mel Erly," Ty said after we were settled in the kitchen. "I made a phone call. He's still behind bars."

I was eating a turkey sandwich. Not wanting to admit that I'd spoken to the reporter Zoë had hung up on only hours earlier, I didn't tell them that I already knew about Mel.

Ty sat next to me, his long legs stretched out in front of him. He was drinking a Smuttynose from the bottle. Just seeing him took my breath away. Everything about him appealed to me—his brains, his kindness, his looks. His eyes were dark and observant. His hair was deep brown and cut short. The bulk of his Homeland Security work was overseeing emergency responder training. With his spending so much time outdoors, his skin had weathered to a nut brown. Tonight, he wore jeans and a dark green collared T-shirt.

Zoë sat on the other side of the table, hunched over, staring into the middle distance. Her eyes were puffy and red. "Then he must have hired someone. He's a thug."

"I'm sure the police are looking into that possibility," Ty said.

"But you don't think that's what happened," she said. Her tone had an edge, as if she were daring him to disagree with her.

"A rolling pin is a weapon of opportunity, not an assassin's tool."

"Maybe the killer brought a gun, then when he got there, he used the rolling pin instead to throw the police off the trail."

Ty shook his head. "Not likely."

"Why not?"

"Are you sure you want to talk about this now?" Ty asked. He finished his beer and placed the empty on the table.

Zoë stood up, grabbed the bottle, and stomped to the recycle bin, then grabbed a replacement from the fridge and handed it to Ty.

"I'm sorry I sounded so . . . what . . . impatient? Irritated? I always want to talk about everything, no matter what," she said.

"Thanks," he said, tipping the bottle toward her. "No problem."

"So, talk to me. What's wrong with my theory?"

Ty said, "A hired killer wouldn't bother with the kind of subterfuge you described. One bullet to the back of the head, boom, he's outta there. That's what professionals do. Sure, sometimes they mutilate the body to send a message, but that doesn't figure into this case. Trying to confuse the police is too risky because staging a crime scene isn't easy, and professionals know that. If Mel called on a friend to do it, not a pro, he'd have been even more eager to get in and out than an assassin, and with as little fanfare as possible."

Zoë looked unconvinced. "Maybe it's a stupid professional. You hear all the time how criminals are stupid."

"Unquestionably, many criminals are stupid, but not that kind of stupid. Almost all hired killers, professional or semiprofessional, are risk-averse."

She sighed. "I suppose you're right."

I pushed my plate aside. "Wouldn't whoever killed Frankie have been covered in blood?"

"Probably," Ty said. "Regardless, if I were running the investigation, I'd be working on the premise that this was a crime of passion, not a hit, until I heard otherwise."

Zoë looked forlorn. "I just don't understand how someone could have killed him."

"Did he ever mention any friends besides Curt?" I asked.

"No."

"How about girls? Was Frankie dating anyone?"

"No. He talked about wishing he met more girls, but that was it." She looked at me, then Ty. "You said that if you were running the investigation, you'd assume this was a crime of passion. That's why Josie is asking about girls. What else would you look at?"

"I'd want to know about his relationships with everyone in his orbit—his family, co-workers, buddies, even the mailman. Unless we're talking about a crazy person, and I don't think we are, this level of anger usually isn't a secret."

She nodded, sighed again, and looked at each of us. "Do you know anything about Chief Hunter?"

"He's retired NYPD," I said. "A captain. Homicide."

"The city took its time replacing me," Ty said. "That's a good sign."

Zoë sighed. "I hope he's good enough," she said.

CHAPTER NINE

T he next morning dawned with the golden warmth of Indian summer. I cranked open the window over the kitchen sink. The air was fresh and bright. There was no wind. The thermometer Ty had installed outside the window read seventy-one degrees, downright balmy for a New Hampshire morning in September. I looked out into the woods. Some leaves glowed in garnet red, others in canary yellow.

I made coffee for one. Ty was long gone, up to Presque Isle for the rest of the week. Through the side window I noticed Zoë leaning into her car, buckling Jake into his car seat. I stepped onto my covered porch and called to her. "Hey, Zoë. You're leaving early. I was going to pop over to see you. How are you doing?"

She shrugged. "I couldn't sleep, so I decided to get an early start." She closed the car door and crossed the driveway so she wouldn't have to shout. "Do you think it's tacky that I'm sending them to school? I mean, I can't even think about the funeral yet, you know?"

"I think you're smart. There's no point in keeping them home. How about you? What are you going to do to keep yourself from fretting?"

"I'm going to show up with them and let the principal put me to work. They've got to need an extra set of hands somewhere."

"If they don't, I do. Eric always needs help setting up for the tag sale."

"It's only Wednesday. Does he really start setting up this early?"

"We're always either setting up or breaking down," I said. "I keep trying to think of ways we can only tweak it from one week to the next, but it never looks fresh unless we reshelve everything and start from scratch. So yes, he starts setting up today. And yes, you have a job anytime you want one."

Her eyes moistened. "Thank you, Josie." She took a step back toward her car, then paused, turned full around to face me, and said, "Can you believe this weather? I figure God's so glad to get Frankie up in heaven, he's shining down on us."

Tears sprang to my eyes. "Oh, Zoë."

Her lip trembled. Even with worry lines furrowing her brow and a downturned mouth, she was beautiful. Her raven-colored hair hung in lush waves to her shoulders. Her skin was radiant, her figure willowy and graceful.

"You know, Josie, I'm a rule-follower," she said. "Line up single file, I do it. Line up by height, no problem. And you know what it's got me? More heartache than I ever would have had if I'd just gone after a good time. Who makes the frigging rules anyway?" She took in a breath and rubbed her temple, as if she had a headache. "Don't mind me. I'm a little upset."

"It would be odd if you weren't. Come for dinner. Ty's in upstate Maine. We can share a martini and toast to better days."

"Thanks . . . great . . . but let's do it at my place, okay? So I can keep the kids on a regular schedule."

I glanced at them. Jake was absorbed in a book. Emma was talking softly to her teddy monkey, a battered stuffed animal she'd found in the attic and christened Mary-Rose. "Sounds good. I'll bring everything."

"Can we tell good Frankie stories?" she asked.

"You bet. And there are a lot of them. Do you remember the time he—"

I broke off as Chief Hunter drove up. He parked in back of my car and stepped out. His jacket was dark green, his shirt yellow, his slacks brown, and his tie was gold with brown and green dots. He wore dark-tinted sunglasses, and I couldn't see his eyes as he approached us. He nodded at me, then turned to Zoë.

"I'm glad I caught you," he told her. "I interviewed Mr. Erly last evening. He hasn't made bail, and from what he told me, he doesn't expect to. We've just finished tracking down his known associates." He removed his sunglasses and blinked several times as his eyes adjusted to the light. His scar looked bloodred in the harsh daylight. "I'm convinced that he had nothing to do with the murder."

She held his gaze and nodded, but she didn't reply.

"I wanted you to know that I took your concern seriously," he continued. "If you have any other thoughts, please get in touch right away."

"I will," she said. "And if you learn anything, anything at all, please tell me. I can deal with anything, but I hate not knowing. Thank you for taking my comments seriously."

She reached out her hand, and he took it and held it for an extra beat.

"I'll keep you as up-to-date as I can," he said.

"Thank you."

He nodded at me, and Zoë and I watched him back out and head off toward Rocky Point.

"He seems awfully nice, doesn't he?" Zoë remarked.

"And sensitive. And thoughtful."

She nodded. "I don't know what I would have done last night without you and Ty," she said, her tone soft and ripe with emotion. "Thank you."

As I stood in the early morning sunlight, I tried and failed to formulate words of comfort. Her shoulders began to shake, and she turned her back to her children. After several seconds, she stopped crying.

"I wish I could think of what to say," I told her.

"You have. You do." She touched my arm. "You're such a great friend, Josie."

"You, too," I whispered, fighting tears. "You, too."

She offered a wavering smile, enough to reassure me that for the moment at least, she would be all right. After she'd driven away, I remained where I was, staring over the stone wall and into the forest. Through slashes of sunlight, I could see deep into the woods. The turning leaves formed a mosaic of deep reds and rich golds and bright oranges, lit, perhaps as Zoë thought, by the will of God. I stood for several moments, transfixed, and then I drove to work.

Three people, two men and a woman, lay in wait as I pulled into my company's parking lot. I recognized the woman as a New York reporter named Bertie Rose, a journalist with the ethics of a cockroach. The others were strangers. All three ran after my car as I drove toward my building, shouting questions and snapping photographs. I parked near the front entrance, and one of the men tried to open the passenger's door, but couldn't because it was locked. Their clamoring felt like a full-on assault. My pulse began to race. I forced myself to breathe deeply, to try to calm myself.

Years ago, I'd been the prosecutor's star witness in a price-fixing scandal that had rocked Frisco's, the high-end New York City antiques auction house where I'd worked. I'd been the whistle-blower, and as a result I'd been shunned by most of my friends, treated like a pariah at work, and ultimately dismissed from my dream job because, according to the feckless acting CEO, I wasn't a team player.

Everything about that era was horrible—and through it all, my nemesis had been Bertie, a devil-woman who stalked me for *New York Monthly* and made my life a living hell. Back then she'd pretended to be my ally, a lie it had had taken me weeks to uncover, damn her eyes. Now, here she was again, standing in my parking lot, pounding on my car window, her strident voice yelling something about the Whitestones, and had I talked to them, and did I know who killed their caretaker, and what did the murder scene look like. The men shouted, too, asking whether I knew Frankie well and what I thought had happened.

I ignored them all, emotionally distancing myself the way I'd learned to do, protecting myself from their rabid attacks, focusing instead on how to handle their assault. Once I had decided what to say to them and what to do as a follow-up, I grabbed my tote bag and prepared to exit my vehicle.

They backed away enough to allow me to step out, but not one inch farther. I locked my car and, with my front door key in hand, edged my way to the building's entrance. I turned to face them. I held up a palm, and they quieted down, smiling, holding digital recorders in outstretched arms, ready to memorialize my every word.

"Bertie, I know you're from *New York Monthly*," I said, managing to keep my tone civil. "Who are you guys?"

"Mark Jenson, *Manchester Sentinel*," one man said, naming New Hampshire's largest-circulation newspaper.

"Dwayne Malloy, *Boston Trumpet*. Tell us what happened."

The *Trumpet* was a tabloid that mostly featured stories about babies born with three heads and aliens camping out in suburban backyards.

"You're all trespassing on private property," I said politely. "Get out now. As soon as I'm inside, I'm calling the police."

Ignoring their clamorous protests, I turned my back to them and entered, shutting the door without slamming it. I spun the dead bolt and deactivated the alarms, then ran to the window. They were leaving; probably, I thought, to loiter on the public street.

The immediate crisis over, I began to shake, but I also smiled. I felt proud of how I'd handled myself. Previously, in the face of a media onslaught, I would have panicked or become a quivering mass of helplessness. Now, I was in control.

I called Chief Hunter's cell phone and got him. Three minutes later, I'd won his commitment to send a police officer to remind the reporters that my office and my home were private property. Secretly, I wanted the evil Bertie to ignore our warning, scuffle with the officer, and end up behind bars. That would be a trial where I'd relish testifying.

"Thank you for talking to Wes Smith," he said before he hung up. "His article is exactly what I'd hoped for."

"Any payoff yet?"

"Thanks again, Josie," he said.

I took the hint. "Glad to help," I replied.

Upstairs in my private office, I turned on my computer. As soon as it booted up, I went to the *Seacoast Star* Web site and read Wes's front-page article.

Whitestone Caretaker Murdered
Was the Motive Anger or Gain?

The article first presented the facts. I learned two things. First, while the police had collected a mishmash of fingerprints from all over the lighthouse, including several on the sill by the open window in the kitchen, and were sorting through them, using them to prove who'd wielded the rolling pin was probably going to be a bust. The prints found on it were smudged beyond recognition. Second, the rolling pin had been positively identified as being owned by the Whitestones. Ashley had been able to recall that there was a small burned spot near one of the handles, and Maddie, reached at her apartment in New York City, had confirmed it.

Wes concluded with a question: "Frankie Winterelli lived among us in the Seacoast region for less than two years. If this murder resulted from anger, as many in the police theorize, what do you know that could explain it? The police need your help." No wonder Chief Hunter thanked me.

CHAPTER TEN

I glanced at the time display on my computer monitor. It was a quarter to nine, too early for my pal Shelley to be at work. It was probably too early to call Shelley, period. She was not a morning person. As far as I knew, it was she who had invented the disco nap. She slept for several hours in the early evening, so she could go out clubbing at ten or eleven, get to sleep at four or five, and still perform at full throttle the next day.

During the dark days of the trial and its aftermath, Shelley had stayed neutral, no easy task when most of her colleagues were gunning for me. We rarely saw each other anymore since I only got to New York City once or twice a year, and to Manhattan-centric Shelley, Rocky Point might as well have been located in the Antipodes. Shelley still worked at Frisco's, and her day started around ten. I decided she'd forgive me and called her at home.

Six rings later, her sleepy voice said, "Hello."

"Shelley, it's Josie. Wake up—I need a favor."

"Jeez, Josie, what time is it?"

"Almost nine."

"In the morning?"

I smiled. "Yes. It's Wednesday."

"You're cruel. . . . It's ten to nine, which means you've just robbed me of ten minutes' sleep."

"I need you."

"Sigh, sigh, sigh. Hold on while I throw some water on my face."

I put the phone on speaker and spun around to face my window. The old maple was alive with color.

Two minutes later, Shelley was back. "Okay. This better be good, my friend."

I crossed my fingers for luck. I knew for a fact that Shelley hobnobbed with all the players in the rarefied New York City arts and antiques world—including the magazine editors who followed the trends. "Do you know anyone at a top-drawer magazine who might be interested in an *In Cold Blood* sort of exposé?"

"Is this about the Whitestones?"

"The murder at their lighthouse, yeah. I'm trying to help out a local reporter."

"That doesn't sound like you—helping a reporter? Are you sure you aren't calling me to come help tar and feather him? Has the frozen tundra finally turned your brain to ice?"

"First of all, it's over seventy today and absolutely gorgeous. Second of all, Bertie from *New York Monthly* is here, and after me again."

"Ah! Your Machiavellian plan becomes clear. You're out to screw her by giving an exclusive to someone else."

Shelley was as quick as ever, even half-asleep. "Do you think it will work?" I asked.

"It will if you give Ray Austin a call. He's an editor at *Metropolitan,* and he'd love a story like this." She chuckled. "What am I saying—anyone would love a story like this."

Metropolitan was a well-respected, *Vanity Fair*–like monthly magazine, filled with long, thoughtful features delving into the stories behind the news as it affected New York City's *Town and Country* set. It was a perfect fit for what I had in mind.

"Great. Thanks, Shelley."

"Have your reporter buddy call and use my name. Ray's a hottie—*and* a good dancer."

"Shelley, you devil. Are you two an item?"

"I wish. He's happily married to Lucy Mattin, the shoe designer. Have you got a pen?"

"I'm ready!" I said, exhilarated. I wrote down Ray Austin's contact information. "This is exactly what I was hoping for. Shelley, you're a peach!"

"This is my favorite kind of networking—win-win all around.

You're thanking me, and Ray will, too. How can a girl lose? Plus, the next time you're in town you can buy me a drink."

"You got it."

I asked her about life at Frisco's, and she told me about the latest power play unfolding in the decorative arts department. I listened with pleasure, enjoying her dry observations about co-workers who were weasels and bosses with unfettered ambition. She asked me about Ty, line dancing, a hobby we shared, and my business.

"Someday you've got to come up here, Shelley, and see what you're missing. Seriously—you ever decide to move, you have a job. Don't dismiss it out of hand just because it's not New York. My company's growing. In a smaller house, you'd have more opportunity to really shine."

"Send a relocation video and I promise I'll watch it some night. I always love a good comedy."

I laughed. "You're xenophobic, you know that, right?"

"Xenophobic because I don't want to leave the big city for a teeny tiny, but no doubt adorable, coastal town? Josie, honey, you've been gone too long. Take a couple of martinis and come to brunch."

I laughed again, as enamored as ever with Shelley. I missed her.

We chatted awhile longer, and then she had to get ready for work. As I hung up, I had the incredibly comforting thought that while I missed her, I no longer missed my previous life at all. I loved visiting New York City, but I had found my home in Rocky Point. I fit in. I had friends. I loved my life. And I loved my plan to help Wes. I dialed his number and got him.

"Whatcha got?" he asked, skipping the pleasantries, as usual.

"An opportunity for you. A big-time major-league opportunity." I described my story idea and told him about the *Metropolitan* editor who might be receptive to the project.

"What's the catch?"

"No catch."

I could hear him breathing. After several seconds, he said, "This is bonzo, Josie. I mean, really, really bonzo. But I don't get it. What do you want in return?"

Bonzo, I translated silently, *Wes-speak for awesome.* "Nothing. Well, maybe some information, just like always, but nothing else."

"Why are you doing this?"

I thought for a moment about how much to reveal, watching as my maple's burnished leaves fluttered in a passing breeze. I decided to tell him the truth. "You're a good guy, Wes, not just a good reporter. Many journalists aren't. I want to reward your integrity and send a signal to the others, the vultures, that if I have anything to say about it, the good guys will always come out on top."

"Jeez . . . *Metropolitan* . . . Josie, I'm telling you, you're the bomb, the nuclear bomb," he said, sounding stunned, then energized. "I won't forget this."

I laughed, then gave him Ray Austin's name and number and Shelley's name. I added, "When you're pitching the story, you can tell him I've promised you an exclusive."

I was sitting nearby as Sasha explained the Chinese dinner set's valuation to its owner, Joan Scott, finding a measure of solace in the routine of work. Cara told me that Chief Hunter was on line two. It was nine thirty in the morning.

"I just got the word from the techs," he said. "They're on schedule, so if you're okay with it, I can pick you up at noon."

"Why don't I just meet you at the lighthouse?"

"I have some more questions. I thought we could talk en route."

What else could he possibly have to ask me? I wondered. I'd already told him everything I knew. I looked around the office. Sasha and Joan sat within arm's reach, both politely waiting for me to rejoin their conversation. I wanted to ask Chief Hunter for details but didn't. Both women were listening in, and who could blame them? An open office was no place for a private conversation.

"Sure," I said, feeling as if I were volunteering for a root canal, "noon's good."

I hung up, then told Joan and Sasha, "Sorry about that."

I'd met Joan for the first time this morning. She was tall and thin, with intelligent blue eyes and salt-and-pepper hair. She was a retired scientist, now interested in a different kind of research—genealogy.

She'd traced her family's ownership of the dinnerware to General Lingan.

"You were saying that the serving pieces added value to the set, Sasha," I said, to ease us back into the appraisal.

"Exactly. Some of the larger and unusually shaped pieces are quite rare. Especially the octagonal platter and what you call the leaf plates." She smiled. "You said you weren't planning on selling, though, is that correct?"

"That's right. Part of why I want this appraisal is that I'm curious," she said, laughing. "That's the scientist in me—I'm curious about everything! But another part is that we use the dishes all the time, and since they date from the eighteenth century, I figured I ought to be certain that I'm not risking a fortune every time I wash a plate!"

"One of the things I looked into was the association to General Lingan," Sasha said. She turned to me. "The general bought the set from merchant ships when they docked in Baltimore, and the set has been passed down in Ms. Scott's family from generation to generation ever since." She took in a breath, and I could tell she was worried that Joan wouldn't like what she heard. "General Lingan is, in fact, considered an important Revolutionary War figure, but the association probably won't boost the selling price unless we happen to find someone who wants the dishes who also happens to value the connection. That's not likely. At auction, if properly marketed and with a little luck, I would expect the set to sell for around two thousand dollars . . . maybe twenty-five hundred."

Joan nodded. "Not a fortune, but not nothing."

"And who can put a price on the heritage?" I asked.

"You've got that right." She smiled again, stood up, and shook Sasha's hand, then mine. "Thanks so much."

Sasha asked Cara to page Eric, and I watched as he wheeled the carefully boxed china to her car.

"Good job, Sasha," I said, and she smiled shyly and thanked me.

Eric was almost through loading it into the trunk for her when Lenny Wilton, the scrimshander, drove into the lot.

"Lenny's here," I announced.

"He gives such great service," Gretchen said.

Lenny pushed open the door, setting Gretchen's wind chimes

jingling. He was carrying a duffle bag, looking for all the world as if he'd stepped off the pages of an Abercrombie & Fitch catalogue. He was about twenty-five, tall, and blond, and he didn't walk, he strutted. His features were symmetrical, his hair a little long. He was a hunk.

When he'd first stopped by to introduce himself, about three years earlier, Gretchen had lasered in on him like a cat to cream. He'd been cordial but uninterested. I'd shaken my head over it. Gretchen, who could charm a statue to life, and who, until she'd met her boyfriend, Jack, had an internal radar system for spotting single, attractive men that would put NASA to shame, had got nowhere. All Lenny seemed to care about was business.

She'd shrugged off his indifference with a good-natured "Story of my life."

I remembered thinking that a man had to be insane not to pursue Gretchen like a hound dog. She was beautiful, sweet, hardworking, and kind. It was still a mystery to me why she'd had so much trouble meeting good men, a moot question now that she and Jack were a couple.

"Hi, Lenny," I said. "I hear your barrettes are selling like hotcakes."

"Which means your customers have great taste!"

"Obviously!" I said, smiling.

"Here you go," he said, extracting a box from his bag and hoisting it onto Gretchen's desk. "There are two new designs—a winter scene and a Christmas one."

"Great!" Gretchen said. "Let's take a look."

The barrettes were beautiful. There were four dozen each of three designs, one a Currier and Ives–style, skating-on-the-village-pond design; the second a gaily decorated Victorian home, complete with a doily-draped sofa, poinsettias, and boughs of holly; and the third a sailboat leaping over swells, each signed LEON, Lenny's branding for his low-end scrims. The name Leon came from combining the first two letters of his first name with the last two letters of his last name, a clever way, I thought, of differentiating his machine-made scrims from his custom-made, high-end offerings.

Gretchen, Cara, and I oohed and aahed; then Gretchen confirmed the count and handed him a check. He nodded, chatted for a minute about the beautiful weather, and left.

"The workmanship is spectacular," Cara said, examining a barrette close up.

"Hard to believe it's machine-made," I said. "Those new designs are fab. I think we should put out three separate baskets so it's obvious there are three different designs. I bet lots of people will buy more than one."

Gretchen loved the idea and went to show the new designs to Eric.

I wandered upstairs, unmotivated and unfocused. I spent the next two hours moving papers around on my desk, unable to concentrate on work. Finally, I gave up trying. I couldn't stop thinking about Frankie. I wanted to know how he'd lived the last year of his life, whom he had spent time with, and what he did when he wasn't working. Then I realized that I had an untapped source of information at hand—Eric.

CHAPTER ELEVEN

T he tag sale venue looked barren and unwelcoming. Rows of folding tables stood uncovered and empty. Nothing hung on the walls. The incandescent track lighting was off, and the fluorescent lighting was harsh.

I saw Eric near the front, stooped over. He was using a hose attachment on the Shop-Vac to clean the baseboards. The door and windows were open, and the breeze blowing through was refreshing.

"Hey, Eric," I said, shouting to be heard over the drone of the vacuum cleaner.

He looked up, startled, then switched off the machine. "Hi, Josie."

"Sorry to interrupt, but I'm hoping you won't mind if I ask you a couple of things about Frankie."

"Okay," he said, his expression somber.

"I'm trying to understand how this could have happened, to figure out who could possibly have wanted to kill him. Did he ever mention a man named Mel? Mel Erly?"

Eric shook his head. "No, I don't know that name."

I nodded. "How about girls? Was he dating anyone?"

"No."

"I don't mean to pry . . . but were you two close? I mean, would he have confided in you if he were seeing someone?"

"I think so. We hung out pretty often."

"Really? I didn't know." I smiled. "Not that there's any reason why I should! What kinds of things did you do?"

"We went out for burgers a lot, you know, to a sports bar to watch a game or something. We went bowling a few times. He was pretty good. Once we went fishing. We caught some bluefish."

"Did he talk about any of his other friends?"

"You mean like Curt? Sure. Curt usually came with us."

"Any other friends come to mind?"

He shook his head. "Not that I know of."

"And nothing about girls?"

"I know he was hoping to meet someone."

"What did he say about it?"

Eric shrugged. "That it was hard to meet nice girls, especially since his work was solitary. I mean, when he worked at Jackson's Landscaping, he was with a crew of guys taking care of houses where usually the people weren't home. At the Whitestones', he was all alone except for Ashley. So he had this idea to go where he thought nice girls would be."

"That's smart, isn't it? Where did he try?"

Eric smiled. "The library."

"That's great!"

"Not really. You're not allowed to talk in a library."

I laughed. "So then what did he do?"

"He went to church events. I went with him a couple of times." He stared at his boots. "I wanted to meet a nice girl, too."

"How did it work out?" I asked, thinking that I was learning about a whole new set of relationships Frankie might have had. Who knew how many friends—or enemies—he might have made at church?

His cheeks reddened. "Good. For me, I mean. Last February we went to a potluck singles dinner at Rocky Point Congregational Church." He raised his eyes to mine, maybe checking whether I was getting ready to tease him, saw that I wasn't, and added, "I met a girl. We're still seeing each other."

"That's wonderful, Eric," I said, delighted and surprised.

He smiled. "Her name's Grace."

"What a beautiful name! What does she do?"

"She's a teacher's aide, and she goes to night school. She wants to be an elementary school teacher."

"I look forward to meeting her," I said. "How about Frankie? Did he meet anyone?"

Eric shook his head. "No—but just yesterday he told me he'd

volunteered to work at the church's booth at the Harvest Festival, so he was still trying, you know?"

I nodded. "What else did he talk about? Did he mention any other plans?"

"He was thinking about getting a dog. He said he was finally feeling ready to settle in. He wanted to know about breeds and what kind I thought he should get. I told him about Jet—my black Lab—how smart he is and all."

I shut my eyes, and swallowed several times, determined to keep from crying. *How sad is that?* I thought. *Frankie was ready to put down roots, and instead, someone killed him.*

"Have you told the police all this?" I asked.

He nodded. "Last night. Officer Brownley came to see me at home."

The PA speaker crackled, followed by Cara's voice. "Chief Hunter is here, Josie."

I patted Eric's arm, thanked him, and headed to the front.

I took my time crossing the dimly lit warehouse. As I walked over the daddy-longleg shadows that striped the concrete floor, I passed shelves packed with inventory, crates stacked like bricks, worktables, and wall-mounted rolls of bubble wrap. I paused at the door that led to the main office, wanting to finish assimilating everything I'd just learned.

The staff and congregants at Rocky Point Congregational Church knew Frankie in a way I didn't. I wondered whether he'd offended any young women—or, as I thought about it, their boyfriends, fathers, or brothers. Up until this moment, I'd thought Eric lived a mostly solitary life, sharing a big, old white elephant of a house with his mother and his dog, enduring a life I couldn't have borne. I'd long since concluded that his mother, a whining complainer with the personality of an emery board, was the luckiest woman alive to have gentle, caring Eric as her son. Not many young men would excuse her bad temper as a by-product of her hard life, but Eric did. Now I knew that Eric had a life that stretched beyond her reach. Good for him.

I pushed through the door and greeted Chief Hunter.

Before we left, I called everyone together, including Eric.

"Have any of you been approached by reporters?" I asked.

They all nodded.

"It's not going to stop anytime soon," I said, explaining that I anticipated that the story would garner increasing worldwide attention. "Talk to the reporters. Don't talk to them. It's totally up to you. I just want you to know that you're under no obligation to do so. If you don't want to talk to them, all you need to do is either keep quiet or keep repeating 'no comment,' over and over again. If they're on private property, you can order them to leave, explaining that if they don't, you'll call the police. They can dig and claw and scratch trying to find dirt or scandal or secrets, but they can't trespass. They're not allowed on Prescott's property."

From their expressions, I could tell they were reacting as expected—most of them. Sasha was anxious, worrying a twist of hair. Gretchen was excited. Her eyes sparkled as she anticipated being in the thick of a media crush. Fred was detached and analytical, processing the information. He leaned back in his chair, his lips pursed, his eyes missing nothing. Cara looked on, her eyes big, her mouth slightly open, her uneasiness apparent. Eric didn't look shy, though, as I would have anticipated. He looked afraid. The blood had drained from his face, and he was biting his lip. That reporters were digging around was irritating, for sure—but there was only one reason I could think of why their presence might be scary: Eric had something to hide.

CHAPTER TWELVE

C hief Hunter took the scenic route, turning onto Ocean Avenue at the first opportunity. I lowered the visor against the sun's midday glare, the brightness welcome after yesterday's bone-chilling rain.

"I spoke to Mrs. Whitestone," he said. "She flew in this morning and will meet us at the lighthouse."

"It's got to be a nightmare," I said, "having someone killed in your house."

"Yeah," he agreed. After a short pause, he added, "So . . . I mentioned that I had a couple of questions."

I turned toward him and studied his face, hoping to get an indication of where this was heading. My eyes were drawn to his scar. It ran on the outside of his eyebrow in a loose zigzag pattern. The shape was what I would expect if he'd been attacked by someone wielding a broken beer bottle. If that's what happened, I wondered how the perpetrator had been stopped from doing even more damage, and whether the incident had occurred in a barroom brawl or in a domestic dispute while he was on duty.

"Right," I said, turning back to watch the glimmering ocean. Golden stars glinted on the midnight blue water. "I have something to tell you, too."

"You first."

"I asked Eric about whether Frankie had any other friends except Curt, and we got talking about girls." I repeated what Eric told me about meeting nice girls at church.

"Thanks," he said. "Why did you ask him about friends?"

"Because I thought he might know something. I was right."

"You shouldn't be questioning people."

"Eric's not 'people,' not the way you mean."

Chief Hunter didn't speak for several seconds, long enough so I began to wonder if he was waiting for me to say something.

"You told me how it came about that Mr. Winterelli got the job as caretaker," he said finally. "Do you know how Ms. Morse became the Whitestones' housekeeper?"

Relieved that he'd let the issue of my talking to Eric slide, I said, "Yes, actually, I do. It was last July, the day I went with the White-stones to the Sea View Gallery exhibition opening. The show was called *Made in America: An Artisan's View of the Coast*. Greg had a nice selection of American-crafted objects, all sorts of things—paintings, jewelry, pottery, and some scrimshaw. Ashley's work was represented. The Whitestones had just decided to take my advice and buy a spectacular Lenny Wilton scrimmed tooth when Ashley struck up a conversation with us. She was enthralling—when she gets going about the history and lore of scrimshaw, she's riveting. Anyway, one thing led to another, and they ended up offering her the job, and she took it."

"That sounds like you're doing a fair amount of editing. Fill in the blanks. Did they buy one of her scrimshaws?"

I smiled, remembering how Maddie had confessed to me that she'd gone back to the gallery the next day to get one of Ashley's scrimmed teeth. "Yes."

"Against your wishes."

"That's too strong. Against my advice would be a better way to put it—but that's still misleading. Guy told me he was interested in building a world-class collection of maritime art and artifacts. I mean no disrespect to Ashley, but as I explained to you yesterday, the quality of her work just isn't on par with that standard."

"Why did they buy it, then?"

"Maddie told me that when she went to the gallery to pick up the Wilton tooth, she and Greg got talking about local artists. Greg contrasted Lenny Wilton's situation with Ashley's. They're both serious scrimshanders, but there the resemblance ends. Lenny's an artistic and business force to be reckoned with. Ashley is a hold-your-pinky-in-the-air artiste with no business sense at all. He's twelve or fifteen years younger than she is, but his scrimmed teeth sell for more than six times what hers do. He's won a dozen awards, holds patents for a scrimming machine, is represented in major museums, has had one-man exhibitions in Tokyo and New York, and has a growing business selling low-end, high-quality trinkets under the brand name Leon. Until the Whitestones hired her, Ashley had trouble making ends meet."

As we approached Lighthouse Lane, I kept my eyes on the undulating ocean. The rhythmic ebb and flow was hypnotic. If I squinted, specks of shimmering sunlight glinted like flickering candles.

"Maddie has a soft heart," I continued. "After she heard about Ashley's situation, she bought one of her objects—and she offered her the job as Rocky Point Light's housekeeper. It was a perfect opportunity for Ashley. The cottage that comes with the position is big enough so that she can use it as her studio as well as her living space, and since the Whitestones aren't often at the lighthouse, she has plenty of time for her art. No surprise—Ashley accepted the offer, and she's been there ever since."

"How long has she been exhibiting at Sea View Gallery?"

"I don't know."

"What's Greg Donovan's reputation in the field?"

I turned to look at him. "In what way?"

"Is he an honest businessman?"

"I have no reason to think he's not."

"You sound like you're hedging. What's your hesitation?"

I chose my words carefully. "Greg's been in business for a long time. I've never heard anything to suggest that he's not completely on the up-and-up. If he wasn't paying his artists, for example, I'd know it."

Chief Hunter didn't respond for several seconds. "You don't like him."

"Not much, no. But that has nothing to do with your investigation."

"Maybe so, maybe not. What's your issue with him?"

"You're trying to get me to gossip some more," I said.

"I'm trying to conduct a proper investigation. Why don't you like him?"

"I don't know exactly. He's fake, for one thing. It sounds awful to say, but the plain truth is that being around him makes my skin crawl."

He nodded. "Thanks for telling me."

He turned onto Lighthouse Lane. About a quarter mile up the road, we came to the massive gates. A patrol car blocked the entry. A young officer I knew by sight got out of the car and approached us. She was tall and thin and so fair her skin appeared translucent. Her hair was platinum blond, and she wore it in a high bun. Tendrils trailed from under her cap. She wore no makeup. Her badge read: OFFICER F. MEADE.

Chief Hunter lowered his window. "Anything?" he asked her.

"Yes, sir. Several reporters have been by. Most left without incident, but two had . . . well . . . a pretty combative attitude. One, a producer from a Portland TV station, wanted to shoot some background color—that's what he called it, background color. The other, a reporter from a magazine, tried to sneak in while she thought I wasn't looking." She consulted her notebook. "She's from *New York Monthly.*"

Bertie, I thought.

I followed Chief Hunter's eyes as he surveyed the tall stone wall that stretched along the road, then curved into the forest. It would be impossible for one police officer—or even a dozen—to guard the entire perimeter. After a moment, he said, "You need help, you holler, okay?"

"Yes, sir. One other thing. Mrs. Whitestone is here."

He nodded, acknowledging that he heard her, raised the window, and waited while she backed her car up so we could turn in.

His phone rang, and he put in his earpiece and answered with a crisp "Chief Hunter." He listened for a minute, thanked the caller, then said to me, "Citizen calls are trickling in about Mr. Winterelli."

"From Wes's article?" I asked.

"Looks that way. We just got an anonymous call from someone who said that Mr. Winterelli got into a fracas over the summer. About a girl. Do you know anything about it?"

"No, I haven't heard of anything like that. If there'd been a scuffle and Eric knew about it, I think he would have told me."

"We'll check it out."

As we passed the turnoff to Frankie's and Ashley's cottages, a fresh wave of sadness washed over me. Today was a perfect September day, warm and sunny and filled with promise, one of God's days, my mother would have said. A day of easy living, a day to cherish before the long, hard winter provided an unremitting test of endurance. *Is it better to die in darkness and cold than in bright light and warmth?* I wondered, then realized that it didn't matter—dead is dead. *Poor Frankie.*

CHAPTER THIRTEEN

W e came to a stop in back of a black stretch limo parked in front of the lighthouse. As I stepped out of the SUV, video-recorder bag in hand, the shiny red front door opened. Maddie stood on the threshold, smiling, waiting for us to join her. I hoisted the bag onto my shoulder and grabbed my tote bag.

"Josie," she said, her Slovenian accent strong and appealing. Her chestnut brown hair was long and straight. Her red silk blouse, black pencil skirt, and black suede high-heeled boots had been fitted by experts. She looked magnificent.

"Hi, Maddie," I said. She stepped back into the enclosed vestibule, a bulwark the Whitestones had added during the renovation to protect visitors from the sometimes brutal New England weather.

"Have you met Chief Hunter?" I asked.

"We spoke on the phone. How do you do?" She offered her hand, and they shook. "Come in, please."

The atrium floor was laid with reclaimed oak. A four-foot-wide compass made of rosewood and mahogany had been inlaid at an angle. Lights glittered in the ceiling twenty-five feet overhead. Guy had told me the pattern replicated the night sky as it would have appeared to a sailor passing Rocky Point Light on a midsummer's night.

To the left and right were arched entrances into the circular open-plan living areas. On the left was the living room, then a small area Guy used as his downstairs office, then a game room, then the kitchen. On the right was a parlor, then a book-lined reading room, then the dining room, then the kitchen. A short hallway in front of me led directly to the kitchen.

A central core housed a curved staircase three times as large as the one at Prescott's. It spiraled up three levels, passing the master bedroom suite, which comprised the entire second floor, then two guest rooms, each with its own bathroom, on the third floor, ending at a sitting room located directly under the rotating beacon. The beacon sat atop the widow's walk and was accessed through a pull-down ladder. A waist-high railing at each landing provided dramatic 360-degree views down into the living space below and out over the ocean and forests through the walls of windows.

"I know you want to start right away," Maddie said. She handed me a key and a slip of paper. "The key, it is for the front door," she explained. "Here is the alarm code and the directions."

"You're not staying here?" Chief Hunter asked.

She shook her head. "No." She glanced over her shoulder, toward the kitchen. "I'm not comfortable . . . I'm at the Forsythia Inn in Portsmouth."

"I understand," he said. "How long will you be in town?"

"A few days at least. Certainly until Guy joins me. We want to help in any way we can." To me, she added, "You don't need me now, do you, Josie? I have some work to do—it sounds . . . so . . . I don't know . . . with Frankie just dead—" She broke off her sentence, paused, then continued. "I'm chairing the Golden Lights ball, a charity fundraiser, this coming December, and our invitations needed to go to the printer yesterday. I'd like to check into my room and finalize them."

"That's fine," I said. "I won't have the inventory to show you for several hours at the earliest."

"I'll come back after I finish. I'm going to pack some things. Guy and I were planning on spending one more weekend here before closing the place up for the winter—but now, I don't know . . . so I thought I should go ahead and take what I want while I'm here." She sighed. "Also for later, Josie—I want to consult you about a Winslow Homer etching I'm thinking of buying Guy for his birthday. May I show you the photographs of it?"

My heart gave an extra thump. Winslow Homer was a dominant figure in nineteenth-century American art. One of his era's most important proponents of realism, he had achieved popularity during his lifetime and near-icon status after his death. "Are you kidding me? I'd love to see them! Who's the seller?"

"Some man who bought it from a woman. The first seller, I don't know her name, she found it when she was cleaning out the attic of her family's home. She wanted to sell it quickly and without a middleman—so she did, to this fellow, who I think is a kind of antiques peddler of some sort, I don't know. He told me he read about Guy's collection in the *Antiques Insights* article, so he called him." She smiled, looking devilish and proud. "I picked up the phone, so Guy doesn't know anything about it! I am very clever, yes?" She laughed. "It would be a perfect gift. He wants two hundred and fifty thousand dollars. What do you think, Josie? Is that a fair price?"

"I'd need to see it, of course, but on the face of it . . . maybe. If it's an original, it's a spectacular find, and that's a better than spectacular price—but that's a big if. What's the subject matter?"

"A man and a boy in a small boat. They have a net filled with fish. The ocean is . . . I don't know the word . . . angry."

"The subject matter is right, but that doesn't mean anything. I'll let you know what I think as soon as I look at the photos. You'll e-mail them to me?"

"Yes, of course. Thank you, Josie." As Maddie turned to leave, her expression grew solemn. "I still can't believe it . . . Frankie . . . Do you know his family?"

"Yes. His aunt, Zoë Winterelli."

"Would you give me her address, please? I'd like to write a note, telling her how much we valued Frankie's work, and how much we enjoyed getting to know him."

I assured her that I would. As soon as she stepped outside, a short man with gray hair hurried around her limo to open the rear door, and I watched until they were out of sight. "How long do you need here?" Chief Hunter asked, recalling my attention.

"An hour, maybe two. I don't think it will take longer than that. I'm not actually appraising anything. I'm just recording what's here to create an initial inventory."

"How about if I call you in an hour and see how you're doing?"

"That's fine," I said, and as soon as he left, I slid my tote bag and camera carrying case out of the way under a table in the front hall and stepped into the living room.

I started with a long, low display case positioned as a room divider. Inside, there were two handcrafted boat replicas, one in teak and one in mahogany; the boat-in-a-bottle they'd bought at auction from Prescott's; five ship's bells; the Frederick Myrick tooth that Maddie and Guy had bought from me, and the two teeth by Lenny Wilton and Ashley Morse they'd purchased at Sea View Gallery; two nautical clocks; and a logbook from a Nantucket whaler, the *Planter*.

Three paintings hung on the inside wall, all nineteenth-century oils of coastal or ocean scenes: a J. M. W. Turner, a Thomas Chambers, and a Charles Henry Gifford. I recorded each object from all sides, describing what I saw in minute detail, then scanned the room to see if I'd missed anything. I hadn't.

I recorded a ship's bell that Guy used as a paperweight, a captain's desk, and, in the game room, a handcrafted chess table. I paused at the entrance to the kitchen, dreading entering the room where Frankie had been killed but knowing that I couldn't skip it—the Whitestones had hung a beautiful Robert Salmon rendering of Boston Harbor there, and I needed to record it. I took a deep breath before stepping into the room.

The floor was streaked with dirty footprints. Dried blood provided mute testimony to the violence that had occurred the day before. I closed my eyes to escape my memories of the macabre scene, then opened them—closing them only made the images more garish.

The kitchen was decorated in silver and black. The cabinets were crafted from cocobolo wood, the appliances were stainless steel, and the counters were black granite, flecked with silver. A porcelain cookie jar in the shape of a jaunty-looking sea captain smoking a pipe sat on the counter. The MADE IN CHINA mark told me it was a modern repro. Four small watercolors showing Rocky Point Light in different seasons hung in the in-room dining area along with the magnificent Robert Salmon oil. They, and several locally produced baskets suspended from an over-island wrought-iron pot rack, were worth recording.

Stepping into the dining room, I exhaled, feeling as if I'd held my breath the whole time I'd been in the kitchen. I was glad to be out of there.

I recorded a Fitz Hugh Lane oil of ships sailing into port that hung over the sideboard and a scrimmed ditty box that sat on top, and then I was done with the ground floor.

I climbed the spiral staircase to the next level, pausing briefly on the landing to admire the riot of color visible through the windows. Most of the furnishings and decor in the Whitestones' bedroom suite were contemporary. I recorded only two paintings and three inlaid tea boxes nicely displayed on a small table.

On the guest level, one up, I memorialized a navigational map dated 1634 featuring hand-colored images of sea serpents, giant squid, whales, and other fearsome creatures of the sea.

In the small sitting room at the top, I opened the accordion file Guy had told me contained the collection's documentation. I sat cross-legged on a toile-covered window seat and flipped through the papers. I was impressed—he was thorough and organized. Each receipt, certificate of authentication, or written appraisal had a photograph of the object it related to attached. I went through the papers one by one, confirming I'd recorded the object each referred to. Everything correlated beautifully, and then it didn't.

A receipt from Sea View Gallery indicated that Guy had purchased a second Myrick tooth featuring the *Susan*—a tooth I hadn't seen, or until this moment heard of. He paid $25,350 on August thirtieth. There was, it seemed, no record of its provenance.

I stared out over the glass-smooth, cerulean ocean for a moment, then reread the meager description:

FREDERICK MYRICK SCRIMMED TOOTH OF WHALING SCENE
FROM THE *SUSAN*, CIRCA 1826.

They bought a second Myrick? I asked myself. Myricks were the gold standard of nineteenth-century sailor-scrimmed objects. Frederick Myrick was one of history's most prolific and respected scrimshanders. He created an unknown number of scrimmed objects—perhaps as many as thirty-five or forty teeth, an astonishing output—in the three years he spent at sea aboard the *Susan,* from 1826 to 1829. Oddly, once he left whaling and took up farming, he never scrimmed again. Some experts wondered whether he was that productive for real or whether he had help, or even if—perish the thought—he'd traced his designs.

From the photograph of the missing tooth, I could see that the design illustrated a typical theme, sailors at work on the *Susan*. I tipped the photograph to better catch the light. A couplet attributed to Myrick and found on several of his scrimmed objects ran along the long curve. "Death to the living, long life to the killers, Success to sailors wives and greasy luck to whalers," it read. A compass etched on the reverse side was meticulously rendered. A dark-colored material, tobacco juice, maybe, or soot, saturated the etched areas, and decorative accents had been scrimmed along the outer edge. Additional highlight lines ran along the ship, mast, and sails. The layout, style, and coloration looked similar to other Myrick teeth I'd seen. I was setting the receipt aside when from somewhere inside the lighthouse I heard a soft patter and froze.

A door clicked closed. I heard shuffling sounds, then a pitterpat of soft tapping, maybe someone walking across the hardwood flooring, then, as if I'd fallen into a vacuum-sealed capsule, utter silence.

Who was here? It couldn't be the police. They didn't have a key. It couldn't be Ashley. She was at the police station. *It has to be Maddie,* I thought. Maddie had quickly approved the Golden Lights ball invitation, and now she was back to pack up.

I tiptoed across the room to the front window. Her limo wasn't there, but an old blue Chevy was. Rust had corroded parts of the door panels, a inevitable consequence of driving on the salt that keeps our roads passable through the long New Hampshire winters. I didn't recognize the car.

My hands grew moist, and spiky shivers raced up my spine. My tote bag was downstairs in the entryway, and my cell phone was in it. I looked around for a phone. There was none in sight. I made a mental note to carry my phone on my belt from now on. Steps sounded again, and my heart stopped, then began thudding. I caught my bottom lip in my teeth and edged closer to the staircase. Except for an emergency rope ladder, it was the only way out. Soundlessly, I started down the steps. Halfway down, the step groaned under my weight. I froze again and stood holding my breath, listening for signs that whoever was inside had heard me moving.

Papers rustled.

I wiped my hands against my jean-clad thighs to dry them off, then, leaning heavily on the railing so it, not the step, would bear most of my weight, I lowered myself to the next step. At the landing, I paused to listen.

I heard a subdued whirr, a machine sound, maybe the refrigerator cycling on. I pressed an ear against each of the two guest room doors. Silence.

Taking a deep breath and holding it, I looked over the railing into the open living area. Ashley stood by Guy's desk, a stack of papers in her hands, a bottle of furniture polish and a chamois nearby.

"Ashley!" I called.

She didn't respond, and I called again. I couldn't understand why she wasn't reacting—then I saw that she was wearing earphones. A thin white wire led to an iPod clipped to her belt. I ran down the remaining stairs and caught her eye.

She gasped and dropped the papers. "Oh, my God, Josie!" she said, pulling the earphones from her ears. "You scared me to death!"

"You and me both. Sorry to startle you. I didn't hear you drive up, but then I heard noises inside."

"I didn't see your car. I thought the lighthouse was empty."

"Chief Hunter drove me. He'll be back soon."

"Wow." She pressed her hand against her chest. "My heart is still pounding."

"Yeah, mine, too."

"Have you already started the appraisal?" she asked.

I nodded and bent to pick up several sheets of paper that had fluttered near my feet. She scooped up the rest and placed them on Guy's desk under the ship's bell paperweight.

"Yes, the police asked me not to delay. I'm almost done, so I'll be out of your hair in a few minutes," I said.

"No problem. I can come back anytime. It's easier for me to work if the place is empty."

"Makes sense. Do you want me to call when I'm done?"

"To tell you the truth, I'd just as soon come in tomorrow. I came straight here from the police station, and I'm beat."

"Was it bad?"

"Yeah."

I sighed and nodded. "My staff and I are going to be in and out over the next few days. I don't know my exact schedule yet. Why don't I call you when I'm en route so you won't be surprised?"

"That's fine. Or not . . . really, it's no big deal." She waved good-bye as she left.

I sat on a step to allow my still-racing pulse to quiet. I heard Ashley drive away. After a while, I went to one of the study windows and stood with my forehead pressed against the glass, watching the ocean twinkle with diamond-studded glints.

"Back to work," I said aloud.

As I walked past the desk, my eyes came to Ashley's chamois. I touched the soft fabric. My mother had kept her cherished Baccarat crystal rolled in chamois. Every holiday she and I unrolled the glasses, oohing and ahhing as if we were seeing them for the first time. When I was twelve, we'd spent so long aiming the crystal under the chandelier light to make prisms on the walls, my dad came in to see what we were up to. Eleven months later, on a raw November afternoon, my mother died of a grisly cancer, leaving me and my father alone. The next week, he'd asked me to set the table the way she always had, using the Minton china, the Lunt silver, and the Baccarat crystal they'd received as wedding gifts.

"You aced your biology test, and I don't want celebrating your accomplishment to get lost in our grief," he'd said.

I'd shaken my head, stunned that he could even think of such a thing at such a time. *How can he imagine I care about biology or tests when I feel like my heart's been ripped out of my chest?* I'd wondered that day. I'd turned away, unable to stop weeping.

"She'd be beside herself, Josie," he'd said, "to think that we didn't continue our family traditions. And one of our most important traditions is celebrating everything we can."

We used those Baccarat glasses nearly every week. When I got a part in the school play, out they came. When my dad closed a deal with a new client, the table was set to the max. Chamois was, to me, an enduring symbol of love and celebration and my parents.

My cell phone rang, chasing away the memory, and I raced to reach my bag. It was Chief Hunter, and he said he was about two minutes away and asked how was I doing timewise. I told him I was done. I tore back upstairs, scooped up the file I'd left on the window seat, and was at the door before his SUV came into view.

CHAPTER FOURTEEN

scrimmed tooth is missing," I said.

Chief Hunter stood with his arms folded as I explained. "What would you do if this was a regular appraisal?" he asked.

"Search to be sure it wasn't simply overlooked. For example, maybe the Whitestones moved it to a bureau drawer. If I didn't find it, I'd call the owner."

"Let's do it."

We started at the top and worked our way down. We looked on every shelf, in every drawer and closet, and under every piece of furniture. The tooth wasn't there.

"Where do you think it is?" he asked.

I made a "beats me" face. "Maybe they took it to New York."

"Why would they do that?"

"To get it appraised. They bought it without provenance."

"Wouldn't they hire you to appraise it?"

"Yes."

"So where is it?" he asked.

"Maybe they took it to New York to show someone."

"Who?"

"A friend."

"Why?"

"I don't know." I shrugged and looked out the window. A squirrel was on its hind legs, listening to something I couldn't hear. I glanced back at Chief Hunter. He was waiting for me to say something, to explain. I didn't want to express my fear; to speak the words aloud would make it real. "Maybe someone stole it," I said.

He nodded. "I'll call Mrs. Whitestone."

I stood nearby and listened in as he received the expected news—Maddie had no idea where the missing tooth was. The last time she recalled seeing it was Saturday night when Guy had brought all four scrimshaw teeth out of the display cabinet to show some friends who'd come by for drinks. She saw Guy put them back.

I waved my hand to get his attention.

"Hold on," he said, looking at me.

"Ask her which display cabinet and which shelf." I pointed to the case in Guy's study. "Do you see? All the shelves are full. There's no spot for it."

He stared at the glass-fronted display case for a moment, then spoke into the phone.

"Mrs. Whitestone . . . thanks for holding." He repeated my question, then listened to her reply. He thanked her again and ended the call with a promise to keep her posted. "That case, third shelf," he told me, pointing. "In between the two clocks."

"Someone adjusted the position of everything else so there wouldn't be a gap," I said, looking at the shelf.

He leaned back on his heels, assessing the situation. "If you were going to remove a scrimmed tooth from the case, what would you do? Exactly. Would you squat? Sit on the floor? Describe it to me."

I followed his gaze. "I'd kneel on the floor, put on plastic gloves, and position bubble wrap next to me so I could move each tooth directly from the case onto the bubble wrap. My goal would be to touch it as little as possible."

"Why plastic gloves?"

"Oil from skin discolors ivory."

"So your fingerprints, if you weren't wearing gloves, would be on the knob to open the door and maybe the shelf."

"Possibly on the door molding, as well, if I pushed it shut without using the knob."

He nodded. "I'll call in the tech team to check. We did handles, but not door molding or the insides of the cases."

"Can I pack up everything else?"

"Better not. I want them to check the objects themselves, too."

I nodded. "Okay. They know to use archival processes, right?"

"Yes. They've done similar projects before, so they tell me. I'll have them call you if they have any questions."

I consulted the alarm instructions Maddie had given me, then set it and locked the door as we left.

"Probably Frankie got caught up in the middle of a robbery, just like we thought. But why would the thief steal that one tooth? There are more valuable objects in plain sight," I said, thinking aloud.

"Can you think of a reason why?"

I considered his question. "Maybe the thief was interrupted."

He glanced at me. "I'd like to stop by Ms. Morse's cottage on our way out to see if she knows anything about it. It won't take long. I'm thinking I'd like you to come in with me. Having a civilian in the room might make my questions seem more like conversation than interrogation. You okay with that?"

"Sure," I said, not knowing what else to say.

The more I learned about Chief Hunter's style and abilities, the more impressed I became. He was forthcoming without being indiscreet, trusting while always validating, protective without being patronizing, and simultaneously intuitive and respectful of science. He was a foe to be reckoned with and an ally to be valued.

Ashley opened the door wearing her working smock. The living room cum studio was unnaturally bright. It took several seconds for my eyes to adjust, and when they did, I discovered the explanation: Grow lamps hung from sliding tracks, and they were all on. It was dazzling.

"Sorry to interrupt you," Chief Hunter said. "We'll only be a minute."

She nodded, looking wary. I didn't blame her. I'd feel on edge, too, if a police chief showed up at my door—especially since she'd just returned from a stint at the station.

She stepped away from her worktable into a small area that had been set up as a sitting room. A hunter green love seat sat on hardwood flooring, facing a TV mounted on the far wall. Two ladder-back chairs were nearby. A square glass-topped coffee table was in front of the love seat. Nothing was on it. There were no books or magazines in sight. There were no plants. There was no art on the walls. There were no rugs. A fieldstone fireplace matched the outside of the house. The hearth was ash free. A built-in storage cubby was filled with logs and kindling.

On the side of the room near her worktable, every inch of wall space was covered with thumbtacked photographs, museum catalogue pages, and computer printouts of famous scrimmed scenes. The table sat flush against the outside wall. On the floor in front of it, a teak platform was perched on a fixed roller. Four work lights were clamped along the sides, two per end, their lamps aimed up. Small ceramic pots rested in a trench on one side. Calligraphy labels read CANDLE BLACK, TOBACCO JUICE, and INK. Brushes, an antique knife with an elaborately carved ivory handle, sail needles, an échoppe—an etching tool used to create swelling lines—and sharpened shards of bone sat nearby. A stack of hair-thin onionskin paper was in a tray alongside a stack of neatly folded chamois. Three oval-shaped pieces of bone, about two inches by one, lay in the center of the work area, all partially scrimmed. The design on all three was identical. At the top and bottom, ornate borders, suggestive of pointy waves and rope, had been etched. A waving banner just below the top border read, USS CONSTITUTION, and below it, a ship sailed toward the viewer, sails aflutter in the wind. Toward the bottom, just above the lower border, another banner fluttered. The elements that were completed were minutely detailed. I wondered if Ashley would add her signature extra lines.

"Are they pendants?" I asked, nodding toward the objects.

"Yes. I'll drill holes after the scrimming is done. Greg thought that less expensive items might sell well, so we're going to test it."

"That's a great idea."

"Thanks," she said. She tucked her ashen hair behind her ear. "I've never mass-produced anything before. I've only done about a dozen so far. Greg says it's too early to tell how well they'll sell, but I've got my fingers crossed."

I looked at the pendants again. I wanted to offer another compliment, a specific one, and I wanted it to be sincere. "The ship's amazing," I said, pointing toward it. "It's not easy to convey that sense of power in such a small format."

"Thanks," she repeated, blushing and smiling. "Would Prescott's be interested in trying some out? I know you carry Lenny's Leon barrettes."

"What's the price point?"

"Ten dollars."

"Wholesale?" I asked, shocked. We'd need to charge thirty dollars retail for the deal to make financial sense. I'd expected her to match Lenny's Leon brand strategy and market them as three- or five-dollar impulse buys.

Her smile faded to nothing. "Yes. Scrimming them is very time-consuming."

"I understand. I'm sorry, but that won't work for the tag sale." I pointed toward one, wanting to change the subject, afraid that I might have angered her. "Do you use resin or contemporary materials?"

She shook her head. "Oh, no, I only use fossil bone and baleen. Well, sometimes I use ivory, but never elephant ivory. I'm very careful with what I buy."

I nodded. "Poaching is horrendous."

"And unnecessary," she added earnestly. "There's no need to kill animals when so much fossil material exists."

"Baleen was used in corset stays, right?"

"Right, and umbrellas and buggy whips. It's supple in a way that—" She seemed to recall why I was there and turned worried eyes toward Chief Hunter. "Sorry . . . I'm easy to distract if you get me talking about scrimshaw."

"It's interesting," Chief Hunter said, smiling. "As you know, Ms. Prescott is appraising the Whitestones' maritime collection. It seems that one of their scrimmed teeth has gone missing."

He spoke easily, sounding as unconcerned as if he were talking about a sock that mysteriously vanished between the washer and the dryer, not an antique worth tens of thousands of dollars that had disappeared during a murder investigation.

"Do you know where it is?" Chief Hunter asked.

"Me? No! My God, no!"

"When did you see it last?"

"I don't know. I mean, I cleaned up each day of the weekend—but I just was in for a quick tidying up, you know? I haven't dusted anything in any of the display cases for days."

"Can you come any closer to an exact time?" he asked.

She looked down, thinking. "Last Thursday, the day before the Whitestones arrived for the weekend. I did a thorough cleaning that day." She looked from Chief Hunter to me, then back. "Which tooth is missing?"

"Josie, would you tell her? You can describe it more succinctly than I can," Chief Hunter said.

"The Myrick the Whitestones bought from Sea View Gallery."

"Oh, no!" she exclaimed. "Are you serious?"

"You have no information about its whereabouts?" he asked.

"No . . . of course not. Why would you ask me that?"

"You work here," he said, shrugging.

"No," she repeated. Her eyes never left his face.

"When you were down at the station, you mentioned seeing Mr. Winterelli the morning of his death. You said he was with Curt Grimes. Where were you when you saw him?"

"Here," she said, gesturing toward her worktable. "I was here working, and I happened to look up and notice the foliage."

She looked out the window, and I followed her gaze. Part of Frankie's cottage roof and chimney were visible over the treetops. Boston ferns grew amid a tangle of bushes close in. A stand of tulip poplars, their leaves a soft gold, gave way to maples, elms, and oaks. By looking hard I could see bits of Frankie's lawn chairs, the ones I'd noticed yesterday.

"The colors are extraordinary this year, and the change has come early," she continued, "so my attention got caught. Then something moved. It was Frankie and Curt arriving. They got out of their cars and walked into the house." She shrugged. "I only saw them for a second or two through the trees."

"Did you notice whether either man was carrying anything?" Chief Hunter asked.

"No," she said, "but I don't know that I would have from so far away."

"Let's look at it from the other side. Can you think of any reason why Mr. Winterelli might have removed the tooth?"

"No, absolutely not. Frankie knew he wasn't supposed to go any-where near the display cases."

"Maybe he picked it up to admire it while he and Mr. Grimes were inside hanging the door. Do you know if he was into scrimshaw? For example, did you ever talk to him about your work?"

Her nose wrinkled as if she'd sniffed a rotten egg. "No," she said, her voice frosty.

I gathered that the thought that an artist like her would discuss art with a caretaker like him was beyond distasteful—it was insulting.

Chief Hunter cocked his head. "What did you think of him?"

"Frankie?" she asked, turning to face the chief straight on. She shrugged. "He seemed competent enough."

Chief Hunter nodded. "Thanks for your time."

"Can I ask you a question having nothing to do with anything?" I asked her, smiling. "I'm curious about something."

"Sure." Her blond hair appeared nearly white under the harsh glare of the grow lights. Her eyes met mine, her expression guarded.

"How come it's so bright in here? I thought most artists preferred northern light."

She relaxed. "In order to achieve authenticity, I try to replicate the entire scrimming experience. I only use period-appropriate materials and techniques—like sail needles or bone shards. I work with the motion of the sea," she said, pointing to the rocking platform, "and under varying lighting conditions depending on the weather." She opened her arms wide and looked all around. "This approximates a bright sunny day on the open ocean."

"Wow," I said. "I'm impressed."

"Thanks. I take it all very seriously. I found a whaling ship's log that tracked the weather day by day in the 1820s. I follow it meticulously, adjusting the lighting as needed, so some days I work under clouds, some under partial sun, and so on. The objects look much richer when scrimmed under realistic conditions."

"How do you adjust for rough seas or rain?" I asked.

She smiled. "I don't! If it was bad weather, I might scrim for a few minutes with the platform really rocking, but since scrimming was a hobby for sailors, I assume that the masters didn't work in adverse conditions. They'd be busy keeping the ship afloat!"

I extended a hand. "Thank you, Ashley. As I said—I'm impressed."

"Is that true?" Chief Hunter asked as we headed out. "Are you impressed?"

"Absolutely. Her dedication to her art is inspiring."

He glanced at me, and from his expression, I got the impression he was trying to gauge whether I was sincere, but before he could say anything, we reached the end of the drive. Officer Meade's car was still in place, preventing vehicles from turning onto the lighthouse property and blocking our access to Lighthouse Lane, but she wasn't in sight. I lowered my window and heard a muddle of voices. Chief Hunter tapped his horn, and she stepped into view, registered who was beeping, and hustled toward us. Chief Hunter lowered his window.

"Sorry," Officer Meade said. "I'll move the vehicle right away."

"What's going on?"

"Media," she said, dismissing them with a wave. "The onslaught is growing."

"How many?"

"Eight right now. They come and go."

He nodded. "Don't forget to call if you need help."

She said she would. Once she was at her car, she said something I couldn't hear to people I couldn't see, then got in and drove forward, allowing us to exit. Cameras were raised and photographs of us were taken as we passed the clutch of journalists. Two men ran after us shouting questions as we drove past. Through my side mirror, I watched a stocky man in his fifties jot down the SUV's license plate number.

"Did you bring the receipt for the missing tooth?" Chief Hunter asked.

"Yes." I patted the accordion folder. "One thing . . . its description is a little sketchy."

"In what way?"

"Apparently the tooth was sold without provenance. I'm curious why Greg didn't get the tooth appraised."

Chief Hunter glanced at his watch, then confirmed the time with the dash clock. It was almost three.

"Do you have time to stop at Sea View Gallery?" he asked. "I'm thinking that maybe Mr. Donovan knows something that didn't get written on the receipt, and if so, you can help me get the info 'cause you know the questions to ask."

"I have the time, but you should go in alone."

"Why?"

"I'm competition. If I'm there, he'll tell you as little as possible."

"Good point. You can wait in the car. If I need you, you're there. If I need the receipt, I can get it." He glanced at me. "Why would Mr. Donovan have skipped getting an appraisal?"

"Maybe he was in a hurry and he figured that what the collectors didn't know wouldn't hurt them." I shrugged. "Or that they might not care."

"That doesn't seem to apply in this case. From what you've told me, the Whitestones know—and care," Chief Hunter said.

"Yes, but they're new to the game. They might not recognize that the work was sloppy."

As we drove into Rocky Point, I was wishing that I could be a fly on the wall of what would probably be a discomforting conversation. Greg didn't know it yet, but he was about to be embarrassed.

CHAPTER FIFTEEN

C hief Hunter parallel-parked at a two-hour spot across the street and five doors down from Sea View Gallery. I had a clear view of the front door, but people inside looking out couldn't see me. No one but Chief Hunter entered or exited.

Ten minutes passed. A marked patrol car drove up and double-parked, boxing us in. A uniformed police officer, the same young patrolman who'd driven Officer Brownley yesterday, stepped out. He circled the car to approach me curbside.

"Ms. Prescott?" he asked. "Chief Hunter is going to be tied up for longer than he thought, and he asked me to run you back to your office."

"Sure," I said, astounded, moving into the patrol car's backseat.

A thick wire mesh grate topped the front seat, imprisoning me. The window and door controls had been disabled. Sitting alone in the rear with no way out, I felt the sides closing in on me.

"Is everything okay?" I asked.

"Yes, absolutely," he said, giving me no information.

I looked into the gallery as we passed. Chief Hunter stood in the center talking to Greg, Lenny Wilton, and Curt Grimes. I wondered what they were discussing.

Curt, about six feet tall and lean, was sinewy, with iron claws for hands. He was rocking back and forth as if the floor were covered with smoldering rocks. He was squeezing something in his right hand, an exercise ball, probably.

The officer didn't ask any questions, and I didn't volunteer anything. As we approached my parking lot, I saw a knot of reporters turn as if they shared one eye. Bertie wasn't there. I looked down, pretending the journalists didn't exist. The policeman pulled to a stop at the front door.

"Thanks for the ride," I said.

He got out and opened my door. I was glad to be back. *The first thing I'll do,* I thought, *is scan the documentation and upload the video. When in doubt, create a backup. Then I'll call Wes.* I had questions.

Sasha was holding a gleaming silver sugar bowl. She looked worried. "I don't know what to tell her," she said to Fred.

"Tell her the truth," Fred said. "You have no choice."

"Maybe I should limit my comments to value alone and skip discussing its history."

"She's a grown-up—tell her the truth. It's an obligation of an appraiser."

"No, it's not! We only tell things we can prove, and we can't prove this."

To the uninitiated, Fred and Sasha's bickering might smack of disrespect, but I knew better. Their communication style suited them, and their disagreements were always professional, never personal.

"It's an appraisal, Sasha," he insisted, "not a love fest."

"A love fest?" I repeated, laughing. "Do we run them often?"

Fred gave a cocky grin, one corner of his mouth higher than the other. "Not often enough," he said.

Gretchen, who'd been listening in, giggled, her green eyes twinkling with appreciation.

"The sugar bowl was made for a Sheraton hotel around 1950," Fred said, "and Sasha's afraid to tell the owner that it was probably stolen."

"I'm not afraid exactly," Sasha protested. "I'm just concerned that she'll be disappointed." She turned to me. "Mo Heedles is a lovely woman, and this sugar bowl is a cherished heirloom. She got it from her mother." She sighed and glanced at her watch. "I told her to come back at four thirty."

I leaned over so I could see the Mickey Mouse clock on Gretchen's desk. "So you have about a minute and a half to decide how to handle it," I said.

"How can I tell that nice lady that her mother was a thief?"

"You don't know how she got the bowl," Fred said. "Maybe her mother got it as a present from a friend for Christmas one year, so the unknown friend's the thief, not Ms. Heedles's mother."

"That's true," Sasha said, perking up.

"She won't be the first person to hear that her object has a less than righteous history," Fred added.

I lowered the timbre of my voice, mimicking a male TV host concluding a story about a dastardly event. "And this, ladies and gentlemen, is the underbelly of the antiques appraisal business."

Sasha sighed again.

The phone rang, and Cara answered with her pleasant stock greeting. "Prescott's. This is Cara. May I help you?"

Her eyes met mine, and she nodded. "Hold a moment, please." Then to me, "It's that reporter, Wes Smith. You said you didn't want to talk to any journalists, but I know you've spoken to him in the past."

"Good thinking, Cara," I said. "I'll take it in the warehouse." I pushed open the heavy door and grabbed the phone mounted on the wall by the worktable. "Hi, Wes," I said. "I was just about to call you."

"I have info. We need to meet."

"I can't leave now. I just got back. Tell me on the phone."

"I can't." He lowered his voice, adding drama. "It's about Frankie and a girl."

"What girl?"

"Not on the phone."

I considered whether I could leave. I had to talk to my staff, but that would only take a few minutes. "Five o'clock," I said. "I can meet you at five."

"Done. Our dune at five. See ya," he said and hung up.

———

Frankie and a girl? I repeated to myself. *What girl?* Eric said that Frankie hadn't had any luck meeting a girl, and then I recalled that Eric had seemed frightened.

Back in the front office, I was greeted with laughter. A pleasant-looking middle-aged woman had tears running down her cheeks, she was laughing so hard. Sasha looked bemused.

"This is Mo Heedles," Sasha said.

Ms. Heedles nodded in my direction, gasping, trying to still her laughter.

"You told her about the Sheraton connection, I see," I said, and Ms. Heedles began laughing hard again.

"I asked if she knew of anyone who might have a link to a Sheraton Hotel. It seems that her mother was married at the Sheraton in Boston."

"She must have swiped it herself!" Ms. Heedles managed between gales of laughter. "No wonder she loved it so much!" She swept her tears away and smiled. Little crinkly lines gathered at the corners of her eyes. "I wish she was still alive to share the joke." She thanked us, picked up her mother's illicit souvenir, and departed, her musical chuckles mingling with the tinkles from the wind chimes.

Seated at the guest table near the front window, I described the scope of the Whitestone appraisal to my staff.

"The first thing we need to do is create a written inventory. Since we're helping the police on this one, we have no time to waste. Fred, can you take it on?"

"Absolutely," he said.

"E-mail it to me as soon as it's done."

"Will do."

"Meanwhile, Sasha, you'll need to review the recording, too, and look through the documentation to establish the protocols. Put together a list of which experts we'll need to consult, which tests we can do in-house, and which we'll need to outsource by noon tomorrow. That's when I'm hoping we can pack up everything and get started. What do you think? Is that a realistic timeline?"

"I think so," she said. "All of our scrimshaw contacts are current, and we have our standard oil painting and maritime artifact protocols in place, so it should be a pretty straight-ahead process."

I wish, I thought as I climbed the stairs to my office. I had a nagging sense that nothing about this appraisal would be straight-ahead.

CHAPTER SIXTEEN

Wes was standing at the top of the dune staring out over the ocean when I drove up. He wore jeans that sagged at the rear and a blue button-down shirt with the cuffs rolled up. He turned to watch as I walked up the shifting sand. Wes was about twenty-five but looked younger. He was plump but not fat, more soft than chunky. His skin was pasty white, as if he hadn't been outside in the fresh air for months.

The clouds were thicker at the shore than they'd been inland. At the water's edge, two girls, maybe thirteen or fourteen, ambled along, engrossed in conversation. They were barefoot, their sandals dangling from their fingers. To the north, a man in shorts was tossing a Frisbee for his dog, a golden retriever.

"Did you e-mail me some photos?" he asked as I reached the summit.

"Hi, Wes," I said. "I will."

"I need them now, Josie! I'm on deadline."

"You said you had news about Frankie and a girl," I said, ignoring his demand.

Wes sighed, tacitly agreeing to put his request on the back burner. "Her name is Lu-Ann. Lu-Ann Foland. She and Frankie went out once, and her ex-husband, his name is Timmy Foland, he found out about it and went nuts. This was last March. He hunted Frankie down, finally finding him at a bowling alley in Durham. He taunted him some, and they ended up taking it outside. Punches were thrown, but neither guy was much good at fighting, and everything would have blown over except the owner of the bowling alley called the cops. At the sound of the siren, Frankie ran off and left Foland to take the heat—which he did. He refused to give them Frankie's name since it would have implicated his ex—he actually told the cops that he wouldn't sully a woman's good name." Wes grinned. "He said 'sully.' Foland got off with a warning. Lu-Ann, always glad for an opportunity to screw with her ex, passed Frankie's name to the cops as a tip."

I wondered why Eric hadn't mentioned it when we were talking about Frankie and dating.

"From last March?" I asked. "Doesn't it seem a little far-fetched that Timmy Foland could be a suspect? From a fight six months ago during which no one got hurt or arrested?"

"Yeah, the cops think so, too. Plus, Foland has an alibi. He's a welder, and he was on the shop floor when Frankie was killed." Wes lowered his voice. "The truth is that I mentioned it as a decoy. What I wanted to ask you about is so confidential, I didn't want to risk saying anything about it on the phone." His eyes were big with news. "Greg Donovan is at the police station."

"You're kidding! How come?"

"Don't you know?"

"No. I have no idea."

"Weren't you there when Chief Hunter began his interview with him?" he asked.

"How can you possibly know that?"

"A call went out over the radio for a cop to come get you."

Check, I thought, astounded for the thousandth time at how plugged-in Wes was.

"So?" he prompted, waggling his fingers. "What do you know?"

"Nothing." I shrugged. "They often videotape people's statements. Probably that's why they asked him to come in."

"Did they tape yours?"

"Yes."

"And you didn't think that was ominous?" he asked.

I pursed my lips. Wes used innuendo like a pickax to dredge out unspoken fears.

"No," I said. "I was cooperating with a homicide investigation. Videotaping is standard operating procedure in Rocky Point, Wes, not a precursor of doom."

"Maybe . . . but why do you think they're interviewing Greg Donovan at all? How is he connected to Frankie?" Wes asked.

"He isn't. I mean, Greg said he'd never met him."

"Then why are the police interviewing him?" he asked again.

"He sold the Whitestones some objects, one of which—a scrimmed tooth—is missing."

"What!" Wes exclaimed, extracting a grimy piece of notebook paper from his pocket. "Tell me."

I described the missing tooth, explaining, "Even though it was sold without provenance, it still could be genuine. No one knows for sure how many teeth Myrick scrimmed, and rare objects are discovered all the time, in an estate sale, for example. Once it enters the marketplace without provenance . . ." I flipped open my hands and shrugged.

"But if it has no provenance, weren't they stupid to buy it for that much money?"

I shrugged. "Stupid is the wrong term. Impulsive, maybe."

"You would have told them not to buy it, right?"

"I would have encouraged them to have it authenticated."

"Why didn't they?"

"I don't know."

Wes made a note, then said, "This would make a great sidebar—bullet points on how to tell if your scrimmed object is the real McCoy."

I shook my head. "There are too many variables that nonexperts can't test. Heck, Wes, some of the tests are so technologically advanced, we use outside experts."

"Love it, love it!" he said, continuing to write. "Mysterious and exotic."

"It's not mysterious *or* exotic! It's analytical."

"So is there a photo of the missing tooth?" he asked. From his eager look, I knew the sidebar title would read something like "Is My Antique Worth Millions? Science Reveals All," which, as I thought about it, was a pretty good take on the process.

"Yes. I'll send it to you."

He shot me a quick smile. "Thanks." He wrote for another few seconds, then asked, "What else are you going to do to find the missing tooth?"

"Once we confirm it wasn't simply relocated or misplaced, I'll list it as stolen with all the official stolen art registries."

"Gotcha. Will you send me the names?"

"Okay," I agreed.

"Anything else?"

"Have they finished the autopsy?" I asked.

"Not all the tests are back yet, but they've confirmed that Frankie hadn't been drinking or doing any drugs."

I smiled. "I knew it!"

"Also, they've narrowed the time of death to between eleven and two, probably closer to eleven."

"That can't be—he didn't leave my building until noon."

"Really? Great." He jotted a note, then looked up. "You said you were about to call me—how come?"

"I was wondering about alibis. Have you learned anything?" I asked.

"Not yet. Soon, though. Give me something on the Whitestones. Did you speak to either of them today?"

"Maddie is in town. I'll be sending her an inventory of their collection so she can let me know if anything else is missing." I paused and scanned the beach. The two girls, the man, and the dog were gone. Gentle swells crashed against the jetty, wetting the craggy rocks a little higher and a little closer to shore with each pass. The tide was coming in. "I know we need to think about alibis, but it seems to me that it all comes down to motive, you know?"

"The motive is hatred, right? I'm telling you, Josie, the medical examiner's report reads like a trashy novel—those wounds were brutal. I don't think the question is what's the motive—the question is who had that motive. You know what I mean? Usually things are just what they appear to be."

I nodded. "That's true, isn't it? Sometimes it's us who interpret events to suit our own agendas, discounting the parts we don't want to believe or that we think are wrong, and filling in the blanks with whatever supports our point of view."

Wes narrowed his eyes, concentrating. "Like what?"

"Like the time I decided that I hadn't been cast in the school play because I wasn't as tall as the girl who got the part." I smiled and shook my head. "My father pointed out to me that it was just possible that the other girl did a better job at the audition."

Wes laughed. "What did you say to that?"

"I was shocked, really shocked. I know it sounds stupid, but it had never even occurred to me that she might have been better than me. Isn't that something? Talk about narcissistic! The arrogance of youth—which, as you and I both know, isn't limited to young people. Of course my dad was a hundred percent right. She did do better at the audition. She did a great job in the show, too."

"Did you resent it?" Wes asked.

"No, not once the shock wore off. It was a good lesson. If I hadn't had that realization, I might have tried to be an actress. Instead, I tried out for a couple more parts, took a few classes, and noticed a trend—there were lots of girls better than me." I chuckled. "Perseverance is all well and good, but not if you lack the innate talent. I decided that I needed a new career aspiration. I'm lucky—I found a field I love, and it's a good fit with my abilities. You, too, right?"

"Yeah, but writing is all I ever wanted to do."

"Speaking of which, did you reach Ray Austin?"

"He wants to see a proposal," he said, grinning. "I'm pretty stoked." I could tell from his tone of voice, though, that he felt anxious, too.

I patted his arm. "Oh, Wes! I'm so pleased. You'll do a great job."

"Thanks. To tell you the truth, I'm not just stoked . . . I'm *wicked* stoked."

"Way to go, Wes!" I smiled. "I've got to get back."

"Don't forget to send me those photos and the stolen art organizations' names."

"You're relentless, Wes."

"Thanks," he said again, flashing an appreciative grin.

I laughed, waved good-bye, and slid down the dune.

My cell phone rang. It was the Rocky Point police station number. I was tempted to let the call go to voice mail. I wanted to go home and get dinner organized, see Zoë and her kids, and talk to Ty. Instead, I slipped in my earpiece and took the call. It was Chief Hunter.

"I could use some help," he said. "Any chance you can stop by the station for a half hour or so?"

According to the dash clock, it was five thirty. "Okay," I said, resigned to doing the right thing. "What's it about?"

"Antiques. Something smells fishy to me."

Something smelling fishy when it came to antiques could mean anything from an easy-to-spot bad repro being passed off as a valuable original to a motive for murder. My curiosity gland was working double time.

"I'm on my way," I said and turned south.

CHAPTER SEVENTEEN

I called Zoë to ask how she was doing and tell her to go
ahead and feed the kids; I hoped to get there, leftover
Chicken Florentine in hand, around seven, maybe seven
thirty, I said. She was fine with that, and she wanted, she said, to fill
me in on her day.

"Tell me now."

"Nope, only over a Lemon Drop."

"God, doesn't that sound good."

"See ya," she said and hung up.

I turned into the Rocky Point police station lot. The phone still in
my hand, I sat for a moment, looking across the street into the wild
roses and scrambled vines that lined the sandy shoulder, wondering
how Ty's work was going, wishing he were home and that I could
tell him everything. I called and got his voice mail.

"This is a nothing special message," I told him. "I just felt like
hearing your voice. I love you."

Inside, I approached the counter. Cathy, the civilian admin, told
me that Chief Hunter was expecting me and would be right out. She
buzzed him, and within seconds his office door opened and he
waved me in.

I hadn't been in the police chief's private office since Ty had left
the job. The ash cabinets, bookshelves, and desk were the same, and
so was the tan and brown nubby carpet, but the artwork was different. Instead of Ty's photographs of Rocky Point, Chief Hunter had
hung three reproductions of Norman Rockwell illustrations, *The Gos-
sips, Gramps at the Plate,* and *Doctor and the Doll.*

"You weren't kidding when you said you were a Rockwell fan," I commented.

"Like them?"

"Love them."

He smiled and pointed to a guest chair, waited for me to sit, then sat across from me.

"Thanks for coming in." He leaned back. "I'm out of my depth in questioning Mr. Donovan about the missing tooth. I'm hoping you'll jump in and help. I have this niggling sense that I'm not getting the full story because I'm not asking the right questions."

"What in particular is troubling you?"

"Talk to me about pickers."

"Pickers are independent itinerant sellers. Some specialize; others sell whatever they pick up."

"Do you deal with them?"

"All the time."

"Know anyone named Sam?"

"Sam who?"

"Don't know. Mr. Donovan claims he knows very little about him—except that Sam often brought him rare maritime artifacts and that he has the communication talents of a hood ornament. Sam no-last-name was the source of the undocumented Myrick tooth. Because he'd done business with Sam before with no problem, he didn't hesitate to buy it. He paid seven thousand dollars. Does it sound right to you? Would you give a man whose last name you don't know thousands of dollars in cash?"

"It's not unusual for pickers to be . . . secretive."

"Is he a fence, or is he avoiding the tax man?"

I shrugged. "Depends on the picker."

"How do you protect yourself?" he asked.

"We rarely buy expensive objects from pickers, partly because, in my experience, it rarely comes up—that's not their specialty. Sam sounds like an aberration. Sometimes we get lucky and in a box of miscellaneous things there's a rare object, but usually their goods are more prosaic than distinctive." I paused. "May I ask you a question? Greg doesn't deal in antiques, so why would this picker go to him?"

"Maybe for just that reason. If he doesn't deal in antiques much, he's likely to be a less discerning buyer than, say, you," Chief Hunter said.

"That's possible, I suppose, but not likely. Not if we're talking thousands of dollars. That's pretty rich for most nonexperts' blood. I wouldn't have thought that Greg was that much of a risk-taker."

"Do you think he knew it was a fake?"

"I'd hate to think that about him," I said.

"What about the receipt he gave the Whitestones? What does it indicate to you?"

I shrugged. "At a guess, probably it's nothing more than laziness. If Greg knew the tooth was a phony, he would have faked a provenance."

"If you were me, how would you figure out who Sam is?"

I thought for a moment. "Can't you trace his phone number and learn his name that way?"

"It tracks to a disposable cell phone, the kind you buy in a discount store and add pay-as-you-go minutes to."

"Isn't that kind of suspicious in itself?" I asked.

"It's pretty common for people with no credit or bad credit."

I nodded again. "Or people who want to stay below the radar for some reason because they're suspicious of government interference. That's consistent with the pickers I know."

"What is it about pickers that makes them want to avoid mainstream living?"

"From what I've observed, they're either relentlessly private, the rugged individualist type, or they're paranoid."

Chief Hunter nodded slowly, his interest fully engaged. "Someone doing business, presumably eager to sell to the highest bidder . . . you'd think he'd be easy to find, wouldn't you?"

"Not necessarily. Pickers want to move their inventory quickly and without hassles. They're not businesspeople, per se. Some might be, but usually that's not what they're about."

He nodded. "Back to that Myrick tooth. Mr. Donovan said Myrick's style is distinctive." He consulted his notes. " 'It's detailed, yet with a tidy folk art feel.' What do you think? Is that right?"

"Yes, but lots of scrimshanders used that style. You'd still need to authenticate it."

"He called in Ms. Morse for that part."

"Ashley?" I exclaimed. "I didn't know Ashley did appraisals."

"I spoke to her just before I called you," Chief Hunter said. He glanced at his notes again. "She consulted a reference book to confirm that the etching style was similar to known Myrick scrimshaw, which was just a matter of form since she recognized the master's work on sight."

I didn't respond. If I'd been alone, I would have chortled.

"Then she did the hot pin test. I didn't ask her to explain—I was hoping you'd translate."

"Sure. It's a tried-and-true, low-tech way to discover if the material is plastic or resin. The way it works is that you take a pin and heat the tip until it's red-hot. Insert it somewhere it won't show, and voilà! If it's ivory, the pin won't penetrate. If it's plastic, the pin will slide through easily."

"So in this case, Ms. Morse was able to demonstrate that the tooth was real."

"Not necessarily. Assuming it passed the hot pin test, all that proves is that the object *isn't* made of plastic or resin. She might also conclude that it *probably* was made of ivory or bone. I bet her next step was examining the tooth under a loupe, am I right?"

"Yes. What was she looking for?"

"Grain. Ivory has a grain pattern in it, but bone doesn't. Sometimes bone resists the pin in a hot pin test just like ivory, but under magnification, you can see that it's completely free of grain. Also, it shows pockmarks where marrow and blood were."

"So if she saw grain, she knows it's real?"

"No, all she knows is that it's ivory. The tooth could still could be a modern-day scrim. What did she do next?"

"Nothing. That was it. How about you? What would you recommend as a next step?"

"If we think a scrimmed object might have significant value, we send it out for spectroscopic analysis."

"You're kidding."

"No. Just last year spectroscopic analysis proved that a tooth we were appraising, purported to have been scrimmed in 1810, was a modern repro. The ivory was only about fifty years old. It was one of the best fakes I've ever seen."

He tapped his pencil on the desk's edge. "Let's say the ivory dated right. Then what?"

"The next step is verifying the location of all known examples of the artist's work."

"Can you do that?"

"If there's a finite number of extant examples, and it's rare that they come on the market, yes." I held up a finger. "However, in this case, no one knows how many Myrick teeth were scrimmed, so it's completely plausible that a previously unknown tooth might surface."

"How do you handle it?"

"I'd trace the ownership of this particular tooth."

"How?"

"By asking Sam, the picker, where he got it."

"Would he tell you?" he asked.

"Not without what we might call encouragement."

"Which means?"

"Cash," I said.

"Won't that just motivate him to tell you what you want to hear— like he got it from a man named John Smith who found it when Aunt Mabel died, wink wink?"

"Yes, which is why we appraisers have to become adept at sniffing out liars." I shifted in my seat. "I wouldn't make it adversarial, I'd make it collaborative, but that's my business model—other dealers might take a different approach. I'd tell the picker the truth, that this object might be rare and valuable. I'd offer him a bonus based on the selling price—if he helps me verify provenance."

"What do you think of Mr. Donovan and Ms. Morse's approach? I'm asking for your expert opinion."

"Not for quotation?" I asked.

"Fair enough."

"I'm shocked and disappointed. Even if Greg doesn't deal in antiques much, he should know better. So should Ashley. No way could either of them think a book, a hot pin test, and a loupe represent a proper appraisal of a previously undocumented tooth alleged to have been scrimmed by Myrick."

"You told me he was a reputable businessman."

"Yeah. Goes to show you," I said.

Chief Hunter nodded and stood up. "Thanks for coming in."

"Now what do you do?" I asked.

"Check into the anatomy of repute."

I nodded, thinking that was a pretty fancy way of saying that Greg was in for it.

CHAPTER EIGHTEEN

I had just arrived home when Ty called. It was six forty-five. He sounded beat.

"Your message was great," he said. "I love you, too."

I smiled, switched on the kitchen light, and sat at the round table that overlooked the meadow. The thick clouds at the coast hadn't moved inland. Out over the vast field of grass and wildflowers, the sky was streaked with red. According to the sailor's lore I'd learned from my dad—red sky at night, sailor's delight—tomorrow would be warm and clear.

"I'm eating a sub," Ty added, "from the local pizza joint. An Italian sandwich, they call it."

When I'd moved back to New England, I'd had to relearn that those long sandwiches were called subs. In New York, they were called heroes. Speaking the proper dialect—doing as the Romans did—was, I knew, an important part of fitting in, and from the first moment I'd arrived in Rocky Point, I'd been determined to do just that.

"What kind?" I asked.

"Turkey."

"Is it good?"

"No." He paused, then said, "I miss your cooking."

"That's a good thing, because I miss cooking for you."

He asked about my day, and I told him about the missing tooth, Greg's slipshod appraisal process, and the medical examiner's report stating that Frankie had been clean and sober when he died. Then I asked for his news.

Ty said that the new training program he was using for the first time was working better than expected, and that with any luck he'd finish up by noon on Friday.

We agreed to talk before bed, and after we were done, I sat for a long time looking out into the meadow. Orange butterfly milkweed, bluebells of Scotland, and yellow Jerusalem artichokes shimmered in the muted twilight. It would be dark within minutes. I took a deep breath and stood up. I had promises to keep.

Fred had sent the Whitestone inventory to my home e-mail. I read it over and found no errors or omissions, and I forwarded it to Maddie, cc-ing Chief Hunter. I right-clicked on the photo from the Sea View Gallery documentation showing the missing Myrick tooth, saved it to my desktop, and e-mailed it to Wes with a suggested caption: "This scrimmed tooth, attributed to the celebrated scrimshander Frederick Myrick, is missing from the Whitestones' lighthouse residence." I also e-mailed him several photos of other objects in the collection and the names of the stolen art registries, telling him I'd let him know as soon as I had confirmation that the tooth was, in fact, missing.

Maddie had e-mailed two photos of the Winslow Homer etching she was considering buying. One photo showed the print, frame and all; the second, the unmarked, standard-issue brown paper backing. The print was black-and-white, an etching referencing Homer's oil painting *The Herring Net*.

I'd studied the painting, which was in the Chicago Institute of Art's permanent collection, during a course on American artists in college. It had been a favorite of my professor. I hadn't known that Homer had created an etching based on it, but it didn't surprise me. He often painted studies in watercolor before turning to oil, and he often painted the same or similar subjects over and over again, sometimes with modifications, sometimes without.

I leaned back to view the photograph from a little distance. The man hauling in the net was bowed over, his weariness apparent in the set of his shoulders. The boy unloading the catch had his back to us. The sea was choppy. The mother ship was far away, too far for so late in the day. I wanted the man to finish up, to get back to his ship before night fell or fog rolled in. It was a masterful commentary on man's epic struggle for survival.

Something was off about the boat. I right-clicked and enlarged the photo. The front of the boat was rising on a swell. The chop lapped high on the right side. Darker lines edged the boat on the left, drawing my attention away from the primary elements—the man and the rough sea. Still, despite the odd lines, the rendering was detailed and precise. Before making any judgments, I needed to see the etching itself. Those too-dark lines might be a function of nothing more ominous than a poor-resolution photograph or scanner.

I hit REPLY and suggested to Maddie that she ask the seller to bring the painting to my office for authentication and valuation. I hit SEND, then turned off the computer. It was time to make a pitcher of Lemon Drops.

"So, you tease," I said when Zoë and I were settled in her living room with our Lemon Drops, "how was your day?"

"Better than I expected. I managed to go the whole day without crying." She teared up. "Being around children was a godsend."

"What did they have you do?"

"Origami. Not to sound immodest, but I've been crowned the origami queen in Jake's second-grade class."

"I didn't know you did origami, Your Majesty."

"I'm a monarch of many talents."

"You're hired for the Harvest Festival."

"I thought you were doing face painting."

"We are. I've just added origami."

"I can't. Jake and Emma are too distracting, and origami, my friend, requires laserlike focus."

"The festival organizers are providing child care. In addition to your salary, I'll pay the fee."

"You seem oddly keen to include me. What gives?"

"I'm questioning my face-painting ability. A debacle will blow my company's reputation as an arbiter of art. You are what might be called a safety net. If things go badly, we'll nix the face painting and go exclusively with origami."

"I liked it when you called me 'Your Majesty.'"

"We'll make an official sign. Is that a yes?"

"You bet," she said, tearing up again. "Thanks, Josie."

I raised my glass. "Here's to silver light in the dark of night."

"To silver light," Zoë said, clinking my glass. After a long minute, she added, "I heard on the radio a valuable antique is missing from the Whitestones' collection. Do you know anything about that?"

"Not much, no."

"So the next thing I should expect to hear is a rumor that Frankie's a thief, right, that it was an inside job?"

"Oh, God, Zoë, I hope not."

She nodded and sipped her Lemon Drop. "Do you think he did it?" she whispered, looking down into her drink, seemingly fascinated by the pale yellow swirling froth.

"No," I said, meaning it. "I really don't. The medical examiner found no evidence of drugs or alcohol."

Her eyes flew to my face, and she stared at me for a moment, her eyes moist. "I hadn't heard. Really? That's wonderful news!"

I nodded. "I don't think the report has been officially released yet. I got the update from Wes, that reporter."

"Thank God. I don't think I could have borne it if I'd been wrong to trust him, if he'd gone back to doing drugs or something. I just don't think I could have borne it. How could I trust myself, my judgments about people, ever again?"

I reached out a hand and patted hers. "You weren't wrong," I said. "Even if you were, well, you're not omniscient."

"I hate this," she said, her voice thick with emotion. "I just hate it."

It was only later, after we finished the warmed-over chicken and emptied the pitcher of Lemon Drops, after I'd exchanged good-night wishes with Ty and blown him kisses over the phone, after I'd showered and was snuggled into bed with Rex Stout's *And Be a Villain,* that I realized how absurd it was that Greg had consulted Ashley, not me or someone like me, for an appraisal of a Myrick tooth. Not only was I an antiques appraiser by training and trade, but I'd just sold a comparable object months earlier. The only possible explanation was that he had something to hide.

CHAPTER NINETEEN

T he next morning, Thursday, my head filled with questions I couldn't answer, I headed straight to the tag sale room to find Eric. First, though, I had to get by the gauntlet of sharklike journalists.

Bertie, the *New York Monthly* reporter, sat in her car blocking my driveway. As soon as I stepped onto my porch, she was on the street, toenail-close to the property line, barking questions. I ignored her. I got behind the wheel and started my engine. I began backing out. She held her ground. I put the car in park and stepped out to face her, my cell phone in hand.

"If you don't move your car," I said, "I'll call the police."

She smiled. "Just tell me how you're doing," she said, sounding as if she and I were old friends and she was concerned about my well-being. Her tone implied that not answering her would be rather boorish.

I scrolled through my call log, found Chief Hunter's number, and held the unit up above my head. "In five seconds, if you're not in your car and backing up, I make the call."

"I'm on public property, Josie."

"Five, four, three . . ." I finished the count silently and hit the call-back button.

She scooted into her car and drove away. I disconnected the call a nanosecond before it rang.

Score one for the home team, I thought.

Eric was wheeling a cart filled with inventory toward the front of the tag sale room. I spotted silver thimbles, souvenir shot glasses, amethyst and green glass doorknobs, brass bookends, miniature birds, wooden tools, Hummel figurines, jelly molds, and metal cocktail shakers. No item would sell for more than a hundred dollars, and many of them were priced below ten dollars. At those price points, some objects were real bargains, and a couple of things would be tell-all-your-friends finds for collectors. That was by design. We always seeded the stock with a couple of bargain-priced rare finds; it kept serious collectors coming back, and it built our reputation as an antiques and collectibles source worth visiting over and over again.

"Hey, Eric. You're starting early!" I said.

"Yeah. We have a lot of smalls this week."

With dozens of little objects all in one place, it was hard for customers to see the trees for the forest. It took careful arranging to ensure each piece showed to advantage—and careful arranging required more time.

"Do you have enough help coming in?" I asked.

"I think so. Everyone should be here at ten. I've asked Cara to supervise them while I do the Duncan pickup."

The Duncans, a couple retiring to North Carolina, didn't have any antiques, but they did have very high-quality furnishings and decorative objects dating from the seventies and eighties, perfect fodder for the tag sale.

"Great," I said, thrilled at yet another example of Eric showing initiative and care. Cara had started at Prescott's working part-time at the tag sale, and she knew enough about merchandizing to get the display process started.

I paused, uncertain how to segue into my question. I took a deep breath. "May I ask you something?"

Something in my tone caused him to stop and look up. A crease appeared between his brows. "Okay," he said.

"You know how you told me that Frankie hadn't met any girls? I heard a rumor that he got into some kind of brawl over a girl named Lu-Ann Foland. Is it true?"

He looked guilty but unrepentant, as if I'd caught him at the beach after he'd called in sick—he'd broken the rules, but the benny was completely worth whatever punishment or recriminations were coming his way.

"I can't say."

"Can't or won't?"

He shook his head.

"How come?" I asked.

"I promised."

"You promised Frankie you wouldn't talk about his fight with Lu-Ann's ex-husband?" I asked. "Why?"

He looked down. He didn't speak for several seconds, and tempted though I was to try to persuade him to open up, I didn't. From my years' experience negotiating, I knew the power of silence. When it's the other guy's turn to talk, let him.

"I gave my word."

By waiting, I received confirmation that, if nothing else, there was a tale to tell.

"To Frankie?" I asked.

Eric nodded.

"You're a good friend, Eric—but it's a murder investigation. It may be related . . . and now that he's died . . . you don't need to keep the promise anymore."

"It was a long time ago," he said. "It can't possibly be related to his murder."

"Sometimes emotions fester for a long time, so there's no way to know whether it is or not."

He continued ruminating, seemingly studying the oak flooring.

"Really, Eric, you need to tell," I nudged. "If you don't want to talk about it with me, tell the police."

He sighed heavily and picked at a hangnail. "It can't be relevant," he said finally. "There was no fight."

I stared at him, confused. "I heard the police were called."

"Yeah, the bowling alley manager called them as soon as Frankie and Timmy went outside. But nothing happened. *That's* what Frankie made me swear never to tell. Timmy shoved him a couple of times, and Frankie didn't shove back. The cops came, and Frankie just ran off. He told me later that he was scared of violating his parole, but he didn't want it to get around that he'd shied away from a fight, so he made me promise never to tell. Timmy talked smack for a few days, but when he realized that Lu-Ann and Frankie really weren't dating, he shrugged it off. Frankie and Lu-Ann only went out once. It was—and is—a lot of noise about nothing."

A tempest in a teapot, I thought. I nodded, but before I could comment, someone rapped a "shave and a haircut, two bits" knock on the outside door. Eric and I both turned at the sound. Curt Grimes waved.

"Curt's going to help me with the pickup," Eric said, his eyes gravitating to the wall clock. "We should get going."

"Thanks, Eric, for telling me about it. You did the right thing."

"I guess," he said, walking to the door.

Curt stepped inside.

"Hi, Curt," I said. "Thanks for helping us out today."

"Glad to." He stood by the door, bouncing a little, as if he were standing on tightly coiled Slinkys.

"I'll get the keys to the truck," Eric told him. "You can meet me out front."

"You go ahead," I offered. "I'll lock up."

"Thanks," Eric said. He wheeled the cart to the warehouse door.

"I'll walk around front with you," I said to Curt.

I closed and latched the windows. Outside, I tugged on the doorknob, testing that the lock was secure. It was another beautiful day, sunny with fluffy clouds floating in an azure sky, in the seventies.

"I was wondering," Curt said, breaking into my thoughts, "can I stop by and show you some collectibles? I got some nice repros, perfect for your tag sale. I'm expanding my sell-to list." He winked at me, his eyes bright with excitement. "Want to be on it?"

For a moment, I was speechless, shocked. Everything about his sales pitch was obnoxious. His wink was especially offensive.

"We almost never sell reproductions," I said, allowing a bit of umbrage into my voice. "Sorry."

"Sure you do. You've got some scrimshaw barrettes and some cheesy bamboo furniture—you know, fake Colonial stuff, who's to know, right?" He winked again. "I do my homework."

He just called me a liar, I realized, aghast. If a reproduction made

it into the tag sale, it was always labeled as such. Bristling with outrage, I wanted to defend myself, but I didn't. Educating Curt Grimes
was definitely not worth the energy. I let it go.

"Thanks, but no thanks," I said, adding, "I've got to get back to
work. I'm sure Eric will be here in a minute."

I hurried ahead and went in through the front door, feeling as if
I'd just been drenched by a shower of slime.

Upstairs, in my private office, I turned on my computer.

Maddie had e-mailed. The inventory was complete and accurate
as far as she knew, but since it was Guy's collection, she wanted him
to review the list before signing off on it.

I scanned my desk, determined to make a dent in the paperwork
that had piled up over the last couple of days, but I couldn't concentrate. I couldn't get my mind off Zoë. Seeing her cope was like
watching a reflection of myself from years past. I rested my forehead
on my hands as remembered loss took control of my mind. My emotional wounds had healed, but the memories of love lost lingered
like tule fog.

In the first days after my father's death, I'd plodded through life in a
haze of despair. Once Rick left me, the pain became harrowing and
unrelenting. Then a month or so later, while I was languishing on a
park bench overlooking Strawberry Fields in Central Park, a man and
a young girl—a father and daughter, I'd assumed—sat next to me. It
had been a day like today. The sun shone with summer warmth, and
the temperature hovered near seventy-five. The man was in his early
thirties. His tie was loosened, and he'd draped his jacket over the back
of the bench. The girl looked to be about eight. She wore a plaid
pleated skirt, a white blouse with a Peter Pan collar, and a navy blue
blazer, a school uniform, I'd been certain. From their conversation, I
could tell that he'd just picked her up from school.

"We should stop at the store. There's no food in the house," the
man said. "What do you think of spaghetti and meatballs for dinner?"

I'd glanced at her in time to see a devilish gleam transform her
eyes. "Let's have ice cream." She giggled.

"Ice cream!" he said, sounding over-the-top shocked and dismayed, yet I could see from his twinkling eyes that he was playing along. "Well, then, what should we have for dessert?"

"Spaghetti and meatballs!"

He'd laughed and said, "Done!"

I burst out laughing, suddenly a participant in their homey conversation.

The man could have perceived it as encroaching, but he hadn't. He'd smiled and nodded at me as they left. In those few seconds, I'd realized that my purgatory of despair and isolation would end, and that someday I would once again experience joy.

I picked up a small framed photo of Ty. I'd taken the shot five years earlier. He was in his backyard, planting a lilac bush to celebrate our one-month anniversary of being together.

"We'll be able to watch it grow," he'd said.

"I gotta tell you, Ty . . . this is like the most romantic thing I've ever heard of. You went and bought a lilac bush to commemorate our one-month anniversary. Gosh, jeepers."

"Gosh, jeepers?"

"A perfectly good expression, according to my mother." I'd smiled, reached up, and touched his cheek, drawing my finger along his strong jawline. "Why a lilac bush?"

"I like lilacs."

Never overlook the obvious, I'd reminded myself. "Good reason. So do I. Thank you."

"I love you, Josie."

"I love you, too, Ty."

I replaced the photo, calmer just for looking at his picture and recalling his tenderness and caring.

There was nothing I could do for Zoë except be with her when she wanted company, listen if she wanted to talk, offer opportunities for her to distract herself like being the origami queen at the Harvest Festival, and help the police in any way I could. I sighed and turned back to the mound of paperwork.

The first item I picked up was last week's sales report, and I flipped through it without seeing a thing. The question I'd posed to myself as I was drifting off to sleep last night nagged at me. Why had Greg arranged such a superficial appraisal of a tooth alleged to be a

Myrick? That he believed Ashley's appraisal to be sufficient made no sense—and if something made no sense, usually it wasn't true.

If Greg had been able to authenticate the tooth as a genuine Myrick, it would have added tens of thousands of dollars to his selling price and brought him priceless publicity as the discoverer of a previously unknown Myrick. And if it had been shown to be a phony, well, that's the way the cookie crumbles sometimes in the antiques biz. Not doing a proper appraisal was a surefire way to tarnish your reputation— why would people allow you to sell their objects if they didn't have confidence that you'd get them the best price? He had to have a good reason to have skipped such a crucial step.

Maybe he didn't have the cash to pay for an appraisal. I shook my head. That wasn't the answer.

Greg had owned and operated Sea View Gallery for more than two decades. Even if he was in a cash crunch, he would have done what we all do as a matter of course under those circumstances— spread the risk by sharing the potential reward. Just last week, I'd agreed to appraise what the owner of the Darling Gallery in Bangor, Maine, and I hoped was a Rembrandt etching. They lacked both the expertise and the cash on hand to handle the appraisal themselves, and my company had both. Prescott's agreed to pay all the costs— including sending the print to Milan for chemical testing, if we got that far—and in return, the Darling Gallery agreed to pay us 19 percent of the final selling price, subject to a reserve we'd agree on later, once we knew the object's value. Those kinds of partnerships were standard operating procedure in the industry.

Greg hadn't done that. Instead he'd hired Ashley Morse, a scrimshander, not an antiques appraiser or maritime artifact adviser. The only logical answer was the first one that had occurred to me: The tooth was counterfeit, and he knew it. He didn't bother with faking the provenance because he had a live one about to leave town— Guy Whitestone.

Either his picker, Sam, and he were in it together, or he'd bought the tooth as a repro and cooked up the scheme on his own. Greg probably decided that it would be flying in the face of providence to pass up an opportunity to make more than seventeen thousand dollars overnight—assuming he really had paid Sam seven thousand—

for little work and less risk. He might have rationalized it by telling himself that not only wouldn't it hurt anyone, no one would ever be the wiser.

If that's what happened, if Greg intended to deceive Guy, choosing Ashley to do the appraisal was understandable.

As a novice in the ways of high-end antiques appraisals, Guy would have no reason to question Ashley's bona fides as an appraiser. Her background as a scrimshander would be reason enough for him to have confidence in the appraisal. Certainly Ashley wouldn't question Greg's choice; that would be to bite the hand that fed her, and if nothing else, Ashley was no fool. She'd know that her three-step appraisal was cursory at best, but she'd also recall the lean times, the years during which she'd only earned a subsistence wage and had struggled to get a gallery to represent her. The last thing she'd do would be to suggest that her savior—the gallery owner who took her on—was a scammer. Probably if Greg said jump, Ashley's only question would be how high.

I swiveled and looked out my window. An antique copper weather vane mounted on the church roof across the way shifted with the wind.

The only question remaining was who else knew the Myrick tooth was bogus. Was Greg operating on his own? Had he partnered with Sam? Or was he part of an even larger conspiracy?

CHAPTER TWENTY

I called Wes and got him.

"Talk to me," he said.

"Hi, Wes. I have a question. Have you learned anything about alibis yet?"

"Yup. Ready? Greg had breakfast at the Rocky Point Diner, arriving about eight thirty and leaving about nine thirty, the same as he did almost every morning. His gallery alarm was turned off at nine forty-five, and he opened for business at ten. His first customer arrived around eleven, and from then until twelve thirty, he was with one or more people every minute. At twelve thirty, after his assistant Suzanne Jardin arrived, he drove to various galleries in Maine, assessing the competition, he says. He didn't go into any of them—he just looked through the windows, seeing how busy they were, getting a feel for their inventory, and so on. He went as far north as Ogunquit, then turned around, getting back to his place at two thirty."

I considered the timeline. Greg's gallery was only about a ten-minute drive from Rocky Point Light, so he would have had plenty of time to get to the lighthouse, kill Frankie, and still drive to Maine and back, peeking into shops not so he could suss out the competition but so the shopkeepers could see him peeking in and alibi him if it came to that.

"Curt Grimes was at the lighthouse with Frankie from eight thirty to nine or so," Wes said, "hanging the door. He drove to Frankie's cottage to borrow a DVD." Wes chuckled. "It's called *The Ten Most Outrageous Sports Bloopers of All Time*. Doesn't that sound totally zez?"

"What does 'zez' mean?" I asked.

"Jazzed. Awesome. Bonzo. You know . . . zez?"

"Oh," I said, smiling at Wes's colorful language, "*that* zez."

"Yeah. So anyway, Curt hung out there for a few minutes. Around nine thirty, he went home—he lives in an apartment in the basement of his sister's house. He had something to eat and watched the DVD. Around noon, he visited three companies, trolling for work. No one needed him, and he got back to his apartment around three. He washed his car, then around four, he took his sister shopping. The police were able to verify his alibi from his sister and staff at the three companies, but it doesn't prove anything because there was enough time between stops for him to have detoured to the light-house. He says he just drove around, that he likes driving, that it relaxes him."

"Interesting," I remarked.

"Who else should I look at?" Wes asked.

"I can't think of anyone."

"Got any news for me?"

"No, not now," I said.

"Okeydokey—catch ya later," he said and hung up.

As I gazed at the weather vane's green patina, I realized that the most logical explanation was probably the correct one—Frankie interrupted a burglary. *Was Curt the thief?* I asked myself.

Apparently, Curt needed money. He'd driven to three companies that day without getting work. Was that typical? Was he desperate?

I made a note to ask Wes about Curt's finances.

After striking out with the third company, maybe he decided that desperate times required desperate measures. According to Wes, Curt would have had ample time to get to the lighthouse. Maybe he called Frankie to say that he'd lost something—his wallet or a tool, for instance—and that he must have dropped it in the lighthouse that morning. Frankie, helping his buddy out, would have let him in. Frankie would have run upstairs to look in the sitting room at the top where they'd been working, while Curt pretended to look by the entranceway, where he'd left his stuff. While Frankie was upstairs, Curt grabbed the Myrick tooth, thinking that if he rearranged the other items on the shelf, the theft wouldn't be noticed right away—and it wasn't. He chose that Myrick tooth either at random or because, for whatever reason, he thought it was the most valuable one. Maybe he heard Greg quote the price to Guy, for example, and didn't know that other easily accessible objects were priced even higher.

Boom—he's caught red-handed. They argue. They fight. Curt kills him.

What happened next? I asked myself.

Probably Curt tried to sell the tooth right away. Had he stopped at a pawnshop or at one of the dozens of antiques shops with WE PAY CASH FOR ANTIQUES & COLLECTIBLES signs in their windows? Had he discovered how little money a scrimshaw tooth unaccompanied by proper documentation would sell for? If so, perhaps he decided that his best shot at avoiding a murder rap was to return it. Would he have driven back to the lighthouse without making an appointment? How could he hope to get in? Unless Frankie had told him he was meeting me at three and would be around the rest of the day. Or unless Curt knew the back door was open.

If Curt drove up and saw my car in addition to Frankie's, what would he have done? He would have rung the doorbell, and when there was no answer, he would have tried the doorknob. *Why did he just drive away at that point?* I asked myself. *Either he didn't know the kitchen door was open, which means he's not the killer, or he didn't remember leaving it open, or he just got spooked.*

I shrugged. I was weaving scenarios based on what-ifs, and that kind of conjecture often led nowhere.

My eyes took in the sun-streaked patterns on the church parking lot next to Prescott's while my brain was busy. I spotted a squirrel darting into the bushes that ranged along the near side. From the set of his jaw, I could tell that he was carrying an acorn. Stockpiling for winter started early in New Hampshire.

Was Curt the kind of person who would steal a valuable object while Frankie was on-site and responsible? It would take a real snake to deceive a friend like that. Recalling Curt's sordid offer to sell me fake goods, I found it easy to cast him in that role.

I needed information. I swiveled back to my desk and called Wes again.

"Wes," I said. "It's me."

Wes's lightning rod, the one he used to capture news, sparked as soon as he heard my voice. "Whatcha got?" he asked.

"Nothing except a few more questions. First, money—can you find out some financial information? I want to know about Curt's overall condition."

"Spell it out for me. What are you looking for?"

I didn't want to voice my suspicions without evidence. I looked out the window again. The weather vane had spun to the east.

"I have nothing to tell you. I want information to help guide my thinking—that's why I called."

"Sketch it for me," he persisted.

"No," I said. I'd been in sixth grade when I learned that secrets, once divulged, were lost forever. Curt might be, in my opinion, a sleaze-bucket, but I didn't want to start a rumor that he was a thief, and maybe even a killer.

"Why not?" Wes asked, sounding shocked.

"Because people's reputations are at risk."

He sighed heavily. "All right. If I learn anything, and if it leads somewhere, I'm your first call, right?"

"I can't promise that, Wes. If I uncover a crime, I'll need to report it to the police."

He sighed again. "Then I'm your second call—and you make it soon enough after the first one so I'm in on everything."

I nodded. "That's fair."

"Okay, then. What else do you want to know?"

"The names of the companies Curt visited the day Frankie was killed."

"Heyer's, Jumbo Container, and Mandy's Candies," he rattled off, "in that order."

I knew them. They were all in Rocky Point. "Thanks, Wes. One more thing . . . I'd like to know everyone Frankie spoke to the day he died. I know he talked to Guy Whitestone midmorning because he told me so when he stopped by my office that day. I also know that I left messages on his cell phone around three thirty. Going back a few days, can you find out the details of all calls in and out, and how long each one lasted?"

"Yup. What's his number?" Wes asked.

I read it off to him, adding his home number, too. "I don't think he used his home phone much, but we ought to check."

"No problemo. I'm on it."

"Thanks, Wes. You know I'll fill you in when I can."

"Yup, thanks. So, I was getting ready to call you. I've got a real shockeroonie. You know that picker, Sam? He's refusing to cooperate. He won't talk to the police. He keeps hanging up on them."

"Why?"

"He says it's none of their beeswax who he does business with and they can go jump in the lake. Or words to that effect."

"He sounds real personable."

"Yeah. The police figure he's one of those off-the-grid, antigovernment loner types," he said, unaware that it was my explanation of pickers that the police were using as a guide. "So, any word on Frankie's replacement?"

"He isn't even buried yet, Wes."

"Yeah, I know. They're releasing the body tomorrow. Do you know about funeral plans?"

I blinked away sudden tears. *Poor Zoë,* I thought. "No."

"I've submitted the proposal to *Metropolitan.*"

"I'll be sending good wishes south."

"How long do you think it will take them to respond?" he asked.

"With this story? I think you'll hear very soon."

"Thanks again, Josie."

We said good-bye, and I pushed the disconnect button to get a new dial tone. I called Zoë. She sounded as if she'd been crying.

"You must be a mind reader," she said, her voice laden with grief. "I just heard from the police. They're releasing Frankie's body tomorrow."

"Oh, Zoë. It's all so horrible."

"No one teaches you how to handle stuff like this, you know?"

"All you can do is just keep on keeping on."

"Except that I have no idea what keeping on looks like when it comes to planning Frankie's funeral. I mean, who thinks to ask a twenty-three-year-old what kind of funeral he wants? Jeez."

"Eric told me that he and Frankie went to the Congregational church together a few times, and Frankie liked it. Maybe you want to talk to the minister there."

"Frankie went to church?"

"Yeah. It started because they wanted to meet nice girls," I said.

"I'll be darned. Did they?"

"Eric did."

"Good for him. But not Frankie."

"I don't think so."

"It figures. That kid never caught a break in his life."

"Yes, he did. He had you for his aunt." Zoë began to cry. After a moment, I asked, "Do you want me to call the minister and ask him to contact you?" More tears. "Or I can make an appointment, then come get you, and we can go to the church together."

"Thank you, Josie," she managed after several seconds. "I just had a thought . . . I'll call the funeral parlor I used when my uncle died. They were terrific to me. Kind, you know? They were kind to me." I heard her inhale. "They'll know who to talk to at the church."

"That makes a lot of sense," I said, then offered again to accompany her.

Zoë said she'd be okay, that having a plan of action was the best medicine.

After I hung up, I kept my hand on the receiver for a moment wishing I'd been more articulate, wishing I had the words to express how much I cared about her, and how much I empathized with her loss.

I shook off the thought, struck by something Wes had just revealed—Sam, the picker, wasn't talking despite the fact that he was the source of the missing tooth. Somehow, in some way, whether as an innocent seller or as an accomplice to a crime, Sam was deeply involved in whatever had led to Frankie's death.

CHAPTER TWENTY-ONE

C ara buzzed up to tell me that Maddie was on the phone. "Thank you for working with the police about the antiques. This whole thing," Maddie said, "it is so . . . so . . . I don't know the word. Beyond bad and sad."

"Heartrending. Wicked."

"Yes. It is those things. Guy and I are so thankful you are helping. I spoke to him just now. Except for that one tooth, the inventory you sent is correct. Would you please tell Chief Hunter for me?"

"Certainly. I'll report the tooth as stolen, too."

"Do you have any news from the police about who killed Frankie—or who stole the tooth?"

"No," I replied. "I wish I did."

She sighed, then said, "The man who owns the Winslow Homer etching agreed to meet me at your office. We said one this afternoon. Is that all right?"

"Yes, that's fine," I said.

"He asked how long the appraisal would take. I told him you'd explain everything." She sighed again. "Guy is flying in tomorrow morning. I will be so glad to have him here. The reporters—they are like . . . like those yellow bees that don't let us eat on the patio, what do you call them?"

"Yellow jackets?"

"Yes! That's exactly right. They are like those yellow jackets around syrup."

I smiled at her simile. When I was a girl, my dad would pour a half inch of Campari into a bowl and place it fifty feet away from our picnic table. Within seconds it would be covered with yellow jackets, and we were able to eat in peace.

"With all those reporters—you feel trapped in your hotel, right?" I asked.

"Exactly."

I recalled the feeling well from my New York days. This time around, I wasn't this story's primary target—the Whitestones were—so I was spared the worst of the harassment.

"Chief Hunter has a police officer here," she said. "Still . . ."

"I understand," I said, knowing how she was feeling—hunted. "I'll see you at one."

"Of course. Thank you again, Josie."

As soon as I hung up, I listed the missing Myrick tooth on the three stolen art and antiques sites we subscribed to, one sponsored by an industry association and the other two run by international law enforcement agencies, one based in Europe, the other associated with Interpol. I described the tooth and uploaded the photograph, listing myself and Chief Hunter as contacts. I also e-mailed Wes that the theft was confirmed.

Within seconds of my clicking SEND, Cara called up. Chief Hunter was on line two, and he said it was urgent. I thanked her and punched the button to take his call.

"The technicians have okayed your packing everything up," Chief Hunter said.

"Great," I said. "We'll get right on it."

"Also, I've run into another wall. Can I stop by and talk to you for a minute?"

"Sure," I replied, flattered at being asked.

"Thanks. I'll be there in ten minutes or so."

Downstairs, I told Sasha and Fred that we were good to go to collect everything on the inventory from the lighthouse. They left through the warehouse to gather packing supplies and crates.

Gretchen was making a fresh pot of coffee and trying not to smile, looking for all the world like a giggly schoolgirl with a secret.

"Why are you looking like the cat that swallowed the canary?" I asked.

She laughed and handed me a mock-up of our next direct mail flyer—the one that would be posted in early October. "Take a look," she said.

Keith, our freelance graphic artist, had designed the cover to look like our tag sale venue door. A smiling ghost gestured the reader in with a wispy wave. When I opened the door—that is, when I un-folded the brochure—it was as if I'd stepped into the tag sale room. I spotted cheerfully ghoulish skeletons hanging from the ceiling, jack-o'-lanterns in corners, and children in Halloween costumes. The tables were packed with festive merchandise. I was entirely charmed.

"Wow," I said looking up. "This is so clever. Who came up with the concept?"

Gretchen's eyes shone with delight. "Jack!" she said, naming her scientist boyfriend.

I laughed. "Tell him I bow before him. Keith, too. This is fantastic!"

Chief Hunter entered. "What's fantastic?" he asked, nodding and smiling at each of us.

I handed him the mock-up. "Take a look."

He scanned it and nodded. "Sharp," he said.

"Way to go, Gretchen!" I said, giving her a double thumbs-up. "We're going upstairs. Would you bring us some coffee?"

"You bet. I'll bring some of the lemon cookies Cara made, too. They're evil!"

"Excellent!" I said. "I love evil cookies before lunch."

Upstairs, Chief Hunter sat on the yellow brocade love seat and stretched his long legs out in front of him. I took the Queen Anne wing chair. Gretchen followed with a gleaming silver tray that she placed on the butler's table.

"I was just about to call you," I told him. "Maddie spoke to Guy—the Myrick tooth is the only missing item. She asked that I tell you. I've already listed it as stolen."

"No surprise there." He paused, his brow wrinkling. "I know that each industry has its own idiosyncrasies, but usually there are some standard procedures, some policies that help me get a handle on what's going on. Not now. Not in this case. What I'm concluding is that the antiques business is pretty . . . shall I say freewheeling?"

"One of the last bastions of pure capitalism," I agreed, nodding.

"If you can't predict what inventory you'll acquire, or how much you'll pay for it, how can you project revenue? Or know how much cash you'll need to buy your products? How can you know how many people to hire? How can you run a business?"

"You've hit the nail on the head. The key to success is managing inventory. It's the toughest thing to do consistently and well. Any antiques dealer will tell you that it's way harder to buy good-quality objects than it is to sell them, so having reliable sources for inventory is one of the keys to success. Lots and lots of sources."

"Like Sam, the picker?"

"Sure. Of course, there are lots of other sources, too."

"And it's all unregulated."

I shrugged. "When you're dealing with antiques, almost by definition, every transaction is unique."

He nodded. "That doesn't apply when you're dealing in reproductions."

"Right—but we don't sell reproductions, or we almost never sell them. The only ones we offer for sale either came to us as part of a bigger deal or they're unusual enough and special enough to merit being included, and they always go to the tag sale. We never put repros up for auction."

"Sam is not forthcoming," he said. "He won't even tell us his last name, let alone where he got the Myrick tooth." He looked at me. "You don't look surprised."

"Sourcing is considered confidential information in most businesses—especially in the antiques business. His recalcitrance doesn't necessarily indicate that he's done something wrong." I opened my palms. "Maybe he bought it from someone who made him promise to keep his name out of it. For example, it could be a prominent citizen who doesn't want the world to know he's selling assets to raise cash. Or the seller has other objects he or she is considering letting go and Sam doesn't want the competition to get wind of it."

Chief Hunter nodded. "How can I shake him loose?"

I considered his question for several moments, gazing at the red and gold Oriental carpet as I nibbled a cookie. Gretchen was right— the cookies were evil, sweet and tart and rich. I raised my eyes to meet his. "As a general rule, pickers don't know much about what they sell. They're pretty low on the antiques seller food chain."

He crossed his ankles. "That makes sense. So you're saying it's likely that he doesn't know anything about the missing tooth except where he got it, right?"

"Right. Probably the tooth was in the bottom of a box he bought at a tag sale somewhere in the middle of nowhere. He just read the signature."

"Or he bought it knowing it was a repro," Chief Hunter said.

"That's possible. What does Greg say?" I asked.

"That Sam sold it as a real Myrick. Period."

I shook my head. "Unlikely," I said.

"Why?" he asked.

"If Greg had believed it was real, he would have arranged for a proper appraisal. He's been dealing in antiques—albeit on the fringes—for twenty years. He has to have known that consulting an artist or an artisan instead of an antiques appraiser is like asking an architect to value a house instead of a real estate appraiser or agent. It's apples and oranges."

"Ms. Morse says that Mr. Donovan told her he wanted the appraisal done in 'a New York minute.' That's a quote."

"I can almost hear him saying it."

"Mr. Donovan said that Ms. Morse was an appropriate choice. He was delighted with her work. Still is. He thinks you—and other appraisers like you—conduct unneeded tests."

"Why would we do that? Or do I even need to ask? To justify our fees, right?"

"He said he'd never accuse you or anyone of jacking up your prices, but his implication was clear."

I pressed my lips together to keep myself from speaking the words that came to me. Cursing Greg wouldn't help me or hurt him. "What was his hurry?" I asked instead.

"The Whitestones were leaving, and he wanted to get the sale in before they 'flew the coop.' I'm quoting again."

"What a miserable excuse for a man he is," I said.

"Does it change your mind? Do you still think Mr. Donovan knew it was a fake, and that's why he had Ms. Morse appraise it?"

I thought for a moment, then shrugged. "I could go either way. It's possible that Greg is telling you the truth and that he was simply out to make a quick buck."

"How about Sam? Do you think he suspected or knew the tooth was a phony?"

"I don't know. Some pickers deal in a wide range of antiques, collectibles, and repros and are straight shooters who will tell you what's what, if they know. Others play it a little closer to the vest. I don't know where Sam fits on that spectrum. Maybe he doesn't know a thing about scrimshaw."

"If it's a fake, who created it?"

"I haven't seen it, so for all I know the design is painted on or it's machine-made. Even if it's real, if it's hand-etched, any competent scrimshander can etch a traced design. There are hundreds of them worldwide." I shrugged. "It could have been scrimmed in Indonesia or Paris or Rio and shipped here."

"You say any scrimshander could have produced it . . . like Ms. Morse."

"Yes, although she'd never do it. She's a purist."

"What can I do to find out if it's a fake and, if so, who faked it?"

"Follow the money," I said.

He nodded. "We're on it. Nothing so far, but that might only mean that it was a cash transaction using money on hand. You keep large amounts of cash here, right? In case of walk-in sellers?"

"Yes."

"So presumably Sam was paid in cash, too."

"For sure. As far as I know, pickers only deal in cash."

"What else can I do to trace it?" he asked.

"Scrimshanders have an association, a newsgroup, and an online forum. When it comes to communications and business, the world has definitely become a smaller place. Track past postings and see if anyone solicited a scrimshander to produce repros."

He made a note. "Good idea. What else?"

"See if anyone tried to sell the missing tooth locally. There are scores of small antiques stores and pawnshops who might remember someone selling a scrimmed tooth."

"We've sent out notices to antiques dealers, pawnshops, and

auction houses in New Hampshire, Massachusetts, and Maine asking for information, but no nibbles yet. What would you do if someone walked in with it?"

"Ask about its history and check if it was stolen."

"Would you make a cash offer on the spot?"

"It depends on what I learned," I said. "It's rare, but I've done it."

"Would many dealers?"

"Sure."

"Who?"

"Most of them. They count on walk-in sellers for inventory."

"So do you," he remarked.

"True, but I don't maintain an open shop, so I have an easier time saying no." I smiled. "I also hold out the promise of a higher payday if they let me do my homework."

He nodded. "I bet you're a killer negotiator."

I smiled and looked down. "Thanks."

"Say someone came in and told you they found the tooth in a box in their cellar—they just moved into the house, so they don't know anything about its history. What would you do?"

"Assuming I've done my due diligence in determining that it's not listed as stolen, I'd buy it."

"For how much?"

"A fraction of what I thought I could get for it. It's business, right?"

"And after you've closed the deal, then you'd appraise it?" he asked.

"You betcha."

He nodded again. "This is a heck of an industry."

"It's not for the faint of heart," I granted.

"What else can I do?"

"Let me talk to Sam," I suggested.

"For what purpose?" he asked.

"We can see what he offers me for sale. Maybe he has another Myrick tooth hidden away."

"What would you say?"

"That I heard that he's the one who sold that tooth to Sea View and that I guarantee him I'll always beat Greg's price."

He leaned forward, grinning like a World War II pilot I once saw in a photo. The pilot had been about to step into his plane to fly a sortie, his eyes ablaze with excitement.

"I like it," he said. "I like it a lot. Let me run it by the ADA. We don't want to risk your getting mixed up in any entrapment charges."

My pulse spiked. I stared at him, wondering if I was blanching before his eyes. I took a deep breath. "We sure don't. That hadn't even occurred to me. It can't be entrapment if all I'm doing is offering to buy things. I make that same offer to people, pickers included, all the time."

"I agree—it's a sting, not a trap. But just for the heck of it, let's cover our bases."

"Then I ought to consult my lawyer."

"Sure. Do you want me to wait downstairs?"

"No," I said, crossing the room to my desk. "He may have questions for you."

He watched as I dialed Max Bixby's number.

Max was a rock, knowledgeable about the law and solidly in my corner. Knowing he was on my side had made countless anxiety-filled moments easier to bear.

"Max," I said, when I had him on the line. "It's Josie."

"Long time no speak, little lady," he said, sliding into his oddly comforting Western cowboy cadence. "What's a-doing?"

"You heard about Frankie? Frankie Winterelli?"

"Terrible," he said, all trace of playfulness gone. "Just terrible."

I described my connection. "The police want me to help trick someone, a picker. I'm a logical choice since I'm in the business, which means he probably won't smell a rat."

"What's the police objective?"

I put the phone on speaker. "I just put you on speaker, Max, so Chief Hunter can join our conversation. Do you two know one another yet? Tuesday was the chief's first day. Chief, this is the best lawyer in town, Max Bixby."

Chief Hunter left the yellow Queen Anne chair and sat in a guest chair near the desk to be close to the phone.

"Chief," Max said by way of greeting. "Welcome to Rocky Point.

Although at this point, you may be ready to turn tail and hustle on out of here."

"It's a heck of a way to start a new job, that's for sure."

"So about this situation . . . can you tell me the police objective in asking Josie for help?"

"My investigation suggests that this seller may be dealing in repros marketed as genuine items. Or he could be on the up-and-up. It's all circumstantial at this point. If Josie asks him to sell her whatever he's got—by observing his sales presentation, as it were, we would hope to learn more about his methods and inventory."

"Do you suspect him of murder?"

"It's early days," he said, giving the kind of answer I'd come to expect from him.

"Thanks for clarifying."

"You're welcome."

"Is this request going to be made via the phone or in person?" Max asked.

"She'll call to set up a meet. Then in person."

Max continued to probe for how exposed I'd be, then asked, "Josie, is this something you want to take on?"

Max spoke, but it was Zoë's sobs I heard. "Yes," I said. "If I can help, I want to."

Max asked Chief Hunter to fax him the ADA's opinion, which he promised to turn around immediately. After the call ended, Chief Hunter stood up, ready to go.

"Thank you," he said.

"Don't thank me yet. I haven't done anything." I came around the desk, prepared to walk him out.

"Good point," he said, his voice echoing as we walked down the stairs into the vast warehouse. "Has the media given you any trouble?"

"Not really. All I have to do is threaten to call you and they flee."

"Good. How's Ms. Winterelli?"

"She's sad. She's really sad."

"I'll call her to see if she has any questions."

"She will. She'll ask you who killed Frankie."

"Yeah, probably."

"What will you tell her?" I asked.

He looked at me. "I'll say that we're making progress."

At his words, goose bumps chased up my arms. "That implies you're close."

"Does it?" he asked wearily, then gave a little shrug as if shaking off an unpleasant thought. "Well, thanks again for offering to help with Sam. I'll get back to you—and your lawyer—as soon as I can."

He was out the door and gone.

CHAPTER TWENTY-TWO

I brought up the photographs Maddie had e-mailed me of *The Herring Net.*

In the original painting—and in this etching—the faces of the man and the boy in the dory could hardly be discerned, yet from their stoic bearing, you could see that they were exhausted and inured. The mother ship, faintly visible in the distance, her sails starkly outlined against the overcast sky, promised sanctuary even as the roiling sea threatened danger. Dusk was gathering, and the last phase of their day's work—rowing back to their ship—had yet to begin. It was an everyman story, an eloquent portrayal of the hard life endured by men who fished for a living in the nineteenth century. Guy, I thought, would love it.

I did some quick research, consulting a proprietary site for price information. Auction results for Homers were all across the board, from more than four million dollars for a watercolor of fishergirls coiling tackle three years ago to as little as $194,000 for a small oil of skaters last year. I closed the site. It was early days to be thinking about price. The first issue was authentication. I glanced at the clock—it was eleven thirty. In an hour and a half, I'd get my first look at an etching purported to have been crafted by one of America's most loved artists.

While I was online, I also researched requests for Myrick repros on the public scrimshanding forums I'd mentioned to Chief Hunter. I found no hint of nefarious dealings. Which didn't prove anything except that the scheme's organizer, if there was a scheme, wasn't a fool.

Maddie arrived first, looking as elegant as always in a gold silk blouse and brown high-waisted, wide-legged slacks.

She greeted us each by name, then asked me, "Have you heard anything from the police?"

As soon as Maddie spoke, I could feel Gretchen's attention shift—she hoped she was about to hear some inside dirt. Gretchen was a celebrity gossip aficionado, but home-grown tidbits were good, too, the more sensational or spicy, the better. I'd overheard her chatting about UFOs and movie stars' divorces often enough to know that her addiction was a harmless, fun hobby. She never repeated secrets or hurtful tales about people she knew; she was too much of an innate caretaker for that. Personally, I found her interest in scandal bewildering.

"Nothing," I replied. "Except that the police are working on lots of different angles."

"I met with Chief Hunter again this morning, and another detective, a woman, a Detective Brownley. They asked about Frankie's friends, but I had no information. It seems—" She broke off as the wind chimes sounded.

A man with watery gray eyes who was carrying a brown-paper-wrapped package entered and stood just inside. He was somewhere around seventy. His hair was mostly white, peppered with a few black strands, and cut short.

"Hi," I said, smiling. "I'm Josie Prescott."

"Where do you want this?" he asked.

"This is Maddie Whitestone. You've spoken to her on the phone." I reached for the package. "That must be heavy. I'll take it."

"I'm okay. Where do you want it?" he asked again.

"There," I said, pointing to the round table near the front windows.

He slid a gnarled finger under the brown paper flap, then pulled it aside.

The etching was encased behind glass and traditionally framed in ornate gilt. I viewed the image as a whole, then examined it a second time using a grid pattern, seeking out anomalies and imperfections. It appeared to be in pristine condition, with no visible tears, repairs, or foxing. The artistry and workmanship were top-notch. You could almost feel the motion of the water, the wind in the sails, the bone-chilling cold, and the man's and boy's fatigue. My eye was drawn to the mother ship, its sails billowing. The ink distribution seemed off, some lines surrounding the sails too thick, others too dark. Perhaps Homer had used an échoppe to achieve a more prominent line on purpose, intending to highlight the struggle awaiting the fishermen facing that long row back. I didn't think I was looking at signs of plate wear, but just to be certain, we'd need to research how many impressions typically were printed from each of Homer's metal plates. Usually several hundred copies could be made before the plate began to show signs of wear, which under certain printing conditions might result in uneven ink distribution.

"So," he asked, "what do you think?"

"So far all I can tell you is that it appears to be in excellent condition."

He turned to Maddie. "Like I said."

"Josie?" she said.

"We need to do a full appraisal—authentication first, then valuation. It will take several days at least, maybe several weeks."

"What?" the seller objected. "No way."

I nodded to convey empathy. This wasn't the first time I'd heard a seller's dismay. "I understand that it can be frustrating," I said. "Not only is the appraisal process not fast, it's not predictable."

He stared at me, maybe trying to intimidate me, maybe just angry at the situation, then turned to face Maddie. "I told you on the phone, I called with a good price for a quick sale."

"We'll be as speedy as we can," I said. "Let me explain how it works. We need to research and test several elements, from Homer's etching and printing work habits to the paper and ink. Some of the tests take time, and if they come back with ambiguous results, we need to add another layer of testing."

"I don't know nothing about any of that. I named my price, and you'll either pay it or not."

"I'm so sorry, but I need the appraisal," Maddie said.

"Any buyer would," I added.

He shook his head, digging in his heels.

Maddie met my eyes. "Josie? Would you buy it?"

I smiled to take the sting out of my words. "No. I never rush into anything. And while a quarter of a million dollars might be a great price if this is a Winslow Homer, it's still a lot of money. I wouldn't buy it until it's authenticated."

"I agree," Maddie said, sounding disappointed. "I'm sorry it didn't work out."

He looked from her to me, then back again. "What if it's worth more?" he asked, sounding suspicious, as if he thought we were setting him up somehow.

"Then Mrs. Whitestone gets a good deal."

"How about me?"

"You get a quarter of a million dollars." I shrugged. "You set the price."

He turned to leave. "Do what you gotta do."

"Okay, then. What can you tell me about it?" I asked.

"Nothing," he said over his shoulder, one hand on the doorknob. "Just what I told her. I bought it off a woman looking to sell. She said she found it in the attic and didn't know nothing."

"How'd you set the price?"

"I've heard of Homer."

In other words, I thought, *he guessed.*

"Gretchen, would you prepare a receipt for . . . what's your name?"

"What do you need my name for?" he asked, his hackles up.

"For the receipt."

"You don't need my name for that. Just write out what I'm leaving here."

I turned to Gretchen, who was watching our exchange with wide eyes. "And attach photos," I told her. "They're in the system—Maddie e-mailed them to me." To him, I asked, "Did you take the photos you sent to Mrs. Whitestone?"

"A guy I know did. I don't know about that stuff. Why?"

"The pictures were good."

He kept his eyes on me, his distrust palpable. Gretchen handed him the neatly organized receipt.

"You've got my phone number, right? You need anything else?" he asked.

"No," I replied. "Thank you."

He left without another word. I watched as he walked across the asphalt toward a brown van on the far side of the lot.

"Did his reaction surprise you?" Maddie asked.

"Not really," I said, turning back. "Sellers come in all shapes and sizes."

She nodded. "Thank you, Josie. I am so curious. I look forward to hearing what you discover."

I turned toward the etching, drawn to its evocative imagery, and nodded. "Me, too."

About an hour later, Sasha and Fred drove into the lot. I ran out to the loading dock to meet the van. Eric was already there, unloading the Whitestones' carefully packaged possessions.

"Mr. Whitestone has a terrific eye," Sasha said.

"I know. It's a great collection. Some of the objects are so unusual," I said. "Any problems?"

"No. It was routine."

"As soon as you're done, come up front. You too, Fred. I want to show you something Maddie Whitestone is considering buying Guy for his birthday."

"There's not much," Eric said. "I can handle it. You guys go ahead."

We thanked him, then trekked through the auction venue, slid open the moving partition, and continued through the warehouse, our footsteps reverberating loudly in the concrete shell.

"Voilà," I said, gesturing toward the Homer I'd relocated to a work-station.

Fred pushed up his glasses as he approached. Sasha stood next to him, then leaned in close, tucking her fine brown hair behind her ear.

After several moments, she asked, "What do you think?"

"I think we need to be careful. The seller wants a quick cash sale, and he has no ownership information beyond saying he'd bought it from a woman cleaning out her attic."

She nodded. It wasn't an unusual story. "There's some question about how many etchings Homer produced," she said. She was in her element and speaking with confidence. "I've heard that there might be as many as ten—maybe even more. As far as I know, though, this isn't one of them."

"I wondered about that," I said. "And didn't Homer usually change things up when he adapted a painting into an etching?"

"Yes. In *Saved,* for instance, Homer clean-wiped the plate to create an ethereal, atmospheric look to the waves and to emphasize the suspended figures. It's a very different look and feel than the original painting."

"He changed the composition, too, didn't he?" I asked.

"Right. In addition to the original painting, he etched two separate versions. The first etching featured a wide view of the ocean with a cliff in the far distance. When he etched the second one, he reversed the figures and adjusted the viewpoint. The modification changed the entire perspective from expansive to intimate. Also, he retooled the ocean, adding mighty waves designed with a curved pattern suggestive of Japanese art. It's spectacular—you can really feel the thrashing water. It's quite a shock seeing how different it is from the original."

"I know that second etching," Fred said. "I've always thought it was bad form that he didn't retitle it. Sure, it shares a theme with the earlier pieces, but it's a mistake to think of it as anything other than new. Homer changed the emphasis, the style, and the environment he portrayed." He shrugged. "It's not a redo."

"That's too extreme a view," Sasha replied, her tone assured. "I agree that it's not merely a repetition, but neither is it totally fresh."

I pointed to the etching. "Do you think this one could be a real find? A previously unknown etching?" I asked.

The three of us stood for a moment staring at it; then Sasha nodded. When she looked at me, I saw the thrill of the hunt in her eyes, and I understood that she thought there was a decent chance that we might be on the verge of living an appraiser's dream—authenticating a previously unknown work by a master.

"Yes," she said, "it's possible. Homer started as a lithographer. He cared about the printing process—he was diligent, and by some reports a perfectionist. He was also reclusive. If he wasn't happy with an etching, he might well have destroyed the plate after just a few impressions were made."

"Or it could be a well-executed forgery," Fred said.

"What should we check first?" I asked.

Sasha shrugged and pursed her lips, thinking. "To save time, we should check the materials. If the paper and ink are right, then we can pursue the more time-consuming aspects of authenticating it."

"An even quicker approach would be to call a few experts and ask if they know if Homer adapted *The Herring Net* into an etching," Fred said.

"I don't want to start the rumor mill," I said. "I think we should keep our research quiet at this point." I looked at Sasha. "After the paper and ink, then what?"

"I know that a New York company printed all of the impressions," she replied. She stared at the back wall, and I could almost see her opening the relevant file cabinet in her brain. "Ritchie. G. W. H. Ritchie. When Homer died, five plates were in Ritchie's possession. We should find out where the others were located."

"Didn't Ritchie make additional impressions after Homer's death?" Fred asked.

Sasha nodded. "If I'm remembering right, and I think I am, the printing company was sold to someone else . . . someone named White . . . and *he* began making new impressions from the five plates. Eventually, the plates were sold to the Met. That happened sometime in the 1940s."

"At this point, it's moot," I said, not wanting us to get distracted by the Metropolitan Museum of Art's purchase. "The first issue isn't how many impressions were made—it's whether *this* etching was made at all. If we can validate that, then we can consider the integrity of this particular example." I pointed to the lines that had struck me as overly bold. "Do you see these? Don't they seem too thick . . . or too something . . . too *present*?"

"Maybe," Sasha said.

"Did Homer use an échoppe?" I asked.

"I don't know," Sasha said. "Do you, Fred?"

"No, sorry."

"Sasha, do you want to take the lead on this one?"

"Sure," she said, smiling.

Fred and I entered the front office, leaving her studying the etching.

"The Whitestone collection is time-sensitive, so don't be shy about asking us for help, okay?" I told Fred as he walked to his desk.

The front door opened. "Max!" I said.

"Howdy, friends," he said, grinning, including us all in his greeting, looking and sounding as if he had all the time in the world and couldn't think of anything he'd rather be doing than visiting. "Got a sec, Josie? There's something we need to talk about."

"Sure," I said, curious about what he and the ADA had figured out. I led the way upstairs.

"Chief Hunter will be here any minute," Max said once we were settled in. "The ADA and I got it nailed down. You're immune from any and all fallout that may result from this initiative. A formal letter of appreciation for your assistance has been issued. You're going to call this seller—Sam, right?—and hopefully entice him to sell you things. You're to tell him that you're open to purchasing good-quality reproductions in addition to antiques."

"For the tag sale?" I asked.

He rubbed his nose, thinking before replying. "Leave it open," he said. "The phrasing is important. Chief Hunter will be bringing some word-for-word phrases for you to use. The gist is that the police are hoping that if you mention that you have customers hungry for good stuff and therefore you're always on the lookout for quality objects—that will be enough for him to offer to sell you repros without you bringing anything specific up."

"You're saying that I should tell Sam I want to snooker customers!" I objected, appalled.

Max leaned back. "No. I'm saying you should imply it."

"Max, stop it!" I exclaimed, laughing.

"Crime-fighting is not for the weak or wary."

My mouth opened, then closed. I couldn't think what to say.

CHAPTER TWENTY-THREE

ara buzzed up. Chief Hunter and Detective Brownley were downstairs. I told her to bring them up, then said to Max, "What's Detective Brownley doing here?"

He shrugged. "I don't know."

We both stood as they entered. I thanked Cara, then watched as Max pulled a third chair up to the desk. Chief Hunter sat in the middle, sitting directly across from me. Detective Brownley nodded hello, then extracted a notebook from her briefcase.

"We didn't get the warrant," Chief Hunter told Max. "So we can't record the conversation. Also, we need to be very careful about the language. The ADA doesn't want her mentioning anything or anyone by name, unless, of course, Sam mentions them first." He turned to me. "So you can't say you heard he sold a Myrick tooth to Sea View Gallery and you'll always beat the price like we talked about before. What you don't want to do is be specific or explicit. Obviously, don't say, 'Do you have any fakes you can sell me?' Or 'Do you have any repros good enough to fool a layman?' Keep your request vague. Intimate, don't state."

I nodded. "I understand."

"Try to get a meeting today—but don't imply any undue urgency."

At first, helping with Sam had seemed easy. Now, as I listened to the restrictions and admonitions, I began to feel daunted at the prospect of messing up something so important. "I'll do my best," I said.

Chief Hunter eased a sheet of paper from his inside jacket pocket and slid it across the desk toward me.

"Take a minute and read this."

Two bulleted lists were printed on official Rocky Point Police letterhead, one under the heading "Do" and the other under the heading "Don't."

The "Do" list read:

- Say you heard he often had "good-quality" objects.
- Ask him to come to you first to sell the good stuff—since you serve serious collectors, you're certain that you can pay more than other dealers.
- Tell him you're interested in all sorts of items at all sorts of price points since you need to keep both the tag sale and your monthly auctions stocked.
- Say you occasionally sell reproductions—especially excellent-quality ones.

The "Don't" list was shorter:

- Avoid saying you've heard he deals in reproductions.
- Avoid revealing who told you about him.

I met Chief Hunter's eyes, then glanced at Detective Brownley. Her pen was poised over her notebook. She was ready to go, an observer, not a participant. She smiled encouragingly. I wished I felt as confident as they looked.

"What should I say if he asks how I got his number?" I asked Chief Hunter.

"How would you normally answer if a picker asked you that?"

"I've never called a picker before, not out of the blue, I mean, where I don't know him. I don't know what I can possibly say to explain my call."

"Let's make up a logical backstory, then. Who might have slipped you his number as a good lead for quality product?"

"Another picker doing me a favor."

"How would it work?" Chief Hunter asked.

"If I said to my picker how great his stuff is and that I wished I had a dozen of him . . ." I shook my head. "Even if he knew Sam, which he probably doesn't, he wouldn't give me his name. He'd buy Sam's antiques, add a little something to the price for his trouble, and resell everything to me. No way would he give me Sam's name."

"Okay. So who would?"

I thought for a moment. "Rose Mayhew would. She owns a small shop in Rocky Point. I buy a lot of things from her—I'm probably her biggest customer."

"Why wouldn't she do what you just described?" Max asked. "Buy and resell?"

"Cash. She's always strapped for cash. She works on very low margins."

Concentration lines appeared on Chief Hunter's forehead. "Why does any seller go to Ms. Mayhew? Why wouldn't they all come directly to you?"

"They don't know that Rose is selling to me. If they learned about it, they'd come to me in a heartbeat, and she'd be out of luck. One of her real strengths is maintaining a network of suppliers. But if a picker approached her with an object that was too rich for her blood, she'd turn him over to me as a favor to us both."

"Why wouldn't she ask you to front the cash?" Chief Hunter asked. "Like that gallery in Maine, Darling, their name was, right?"

"That's a completely different situation. The Darling Gallery lacks expertise as well as cash. We're not buying something for or from them. We're assisting them in an appraisal they can't do on their own. In this case, if Rose asks me to front the cash, she ends up screwed. She'd lose the commission I'd pay her for the referral, and she'd lose her own markup. I mean, think about it . . . if she asked me to buy something, say a Chippendale desk for three thousand dollars, how could she turn around and sell it to me for thirty-five hundred?"

"So she'd turn the picker over to you? What would she get out of it for losing her source?"

"A commission on the sale, and she'd keep her best customer—me—happy."

"There you go," Chief Hunter said. "Tell Sam that without naming any names."

I nodded as I thought it through. "I can do that."

"As you know," Chief Hunter said, turning from me to Max to Detective Brownley, then back to Max again, "we're making the call from this location so Prescott's phone number will show on Sam's caller ID display. We all need to be aware that the call will be on the speakerphone, so there needs to be no rustling of papers, tapping of feet, or jingling of coins. And for God's sake, if you need to sneeze, get out of the room first." He looked at me. "Ready?"

I wished the three of them weren't there. I hate feeling conspicuous, and this was about as bad as I could imagine. It felt as if I were standing on a big, empty stage in a packed theater. "As ready as I'm going to get, I guess," I said.

Chief Hunter handed me a slip of paper with Sam's phone number written on it. I took a deep breath, then another, then punched the button on the unit activating the speakerphone function. The tinny sound of the dial tone startled me, and I realized that muscles in my neck and shoulders were knotted tight. I arched my back for a moment, trying and failing to relax a little, then dialed.

"A-yup," a crotchety voice said.

"Is this Sam?"

"Who wants to know?"

"Josie Prescott from Prescott's Antiques and Auctions in Rocky Point. Do you have a sec to talk?" I asked, thinking I knew that voice. *Who is he?* I asked myself.

"What do you want?"

Sam sounded pugnacious, more suspicious than curious. I found myself fighting an inclination to apologize for some unknown offense. *Absurd!* I told myself. I kept my eyes on my desk blotter.

"I hear you often have good-quality objects," I replied. "I'm a buyer. Cash."

"Who says so?"

"A dealer."

"Which dealer?" he demanded.

My impulse was to back off in the face of his belligerence, but I resisted. My dad once told me that on the street, you should do whatever it takes to get away from aggression, including turning tail and running if necessary, but in business, you need to meet aggression with aggression. Anything else only feeds the other guy's sense of entitlement, empowering him while weakening your own position.

"A good friend in the business who can't afford your stuff and is doing me a favor," I said impatiently. "Don't you want a new customer who pays cash money? I need inventory—and I need it all the time."

"What kind of inventory?"

I smiled. *Bingo,* I thought. *Gotcha.* Now that he'd asked for specifics, the deal was mine. "Anything good."

"You said your company is in antiques? I don't deal in antiques much. Only sometimes."

It's the man with the Winslow Homer, I realized. *The man in the brown van.* Confusion and shock ricocheted through my brain. *Does this change anything?* I asked myself, forcing myself to focus on the most pressing question.

"I said I don't deal in antiques much," he repeated.

No, I thought, *it doesn't change a thing. He doesn't know I've recognized his voice.* "Come and show me what you've got. I have a couple of good customers—*really* good customers—eager to buy."

"What do you buy?"

"A little of everything. Right now, I'd love to get my hands on some pewter serving pieces, wooden tools, and maritime-themed objects. But I'm open to anything."

"When you want me to come?"

"Now is good. Can you come now?" I asked.

After a pause that seemed endless, he said, "Tomorrow afternoon. I can meet you around four tomorrow."

"Not today?"

"No. I'm too far away."

"Tomorrow will work. Let me give you the address," I said, still pretending I hadn't recognized his voice.

"I know where you are. I'll call around three thirty," he said and hung up.

Chief Hunter reached over and tapped the button to end the call. He smiled. "And that, ladies and gentlemen, is how you do that."

CHAPTER TWENTY-FOUR

I know him," I explained, describing how Sam had come to stop by Prescott's. "I just didn't know his name."

"Do you think it's just random happenstance that you connected with him today for the first time?" Chief Hunter asked.

"Probably. I'm always amazed when a new picker shows up and tells me he's been selling in the area for ten or twenty years. I mean, how can he have just discovered me? I've been in business for five years already! Why didn't he stop by years ago?" I shrugged. "People are creatures of habit, pickers included."

"I guess," he said. He offered a hand, and we shook. "Thanks, Josie."

After they left, I flipped through the small stack of WHILE YOU WERE OUT messages that had accumulated over the last two days.

Someone I didn't know named Hideo Yamamoto, curator at the Shipping Heritage Museum in Honolulu, had called late afternoon yesterday about a Myrick-scrimmed tooth the museum was considering acquiring.

It was just after three here, 9:00 A.M. in Hawaii. I brought up the document Sasha had prepared last spring tracing extant Myrick teeth, then called the museum.

Hideo Yamamoto answered with a heavily accented "Yamamoto here."

"Mr. Yamamoto, this is Josie Prescott returning your call."

"Ah, thank you so much for calling. You are very kind."

"It's a pleasure. Am I calling at a convenient time?" I asked, familiar with the Japanese tradition of engaging in a brief exchange of polite small talk before broaching business.

"Yes. And for you?"

"Absolutely," I said.

"Thank you. Please excuse my English. I am, as you can hear from my accent, Japanese. I am a consultant helping the museum expand their collection. You are near New York City?"

"Not so very far from New York. I'm in New Hampshire."

"Ah, I do not know New Hampshire, but I liked New York City very much."

We chatted for several minutes about his one and only visit to New York and my several trips to Japan; then he said, "Thank you again for calling me back so promptly. I am trying to ascertain provenance of a scrimmed tooth. May I speak to you in confidence?"

"Yes, of course," I said. Discussing potential purchases in confidence was common in the industry. If news got out about an object as rare as a newly discovered Myrick tooth, a bidding frenzy might drive the price up before the museum had time to close the deal. "I am glad to do so. You said in your message that it was a Myrick? A Frederick Myrick tooth?"

"That is what the seller says. We are very interested in it. I think . . . that is, I hope . . . what I should say is that it appears the tooth is new to the market."

Coincidences happen, but this would be a whopper. Sure, another unknown Myrick tooth could have surfaced, but in this age of instant communication and frequent flights between the East Coast and the Hawaiian Islands, there was a better than even chance that the tooth stolen from the Whitestones had found its way to Honolulu.

"When did you receive the tooth?" I asked.

"Yesterday."

My heart began to thump. "May I ask how you acquired it?"

"We have reached a tentative arrangement with a reputable dealer who knows of our longtime interest in maritime art and artifacts."

"A local dealer?"

"No, from your part of the country, in Boston."

Boston was close enough to New Hampshire for a thief to drive there, sell the tooth, and get back in three or four hours if the traffic wasn't too bad and he hurried.

"Have you seen the Interpol listing on a stolen Myrick tooth?" I asked.

"No!" he exclaimed. "I know nothing of a stolen tooth. Please tell me."

I gave him the Interpol URL so he could find the listing online. "I posted it on behalf of a client this morning. A collector bought a purported Myrick tooth from a local art gallery not long ago. It is missing, and presumed stolen."

"I must check."

"Do you have photographs of your tooth that you can send me? I have one photo of the stolen tooth from the initial sale, which is also online."

"Yes. I will e-mail them to you now. One moment, please . . . thank you for your patience," Mr. Yamamoto said. "The photographs have been sent."

I opened up the first image, zoomed in, and exhaled, only then realizing that I'd been holding my breath. Mr. Yamamoto's tooth was not the Whitestones'. His tooth's design showed the *Ann,* not the *Susan.*

"It's not the stolen Myrick," I said. "It's a different design."

"Yes, I see your announcement. Ah, that is good news indeed."

Sort of, I thought. I was glad for him that his tooth wasn't the Whitestones', but it would have been a huge relief to me to know that Guy's stolen tooth had been located and was in safe hands.

"There is only one extant Myrick showing the *Ann,* is that correct?" I asked.

"Yes. This, if it is genuine, would be the second. Do you agree that it looks like a typical Myrick?"

I clicked through the photos. Yellow age spots darkened the ivory, as if someone had spilled buttermilk on it and the stains hadn't washed away. A near-black chevron border circled the narrow end of the tooth. Under it, text read, "This was done by Fred Myrick on board the ship *Susan* of Nantucket for Mr. John Joseph Lewis on board the *Ann* of London" followed by "January the 31st, 1829." The word "London" and the date were markedly lighter in hue than the rest of the text. A fishtail border wended its way around the larger end. Etched over the three-sailed ship were the words "The *Ann* of London on the Coast of Japan." The sea was calm, depicted by six stacked, evenly spaced, wavy lines. Darker lines edged the ballooning sails. The deck of the boat was pale and hard to see. The ropes stretching from the sails to the deck showed astonishing detail—I could even see frayed spots. On the reverse side, a compass indicated that the ship was heading south.

"I agree—the design looks right," I told him. I clicked back to the first photo. "It's hard to tell from the photograph, of course, but it appears that some parts of the ivory have yellowed more than other parts, the coloration is uneven, some lines are darker than others, and some of the text has faded. Is that correct?"

"Yes. Did you observe that in the Myrick tooth that is missing?"

"I didn't appraise that tooth, so I can't say."

"But wait, perhaps I am mistaken, but I thought . . . I have my notes here . . . I called you because I read you sold one this year. Is that not correct?"

"Yes, that's right, but the stolen tooth is not one I appraised. In the Myrick tooth I sold, the yellowing is very similar and, according to the curator at the whaling museum I consulted, very typical. This drawing is both a bit paler and a bit darker in places than that one, however."

"Would you agree that the discoloration and light-dark variation in coloration appear consistent with the natural aging process?" he asked.

"Yes, I think so." I paused, staring at the photograph. It looked right, but it didn't feel right, and over the years, I'd learned to trust my hunches. My eye gravitated to the date. "Let me ask you something . . . about the date . . . hold on for a sec." I searched for "January," and then "February," in Sasha's document and found what I was looking for—other teeth Myrick scrimmed during that season. "The other *Ann* tooth, the one known to be genuine, is dated January seventh of the same year as yours. Do you think it's possible that Myrick could have scrimmed a second tooth in only three and a half weeks? I know he was prolific—but that seems astonishingly quick. I've never had to validate a previously unknown Myrick tooth, so I never had cause to look into the timing."

"You make a very interesting observation. I will need to look at the dates of each extant Myrick tooth."

"I know a couple of scrimshanders," I said. "If you think the information would be useful, I could ask them how long it takes to produce a fully scrimmed tooth."

"I would be most appreciative. Can you do so without discussing this object? As I said before, confidentiality is most critical."

"Yes, of course. I'll check with them right away, and I'll keep my questions theoretical."

"Thank you. May I tell you what I have done in testing? If you have the time. I do not want to impose."

"I'd love to hear."

"Thank you so much. I will appreciate your guidance. The tooth passed the hot pin test, of course. I have examined it under good magnification. There are no signs of marrow. The air bubbles are perfectly shaped—they are very round. Also, they are easy to see. There are two small cracks that appear near the narrow end."

"I don't see them in the photo," I said.

"No, they are minute."

"Interesting. Is the etching over or under the cracks?" I asked.

Hairline cracks commonly appear as ivory ages. A nineteenth-century scrimshander wouldn't work on a damaged tooth—there was no need to do so since plenty of undamaged ones were available. An age crack that runs deeper than the engraved lines crossing it can only mean that the scrimshaw was created after the crack appeared, suggesting that the object is a modern forgery.

"They are not related to the illustration."

"Is their placement awkward to the design?" I asked, thinking that a knowledgeable forger might be prescient enough to avoid etching a spot that could later be used to demonstrate the object was a phony.

"No. I have seen Myrick teeth where the design reaches the tip, but I have also seen his work where it does not."

I nodded. He was right. "So that's no help. What will you do next?"

"Spectroscopic analysis."

"I'll hope the test confirms the age."

"Yes, thank you. Is there anything else you would do now? Besides verify and compare the dates of all extant Myrick teeth?"

"I might ask experts if anyone has ever heard a rumor that a second *Ann* tooth exists."

"That is a sensible idea. Have you?"

"No . . . but I don't know that I would. We deal in maritime artifacts a lot because of our coastal location, but I wouldn't qualify as a scrimshaw expert. Do you know Lester Morley?" I asked, naming the curator of the whaling museum we consulted to help us appraise scrimshaw.

"By reputation, of course, but I have never spoken to him."

"I have his phone number if you'd like."

"Thank you. I would be most appreciative."

"Please say hello for me," I requested.

"I will, certainly. Thank you."

"You're more than welcome. This is quite a coup if it is real—a second *Ann*. That's a prospect we don't run into every day of the week."

"Yes—thank you so much."

I told him I would e-mail him what the scrimshanders said about how long scrimming a tooth takes, and I asked if he would let me know the outcome of his research. He assured me that he would. "You have been most helpful," he said.

I called Lenny and Ashley right away and got their voice mails. I left brief messages, just asking that they call me back, then hung up and glanced around my office.

I was eager to be up and doing, not sitting and waiting, and I tried to think of something productive to do but couldn't.

I kept coming back to Curt Grimes. He was in the lighthouse the morning Frankie was killed, and he winked at shady dealings. If Curt had stolen the tooth, I'd bet he'd want to get it out of his hands immediately.

Chief Hunter had told me he'd sent flyers alerting dealers about the missing Myrick tooth and there'd been no response. From personal experience, I knew that there was a world of difference between getting a routine police flyer in the mail and having someone call in person asking questions. A flyer was easy to ignore; a person standing in front of you was not.

I looked up Curt's home address from our personnel spreadsheet.

He lived on Jasper Road, about ten minutes west of Rocky Point Beach.

I unfolded a map of the area and used highlighters to mark the locations: orange for the three companies he'd visited trying to find work the day Frankie was killed, pink for antiques shops he'd be likely to pass, yellow for Rocky Point Light, and blue for his probable routing.

Driving from the lighthouse, he'd pass a mom-and-pop antiques shop near Heyer's, a large antiques shop near Jumbo Container, and two small shops and a high-end interior design cum antiques shop not far from Mandy's Candies.

I sat back and counted pink dots. Five possibilities, shops that would have been easy for Curt to get to, if he was the thief, and if he'd tried to sell the Myrick tooth right away. I reached for the phone to call Chief Hunter and pass on my idea, then paused with the receiver midway to my ear. Instead of accusing Curt Grimes based on nothing except a tenuous theory of the crime and my visceral dislike of the man, I could go to the stores myself.

The shops' owners all knew me and would answer my questions. It couldn't do any harm to ask, and it might do good. I'd only report my findings if I learned anything relevant. I nodded. I found Curt's high school yearbook photo online and printed it out. I wouldn't show it unless someone described him first. I printed out five copies of the Interpol posting, complete with the photo of the stolen tooth, and folded up my highlighted map. *Good,* I thought. I had a plan to prove or disprove my theory, and by showing the photo of the missing tooth, not Curt, I could do it without implicating him until and unless I had cause.

I headed out.

CHAPTER TWENTY-FIVE

F or the first time since the day Frankie died, there were no journalists haunting the entrance to my parking lot. I couldn't think why they'd deserted their post unless a bigger story had come across their desks or there'd been a break in the case. I turned on the local radio station, which was based at Hitchens University.

Chief Hunter was answering reporters' questions in a live broadcast.

I was just in time to hear Bertie ask in a strident, superior tone, "Do you think Josie Prescott is involved in the murder?"

How dare she? I thought, outraged and enraged.

"No," Chief Hunter replied, his voice calm and resolute. "Ms. Prescott has been helping us understand how certain aspects of the antiques business might figure into Mr. Winterelli's murder. I'm grateful to her for her cooperation."

"How do antiques figure into the murder?" Bertie asked, following up.

"I don't know that they do—but as you may be aware, a valuable scrimshaw tooth is missing from the Whitestone collection. We're looking into the possibility that the tooth was stolen and that the theft is related to the murder."

Bedlam erupted as journalists vied to ask the next question. Someone far from the mike called, "Last question."

"Was Frankie the thief?" a male reporter asked, his powerful baritone managing to overpower other, less penetrating voices.

"We have no reason to think so. In closing, let me reiterate how important community assistance is. The photograph of the stolen tooth is posted on our Web site. If anyone knows anything about it," Chief Hunter said, after stating the police department's URL, "please call us right away. If you have any information at all about the murder of Mr. Winterelli—even if you're not sure it's relevant—call us. We need to talk to you. Thank you."

I could picture him staring straight into the camera, his caring expression reassuring viewers that they could trust him with their secrets, that everything would be all right if only they'd call and talk to him. The ability to engender trust was a gift, and Chief Hunter possessed it in spades.

Heyer's Modular Furniture's world headquarters was set on nearly twenty acres of woodlands overlooking a man-made pond. A couple of years earlier, I'd helped the then-CEO, Gerry Fine, decorate his office suite, so I knew the location well. Main Street Antiques sat in a row of high-end shops about a mile before Curt would have reached Heyer's, taking the most direct routing.

The shop was owned by a middle-aged woman named CeCe. CeCe had frosted hair, long nails, and a big personality. Today she was wearing a leopard print top, just a hair too tight, and black leather pants.

"Josie!" she said, beaming, when I walked in. "I was just thinking of you!"

"You were? Why, what did I do?" I joked.

"You were in the wrong place at the wrong time, you poor thing—Rocky Point Light. I was listening to the police chief's press conference. He said they were making progress. Do you know what he meant?"

I shook my head. "I don't have any idea. It was pretty awful, CeCe, that's all I can say."

"I can only imagine. So to what do I owe the honor?"

"I have a question. It's going to sound a little off the wall—but by any chance has someone tried to sell you a scrimshaw tooth in the last couple of days?"

CeCe put her hands on her hips and gave me a tell-me-more look. "The tooth Chief Hunter said was missing?"

Remembering my father's long-ago instruction that when in doubt I should stay quiet and look wise, I smiled, aiming to convey that if only I could talk, ooh la la did I have tales to tell, but nothing could or would pry me open.

"I'm glad to report that no one offered it to me. If they had, I'd have bought it so fast your head would still be spinning!"

I pulled the Interpol printout out of my bag and handed it to her. "In the unlikely event someone comes in with it."

"I got a flyer on this from the police, too," she said, skimming the printout.

"Well, there's no such thing as too much communication, right? I'm just following up for my client."

"That would be the Whitestones, you lucky dog."

"Sorry, CeCe, I'm not at liberty to say."

She waved it away. "I know, I know. Wish I could help."

"Yeah, me, too. I know you would if you could."

We chatted for another minute; then I drove on to the next store on my list, Harlow's Antiques, an industrial-looking shop shaped and designed like a warehouse or a manufacturing facility, with no charm outside and not much inside.

Hal Harlow, the owner, waved to me from off to one side. He was busy with a customer, an attractive woman with a broad smile, discussing, apparently, a kidney-shaped desk. I felt a familiar pang of envy. Hal's shop was huge and ran like a well-oiled machine. The back half was filled with furniture, some run-of-the-mill, used, but a not insignificant proportion fine examples of various periods, styles, and pedigrees.

"Thanks for bringing it in, Ms. O'Loughlin," he said, his voice carrying easily in the open space. "What do you know about its history?"

"Please, call me Terry. I don't know anything, I'm afraid—other than that I love it," Terry said. "It was in my mother's home, but I don't know where or how she acquired it."

The reniform, or kidney-shaped, desk they were discussing was not an uncommon object. Several examples came through my auction house each year. Still, it was a lovely piece—a lady's writing desk, American made, dating from the early to middle twentieth century. Because it had been so popular, it wasn't rare, and unless it held some distinction, like having been owned by a celebrity, we'd estimate its value at between three hundred and five hundred dollars at auction. I was curious what Hal would say.

"I can tell you a little bit about it," Hal said.

He described it almost word-for-word as I would have done, and said that he'd be glad to find it a good home, if she was ever interested in selling it, but that all he could offer her was seventy-five dollars. His offer was fair considering the markup he'd need to add to sell it retail. Seventy-five dollars bought him a little wiggle room to negotiate with her if and when she ever returned.

"That's all?" Terry exclaimed. "I'm so surprised!"

"Supply and demand," Hal said, nodding empathetically. "A lot of them were produced."

Terry smiled and took a deep breath. "Well, so it goes," she said. "I don't really want to sell it anyway because I love it so much, but I thought if it was worth a fortune, well . . . you know!"

"I do indeed," he said. "Thanks again for bringing it in. I'll help you get it back into your van." He smiled at me. "I'll be with you in a sec, Josie."

"Take your time," I told him.

By the time Hal got back to me, I had spotted a fabulous collection of chess sets.

"Hal," I said as he approached me. "What gems you have here! I'm so jealous, I can't stand it."

"Thanks, Josie. I'm about halfway through appraising them. I may be asking you to put them up for auction."

"We'd love it."

"So, what brings you to my humble establishment?" he asked.

"Humble, ha," I remarked, wanting to be certain that he had no illusions that I thought there was anything humble about his business. I handed him a copy of the Interpol posting. "I'm looking for information about this scrimmed tooth. Has anyone been in trying to sell it during the last few days?"

He accepted the paper, stared at it for a moment, and said, "Why are you asking?"

My trouble meter whirred onto high alert, but I kept my voice casual. "I'm following up for a client. It was stolen."

"Who's the client?"

"Who offered to sell it to you?" I asked, hoping to avoid having to answer.

"Lenny Wilton. You know him, right?"

Lenny? I repeated silently. *Lenny? What in God's name did Lenny have to do with anything?* "I do indeed," I said, not letting my jaw drop. "When was that?"

"Mid-August. I remember because I thought his timing was bad. If he'd offered it to me at the beginning of the season, I might have been inclined to buy it. As it was, I tried to work out a consignment deal with him. He wasn't interested. He said he was doing a favor for a friend—the tooth had been in the friend's family forever, but he was strapped and really needed cash."

I nodded. It was a credible explanation, but something was niggling at the corner of my memory.

"That would have been before your customer bought it, right?" Hal asked.

"Yes. What did he say about it—any information?"

"Just that it was a beauty, which I didn't need him to tell me."

I nodded, thanked him, and said, "Let me know about the chess sets."

I sat in my car considering the timeline. Assuming the tooth Lenny tried to sell was the same one that the Whitestones bought, and that was now missing, which was by no means a certainty—how, I wondered, did it get from Lenny's hands into Sam's? I realized that Sam succeeded in closing the deal with Greg about two weeks after Lenny failed with Hal.

I continued my trek to the remaining three shops just in case Curt—or Lenny—had stopped in, but they hadn't. No one had— unless one of the dealers knew the tooth had been stolen and was now covering his or her tracks. I thought about that. All of the shops I'd visited had been in business longer than I'd been in New Hampshire. If any of them dealt in stolen goods, I'd never heard even a whisper about it. I shook my head. My idea had been sound, but like many appraisal approaches, my research led nowhere.

I drove around the corner, out of sight of the last shop I'd visited, and called Chief Hunter. Cathy told me he wasn't available and put me through to his voice mail. I shut my eyes to concentrate.

"I want to tell you something I just learned." I reported on my conversation with Hal, then added, "If the tooth Lenny tried to sell to Hal is the one Greg bought, it adds credibility that the tooth is, in fact, real. With Lenny's contacts, it's completely plausible that he knows someone who owned a rare scrimmed tooth and wanted to sell it privately."

I hoped Chief Hunter wouldn't be too angry with me for acting on my own.

Cara called as I was driving toward the interstate, ready to return to my office. Lenny Wilton, she said, had returned my phone call.

I called him back and reached him. "I'm hoping you can answer a few scrimshanding questions," I said. "Any chance I can stop by? I'm pretty close."

"Sure," he said. "Anytime."

I took the interstate north to Greenland, then stuck to back roads the rest of the way. I turned onto the paved road that traversed Lenny's property—a compound, really—and found him waiting for me on his wraparound deck.

"Welcome!" he called.

I'd never been to his studio, but I'd heard about it. Maddie White-stone, who'd been there to look at some of his larger scrimmed pieces, told me that his water wall was the most unusual one she'd ever seen.

The studio was big, about forty by thirty feet with soaring ceilings and bamboo floors. Storage units, some ten feet high, others more like credenzas, ringed the room. A couch-sized window seat fitted with canvas pillows ran along the outside wall, under a double-high bay window. The view was astonishing—everywhere I looked I saw a panoply of sunlit gold and red, the colors of passion. I'd never seen anything like it.

"Wow," I said.

Lenny nodded. "I know. This time of year, it's hard to get any work done."

"I don't usually get speechless at a view, but all I can think to say is 'wow.'"

"It's nice, isn't it?"

"Nice doesn't even begin to do it justice, Lenny. Wow."

He smiled broadly, pleased with my reaction. "Let me show you the rest of the place."

A wet bar, complete with mini fridge and microwave, was off to one side. The bathroom featured a steam room and a double-sized, extra-deep soaking spa tub. A sleeper sofa faced the flat-screen TV, which was mounted over the wood-burning fireplace. Fanned issues of *Architectural Digest* and *Scrimshanding Gazette* sat on a rosewood coffee table. Surrounding the fireplace, ripples of water gently trickled down the black ridged granite into matching troughs. Maddie was right. It was unique. Dozens of scrimmed objects covered worktables that stretched along the perimeter. There were piles of barrettes, three teeth in various stages of completion, and two large pieces of scrimmed bone mounted on exotic wood stands. Scrimming machines were attached to the tables by vises. The feel of the place was busy and productive. The style was contemporary in both design and decor, and I could have happily moved into the space and never left.

"Wow," I said again.

"Thanks. I love it. So . . . what can I tell you about scrimshaw?"

"Two questions, one embarrassing to ask, the other not."

He tilted his head back. "Okay . . . I'll bite. Start with the embarrassing one."

"You may be aware that one of Guy Whitestone's scrimmed teeth is missing. I'm helping the police on certain aspects of the investigation. I just spoke to Hal Harlow."

"And?" he said, waiting for me to continue.

"Do you remember talking to him about a Myrick tooth?"

"Sure, I remember," Lenny said. "What about it?"

"He said you were trying to sell it for a friend. I'm hoping you can tell me a little more about the situation."

"I didn't just go to Harlow's. I went to half a dozen places. The friend I referred to told me he felt a little awkward about having to sell a family heirloom. I was glad to help him out—but I didn't do much for him, I'm afraid. He was only interested in cash offers, and I didn't get any. It just occurred to me—I should have gone to Prescott's, right?"

I smiled. "Always. Prescott's should always be your first stop!" After a moment, I asked, "What did you do then?"

"I returned the tooth to him with my regrets that I hadn't been more successful."

"What's his name?"

"There I'm going to have to not be so helpful, Josie," Lenny said regretfully. "He swore me to secrecy."

I looked at him straight on and saw no hint of guile, nervousness, or anxiety. "That tooth may figure in a murder investigation."

"How is a tooth I tried to sell for a friend connected to Frankie's murder?" Lenny asked, sounding puzzled.

"I don't know."

"Sorry. Until you do—or more specifically, until the police do and ask me about it—I'm keeping my word to my friend."

I nodded. "To tell you the truth, I don't blame you."

"It can't be the same tooth," he said.

"How do you know?"

"My friend would have told me if it sold."

I nodded. His point made sense. "Here's my nonembarrassing question. How long would it have taken Myrick to scrim a tooth?"

Lenny smiled. "Believe it or not, that was the subject of a discussion on the scrimshanding forum last spring. Not about Myrick in particular, but with any of the guys who scrimmed on whalers back in the nineteenth century. The consensus was twenty-seven hours."

"Really? How did you settle on that? I mean, it's not an even number or anything."

"Call it an educated average. Several scrimshanders timed themselves scrimming a tooth while duplicating, as best they could, seafaring conditions. After they were done, some others of us assessed their methodology. We discounted some timings because they made it too hard on themselves, and we penalized others because they made it too easy. Then we averaged it out. It's not a scientific study, of course. There were no controls or verifications. But it's interesting nonetheless. I'm writing an article about the process we used for *Smithsonian*."

"I'm fascinated, Lenny. Do you know over how many days the twenty-seven hours would have been spread?"

"A couple of weeks, at least. Given their work shifts, there's no way anyone would have been able to scrim for more than a couple of hours a day. Most of them probably did it far less often than that. When you think about it, there's no reason to think they scrimmed more than occasionally—after all, it was a hobby, not their livelihood. In my article, I compare it to knitting. Some knitters do it daily. Some do it feverishly, in bursts, to make Christmas presents, for instance, after procrastinating for months, and some do it rarely, only when the mood strikes."

"Your article sounds amazing. I'll look for it."

We talked awhile longer about scrimming and his new holiday barrette designs; then I thanked him again and left.

Lenny, I thought, walked a fine line with acuity and perfect balance. He was true to his art and simultaneously a clever businessman. It wasn't easy to accomplish—just ask Ashley. I thought he was right about his friend's tooth being different from Guy's, but it was odd that so many previously unknown Myricks seemed to be surfacing at the same time. I also thought he was probably right on the mark about how long it took to scrim a tooth, but before I passed on the information to Mr. Yamamoto, I thought it would be prudent to get a second opinion. I called Ashley again, and this time I got her.

She almost snapped at me. She sounded beyond irritated, maybe at being interrupted, or maybe because the scrimming gods weren't cooperating with her work.

"I'm sorry to disturb you. I have a quick question," I said. "How long would you guesstimate that it took Myrick or another scrimshander of that period to scrim a tooth?"

"Why?"

"I'm getting ready to write an intro to an appraisal," I replied, coming up with a credible excuse on the fly, "and I'd like to add that scrimming was—and is—labor-intensive, but only if it is, of course."

"It's one of the most labor-intensive crafts there is."

"Have you ever timed yourself?"

"Of course. Work records are crucial to artists. It takes me forty hours, minimum, to scrim a tooth."

I thanked her, and she hung up without saying good-bye. I would have bet that by the time I tossed my phone into my purse, she was already back at her worktable, deep in the zone.

I contrasted my brief conversation with Ashley with my longer one with Lenny. She was moody, a function of her artistic temperament, I supposed, unlike Lenny, who was as even-tempered as he was talented.

An article in *Smithsonian*. From a promotion perspective, it didn't get much better than that. *Way to go, Lenny,* I thought.

CHAPTER TWENTY-SIX

I 'd barely finished drafting the e-mail reporting my findings to Mr. Yamamoto—findings that would neither validate nor invalidate the authenticity of his object—when Wes called with an urgent request to meet. It was almost five thirty.

"I've got news about what you asked me—a real info-bomb, but I can't tell you on the phone," he said, his tone hushed and urgent.

I glanced around my desk. The mounds of paperwork had grown higher. *Tomorrow's another day,* I rationalized. "Do you want to meet at our dune in twenty minutes?"

"Yes," he said, and hung up.

The temperature had dropped, and standing high above the shore on top of the dune with a stiff breeze blowing in off the ocean, I felt the chill of coming winter. No one was on the beach.

Wes drove up, jerking to a stop on the sandy shoulder. As soon as he stepped out of his car, I saw the fervor in his eyes.

"I got news about your pal Zoë," he said when he'd reached me at the top of the dune. "It looks like she might be implicated in Frankie's murder."

My mouth opened, then closed. "That's ridiculous!" I said, when I could finally speak.

He nodded, thrilled at my reaction. "When I say I have an info-bomb, I'm not just whistling Dixie, huh? Like you asked, I checked Frankie's phone logs. Just for the heck of it, I went back a week." He paused for effect. "The night before Frankie died, remember how that lowlife friend of his, Mel Erly, called Zoë trying to get Frankie's number so he could ask him to bail him out? Well, guess what . . . Zoë forgot to mention that as soon as she hung up from Erly, she called Frankie to give him hell for ever in his lifetime having had a friend as disgusting as Mel Erly."

"How do you know why she called him?" I asked.

"Apparently, now that the police have cleared away a lot of brush they're going back and reinterviewing everyone. Including Zoë. Today is the first time they've asked her specifically about that phone call. According to my police source, she admits that she and Frankie really got into it. He was completely pissed at an accusation that felt to him like old news, but she couldn't stop herself—she was rip-roaring angry—and the call ended on a more than sour note. Because she hid that she spoke to him that night, the police are wondering if she has something else to hide, like maybe she went to see him the next day and her harangue turned physical. Maybe Frankie tried to get away from her. He pushes past her. Now she's feeling dissed on top of everything else. She pushes back. He shoves her. She shoves back. It escalates until finally she whacks him."

I laughed. "That sounds like a bad made-for-TV movie script, Wes. It's not the least bit believable. Sure, Zoë has a temper, but she flares up, and that's that. I guarantee you that as soon as she vented, it was over and forgotten."

"Maybe, maybe not," he said, unpersuaded by my out-of-hand dismissal. "The police think it's believable."

"They can't! It's farcical."

"A single mother worn down by life—"

He broke off and shrugged, and I began to wonder whether he could possibly have persuaded himself that there was even a grain of truth to such a ludicrous assertion. Sure, Zoë was a single mother. Of course, that was tough, and some days, when her kids were non-stop demanding, I'd see the strain in her face. But to think that having a hard day could lead to murder was preposterous.

I looked deep into Wes's eyes. He wasn't joking around. *Bad just keeps getting worse,* I thought. His sober demeanor made me want to leap off the dune and rush to Zoë's side, to check that she was okay, to see whether she needed me, to offer my unconditional support.

"If you publish any hint of this, Wes, I'll never talk to you again. You heard it here first—Zoë didn't do it."

He nodded, unperturbed by my threat. "I don't know whether

they really consider her to be a suspect or not, but I do know they're interviewing her again—and as you know, that's always serious."

I shrugged, eager to get to my phone and call her. "What about other calls to or from Frankie's phone?" I asked.

"Frankie called Greg from the lighthouse at eight thirty the day he died."

"He did? What does Greg say about it?"

Wes's eyes fired up again. "Greg is denying it. He insists he never spoke to Frankie ever, that he never met him." Wes consulted his notepaper. "Frankie called Curt just about noon from his cell phone. It looks like Frankie called while he was still at your place, or close by." He looked up. "They can tell by which cell phone tower routed the call."

"What does Curt say the call was about?"

"He doesn't. He said Frankie left a message asking him to call him back, and he hadn't gotten around to it by the time he heard Frankie was dead."

I looked at Wes. "That seems off, doesn't it? I mean, Curt went to all those businesses hoping for work . . . Frankie often had jobs for him . . . wouldn't he have called him back right away?"

"Yeah. The police think so, too. They've pushed him on it, but so far, no dice. Curt didn't call from his cell phone, that's for sure."

"What other phones could he have used?" I asked.

"Who knows? Any pay phone en route, I guess. But neither his cell nor his home phone showed any callbacks. He didn't use his sister's phone either. Plus, why would he try to hide that he called Frankie back?"

I nodded, my brain reviewing the possibilities.

"What are you thinking?" Wes asked, interrupting my ruminations.

"Nothing . . . just trying to see how it all might fit together. Were there any other calls?"

"Nope—but I have some info about money. You asked about Curt. While I was at it, I checked out other people, too. Let me start with Frankie." He consulted his notes. "He wrote two checks a month, one to his cable TV company and one for his cell phone. He paid his car insurance annually. His residence and health insurance were covered by the Whitestones, his car was paid for, and for everything else he used cash. He had twenty percent of his pay automatically transferred to a savings account, and he withdrew five hundred dollars in cash from his checking account at the start of every month. He tried to make it last for the entire month, but it rarely did. Toward the end of some months he withdrew another fifty dollars. Other months he took out an extra hundred."

"So?" I asked. "That all sounds pretty reasonable—and it looks as if my instinct was right. Frankie was showing real maturity."

Wes grinned. Here came another of his infamous shockeroonies, I could just tell.

"The Friday before he was killed—the Friday before Labor Day—he withdrew two thousand dollars cash from savings. The cash is missing. There's no sign of it."

I stared at him, stricken.

"You're thinking blackmail, right?" he asked. "Tell me how it might work."

"No."

"No you're not thinking of it? Or no you won't tell me about it? 'Cause you don't need to accuse anyone of anything." When I still hesitated, he added, grinning again, "You have to. It's part of our deal—I got the *Metropolitan* gig."

"Oh, Wes! I'm so pleased. That's just great." I play-punched his arm. "Way to go, Wes!"

"So . . . ?"

"I don't have any idea how a scheme might work where Frankie ends up being blackmailed to the tune of two thousand dollars. That would require him being involved in some kind of criminal act—and getting caught by an associate or having an associate turn on him." I shrugged. "Was the Myrick real and Frankie somehow got hold of a repro and switched them? If so, where's the fake now? Why did someone steal it?" I held up my hand as Wes began to speak. "I can make up scenarios to answer my own questions, but that's all it is—invention. You want supposition? Okay, here goes . . . just remember you can't ever quote me about it, okay?"

"Yeah, yeah," Wes said.

"Curt learns that Greg plans to sell the Myrick to Guy for a boatload of money. One day while he's working in the gallery, Curt takes photos of the tooth. Curt knows Lenny can do anything and commissions a repro based on the photos. Curt convinces Frankie to switch them. Curt then tries and fails to sell the real Myrick and puts it . . . somewhere . . . the trunk of his car, his closet, his sister's pantry . . . somewhere. Curt then tells Frankie that he taped their conversation about switching the teeth and Frankie better pay up or else."

Wes, furiously taking notes, paused and looked up. "Do you think that's what happened?"

"No. It seems pretty darn far-fetched to me, and out of character for both of them. Curt doesn't have the wherewithal to pull it off, and Frankie wouldn't have done it. I'm telling you, Wes, Frankie was a changed man." I thought for a moment. "Any news from the police about fingerprints?"

He nodded. "None are on the display case or objects except those that should be there—Guy Whitestone's and Ashley Morse's. They found Ashley's and the Whitestones' prints all over the lighthouse, ditto from the weekend's guests, including Lenny Wilton, who was there for a barbecue on Labor Day. Curt's and Frankie's are in various places, too."

"And nothing had been wiped down?"

"Right."

"What about other people's bank records? Did Curt's—or anyone's—account go up by two thousand dollars?" I asked, although I knew extorted money would more likely get slipped into a sock drawer than deposited in a bank.

"Nope. Curt doesn't have one."

"Curt doesn't have a bank account?" I asked.

"Lots of people don't. He helps his sister out with the bills by giving her cash. If he needs a check for something, she writes it for him out of her account." Wes consulted his notes. "He told the police he was thinking of opening a checking account after hearing from Frankie how easy it was, but he hadn't got around to it yet."

"Interesting. Frankie was a good influence in a lot of ways." I sighed. Thinking aloud, I added, "Couldn't Frankie have used the two thousand dollars to buy something?"

"Sure. What?"

"I don't know . . . clothes . . . a vacation . . . a new sound system for his car . . . something."

"Except that he doesn't have any new clothes, and his car hasn't been in the shop for months, and there were no receipts or work orders or airline tickets in his house. If he bought something—where is it?"

I nodded, heartsick. "I don't know."

"I hear you talked to Sam, the picker," Wes said.

I shook my head, amazed once again at the breadth of Wes's contacts, and filled him in. "We'll know more tomorrow. I'm scheduled to meet him at four."

"This is great stuff, Josie," he said. "Where will you meet him? At your loading dock, right, because you don't bring strangers into the warehouse?"

"Probably, although if it's cold we might meet in the front office. Why?"

" 'Cause I want a photograph, and if you meet him out back, I can be in the woods with a camera."

An image of the nonoutdoorsman Wes perched in a tree popped into my head, and I chuckled.

"What's so funny?" Wes asked.

"A picture of you . . . in a tree," I said, giggling.

"It's not funny," he said with dignity. "It's good journalism. Besides, *Metropolitan* pays extra for photos."

"That's excellent! Really, Wes, I'm so pleased for you."

"Thanks. Are the police going to be there?"

"What happened to your police source?"

"I'm confirming a report," he said with dignity.

"Yes."

"Call me as soon as you confirm the location, okay?"

"Okay—and you'll tell me if you learn anything else?"

"You betcha," he said, jiffling down the dune. "You, too, right?"

I agreed, and watched as he drove away. I stood looking out over the near-black ocean. *Two thousand dollars.* Where was it? The situation was confusing and distressing, and the more I thought about it, the more dismayed I became. I wished I could see Ty, but he wouldn't be back until tomorrow. I sighed and headed home to my empty house.

CHAPTER TWENTY-SEVEN

C hief Hunter's SUV was parked in back of Zoë's car. With no other car in sight, I concluded that she didn't have a lawyer with her. She was meeting with the police, and as emotionally upset as she was, it might not have occurred to her to get one. I needed to intervene, but I didn't want to intrude. I called her.

"Zoë," I said, "it's me. I just got home. That's Chief Hunter's SUV, isn't it? Is he with you?"

"Yes. We're talking about things."

"You should have a lawyer, Zoë. Do you want me to call Max?"

"I don't need a lawyer. We're not having that kind of conversation."

"What kind of conversation are you having?" I asked.

"The kind I haven't had with a man in years," she said, whispering. "Years and years and years. We're talking about stuff that matters."

"Like what?"

"Like losing things you love."

"Are you sure you're okay?"

"I am. I'm good." I could hear the sounds of her puttering, a soft clap as a cup was placed on a saucer, the refrigerator door opening, then closing, and water running. "He's a widower. His wife died two years ago of lung cancer. She was a dancer. On Broadway. She was only thirty-three when she died. He said a lot of dancers smoke."

How heartbreaking, I thought, picturing him as I knew him, in command, strong, and reliable, and thinking that competence can be a great cover for grief—when you're capable and adept, no one questions what's going on inside of you. "I've heard that before about dancers," I said. "It's crazy, isn't it? Athletes smoking? It's nuts."

"Yeah. Anyway. I'm fine . . . he's an interesting man."

"I'm glad, Zoë." I looked at the golden glow of the lamp in my bedroom. *Leave a light on for me.* "I'll be home all night. You shout if you want me, okay?"

Inside, I turned on lights, put on Vivaldi's *Four Seasons,* and made myself a Lemon Drop. I stood at my kitchen sink staring out over the meadow and into the nearly impenetrable, distant woods, thinking about loss and love. "Here's to silver light in the dark of night," I toasted aloud, thinking of my father and my mother, and the life I lost in New York City, and Ty and Zoë and the life I'd gained in New Hampshire.

Ty called around nine. "How's Presque Isle?" I asked.

"The place is beautiful, and my training's going well. I'll be home by six tomorrow."

"That's great. I miss you."

"I miss you, too. You sound, I don't know . . . preoccupied."

"I am. I've been sitting here thinking." I told him about recognizing Sam's voice and my conversations with Lenny, Ashley, and Wes, then added, "For the last hour or so, I've been thinking of secrets. Frankie had a secret . . . he took two thousand dollars out of his bank account, and no one knows why. Two thousand dollars! That's a huge amount of money for a young man . . . heck, it's a big number for most everyone. I can't imagine what he did with the money—except pay a blackmailer, and I can't believe Frankie did something blackmailable."

"Have you asked Zoë?"

"No. I was going to, but she's busy. Chief Hunter is there." I got up and peeked out the side window. "He's been there for hours." I repeated what Zoë said about their conversation, and Ty chuckled.

"He's a quick mover," he said.

"You waited until after the investigation to ask me out."

"You were a suspect."

I cringed, remembering the horror of finding myself a suspect in Mr. Grant's murder. "So that means that Chief Hunter doesn't think Zoë is one?"

"Hard to say. He could be trying to loosen her tongue."

"Why didn't you try that?"

"I knew I couldn't trust myself around you. You're too damn hot. I didn't want to socialize unless I knew I could, well, socialize."

I laughed. "I love you so much, Ty."

I could feel his smile. "Me, too."

"I wish I could talk to her," I said. "I don't even know what funeral plans she's made. I feel completely out of touch." A car engine fired up, and I returned to the window. "He's leaving."

"So now you can call her and find out that I'm right. If she tells you anything important, call me back."

"I'll call you back regardless."

"Oh, yeah? Why's that?"

"'Cause I want to kiss you good night."

He told me that while that was an excellent idea and he'd look forward to it, he preferred the real thing. Then our call ended, and I sat for several seconds savoring the solace and security of his love, and then I called Zoë.

"Come over," she said, "and I'll tell you everything."

"Tea or Lemon Drops?" I asked.

"Lemon Drops."

"Done."

As I poured ingredients into a thermos, I thought once again how lucky I was to have a friend like Zoë.

"What a day," Zoë said.

She'd built a small fire, and I was sitting cross-legged on the floor near it. The temperature had dropped into the low forties, and the warmth was welcome. She sighed, her eyes steady on the flickering flames.

"The funeral will be Monday. Your idea of contacting the minister at the Congregational church was a good one. The funeral parlor put us in touch. His name is Harold Emery. Even though Frankie hadn't been a regular churchgoer, he considered him one of his flock. That's what Reverend Emery said, one of his flock. Kind of old-fashioned, you know? I like that. He told me Frankie had been quite active in the Singles Club . . . who knew? The woman who runs it—she's the activity manager at the church, her name is Ellen. She's asked if she can deliver a eulogy, and I said okay. Do you think that I did the right thing? I mean, if she talks about how Frankie wanted to meet girls, it has the potential to be really embarrassing, you know, and Frankie would hate that. What do you think?"

"I think it will be lovely."

She nodded. "Yeah, that's what I think, too. Chief Hunter said Frankie must have made quite an impression for her to be volunteering like that, but I don't know. Maybe it's just any young man showing up, you know? There are always more women than men at those sorts of events."

"No, I think he's right. Frankie was a really good kid, Zoë."

Her eyes filled, but she didn't cry. She nodded, still watching the orange flames as they licked the wood. I forgot to tell them I spoke to Frankie the night before he died."

How does Wes do it? I wondered yet again.

"Did he suspect you of hiding it on purpose?"

"No. At first I was a little scared that they might think there was something to it, but talking about it wasn't hard at all. I don't know why. I guess because Chief Hunter seems so understanding and all I had to do was tell him the truth. I can't believe I forgot to mention it. Maybe I wanted to forget because it's the last time I spoke to Frankie, and all I did was yell." Wetness striped her cheeks and she took in a deep, mournful breath.

"Frankie knew you—he knew you never simmer, you explode, and that once it's over, it's over for good, that you never hold a grudge. I bet that by the time he hung up the phone, he'd forgotten all about it."

"That's a really kind thing to say, Josie. I hate my temper."

"It's part of who you are. I'd always rather know where I stand with someone than wonder about it."

"God, you're about the best friend a girl can have—you take a major fault and reposition it as a virtue."

"Yeah, that's a little much," I said, smiling. "You do have a temper."

"I'm emotional in all ways. Mercurial. Chief Hunter said his wife was like that, too. She'd cry at the drop of a hat."

"He must like that quality. I do, too."

"Thank you, Josie." She finished her Lemon Drop and slid the glass out of harm's way. "Have you spoken to Wes?"

"Yes."

She turned to me. "I don't want to talk to him, but I want to know everything."

"It's all pretty confusing," I said. "It's possible Curt Grimes is involved somehow." I shrugged. "I'm meeting with Sam, the picker, tomorrow." I paused. "There is one thing Wes told me that's pretty odd. Frankie withdrew two thousand dollars a few days before he died. The police can't find any record of a purchase, no receipts or anything—and the cash is gone. Do you have any idea what he did with the money?"

Zoë stared at me for several seconds, then shook her head. "No. Two thousand dollars? That's a lot of money." She took a deep breath. "Are you thinking he was getting back into drugs?"

I shook my head. "No. There's no sign of it."

"Then what?"

"Maybe he lost money gambling."

"Frankie? He didn't know a club from a spade!"

"That would explain his losses."

She laughed, one short burst, then sobered up and said, "You're thinking something else, aren't you? Something worse. Tell me."

I didn't want to reveal my dark thoughts, but I knew that if I were in her place, I'd want to know.

"What is it, Josie?" she asked, reading the ambivalence on my face.

"The only other thing I can think of is blackmail. I don't think Frankie was involved with stealing the Myrick tooth, but if he was, maybe someone else, maybe Curt, found out about it and put the hard touch on him."

Zoë sighed. After several seconds, she remarked, "I guess I didn't know him as well as I thought I did."

"You can't say that yet, Zoë."

"Sure I can. Where's the missing money?"

"I don't know," I said, turning to look into the red and yellow embers of the dying fire. I finished my drink. "I've got to go. I'm beat."

She stood up and stretched, a panther move, sleek and long and dancer-smooth. "Thanks, Josie. I may not like the news, but I'd hate not knowing more. And it means the world to me to have you here."

"One day at a time, right?" I asked.

She saw me to the door, and we hugged; then, thermos in hand, I stepped onto the porch and stood for a moment listening to the night sounds. It was so cold that I could see my breath. Winter was definitely on its way. An owl hooted, low and loud, close by. I heard a car engine drawing near, slowly, as if it were crawling along looking for an address.

Suddenly, I felt conspicuous. I was standing in the circle of pale yellow light cast by the overhead lamp. I scurried behind a porch column, out of the direct illumination.

The car's headlight beams penetrated the tall, thick bushes that Zoë's uncle, my original landlord, Mr. Winterelli, had planted along the road as a privacy hedge. The car stopped, its engine idling. After several seconds, it inched along, pausing just short of our shared driveway, next to our mailboxes. If the driver was looking for Zoë or me, he'd found us.

It was terrifying.

Slices of moonlight stippled the street and lawn. Unnatural-looking shadows striped the forest across the way. The owl hooted again.

I shivered, more from fear than cold.

Taking in a deep breath, and holding it, I peeked around the column trying to identify the car or its driver. Only the hood was visible. I could tell that it was medium-sized, boxy and dark. The driver was tall and narrow, and he—or she—seemed to be alone in the front. The car backed up, pulled a U-turn, and drove off the way it had come.

I didn't hesitate—I leapt off the porch and sprinted across the driveway and my tiny lawn. Inside my house, I double-locked the door, set the night alarm, and leaned against the wall waiting for my pounding pulse to quiet.

"Probably the driver was lost," I said aloud to the empty house.

My bracing comment had no effect on the fear rippling up and down my spine. It was absurd, I chided myself, to allow a slow-moving car to so completely discombobulate me. Somehow, though, it didn't feel as if the driver was lost and searching for an address. It felt as if someone was stalking me.

CHAPTER TWENTY-EIGHT

T he next morning, I was sitting at my kitchen table, sipping orange juice and waiting for my toast to pop, when the doorbell rang. I glanced at the wall clock. It was seven fifteen, too early for anyone except Zoë to be calling, and she would have used the kitchen door.

With memories of last night's mystery car fresh in my mind, I crept down the hallway, edged sideways to the front door, and moved my right eye just enough to see out. Standing on my porch was Curt Grimes. He saw me through the door window at the same moment that I saw him. He smiled like we were buddies and waved.

I opened the door the two inches the chain lock allowed.

"Hey, Josie," he said. "I'm an early bird hoping to catch a worm."

I didn't respond. Yesterday he called me a liar. Today he called me a worm.

"I knew you'd be up already. CEOs always get an early start." He winked.

When I didn't comment, he added, "I thought I'd check if you had any work you needed doing." He glanced around the porch and toward the side yard. "Here, or at your office."

"Here, no. At work, you need to talk to Eric." I took a step back. "Bye-bye," I said, closing the door.

I reached the front window just in time to see Curt disappear around the hedge. From this angle, I could see his car parked next to the bushes. It was dark green and boxy shaped. He got behind the wheel. Within seconds, he'd driven off. Glancing toward Zoë's house,

I saw that she was outside already, buckling the kids into their car seats. I stepped outside to say hey.

Chief Hunter turned into our driveway and parked in back of my car. He said hello to me, then turned to Zoë and smiled at her. She smiled at him over the roof of her car, and in that moment, watching as their eyes connected and held fast, seeing their expressions soften, I felt the depth of their newly forged bond.

Sometimes it happened like that, I knew. It had happened like that with me and Ty. I could still recall the instantaneous and irresistible tug of attraction I'd felt the first time I'd met him, an overpowering pull of like-minded souls that had drawn me toward him, like steel to a magnet. I wanted Ty with me now. I wanted to feel his arms around me, to have him hold me fast and secure.

"I've got to go," Zoë said.

"I'll call you later," Chief Hunter said to her, and she smiled again and nodded.

He leaned over to speak to the kids through the open back door, then turned to me. "Do you have a minute? Want to go inside?"

"Sure," I said.

I looked back at Zoë as I closed the door. She smiled at me and I smiled back, and although nothing was said, much was understood.

My conversation with Chief Hunter was brief. He said he'd stopped by on his way to the station to ask if I'd thought of anything else or had any new ideas they could look into. He sat with his back to the wall and crossed his legs, his right calf resting on his left thigh. He held a mug of coffee in both hands.

"No," I said, "except maybe. Curt Grimes was just here. He said he was looking for work." I explained about the car that had spooked me last night, and said that the one Curt was driving today looked similar.

"Why didn't you call us last night?" he asked.

I shrugged. "The car left. Nothing happened."

"If you see that car again, or if anything scares you, call me. Even if you think it's no big deal."

I met his eyes and saw concern. "Okay," I promised.

"So . . . What do you think Mr. Grimes really wanted this morning?"

I shrugged again. "I have no idea. Maybe work, just like he said."

"You think he's involved somehow. How?"

I shook my head. "That's too strong. I wouldn't be surprised if he's involved, that's all."

"Frankie withdrew two thousand dollars a few days before he died. What do you think he did with it?"

"I don't know," I said, thinking that Wes had, once again, scooped the police.

"That's a lot of cash. Do you think he was being blackmailed?"

"No!" I said, aware my tone had sharpened.

He finished his coffee and slid the mug into the center of the table. "Thanks for the coffee." He stood up.

"You're welcome." I walked his mug to the sink. "I know you released the photograph of the tooth yesterday. Are you surprised no one has reported having seen it?"

"Someone will," he said.

"How do you know?"

"Because someone has worked with it or owned it or considered buying it." He grinned. "And most people want to help the police, so they'll call."

I thought about that for a moment. "Good point."

"About this afternoon," Chief Hunter said. "We need to go over the details. The judge still won't give us a warrant, so Detective Brownley and I need to be close enough to hear but hidden from sight. Where would you normally meet a picker?"

"Since the weather is fairly mild, my usual procedure would be to meet with him outside by the loading dock. That will work in this case, because I can leave the sliding door up. You and Detective Brownley can stand just inside, behind a stack of crates. With the lights off, no one will see you, but you'll see us and you should be able to hear everything."

"Would you normally leave the door up?"

"No."

"Won't he be suspicious?"

"He doesn't know us," I said. "All he'll see is the staging area—there are worktables, some shelving, boxes and crates." I shrugged. "I don't think it will look odd at all."

He nodded. "Okay, then. You know what to do, right?"

"Look at what he's brought me and try to find out as much about the history of the objects as I can without arousing his suspicion."

"Don't just try to not arouse his suspicion—*don't*. Don't ask anything you wouldn't normally ask a picker. If he's skittish, and I have every reason to think he will be, ask less."

I nodded. "It's all right to buy things, right?"

"Would you normally?"

"Almost certainly. At least something, no matter how junky the stuff he brings is."

He looked mildly amused. "After all you've told me about only buying quality, now you tell me you buy junk?"

I smiled. "Only sometimes. If I don't buy something now he might not call on me again."

"If he's selling subquality goods, why would you want him to?"

"We're not dealing with set items of predictable quality. About a year ago, a picker who'd been stopping by our place about once a month with a boxful of dreck—chipped china, books with missing pages, that sort of thing, unsalable objects—brought in a black metal coffeepot with a hinged lid and claw feet. It turned out to be sterling silver. God only knows if it had ever been polished. I'd always found something to buy from him. I'd spend a dollar or three, no more. I was respectful—I never accused him of bringing me trash. I looked at everything, selected something, and paid in cash. You never know what they'll bring in, and when dealing with a picker, your goal is to get first dibs."

"That's a helluva way to earn a living."

"For him or for me?"

He smiled and didn't reply. "Good coffee," he said.

As we walked to the door, I asked, "Do you think anything will come of the meeting with Sam?"

"Yes."

"Why?"

"Because there's something there to be discovered. We just need to get at it, and I think your insider knowledge will give us the advantage we need."

I nodded. "I'll do my best."

"I'm betting your best is pretty darn good."

I smiled. "Ah, shucks."

CHAPTER TWENTY-NINE

Maddie Whitestone called and invited me to lunch at my favorite Portsmouth restaurant, the Blue Dolphin, and I happily accepted. It would be good to see her again. We agreed to meet at twelve thirty. I knew she'd want an update on the appraisal, so I headed down to the front office.

Sasha was on the phone. Gretchen was showing Cara a shortcut for entering data on spreadsheets. Fred, looking as sharp as always in a gray suit and starched white shirt, with his narrow black tie loosened, was talking to a gray-haired woman he introduced as Ginny Meadows.

Fred explained, "Ms. Meadows brought in these two botanicals."

"Watercolors, right?" I asked as I approached the two gilt-framed paintings. One was a precise rendering of lilies of the valley; the other showed a close-up of leaves.

"Yes," Ginny said, "but they're unsigned, and no one we've asked recognizes the artist. We bought them ages ago at a flea market." She smiled as she looked at them. "Isn't there anything you can tell me about them?"

Fred's eyes gleamed, and I wondered what surprise he had up his sleeve.

"From the style," he said, "I'd say that they were painted in the eighteenth or nineteenth century by a gardening hobbyist. Many young ladies sketched and painted—it was considered a necessary accomplishment for a woman of refinement. Probably these were painted to memorialize a particularly successful growing season, and were intended either to provide a record of the garden or simply for her own pleasure. My guess is that she considered herself more of a horticulturalist than an artist."

"How can you tell?"

"Probably if the paintings were more important to her than the subject matter, she would have signed them. I'm guessing that they're a kind of visual journal."

"Interesting!" Ginny said. "I love that idea!"

"We'll never know for sure—it's an educated guess, is all."

"How much would you value them at? Not that it matters, since these two beauties are going right back up on the living room wall, no matter what you say."

"Based on what I've told you thus far, without knowing more about the artist, the provenance, or the materials, we would only sell them 'as is.' I would expect them to fetch somewhere around fifty dollars each."

Ginny cocked her head and kept her eyes on Fred. "'Based on what I've told you thus far' . . . are you saying there's more?"

"There is indeed. Since the first issue was to try to identify the painter, I removed the backing. Some artists sign their work on the back side," Fred explained. "I didn't find an artist's signature . . . but I did find this." He drew a plastic-encased sheet of paper out from under a stack of files. "It's a letter to a Frenchwoman, Madame de Tessé, dated August 14, 1808, from President Thomas Jefferson. In it he says that he will do his best to get her the plants she requested." Fred pushed up his glasses and grinned. "She asked for some magnolias from South Carolina."

Ginny turned her astonished gaze to the letter. "President Jefferson?"

I followed her eyes and matched Fred's grin. He hadn't said a word to me about this spectacular discovery, so it must have been a last-minute find.

"Looks that way. President Jefferson and Madame de Tessé were pen pals."

Ginny seemed transfixed. "Pen pals."

"Yes. In this letter, President Jefferson acknowledges the receipt of seeds that Madame de Tessé sent him. The seeds came from a tree in her garden outside Paris." Fred looked down at the plastic sheath containing the letter. "'When the tree grows, I will cherish it, as it will remind me daily of the friendship with which you have honored me.'" Fred looked up, smiling broadly, pushing up his glasses again. "I mean, really . . . isn't that great?"

"You're kidding, right?" Ginny asked.

"I'm not," Fred replied, still grinning.

"How did the letter get inside the frame?"

"That's the sixty-four-thousand-dollar question," Fred said, shrugging. "No idea, and it's extremely unlikely we'll ever know."

Ginny looked at me. "I just can't believe it!"

I smiled. "I know, but if Fred says it's true . . . it's true!" I turned to him. "Do you think Madame de Tessé is the artist?"

"That would be really something, wouldn't it? But I have no reason to think so," Fred replied.

"President Jefferson," Ginny murmured, seemingly in shock.

"If you decide to pursue it," Fred said, "the first step would be authenticating the letter, and that should be pretty straight-ahead. President Jefferson was a prolific correspondent, and his letters have been widely studied, so there's no shortage of information available." He picked up the plastic sleeve and stared at the elegant writing. "However, assuming the letter is authentic, valuing it in the context of these watercolors . . . well, that would be, at best, a difficult and expensive endeavor. If, on the other hand, we consider the letter only on its own merit, again, assuming that it's genuine, we're talking a minimum value at auction in the hundreds of thousands of dollars."

Ginny's mouth opened, then closed. "I just can't believe it," she whispered.

Fred smiled and nodded. "It's a wonderful letter filled with sentiment and grace. Any collector would be thrilled to own it. What do you think? Might you want to sell it?"

"I don't know."

"Would you like me to place the letter back inside the frame?"

"Heck, no!" she exclaimed, chuckling. "I can't wait to show it to everyone I know!"

"Keep it safe," Fred said.

"Under lock and key," she agreed.

She thanked Fred, then watched as he slipped the plastic-encased letter into a padded envelope. When she left, she was clutching the envelope to her chest as if it were gold.

"Well done," I said to Fred.

"Thanks."

"You must have fainted when you found that letter."

He grinned. "It was a moment."

"What do you think?" I asked. "Is it the real deal?"

"Between you, me, and the gatepost? Yes."

I nodded. "A visual journal . . . I like that phrase a lot."

"Yeah," he agreed. He leaned back and picked up an inventory. "It's back to the Whitestone appraisal for me."

"I'm having lunch with Maddie. Any tidbits I can pass on?"

"Yeah," he said. "Some good news. I was just analyzing pricing data on one of the bells, and it's even better than I thought."

Fred led the way to a box sitting on a worktable at the back of the warehouse. We'd recently automated our tracking process; glancing at the card Fred had slid into a slot attached to the front of the box, I was glad to see that the system seemed to be working. According to the printed label, Whitestone Box 10 had been removed from the safe by Fred at 9:27 A.M.

"Mr. Whitestone purchased this bell from an antiques shop in York, Maine," Fred said. "It's fifteen inches tall and in near perfect condition, with age-appropriate signs of wear but no scrapes, cracks, or dings. If you look here, in this grape cluster, you'll see the date."

The bell was heavy and ornate with rows of grapevines circling the circumference. "Is it bronze?" I asked.

"Yup—with a natural patina."

Using a loupe, the date was easy to spot: 1787. "It looks European," I said. Typically, American bells from that period were simpler in design.

"Swedish," he said. "There's a name engraved on the inside, Hjoch Company. They made bells for the Royal Swedish Navy. Without tracking down sales or manufacturing records, if there are any extant, there's no way to tell which ship this bell was made for."

I turned it over. "How much did Guy pay?"

"Two hundred and ten dollars."

"My gut tells me that was quite a find."

Fred's lips twisted up into an "Oh, yeah, just wait!" grin. "I haven't quite finished, but I'd be comfortable right now estimating it at six thousand at auction."

I whistled. "You're going to make Guy a very happy man."

"Always a good thing. But there's another object where he didn't do as well. A Nantucket basket purse with a scrimmed topper."

"It's a fake?"

"It's new. There's nothing antique about it."

He lifted the basket purse out of the storage box and placed it on the table. The elliptical-shaped, rattan-weave purse was, at first glance, flawless. The bent oak handle appeared unused and moved smoothly. The rim had been affixed with brass escutcheon pins before weaving, a sign of quality craftsmanship. A conical ivory-colored pin fit snugly into a rattan closure loop. The crudely rendered scrimshaw design on the decorative topper showed a three-masted whaler and two whales. I opened the lid and saw that the purse had been signed on the underside: JANICE WALKER.

"Who's Janice Walker?" I asked.

"She's a basket weaver based on Cape Cod who sells her purses to high-end boutiques from Portland to Cape May. Mr. Whitestone paid one hundred and fifty dollars for it at a flea market."

I made a break-it-to-me-gently face. "And when new, it retails for . . . ?"

"A hundred ten."

"Oops."

"Yeah," he said.

"How new is it?" I asked.

"She's still offering them for sale on her Web site. In her bio, she says she graduated from RISD in 2008," he said, using the common shorthand for one of the nation's premier design schools, the Rhode Island School of Design, "so I'm guessing she can't have been making them for all that long. I'm going to call and see if I can confirm the date, just in case she's the fifth Janice Walker in a long line of basket weavers or something." He shrugged. "I suppose there's a chance the purse was crafted by her great-great-grandmother and looks pristine because it's never been used." He shrugged. "I'll see if I can reach her before you leave for lunch."

"Great. This is very helpful, Fred. Knowing Guy, he won't like to hear it, but he'll be glad to know."

Fred pushed his glasses up. "Cool," he said.

Eric was waiting for me on the landing outside my private office, a folded-up newspaper in his hand. As I climbed the steps, I noted that he looked worried.

"Can we shut the door?" he asked.

"Sure," I said, leading the way toward the wing chairs. "Have a seat."

He perched on the edge of his seat, his feet planted, then unfolded the newspaper, the *Seacoast Star,* tapping his finger on the photograph of the missing scrimmed tooth. "I don't know what to do . . . I've seen this tooth."

"Where?"

"Curt had it in his car one night."

Curt? I repeated silently. "When was that?" I asked, my voice reassuringly calm.

"I'm not sure exactly. A couple of Fridays ago. Two, maybe three."

"How did it come about that you saw it?"

"Grace and I were having pizza at John's—you know John's Pizzeria, right, on Route 1? Anyway, Curt comes in, all excited, and joins us for a beer. When Grace went to the ladies' room, he leaned over and whispered that he had something amazing in his car—a scrimmed tooth Greg bought from a picker. I asked him what he was doing with it, and he said he was going to take some photos so he could use the design in some scrimmed objects of his own. He said he was setting up a business, renting a scrimming machine and all."

"That's really interesting, Eric," I said, my brain reeling. "Did he go to John's to find you, or was it a coincidence?"

"I guess he came on purpose. Grace and I have pizza there most Friday nights. He was pretty excited about the tooth and wanted to tell someone." He looked miserable. "What should I do?"

"You have to call the police."

He shook his head. "I can't. I just can't."

"How come?"

"Curt will kill me. No one I know will ever trust me again."

"You can ask them to keep your name out of it."

He looked forlorn. "It will come out."

"Maybe. I know they'll do their best."

He sighed. "Can I make the call from here?"

I placed the call, and when I had Chief Hunter on the line, I handed the receiver to Eric. In a hesitant voice, Eric told him where he'd seen the tooth, then asked him to please do everything he could to keep his tip anonymous.

As soon as he hung up, I said, "You did the right thing."

Eric left, looking unimpressed with doing the right thing.

Within seconds, Cara buzzed up to tell me that Sam was on line two. I glanced at the gold mantel clock I kept on top of a display case on the far side of the room. It was just shy of eleven. Sam was calling four and a half hours early.

"My schedule changed. Can you meet now?" he asked.

"Sure," I said. "I'll meet you out back at the loading dock."

"Nah. I'll meet you in the Super McCory parking lot, by the side entrance, in about ten minutes."

"I thought you were coming here."

"Let's meet there instead."

"How come?"

I could hear his raspy breathing. "I don't know you."

Four words that changed everything. "Fair enough. I'll be there in ten—maybe fifteen—minutes. I'll get there as quickly as I can."

I called Chief Hunter, and when I told him what Sam said, he asked, "Has this ever happened to you before—where a picker changes things up like this?"

"Yes. More than once. I'm telling you, pickers get twitchy."

"Are you okay with proceeding?"

"Yes."

"Detective Brownley and I will be there in unmarked cars ASAP. Give us a five-minute head start. And call me as soon as you and Sam are done."

I agreed, then texted Wes to give him a heads-up. I doubted that he'd make it to the new location in time to see anything, but a deal was a deal, and I'd promised to keep him posted. I wrote, "Change in plans w/ Sam. McCory's side door. Now. Stay out of sight," then tossed my phone into my tote bag, told Cara I was going out for a while, and left.

As I drove past the small clutch of reporters that had resumed their vigil, I noticed that Bertie wasn't among them.

I hadn't a clue as to whether something had got Sam's dander up or whether this kind of subterfuge was his standard operating procedure. Regardless, I didn't like it. I'd much prefer to be on my home turf, knowing the police were only an arm's length away, out of sight but able to hear every word. The way Sam had set it up, we'd be meeting in a mall parking lot. Chief Hunter and Detective Brownley might be able to see us, but they wouldn't be able to hear, and they'd be too far away to help, if there was trouble. I had to assume I was on my own.

CHAPTER THIRTY

I parked as close to McCory's side door as I could, easing in between a silver VW and a black Mazda. I got out and stretched, doing a 360 to see if I could spot him or his brown van.

The place was busy. Steady streams of shoppers entered and left the store. Two boys, about ten, stood off to the side on a grassy strip separating McCory's from the rest of the mall, tossing a ball back and forth. A young woman, cradling an infant in one arm, hoisted bags of groceries into her trunk.

Within a minute, Sam's brown panel van pulled to a stop, blocking me in. He lowered his window.

"Follow me," he said, sounding irritated.

"I know you. Winslow Homer."

"You gonna follow me or what?"

"Okay," I said.

He led the way to the far side of the complex, parking in front of a store called Betty's Fabrics. I took the space next to him and got out. His eyes were still watery. He wore a red and black plaid flannel jacket zipped to the neck, jeans, and work boots.

"I got some good stuff," he said, throwing open one of the rear doors.

"Yeah?" I asked. "Like what?"

"Like liquor bottle ID tags and lanterns. You said you like pewter and maritime stuff, right?"

He dragged a tattered cardboard box toward me. It contained half a dozen pewter tags, the kind you hang on decanters, and five nineteenth-century hanging lanterns. Some of the tags had chains, some didn't, and all were scratched-up and worn. The lanterns had brass or ceramic bases. All five were dirty.

"Anything special here?" I asked.

"You're the expert," he said sourly. "You tell me."

I picked the objects up one at a time and examined them. The pewter tags were run-of-the-mill, worth a few dollars, no more. The lanterns were well used, in fair to good condition. The most ornate of the lot was speckled with soot. Another, simple and streamlined, was smeared with grease and grime.

"Nothing special, but all interesting," I said. "How much are you looking for?"

"A dollar each for the tags."

I nodded. "How about five for the lot?"

"Okay," he said begrudgingly.

"And the lanterns?"

"Ten each."

He must think I just fell off an onion truck, I thought, but I didn't allow my reaction to show. "Too bad," I said. "That's about what I'd expect to sell them for at the tag sale—after we cleaned them."

"So make me an offer."

"Ten for the lot."

"Forget it."

"Okay. Anything else?"

He snorted. "Got some new stuff. Scrimshaw on what they call fossil ivory. Legal." He pulled a green opaque plastic tub forward. Inside were scores of small white cardboard jewelry boxes. "They're cufflinks."

I examined a pair. The design showed ships scrimmed on oval-shaped ivory set in sterling silver settings with beaded bezels.

"How do I know it's fossil ivory?" I asked. It was easy to say the ivory was fossil—and thus legal. Proving it was harder.

"Don't know."

"Who's the artist?"

"Don't know that neither. I just buy 'em from a guy who sells 'em. You interested or not?"

"How much?" I asked.

His rheumy eyes remained fixed on mine for a long moment. I wondered if he was trying to assess my level of interest. Some pickers price the customer, not the goods.

"Make me a fair offer and they're yours," he said, doing what I would do under the circumstances—try to get the other guy to set the price first.

I picked up two additional pairs and compared them. The image on all three showed a Gloucester schooner at full sail on a choppy sea. The design was a bit side-heavy, with too-bold and too-dark lines outlining the left edge of the sails. Still, the minute elements, the cross-hatching to suggest fast-moving water and the way the sails fluttered in the wind, demonstrated great artistry. The three pairs weren't similar; they were identical. The designs had to have been traced or machine pressed.

"Are they mass-produced?"

"I don't know. You buying or not?" he asked, letting his impatience show.

I was interested, but not if they were ivory, unless I knew for certain that the material had been legally acquired, and given Sam's snippiness, I wasn't optimistic.

"I need proof the ivory's legal."

"What kind of proof?"

"Provenance. Certificates of authenticity. Bills of sale. Something in writing from a known and credible source. Something I can verify."

Sam scratched his neck. "I'll let you know."

"Assuming that works out, I'll need to test the material."

"If you got the paperwork that says it's real, that's the ball game. I don't know if I can get it, but regardless, no testing. I only sell stuff as is."

If the ivory was genuine, and legal, and if the scrimmed design was at least partially handcrafted, the cufflinks would sell like hot cakes during the holidays. We'd be able to move at least three or four dozen pairs by the end of the year, and since they featured a traditional design, they'd sell well forever. I could see a price point of $150 a pair, which meant I could offer Sam as much as fifty.

"Assuming you can get the documentation, name a price that will make it worth my while to take a flyer on a new product," I said, hoping to win his agreement to let me test with the promise of a big payoff.

"A thousand a dozen," he said.

"Ouch," I said, smiling to show I wasn't taking his out-of-the-realm-of-possibility offer as an insult. "I'm thinking five hundred."

He shook his head and lifted his chin. "Nope."

"Six hundred," I said. "And I'll take four dozen."

He stared at me through narrowed eyes. "Done. Give me forty for the lanterns and you can have them, too."

I shook my head. "I can give you fifteen."

"Twenty-five."

"I'm sorry," I said. "I can only go to fifteen."

He glowered at me. "Take 'em," he grumbled.

"Can I buy a few pairs of cufflinks now?" I asked as I transferred the ragged box to my trunk. "While you check on the documentation, I can begin testing them."

"I only sell them by the dozen."

"And I want to buy them by the dozen. But first, I've got to authenticate them."

He looked at me as he chewed it over. "A hundred bucks each."

"Fifty."

"Nope. I'm breaking up a lot," he said.

He had a point, and he had me over a barrel—I wanted to get a closer look at them, and I had no leverage. "Two hundred for three pairs," I said.

"Okay, okay," he said, sounding fed up.

"Pick them from different lots, okay?"

While he did as I asked, muttering under his breath, I pulled $220 from the stash in my pocket. He passed over three small jewelry boxes. I opened each one to confirm the cufflinks were there and as expected, then placed them on my front seat.

"Do you want me to write out our deal?" I asked, handing over the cash.

He counted the money twice, then stuffed the bills in his jeans pocket. "Hell, no," he said, then added, with mordant humor, "I trust you."

He hitched up his pants and headed around the side of his van without speaking another word.

I sat in my car with my hands out of sight and jotted down his license plate number. Once the van had turned out of the mall parking lot, I called Chief Hunter.

"We already got it," he said as soon as I started to give him the van's tag number. "I've got you in sight. I'll be there in a minute."

He pulled into a nearby space and asked me to join him. Once I was settled in, he said, "Start at the beginning."

I described my interaction with Sam, quoting our conversation as close to word for word as I could.

"Don't touch anything," he instructed. "We'll want to check for prints. Officer Meade will be here in a couple of minutes to pick things up. So what did you think of him?"

"He's an old-fashioned grump," I said, thinking that if Detective Brownley had been on-site as planned, she was probably following Sam. "He's been around the block a few times."

"In terms of your arrangement with him . . . what do you do now?"

"Wait to hear from him."

"Will he get the paperwork?" he asked.

"I don't know."

Officer Meade, her blond hair tucked up under her cap, rolled to a stop in the fire lane. She walked over to Chief Hunter's SUV, snapping on plastic gloves. I opened my trunk, and Chief Hunter and I watched as she slid the three small cardboard boxes into individual plastic evidence bags. The bigger box containing the lanterns and pewter tags went into a jumbo-sized bag.

"Thanks," she said, removing her gloves, once everything was secured in her vehicle. She signaled Chief Hunter with a quasi-salute and drove off.

"Have you questioned Curt yet?" I asked.

"No. We're checking into some aspects of Eric's story—whether Curt has registered a business or rented office space, for instance." Seeing my you've-got-to-be-kidding expression, he held up a hand. "I know it's not likely, but I like to be thorough."

Like me, I thought.

He said he'd let me know as soon as the objects I'd purchased from Sam could be returned, and we said our good-byes and climbed into our cars. He headed toward Rocky Point. I turned the other way, toward Portsmouth.

Waiting for the light to change, my mind a whirl of speculation, I realized that Curt would be picked up soon. I grabbed my phone and called Wes.

"It's me," I said by way of greeting. "Are you at McCory's?"

"You bet," he said. "I got some great photos. Now tell me what they mean."

"I have no idea. But I can tell you that Curt is involved in some sort of something, I don't know what. I think he's about to be brought in for questioning."

"Thanks, Josie."

I hoped Wes would get a jump on the story before Bertie put the kibosh on his exclusive. If Bertie got to Curt first, she'd button him up, lulling the poor schmo into trusting her, enveloping him with her faux-motherly concern, convincing him that talking openly to her was as safe as confessing his sins to his priest. I knew. She'd pulled the same routine on me the first time I met her.

My phone rang, startling me.

"Slight change of plans," Chief Hunter said. "Can you go straight to the station?"

I glanced at the dash clock. It was just after noon. "I can come by after lunch," I said.

"This is pretty important."

I trusted his judgment. He wouldn't tell me it was important if it wasn't. "Okay."

I called Maddie, and she was as gracious as ever, insisting that changing our plans was no problem at all, even though I was canceling with just a few minutes' notice. She suggested we meet for drinks instead, and I agreed. I called work to let them know I might be out all afternoon, then kept my eye on the traffic.

I parked near the front door of the station. Chief Hunter got out and stood by his car watching as Curt Grimes drove into the lot with Officer Griffin following in his patrol car.

Wes appeared on foot from the left, shooting photos of Curt as he stepped out of his car. I wondered where Wes had parked. He turned his camera toward Griff and started taking photos of him, too, then Chief Hunter, then me. Wes stopped for a moment to glance at his watch, then resumed his work, shooting several additional photos of Curt as he walked toward him.

Curt frowned, taking it in. He wasn't bouncing or jiggling with barely suppressed energy. He didn't look full of himself at all. He looked uncertain of his ground. He approached Wes and said something. Wes replied; then Curt said something else. Wes nodded and spoke again. I edged closer, hoping to hear what they were saying, but with the thunderous waves pounding the shore just across the street, I couldn't make out a word.

Chief Hunter said something to Curt, and Curt nodded and followed him into the station. Wes walked around the building. He must have left his car in back, I thought. I looked over my shoulder as I entered the station and was just in time to see Bertie drive up in her rented Taurus. I smiled, pleased that Wes had been in on the action, and that she hadn't.

Inside, Chief Hunter said, "Thanks again for coming in, Mr. Grimes. Officer Griffin will get you situated."

As Griff led Curt toward Room One, Chief Hunter asked me, "Can you do your testing of the cufflinks here? I'd like to know if they're real ASAP."

"'Real' is a relative term. I can probably tell you if the scrimshaw is etched or pressed, and maybe I can determine something about the materials, but that's it."

"Anything you can tell me will help." He pushed open the door that led to the back. "When did you call Wes Smith?" he asked, slipping in an assumptive question—not *did* I call, but *when*.

"If the cufflinks need further testing, I can help organize that, too," I said, taking a lesson from Chief Hunter's book. If you don't want to answer a question, change the subject.

He grinned, and when I smiled in return, he said, "Thanks," his tone desert dry.

As I followed him down the corridor, I thought about all the things that might not be as they appeared to be.

CHAPTER THIRTY-ONE

I watched as the police tested the jewelry boxes and cufflinks for fingerprints. The boxes showed only two sets of prints, mine and, presumably, Sam's. The cufflinks showed only mine, which wasn't unexpected since most jewelers and artisans buff their wares before selling them.

Cathy, the civilian admin, found a safety pin in the back of her desk drawer, and an officer who smoked lent me his lighter, so I was able to complete the hot pin test. The material wasn't resin or plastic. The loupe verified that finding—the designs were scrimmed on ivory. An age-dating test would confirm the ivory was fossil, not new, but so far, all signs indicated that Sam had been telling the truth. At Chief Hunter's request, I had Fred drive over with the magnet, file, and acid that would allow me to test the silver.

Chief Hunter and I sat in a small room they used as a lunchroom. The windows were open, and the breeze blowing in was fresh. The fluorescent lighting was strong. I worked on a metal tray.

"What are you doing?" he asked, watching as I ran the magnet over the bezels.

There was no pull.

"Lots of materials aren't magnetic," I explained, "including silver. Of course, just because these bezels aren't responding to the magnet doesn't mean they're made of silver. They could be painted porcelain, for all I know."

I turned the cufflink over and used an ultrathin needle file to scrape through the metal. If the cufflinks were silver-plated, not sterling, my filing would reveal the underlying metal.

They weren't plated.

I placed a drop of acid on the filed spot and watched for the color change.

"It's called the acid test," I said. "This cufflink just passed—it's made of sterling silver."

"So," Chief Hunter said, "it seems Mr. Holt—we got Sam's last name from his vehicle registration—wasn't selling junk. What can you tell about the scrimshaw?"

"It was either etched via a printing process, which means the cufflinks are machine-made, or traced, which means they're handmade but not individually designed. All I know for sure is that the image you see was etched in, not painted on."

"So they're real."

"Like I said before, 'real' is one of those words. It's like 'low-fat'—each company defines it differently. There's no standardization. So far what I can say is that they're decent-quality scrimmed cufflinks using natural materials. If you want to know more, I'll need to analyze the materials further, including testing the age of the ivory."

He nodded. "I'll let you know. We've asked Mr. Holt to come in and talk to us."

"And what did he say to your request?" I asked, having a hard time imagining Sam cooperating with the police.

Chief Hunter smiled a little. "We can be pretty persuasive. We've also asked Greg Donovan to come in to talk to us again."

I stared. "Really? Why?"

"Because he says that Sam Holt sold the Myrick tooth to him. Shortly thereafter, Curt Grimes apparently borrowed the tooth so he could take photos of the design. According to Mr. Grimes's initial statement, he snuck the tooth out of the gallery at the end of his shift and returned it the next day first thing with no one but Eric any the wiser. As a trusted helper, apparently he has the run of the place."

My insurance company would have fits, I thought.

"Within days," Chief Hunter continued, "Ms. Morse appraised the tooth, and Mr. Whitestone bought it. After being on display at the lighthouse for several days, it went missing, probably while Mr. Grimes was on-site. It seems to me that there are more questions I can ask Mr. Donovan—and others—about that sequence of events."

He paused, then added, "I'm telling you all this because I'm hoping you'll help." He pointed at the cufflinks. "For instance, I could tell Mr. Holt that you've tested these cufflinks and that they appear to have been crafted of appropriate, organic materials, and therefore I infer that the tooth he sold Mr. Donovan was also probably real. I can ask for his cooperation based on new evidence suggesting that he has been telling me the truth all along. I'm hoping he'll become an ally instead of an adversary."

I nodded. "That makes sense."

"But I can tell from your expression that you don't think it will work."

"Sam struck me as fairly contrary."

"Yeah, I have that feeling, too. What else can I do to get him to talk?"

I thought about his question for several seconds, then shook my head. "I doubt you can."

Chief Hunter nodded. "What about Mr. Grimes? You said he offered you repros for sale, so there's no question about his committing fraud. Based on Eric's testimony, though, we have the tooth in his car—presumably the genuine article. Maybe he switched it with a phony, or maybe he did just what he told Eric he intended to do. Which doesn't explain where the tooth is now or why it and it alone is missing. If Grimes stole the Myrick tooth from the lighthouse—where is it? From all reports, he hasn't tried to sell it." He paused for a moment. "So, help me think it through. How can I get him to cooperate?"

I thought about smarmy Curt. "I'd consider offering him a deal. Ask Greg to issue him a get-out-of-jail-free card for telling the truth about taking the tooth from the gallery and/or about whether he substituted a fake when he replaced it. Ask Guy to issue a reward with a guarantee of no prosecution for information leading to the safe return of the tooth—then tell Curt about the dual offer and see what happens."

"What if the tooth Mr. Whitestone bought was authentic, but the tooth Curt returns in order to claim the reward is a phony?"

I nodded, following his logic. "We have no way of knowing whether the tooth Guy bought is real or not. It seems to me the first issue is trying to sort through what happened. Until we get the tooth in our hands, we're flying blind."

Chief Hunter looked thoughtful. "I like it. How much should Mr. Whitestone offer?"

"Five thousand. Cash. The offer has to be good enough to justify not sitting on the stolen tooth for a couple of years, then reselling it."

"I'll check it out. What do you think—would a promise of no consequences from Mr. Donovan and a reward from the Whitestones work with Mr. Holt?"

I considered it. "I doubt it. Yes, Sam likes money, but he's paranoid by nature and skeptical by habit. My guess is that he wouldn't trust any deal offered by the police even if it was in writing, even if he heard it on the news."

He nodded and stood up, smiling again. "You've been very helpful—as always. Thanks."

"Does that mean I can go?"

"Yes—but keep your phone on, all right? I expect I'll have more questions."

"Sure."

He asked me to leave the cufflinks at the station until they decided whether they wanted to proceed with a spectroscopic and materials analysis, and I agreed. He handed me a receipt they'd prepared for all the objects I'd purchased from Sam.

I stood up and grabbed my tote bag. I paused midstep as an idea came to me. "I have a suggestion."

"Shoot," Chief Hunter said. He heard me out, then nodded, grinned, and said, "That's a doozy of a suggestion. I like it. Let me set the scene. I'll come get you in a minute."

When Chief Hunter rejoined me in the lunchroom, he said, "We're good to go. Mr. Grimes is waiting in the lobby."

"Great. I hope this works."

"Me, too," he said, leading the way.

We turned the corner to the entryway just as Greg stepped in.

"Josie!" he said, smiling like a politician. "Nice to see a friendly face in this den of iniquity." He turned to Curt, sitting on the bench. Curt's sneer was back in place; he looked fully recovered from his earlier bewilderment. "Hey, Curt."

"Shouldn't it be den of iquity?" I joked. "They're not violating rights; they're protecting them."

"Iquity, huh? I must have been absent from school the day they taught that word."

I smiled. "If it's not a word, it ought to be—like ept! If some people are inept, surely others are ept."

Greg laughed and turned to Chief Hunter. "I present myself to your machinations, as requested. I hope to be ept for you today."

Chief Hunter smiled politely. "We appreciate it. If you'll just have a seat, I'll be with you in one minute." He turned to me. "Thank you again."

He offered a hand, and we shook; then he pushed open the door for me.

"Curt?" I said, turning to face him.

Greg, Chief Hunter, and Curt all looked at me.

"Sorry to break in," I said, turning on a five-hundred-watt smile, a stock model I hoped would fool him. "Could I talk to you for a sec?"

Curt cast an assessing glance at me, then another at Chief Hunter, and then he walked in my direction. "Sure."

I led the way outside. "Any chance you have those repros you mentioned with you? I've changed my mind—I'd love to take a look. I'm sure the police won't mind you taking a minute or two to do some business."

"Sure, sure," he said. "You're in luck—I've got my *best* stuff with me." He winked.

His stressing the word "best" was offensive. I followed him to his car, surprised he didn't scuttle like a bug.

He unhinged the tucked-in flaps of a cardboard box he had in his trunk, and I saw stacks of hand-painted tiles, the kind people use as trivets. Most of them were florals, intended to replicate Italian designs, and a few were Syrian in design and coloration. They sold in flea markets nationwide for about three dollars apiece. They were wholesaled by every novelty distributor for $108 a gross, or seventy-five cents each. I knew because I'd toyed with beefing up the tag sale inventory with objects of this kind for years, but I'd always resisted because not only weren't they antiques or collectibles, they weren't even interesting, uncommon, or particularly well crafted.

"I can give you a great price. Fifty bucks for a dozen. You pick the ones you want—mix and match."

"Thanks," I said, stepping back. His offer was almost six times the going price. It was an insult. "What else do you have?"

"Some belt buckles. Scrimshaw. Good stuff."

He handed me a sample. The rectangular scrimmed surface, maybe ivory, was encased in silver metal, maybe sterling. The image, two whales diving through rough water, was etched. The whales, complete with overly dark borders, were off-center, just a little.

"This is machine-made, right?"

"Yeah. An artist makes the plate, then it's attached to a scrimming machine. We can pop them out like nobody's business."

"Who's 'we'?"

He winked again, and I had to stop myself from running away, he was so obnoxious.

"You know I can't tell you that," he said, and I could tell that he thought his tone was humorous.

"The design is a little askew. Are they all like that?"

"Nah. Learning curve, you know."

He made them himself, I thought.

"Once we get the production solid, I'll be branching out into other designs—traditional scrimshaw stuff just like this one . . . you know . . . ships and compasses, that sort of thing," he said.

Like the design elements he copied from the Myrick tooth he showed Eric, I speculated silently. "Great," I replied, keeping my tone casual. "Did you get the scrimming machine from Lenny Wilton?"

"I don't know any Lennys. I use another guy's machine. I'm his helper, you know?" He winked again when he spoke the word "helper," as if something about him being an apprentice or an assistant was funny. "But don't you worry about anything. *I'm* your contact— and I guarantee I'll do right by you. How many are you thinking of getting?"

"How much are they?"

"A hundred twenty a dozen, ten bucks each."

That wasn't a bad price—even if the material was resin, we could sell them for twenty-nine dollars each, close to the three-to-one markup ratio I try to maintain.

"I'll need to examine the materials," I said. "Can you tell me anything about them?"

"No can do. I'm not the materials buyer. I'm production. You buy them, you can authenticate all you want!" Another wink.

"I'll take three now from different lots, do my testing, and let you know how it works out—but I'm only interested if the design is centered and clean."

"You got it!" Curt said.

He seemed so excited at having landed a sale, I wondered if I was his first customer.

"Have you sold a lot of them?" I asked.

"Not so far." Yet another wink. "But I will."

I handed over the cash, packed up the three buckles, and said, "See ya!"

I watched as Curt reentered the police station, then crossed Ocean Avenue and climbed the soft sand to the top of the dune, glad to stretch my legs and extra glad to get away from him. Rather than risk being seen or overheard talking to Chief Hunter while Curt or Greg was in or around the lobby, I called him. I got his voice mail.

"Well, I was wrong. Curt wasn't selling the same cufflinks as Sam, so I couldn't ask him about his source. A good idea, but no soap. Curt had scrimmed belt buckles, though, which I suspect he made himself. He said he plans on expanding his offerings. In any event, I bought three to test them. I'm going to run inside now and give it a whirl."

I crossed the street and stepped inside the police station. Neither Greg nor Curt was in sight. When I explained to Cathy what I wanted to do, she called Chief Hunter to pass on the message that he should listen to his voice mail and that I was waiting for permission to use the lunchroom for more testing. His okay was immediate. It took me ten minutes to confirm that the materials were either identical or similar to the ivory and silver used in the cufflinks. Using Chief Hunter's parlance, they were "real."

I left the information with Cathy, then returned to the beach. Knife-sharp tension had tightened my neck and shoulder muscles, and I willed myself to relax.

I watched the tide lick barnacle-covered stones, then slip away, in and out, in and out, and as I did, I felt my breathing slow to match the calm and steady rhythm of the sea. The ocean was smooth, like satin, and dark blue, like a midnight sky in summer. No one was around. No boats or ships were in sight. I looked north toward the Rocky Point jetty. Mica sparkled in the granite like sequins on a gown. Waves lapped the edges. I raised and lowered my shoulders and felt the rock-hard tension ease a bit. At the shoreline, I saw tiny pricks—air holes. Clams and mussels had burrowed in the sand.

A memory came to me—clamming for littlenecks with my dad at Nantasket Beach. I'd been about eight. It was early on the Saturday before Labor Day, maybe seven or seven thirty in the morning, and the beach was empty. My mom was at home baking cookies for our last weekend at the beach house before school started while my dad and I walked the hard-packed sand near the surf line. It was cloudy and cool. My dad carried the pitchfork and a bucket half full of ocean water. My job was running ahead seeking out air holes. At every sighting, he'd unearth the clams, and I'd toss them into the bucket. When we figured we had enough, we brought them home, and my mom rinsed them over and over and over again.

After they were clean of sand and grit, she placed them in aluminum foil packets filled with a luscious mixture of butter, garlic, vermouth, parsley, and white wine, a recipe of her own invention—Summer Clams, she'd called it. She'd seal them up, and we'd sit on the patio sipping sweet ice tea and talking about everything under the sun as those packets of clams simmered on the grill, and to this day, I found it hard to imagine that life could get any better than that.

I'd asked about clamming in Rocky Point just after I moved to New Hampshire, and I'd been told that it had been twenty years or more since clamming had been allowed. It made me feel old.

Ty would be on the road, somewhere north of Augusta, Maine, and if all was on schedule, he was only a few hours away from home. I called him.

"Josie!" he said, happiness rippling in his voice. "I'm so tired of driving, I can't even tell you."

"Tell me you can stay close to home next week."

"I can stay close to home next week."

"Excellent!"

"Yeah. I'll be in Portsmouth three days and Laconia two. So what's happening?" he asked.

I told Ty about Eric spotting the tooth in Curt's car, and about my buying Sam's cufflinks and Curt's belt buckles and analyzing the materials for Chief Hunter, then said, "Nothing makes sense. If you were still chief, what would you do?"

"When nothing makes sense, all you can do is keep talking to people and looking under rocks," he said.

"Which must be why Chief Hunter is bringing everyone back in for more questioning. Does it work?" I asked.

"Sometimes."

"What do you do if it doesn't?"

"Think of more questions to ask or more people to talk to or more rocks to look under."

Far out to sea, lines of white marked the windbreak. The ocean had been dead calm only moments earlier, but now the eastern breeze was churning up froth.

"Hurry home," I said. "An east wind is blowing."

"You're standing on a tall dune watching whitecaps in the distance?"

"You are an all-seeing wonder man."

"About time you noticed."

"Ha. As if. I've known that about you forever."

"You're my wonder woman."

I smiled, tickled pink at his compliment. "What do you want for dinner?"

"Half a cow."

"Done."

After we hung up, I stayed on the dune awhile longer listening to the surf, thinking about Myrick teeth, and Winslow Homer etchings, and Curt Grimes.

Had Curt lied when he said he didn't know Lenny, that he used another guy's scrimming machine to make the belt buckles? Was Curt the brains behind whatever scheme was going on? *No way,* I thought. Curt couldn't find his way out of a paper bag without instructions. Curt barely knew scrimshaw from Scrimshank. He was learning the novelty business, but he was a small-time operator with the merchandizing sense of a lizard. He darted here and there, to Prescott's and other shops up and down the coast, hoping to nail a buyer or two, the way a gecko hunts for insects. Unlike Curt's business strategy— selling inferior goods from the trunk of his car—this plan featured high-quality objects sold from a reputable gallery.

Could Sam be the power behind the ploy? He seemed smart and savvy—and Greg said he'd bought the tooth from Sam. I shook my head. I just didn't believe it. Sam was an itinerant merchant, not a manufacturer.

If neither Curt nor Sam was running the show, who was? It had to be someone smart and knowledgeable and confident.

Someone like Lenny, I realized, appalled at the thought.

CHAPTER THIRTY-TWO

I called Wes.

"Curt is involved in wholesaling repros and modern scrimmed objects," I explained, filling him in about Curt's offerings.

"Did you get any photos?" Wes asked.

"No," I said, shaking my head at his audacity.

He sighed heavily, letting me know how disappointed he was in me, then said, "I have a source telling me that Curt stole the Myrick tooth."

My heart fell, then jumped. I crossed my fingers, hoping Eric's name was being kept out of the reports. "Really?" I asked with assumed insouciance.

"Yup. Apparently, he returned it, so I guess it's more correct to say he borrowed it."

"Do you know for sure he returned it?"

"Didn't he?" Wes asked, hoping for a scoop.

"I don't know. Maybe he returned a repro."

"Good one, Josie."

"I'm not saying he did."

"Gotcha. Either way, he's a crook."

"An alleged crook."

"Yeah, yeah. So tell me—what do his belt buckles have to do with Frankie's murder?"

"I don't know," I said.

"What do you think?"

I watched the tide sweep into shore for a moment, then replied, "There's a lot of buying and selling going on—maybe everything is on the up-and-up, but I wonder. Not to state the obvious, but Frankie was killed for a reason."

"I'll see what I can find out about Curt's business dealings."

"Good. There's someone else I'm hoping you'll check out, too—Lenny Wilton."

"Why?"

I couldn't think of how to express the vague worry teasing me. While I had no reason to suspect Lenny of either fraud or murder, neither had I any reason not to. It was shockingly easy to come up with credible and damning scenarios.

Lenny could have set Curt up in business. He might well be the cufflink scrimshander, too. Without question, he could have scrimmed a good-enough fake Myrick to fool anyone conducting as cursory an examination as Ashley's.

I took in a breath, considering how fraud could have led to murder. What if Curt told Frankie what he and Lenny were up to—I could see him bragging, "I'm a player, hanging with the big boys . . . It's easy money . . . I take one tooth out and slip another one in . . . and no one's the wiser," wink, wink. Frankie might have been outraged and determined to protect his employer. If he threatened them with exposure, one or the other of them might have killed Frankie to keep him from spilling the beans.

I shook my head. It was easy to make stuff up, but my conjectures bore no known relationship to fact. Lenny was disciplined and self-contained, and from what I could tell, he was a nice guy and a straight shooter. It took quite a leap of imagination to suggest that Lenny was involved in anything duplicitous, and an even bigger leap to think that he might have killed Frankie. *Still, what harm can it do for Wes to check?* I asked myself.

"I don't have any reason to suspect Lenny," I replied. "So check just 'cause, okay?"

"What do you want to know?"

"His alibi, if he has one, and his financial standing."

"Okeydokey. So," he said, clearing his throat, "thanks, Josie, for calling about Curt. I got some great photos. And an even better quote. 'Frankie was my best friend,' he told me."

"Good," I said. "What do you do now?"

"Write my lead for tomorrow's newspaper article," he said. "I've already done the headline: 'Alleged Thief Questioned in Winterelli Murder.'"

"Yikes," I said. "That's pretty strong stuff."

"Thanks," Wes said, then ended the call with a cheery "Talk later!"

I watched the tide for a while longer, then sidestepped down the dune, ready to head to Portsmouth.

Fred called as I walked down Penhallow toward Bow Street. I'd left my car in an open lot about ten blocks away, so I could try to ease the constricting pressure in my back by stretching my legs.

"I can confirm the bad news," Fred said. "The Janice Walker basket purse is new. The design was introduced last summer, so it's not even one of her early pieces—not that a designer with only a few years under her belt has 'early pieces,' exactly."

"And no family weavers in her past."

"Nada."

"Okay, then," I said. "That's that."

"Sasha wants to talk to you. She has news about the Homer."

He passed her the phone. "Homer didn't use an échoppe," Sasha said. "Or if he did, I can't find evidence of it."

"Was he open about his work habits?" I asked.

"Sort of. He was pretty private in his personal life, but he didn't refuse to talk about his work or anything. Also," she said, her concern evident in her tone, "there's no record of this etching. No prior sales, no current offerings. It's as if it's a one-off."

"Maybe it is," I suggested. "It's possible he hated it and destroyed the plate."

"That's theoretically possible, of course, but it's not likely. First of all, I would expect there to be more than one extant etching—this one isn't marked as an artist's proof. Second, if anyone knew about his decision to destroy the plate, someone would have commented on it as a novel event in the artist's life if nothing else. The printer, the printer's apprentice, another artist—someone. I've checked academic research and dissertations, recent sales, exhibition essays, and catalogues for past and upcoming auctions, and I can't find any hint that this etching even exists, let alone that it comes with a dramatic history like a destroyed plate."

I took in air. "What about the artistic style?"

"Homer didn't use dark border lines, but other than that, there's nothing to indicate that it's *not* an original."

Myrick didn't use highlight lines either, I thought.

"Anything on the materials?"

"The paper and ink appear period-appropriate, but of course, if we decide to proceed, we'll need to test them."

"What do you think we should do at this point?" I asked.

She paused. "I know you don't want word to get out—but I think we need more information. I'd like to call Dr. Swann."

Dr. Milton Swann was a world-renowned Homer expert based in Boston. "I trust your instincts, Sasha, and if your gut is telling you there's something wrong, we should find out about it sooner rather than later. So yes, by all means, call him. On a confidential basis, of course."

"Thank you," she said.

I heard the relief in her voice, and I understood: We shared a sense that something was very rotten in the state of Denmark.

CHAPTER THIRTY-THREE

S tanding across the street from the Blue Dolphin, I counted five reporters by the front door, Bertie included.

A middle-aged man with wavy hair wearing a gray pin-stripe suit and a red tie recognized me. I knew him from an interview he'd conducted on fun summer activities in the seacoast region—my tag sale had made his list. He was a reporter from a Manchester TV station.

"Josie," he called. "Does your meeting with the Whitestones have anything to do with Frankie's murder?"

A young woman with short blond hair wiggled in front of him. "Hi, Josie! I'm with *Antiques Insights*. Can you describe the decor inside Rocky Point Light? Throw me a couple of adjectives, will you? Is it eclectic? Masculine? Earthy?"

Bertie bounded across the street, smiling broadly, aiming her recorder at me like a conductor's baton. "Congratulations on breaking the story that Curt Grimes stole the Myrick tooth, Josie. That's quite a coup. How'd you do it?"

I took in a deep-to-my-toes breath, wondering whether she had a separate source or was following Wes's lead, then crossed the street, ignoring them all. They followed me, jostling for position, hemming me in. My heart pounded against my ribs, but I stared straight ahead and kept walking. I made it, and opened the heavy oak door. Inside, I stood until my throbbing pulse quieted.

"Josie," Frieda, the hostess, said, returning from seating some patrons. "Mr. Whitestone told me you'd be joining them."

At her words, all thoughts of encroaching reporters vanished. I was pleased that Guy was there. I'd been looking forward to telling

Maddie about his great find with the ship's bell, but it would be even more fun telling him directly.

Stepping inside the Blue Dolphin was like going back in time two hundred years. The walls were mellowed brick. The ceilings were low. The lighting was muted. Bulbs designed to look like candles twinkled in glass sconces. The flooring, ancient oak planks, had been polished to a golden sheen. Tables in the dining room were covered with crisp white linen. Silver gleamed. Crystal sparkled.

In the lounge, glass covered the mahogany tabletops. The walls were painted hunter green. Jimmy, the redheaded bartender who'd worked there forever, waved and called hello as I entered.

I liked everything about the place; it had become a kind of home away from home for me, a safe haven where I could always be sure of a warm welcome and friendly chitchat.

Frieda led me to the Whitestones' table, a four-top tucked in a bay window enclosure in the back of the lounge. Guy stood to hold my chair as I approached.

Men with courtly manners always reminded me of my father. My dad had routinely opened doors, held chairs, and stood when my mother or I arrived at or left a table or a room, and after an evening out, he thanked us for a lovely time. It had been a shock to begin dating and discover that almost none of the boys and men I'd met knew or cared about that sort of thing. Guy did, and it put a smile on my face.

I thanked him, greeted Maddie, then turned back to Guy. "I'd say welcome back, except that isn't exactly what I mean."

Freida placed a menu in front of me, saying, "In case you feel like a little something," then slipped away with professional discretion.

"Maddie's been telling me how stressful it's been for her. I'm sure it's been tough for you, too," he said, his baritone resonating with an orator's confidence. "Do you have any news? Are the police getting any closer to an arrest?"

"I get the impression they're focusing more on motive than anything else, but if they've identified a specific suspect, I don't know it."

Jimmy came out from behind the bar. "What can I get you?" he asked, flipping a cocktail napkin in front of me.

Maddie and Guy were drinking martinis.

"I'm starving, actually, so I think I'll have one of your fabulous Caesar salads—with chicken. And sparkling water." Once Jimmy left, I explained, "I missed lunch."

"Do you think the missing Myrick tooth is behind the murder?" Guy asked.

"I wouldn't be the least bit surprised," I said. "I don't know how it figures into anything, but I can't think of any other reason for Frankie to be killed, at least none that makes any sense. I mean, it's not like there's a serial killer on the loose or anything. Someone killed *him* in particular, you know?"

"I know you've just started, but do you have any news on the appraisal?" Guy asked.

"A little bit—I can report on two of your purchases. With one, you're going to be very happy. With the other, not so much."

"Guy hates bad news," Maddie said, sipping her martini, smiling enigmatically. "Be very careful, Josie."

"I don't hate bad news. I hate screwing up. There's a difference. Start with the one that will make me very happy."

I explained Fred's findings about the ship's bell, and he whooped and high-fived me as if I'd told him his profit was in the millions, not the thousands.

"I knew it," he said. "As soon as I saw it, I knew it."

His enthusiasm was contagious, and I smiled.

"The basket purse wasn't such a find, I'm afraid."

"Really? It was in such pristine condition, I was certain you'd tell me it was a killer buy."

"It's new."

"New?" he challenged. "As in, not an antique?"

"Yeah."

His eyes narrowed, and he slapped the table. "Damn! I fell for a fast-talking huckster telling me all about the construction and how well made it was and what a steal he was offering it at. I can't believe it! He snookered me!"

"Well, if that's what he told you, he only spoke the truth. It's a terrific example of beautifully crafted basket work."

"How much did I overpay?"

"Forty dollars. It retails for a hundred ten."

He slapped the table again, frustrated. "I need to determine a price point above which I don't buy unless you look at it. I'll have to think about it." He drank some of his martini, concentrating. "It's just like negotiating to acquire a company," he said. "Lots of times, the founder talks big about how much his firm is worth, how many clients he has, you know the kind of guy I mean—cocky and arrogant . . . and why not? He's built his company up from nothing, and it's his baby. You should see his face when I tell them I'm sending in the suits. Half the time, they remember they're not quite ready for prime time."

I stared at him, his words echoing in my brain. *Not quite ready for prime time.* My mouth opened, then closed. It was as if two pieces of a jigsaw puzzle that hadn't fit no matter which way I turned them suddenly locked into place.

Maddie was talking, but I didn't hear her. My salad and drink arrived, and I ate and drank and thought, and then I pushed my dish away. I stared out the window, past the scrubby brush, over the fast-moving Piscataqua River, into the stands of golden poplars and yellow birch and orange maples that lined the riverbank on the Maine side.

The fraud was all about money. Disparate details flooded my consciousness.

Neither Myrick nor Homer used an échoppe.

Neither man etched dark highlight lines.

Onionskin paper was a historically accurate material.

Then, like an out-of-focus image resolving itself, the answer came to me, and with the answer, confidence. The missing Myrick tooth was a fake, and I knew who had created it.

I looked at Maddie and Guy. No one was speaking. They were watching me.

"Are you all right?" Guy asked.

"Yes—but I have to go. I can't explain now. I'm sorry." I offered money for my meal, but Guy wouldn't hear of it. "I'll be in touch," I said.

Outside, I didn't even notice the reporters as I ran for my car.

CHAPTER THIRTY-FOUR

I 'll wait," I told Cathy at the Rocky Point police station.

"I don't know how long Chief Hunter will be, Josie," she said.

I needed to talk to the chief, and I needed to talk to him now. "Could someone call him or slip him a note? It's important."

I'd known Cathy for as long as I'd been in New Hampshire, five years. I hoped she'd take me seriously.

She must have seen the urgency in my eyes, because she nodded. "Sure," she said. "I'll see he gets a note. You need some paper?"

"Thanks." I accepted the sheet of plain paper that Cathy extracted from a nearby printer and a Rocky Point Police letterhead envelope. I wrote, "I know the missing tooth is a fake—and I know who faked it." I folded the paper into thirds and wrote Chief Hunter's name on the envelope.

"I'll see he gets it right away," Cathy told me.

I sat on the bench across from the bulletin board and waited. The station house was quiet. I wondered if Curt and Greg were still being interviewed.

Chief Hunter appeared at his office door. "Come on in," he said.

I sat on the edge of a guest chair. He sat behind his desk.

"You got me just before I was going to make Mr. Grimes an offer. Mr. Donovan has agreed not to press charges, and Mr. Whitestone has authorized a reward."

Chief Hunter must have called Guy just after I left the Blue Dolphin, I thought.

"I feel really stupid," I said. "I should have realized what happened right away—it's obvious. The Myrick tooth the Whitestones bought from the Sea View Gallery is a fake." I held up a hand to stop him from interrupting. "I've said that it might be phony all along, but I've just realized who created it. Ashley."

"You told me before it could have been produced anywhere, and that she'd never do it because she was a purist."

"I was wrong. I don't know why she did it, but I know she did because of the highlight lines. Ashley's scrimshaw designs always include a too-thick line etched with a tool called an échoppe. It can't possibly be coincidence—the lines are wrong for the designs, so it must be a personal quirk, a signature she can't resist adding. It's a private statement of individuality. Like a tell in poker. No scrim-shander on a whaling ship ever used an échoppe. They only used what was handy, pocket knives, maybe, and sailing needles, that sort of thing. Ashley had an échoppe on her worktable—we saw it. It doesn't fit with her scrimming, yet there it was. As soon as I saw it, I should have realized its significance—the bold, dark highlight lines it created were Ashley's way of branding the nineteenth century-style scrims she created as her own. There is no other reason she'd use a tool that was unavailable to scrimshanders on whaling boats. She wants to be famous, to be successful, but she knows she's not quite ready for prime time."

He rubbed the side of his nose.

"If you look at all of Ashley's designs as a group, you'll see what I'm talking about. I can prepare a visual display and it will be apparent."

"Okay. I'm willing to be convinced."

The layout would demonstrate how the highlight lines of items we thought were fake matched those of objects known to have been etched by Ashley. My expectation was that, taken together, the lines would stand out as if they were lit in neon.

I glanced at the time on my phone. It was about five fifteen. Fred was probably still at work, and Sea View Gallery would still be open. I called him. He understood what I wanted before I finished explaining. I e-mailed photos of the cufflinks and belt buckle, then confirmed that Fred knew how to access the photos we already had of the Homer etching and the three scrimmed teeth in question—the one the Whitestones had purchased as a Myrick from the Sea View Gallery, the Ashley Morse tooth, and the alleged Myrick currently at the Hawaiian museum. I asked Fred to pick up an Ashley Morse bookmark at the gallery and include it, too.

After I was off the phone, I said to Chief Hunter, "Ashley's not the organizer of the scheme. She can't be—she doesn't have the business sense. Ditto Curt."

"Mr. Wilton does."

"Yes," I agreed, "he does. I think Ashley will tell us what's going on. No way could she do a scam like this alone, and no way will she go down alone. And once we clear the brush away about the fraud— we'll have a clear sight line to Frankie's killer." I leaned forward. "I think I know how we can make that happen."

Chief Hunter called someone named Rod and told him to offer Mr. Grimes and Mr. Donovan some coffee and ask them to sit tight for a while longer, then led me past Cathy, now busy at a computer, down the corridor past Interrogation Room One, stopping at a door I'd never noticed before.

The room he led me into was long and narrow, only about eight feet wide, and dimly lit. Opposite the entry door was a window covered with ivory-colored cotton drapes. I could see into the back parking lot through a three-inch gap. Huge two-way mirrors provided unobstructed views into the interrogation rooms on either side. There was a small round table outfitted with two chairs in the center of the space and a watercooler off to one side. Toggles controlled whether audio from the interrogation rooms could be heard in the observation room.

Chief Hunter pointed to a dimmer switch by the door. "You need to keep the lights low in order to see."

Sam was in the room to my left, sitting at a metal table. The other room was empty.

Sam's lips were pressed together, forming one thin line. His arms were crossed in front of his chest. A video recorder mounted on a tripod was aimed at him. The red light wasn't on, so I knew they weren't recording.

"Keep the door shut so no one walking in the corridor will see you," Chief Hunter instructed, then pointed to the transom and showed me how to twirl the attached wand to open or close the slats. "With the slats open, you'll be able to hear conversations in the hall. Ms. Morse will be here in about ten minutes." He reached for the doorknob, then paused. "I'll keep my cell phone handy. If you hear anything that raises a red flag, or if there's a question you think I should ask, text me."

I agreed, and he left.

With the door shut and the slats closed, I called Ty. He was almost home.

I kept my conversation brief, merely telling him that something had come up and I was at the police station helping out, that I didn't know how long I'd be, and that I couldn't wait to see him. "I'll fill you in later. They're about to question people about antiques-related issues, so they think they may need my expertise," I explained.

"About the murder?"

"Not yet. Their focus first is on fraud."

"I won't ask anything else now. You take care of yourself, okay?"

"I will. And Ty, there's leftover Orange Chicken in case you're too hungry to wait for me to get back and broil steaks."

"You're a magnificent woman."

I smiled. "Gee, gosh," I said. "Thanks."

As soon as we hung up, a male police officer I'd never seen before entered Sam's room and sat on a hard-backed chair in the corner. I opened the transom slats and flipped the toggle to listen in.

Sam glared at him, but the officer kept his eyes on Sam's midsection, a neutral zone, and neither man spoke. By squinting, I was able to read the police officer's name tag: D. BROUSSARD. Sam shifted his gaze to the floor. Detective Brownley entered, and Sam looked up and tensed. She stood at the head of the table.

"What's taking so damn long?" Sam asked truculently.

"Sorry for the delay," she said. "We expect to be ready to resume our interview shortly. We've received some very interesting information, and we look forward to hearing what you say about it."

"What information?"

She leaned back and looked at him long and hard. "We're not quite ready to divulge it. We have a few more things to check."

"Check every damn thing you want. I don't give a rat's ass what you check. But let's get it done. I got places to go."

"It shouldn't be too much longer."

"Maybe I should get a lawyer—how'd you like that?"

"It's completely up to you. Would you like to call a lawyer?"

"Hell, no. I don't need no lawyer."

"I'll be back shortly," she said.

"A bunch of hogwash and a waste of time," Sam grumbled under his breath. "How's a man supposed to earn a living, that's what I'd like to know."

She stepped out, leaving the door ajar several inches. The officer noted it but didn't move from his position. I kept my eyes on Sam. The charade I'd helped design was about to begin.

CHAPTER THIRTY-FIVE

s. Morse," Chief Hunter said, his voice wafting up and in through the slats.

I could hear with no problem.

In the next room, Sam looked up, his eyes on the open door.

"Thanks so much," the chief continued. "You've really cooperated above and beyond the call of duty."

"You're welcome," Ashley said.

If all went according to plan, Detective Brownley would quickly escort her away, and the chief would speak his next words while alone in the corridor.

The plan worked.

"We only have a few more things to go over," he said. "We need to talk about Sam Holt's role in all this."

At his words, Sam lurched out of his chair and lunged toward the door. Officer Broussard got there first and blocked his way. He crossed his arms in front of his chest, and Sam stopped in his tracks. The two men stood five feet apart, facing one another.

"What's he saying about me?" Sam demanded.

Officer Broussard didn't speak, and Sam glared at him.

The door in the other interrogation room opened, and Ashley entered, followed by Detective Brownley. I flipped the switch to listen in.

"If you'll have a seat, we won't keep you waiting long," the detective said.

"What's this about?" Ashley asked.

"It will just be a few minutes," Detective Brownley said, smiling. "Thanks again."

She left, and Ashley sat down, choosing a chair that put her back to the cage. After a minute just sitting, she began tapping the tabletop. To my left, Sam sat down again. A muscle in his neck twitched.

Time passed, several minutes at least, before Chief Hunter spoke again.

"Let's see what Mr. Holt has to say now," he said from the hall. "He can't just blow us off, not with Ms. Morse filling in all those blanks."

"Should I go ahead and call Judge Halpern about the warrant?" Detective Brownley asked, out of sight.

"Ask him to stand by," Chief Hunter replied. "We'll need to consult the ADA about the specific charges, but before we do that, let's give Sam a chance to talk turkey."

Sam's fingers curled into fists. "What charges? What's he talking about?"

Officer Broussard stayed silent. It was unnerving. I could feel Sam's tension ratcheting up.

"Mr. Holt, my apologies for keeping you waiting," Chief Hunter said as he entered.

"You're saying there's gonna be charges? What charges?"

"Officer, please start the video recorder," he said.

Officer Broussard pushed a button, and a light glowed red.

"Thank you," the chief told him. "You can go now."

Chief Hunter waited until Officer Broussard left the room. I heard the soft click as the door latched. The chief laid his notepad on the desk.

"Now, Mr. Holt, I have some new information that I'm hoping you can help me understand. First, though, I need to read you this statement explaining your rights."

Chief Hunter slid a sheet of paper toward Sam, who fingered it closer. Sam followed along as the chief read the standard Miranda warning, then asked if he understood his rights.

"Hell, yes, I understand. I already told that woman I didn't want no damn lawyer. Let's just get this done."

"Go ahead and sign the form, then, so we can get going."

He signed the form and slid it back.

"Thank you," Chief Hunter said. "Ms. Morse indicates that you two have been doing business for some time. Is that correct?"

"I told you already, I don't talk about my business."

"Yeah, but that was before. Now that Ms. Morse has spoken to us, I figured that you might want to reconsider. She's been very . . . *open*." He paused, letting the implications sink in. "So . . . she sold you a variety of scrimmed objects. Is that correct?"

Sam glared.

I was impressed with Chief Hunter's acting ability. If I were Sam, it wouldn't in a million years occur to me that Chief Hunter had been thanking Ashley for agreeing to come in—not for answering questions, as he'd implied. I'd be furious that Ashley was throwing me under the bus.

"There's nothing illegal about selling art or artifacts," Chief Hunter said, smiling disarmingly. "Ms. Morse explained how she told you that the objects were either contemporary art or reproductions, right? All legal and aboveboard."

Still Sam stayed quiet.

Chief Hunter looked at his notes, then touched the page with his index finger. "Here's where there might be a little problem. You purchased a repro of a Frederick Myrick scrimmed tooth from her. So far, no problem. But when you resold it to Mr. Donovan as a genuine antique, well, Sam, I'm afraid that at that moment, you crossed a line."

Silence.

"That's fraud," Chief Hunter said, his tone conversational.

"No way," Sam said, and from his crusty tone, I could tell that he was mad as hell.

"No way what?"

"No way this Ms. Morse of yours told you that."

"Where do you say you got the tooth?"

"I'm not telling."

"Ms. Morse says you got it from her."

"Bull."

"She was pretty persuasive," Chief Hunter said.

"I'll tell you what I think. I think you're a damn liar."

Chief Hunter leaned back, taking his time. "If you won't tell me, you won't. Will you at least tell me *why* you won't talk about it?"

"Hell, no. I'm not telling you nothing."

"Maybe I misunderstood," he said, glancing at his notes again. "Maybe she said your contact was Lenny Wilton."

"Don't know him neither."

"Sure you do."

Sam fixed his eyes on him. "Prove it."

I was watching Ashley rat-a-tat-tat the table when Chief Hunter stepped into the observation room. He glanced at her, then jerked his head toward Sam.

"What do you think?" he asked me.

"I think he'll hold his ground. You don't seem to have any leverage."

"Yeah." He looked at Ashley for a moment. "Once I get that layout of yours, I'll ask her some questions about it. In the meantime, I want to consult with the ADA. You all right to hang tight for a while?"

I wanted to see Ty. I wanted to go home. I wanted to check in with Zoë. I was bone weary. More than anything else, though, I was curious.

"Sure," I said.

Fred called to let me know that he'd just e-mailed the layout.

"Were you able to include a bookmark?" I asked.

"Yeah. I picked one randomly. It has the same dark line."

"Great."

"Suzanne was there using a scrimming machine. I've never seen one in action before. It was pretty impressive."

"Was she making belt buckles?"

"Yeah—and I gotta tell you, they didn't look as cheesy as I expected."

Given that Fred was an antiques snob, that tepid praise was, in effect, an over-the-moon endorsement.

"She told me that she'd heard from Curt that you'd ordered a gross," Fred added.

I was glad to learn who Curt's mysterious business associate was—he was using Greg's scrimming machine—and I nearly rolled my eyes as I recalled his cloak-and-dagger attitude, given that evidently he had forgotten to tell Suzanne, Greg's employee, that his involvement was supposed to be secret. Hard on the heels of that first reaction was disgust. I was stunned at Curt's effrontery.

"Jeez, Fred . . . what I told him was that I'd let him know if I wanted any, and if so, how many, after I tested them. I explained we only sold fossil ivory, and that the scrimming had to be executed perfectly."

"I guess he's an optimist," Fred said.

"Or he knows the material is real."

I opened the file Fred had sent. As expected, seeing so many examples on one surface, the highlight lines leapt off the page. I forwarded it to Chief Hunter and settled in to wait.

Sam's eyes were closed, and he was very still. In the other room, Ashley's nerves were showing. Her foot jitterbugged on the floor, and her fingers played an imaginary keyboard on her thighs.

I closed the slats in the transom and called Ty again, then Zoë. Ty said he was exhausted from the drive and about to take a shower. Zoë said she was exhausted from the stress and about to have something to eat. I told them both I missed them and would be home as soon as I could.

I had nothing to do. I reached my hand up to rub my shoulders, hoping to ease the tension that had turned my muscles into thin ridges of steel, without noticeable success.

Time passed.

Sam shifted his position, his eyes still closed.

Ashley began pacing.

Wes texted me, my phone's vibration catching my attention.

"Lenny W worth over a mil. In Bos meeting all day—alibi solid."

"Do police know?" I texted back.

"Yup," Wes replied.

Interesting, I thought, glancing at Ashley. Suddenly, Ashley threw her head back, her fine blond hair splaying out like a lion's mane. Her pacing continued, but faster, ever faster, until it took her only seconds to cover the length of the room. She strode back and forth, back and forth, over and over again, like a big cat in a small cage.

CHAPTER THIRTY-SIX

C hief Hunter entered the room where Ashley continued her agitated pacing. He looked tired. Ashley's eyes didn't leave his face as he got settled at the table and activated the video recorder. She barely blinked.

"Sorry for the delay," he said. He thanked her again, stated the date and time, then slid the Miranda form toward her. "I'm going to read you your rights and ask that you sign a form indicating that you understand. Okay?"

"Sure," she said. She listened, then signed the form without reading it.

"Take a look at this," he asked, showing her a printout of the layout Fred had prepared.

Ashley picked up the display of her work, then looked at Chief Hunter.

"You're very talented," he said.

"I made this tooth. And this bookmark," she said, pointing. "Is that what you mean?"

"Did you scrim or etch the other objects?" Chief Hunter asked.

She didn't reply.

"I think you did . . . and I think you know why I'm asking you to confirm it."

She clamped her jaw tight and didn't speak.

He stared at her, keeping the pressure on, his expression severe and unforgiving.

"Guy Whitestone and the ADA have agreed not to prosecute you for the fraud you are alleged to have perpetrated regarding the counterfeit Myrick tooth," he said. "That one." He used his pencil's eraser to indicate the tooth.

Ashley licked her lips. Her eyes stayed on the layout. "I didn't commit fraud."

"You scrimmed this tooth. It was sold as a Myrick." He shrugged. "According to the ADA, that's fraud."

"I scrimmed it as a repro. That's not fraud."

Well done, I thought. He'd just won her admission that she'd scrimmed the tooth.

"You're saying Mr. Donovan knowingly marketed a repro as a genuine Myrick?"

She licked her lips. "I don't know what he did."

"Sure you do. You saw the tooth on display at his gallery."

She dragged her eyes from the display Fred had prepared to Chief Hunter's face.

"The ADA is willing to work with you," he said. "If you tell us what happened. All of it. The whole deal. The truth, the whole truth, and nothing but the truth."

She licked her lips again. "I didn't do anything wrong."

"Someone did."

"It wasn't my idea," she said.

"Whose idea was it?"

She shook her head.

"On some level, you must have felt proud of yourself," he said. "Your work was good enough to fool people."

"Pride!" she said. "I didn't feel proud. I felt ashamed. I hated doing it. I *hated* it."

He nodded slowly. "I can see that. You only did it for the money."

"Exactly," she said, her anger melting away. She looked years younger, lost, and vulnerable, like a child who's lost her parents at the fair. Her eyes filled again, and she looked aside. "I didn't want to do it. I had no choice. He made me."

"Who?"

She covered her face with her hands and began crying in earnest. She moaned, then moaned again, a sound of hopelessness, all while weeping as if her heart had broken beyond repair.

Was it Lenny? I asked myself. I texted, "Ask her if it's Lenny."

His phone vibrated on the wooden table. He read my message, then spoke quietly. "Ms. Morse?" he said, then repeated it, his voice a little louder as he tried to penetrate her sorrow. "Was it Mr. Wilton?"

She shook her head and continued crying, her shoulders quivering as if she were chilled.

Chief Hunter sat and watched her, his expression thoughtful.

Greg said he had no plans or desire to expand his gallery, yet a business without growth was doomed. If a company isn't growing faster than the rate of inflation, by definition, it's shrinking.

Ashley had no business sense.

Greg did. And if the organizer wasn't Ashley, Lenny, Curt, or Sam—by process of elimination, it had to be Greg.

"Ask her if it's Greg," I texted the chief.

He read my message, then said, "Ms. Morse? Please give me the name."

She groaned, still weeping. She lowered her hands. Her face was splotched with red. Her cheeks were shiny with wetness. She looked wan.

"I'm afraid I need to insist," he said. "The agreement not to prosecute you requires your cooperation."

She stared at him but seemed to be seeing through him, past the here and now, into the bleak future.

"Is it Greg Donovan, Ms. Morse? Is it Mr. Donovan who commissioned the fakes?"

"Yes," she whispered.

I wondered if Ashley would clam up again as Chief Hunter started pushing for specifics, but she didn't. The lid was off, and that was that. She tearfully detailed her arrangement with Greg, blaming the ignorant and uncultured public for her lack of commercial success.

By her own admission, she'd created the designs for contemporary scrimmed objects such as bookmarks, cufflinks, and belt buckles; she'd scrimmed four fake Myrick teeth; and she'd prepared the metal plate replicating Winslow Homer's *The Herring Net*. All told, Greg had paid her fifteen thousand dollars. She insisted that other than the one fake tooth the Whitestones had purchased and the bookmarks stocked by Sea View Gallery, she had no knowledge of where anything else ended up.

According to Ashley, Greg had promised her that no one would ever know of her involvement. Creating repros was embarrassing, she said, for an artist of her caliber, but it wasn't illegal. She felt ashamed, but that was all. It was only later, after she learned that he'd been selling the repros as originals, that the magnitude of what she'd done had sunk in. She'd been horrified.

I kept wanting to look away. Watching her confess was excruciating and depressing, like witnessing the end of hope. As her story unfolded, it became clear that she was a pawn, not a leader. It had been Greg's idea, and it was he who executed it, apparently without remorse or even a second thought. I wondered how he slept at night.

When she'd finished, she sat huddled over, rocking a little as if she were nursing a bad stomachache.

Chief Hunter thanked her, turned off the video recorder, and stepped into the observation room. I listened in as he called Detective Brownley and asked her to escort Ashley to another room, then bring in Greg.

"Do you think she's telling the truth?" Chief Hunter asked me.

"I think so. I think she found herself boxed in, convinced that there was no way out. She might have felt horrified, but since Greg is the keeper of her dreams, she must have decided that she had to do as he asked. If he'd withdrawn his support, she'd have lost everything. It's a horrible position to be in—dependent and powerless."

Detective Brownley appeared and led a deflated Ashley out. Within minutes, she brought a slouching Greg in.

Greg's normally buoyant demeanor was gone. He looked irritable and worn-out. His ice blond hair needed combing. His tie was loosened. The corners of his mouth pointed down.

Chief Hunter thanked me again and left for the interrogation room where Sam still sat.

He turned on the video camera and cleared his throat, waiting for Sam to look up. Sam looked exhausted. Purple-black smudges had appeared beneath his eyes.

"Mr. Holt . . . I'm going to ask you a straight question. I'm hoping you'll give me a straight answer."

Sam's mouth twisted into an ugly sneer, undeterred by the chief's newly minted man-to-man approach. He lowered his chin until it nearly touched his chest. His body language and expression shouted, "Drop dead."

"Mr. Holt, you never sold Greg Donovan the Myrick tooth, did you?"

"Ask him. He'll tell you."

"He got you to lie for him."

Sam scraped back his chair and stood up. "I've been thinking during the time you've kept me here waiting on your convenience, thank you very much, that I've been a fool to stay. Talk about patsies. I don't know nothing about nothing illegal, and I'm not telling you nothing about my business. You gonna arrest me, do it. Otherwise, I'm outta here."

Sam didn't look back or hesitate. He left. The chief punched the OFF button on the camera, then followed him out.

I sat and waited, monitoring the time. Seven minutes after Sam took the bull by the horns, Chief Hunter entered the room where Greg sat, from the look of it, brooding.

"You know, Chief," Greg said as Chief Hunter pushed the RECORD button on the video recorder, "I think we've reached the point where even a good citizen who wants to help the police might tell you to go take a hike."

"I understand that this hasn't been as speedy a process as any of us would like, but it *is* a process."

Greg sighed heavily and glanced at the camera's glowing light. "You've read me my rights. You've told me I'm not under arrest. I've said I didn't want a lawyer. What now?"

"You've been implicated in a scheme to defraud investors and collectors, and I have some questions about it."

Greg's mouth opened, then closed. He sat up straight. "Implicated? By whom?"

"By Ms. Morse. She said you commissioned a counterfeit Homer plate and several phony Myrick teeth."

"That's absurd! I'm the victim here, remember? Sam sold *me* the fake!"

"That's what I'm trying to sort out. Right now all I've got is a he said/she said blame game—it's your word against hers. Can you think of any way to corroborate your side?"

"And Sam's not talking, right?"

"He will."

Greg thought for a moment, then shrugged. "Since you're telling me that she confessed to committing fraud, I'd suggest that you consider your source rather than accuse me of wrongdoing."

"Then let's start with legal activities. Did she create scrims for you to use with a scrimming machine?"

"Sure. I bought a scrimming machine from Lenny Wilton to use with Ashley Morse designs—and I rent the machine out to other people." He opened his palms. "So what? Even if some of those repros are good enough so that some people might try to market them as antiques—what has that got to do with me?"

"Did you ever instruct Ashley Morse to hand-scrim teeth in the style of Myrick? Or suggest she do so?"

"Of course not!"

"Did you ever instruct Ashley Morse to etch a metal plate in the style of Homer? Or suggest she do so?"

"No."

Chief Hunter nodded, then shrugged. "He said . . . she said." He stood up. "I'll be back."

"How much longer do you expect me to sit here as if I were a—," Greg said, breaking off when Chief Hunter held up a hand.

"Right now, Mr. Donovan, you're looking at fraud, grand larceny, and maybe racketeering charges," Chief Hunter said. He kept his eyes on Greg's for a three-count, then added, "Felonies, Mr. Donovan. Felonies."

"Do I need a lawyer?"

"Your call. Do you want a lawyer?"

Greg stared at him for a long moment, then said, "Yes."

"He makes a helluva case," Chief Hunter said to me as he stared at Greg through the one-way mirror. I stood next to him doing the same. "Maybe he's telling the truth. I'd love to get a search warrant for his gallery, but there's no way I could based solely on an alleged co-conspirator's testimony. I need corroboration of Ms. Morse's story."

I saw his point. *Lenny,* I thought. I looked up at him. "Sam didn't deny knowing Lenny. Lenny tried to sell the fake Myrick tooth, or one just like it, to Harlow's, allegedly for a friend. I asked him who his friend is and he refused to tell me. He said that when the police could link it to Frankie's murder, he'd tell them. Has anyone done that? Has anyone asked him?"

He thought for a moment, then said, "Let me check."

He went to a wall phone, and I listened as he consulted Detective Brownley. No one, it seemed, had asked.

"You take Curt Grimes," he instructed her, "and focus on his business dealings with Greg Donovan. I'll call Lenny Wilton." To me, he added, "Follow me." His demeanor was resolute and urgent as he led the way to his office. "Just like before, I want you here in case I need help with technical questions."

He didn't.

He told Lenny he was calling on official business, and as such was taping the call, and Lenny said that he was glad to help. I stayed still, mindful of how sounds carry on a speakerphone.

Lenny repeated what he'd told me: that his friend really wanted privacy and, without one heck of a good reason, he wasn't going to reveal his name. "Can you connect that tooth or my trying to sell it to the murder?" he asked.

"We believe the tooth is central to the murder," Chief Hunter replied, keeping to the literal truth.

"How?"

"I'm not sure yet."

"When you figure it out, let me know."

"I'm asking for your help."

"Sorry," Lenny said.

The call ended cordially.

Chief Hunter said, "Interesting," maybe to me, maybe to himself. He called Detective Brownley, asked for an update, then hung up and said to me, "No surprise. Grimes says he works with Donovan—and lots of other people—and doesn't know anything about fakes." He shook his head. "Any ideas on another collaborator?"

I stared out the window, thinking. "Sam," I said, looking back at him. "He knows where he got the Winslow Homer etching he's trying to sell to Maddie Whitestone. Maybe he'll tell you who's behind it."

"Why would he?"

"I can't imagine."

Chief Hunter nodded. "What have you discovered about the etching?"

"We think it's a phony. We're consulting a Homer expert on Monday."

"Any ideas how to get him to talk? He wouldn't have to go into details. I just need the name."

I stared across the room. "You know how I said before that you don't have any leverage?"

"What about it?"

"You do. You have the ability to give him something he'll value—your ironclad commitment never to talk to him again," I said, smiling. "Promise him that."

"It can't hurt to try," Chief Hunter said, grinning. He tapped the SPEAKER button, then dialed. Sam answered on the first ring. "Don't hang up—it's Chief Hunter. I need to know how you got the Winslow Homer etching you offered to Mrs. Whitestone. I just need the name of the person you got it from. I don't need any details. I never will. Just the name."

"I already told you I'm not talking."

"If you give me the name, I'll be able to stop bugging you. Permanently."

He snorted. "You say that now."

"It's a promise."

"You think I trust you?" he said, his tone making it clear he never had and never would.

"No, but I think you know a low-risk deal when you hear one. What's the worst that can happen? I'm lying, and I'll call you again. Maybe, though, just maybe, I'm telling you the truth. What have you got to lose by giving me the name? Nothing. And you might gain something you want—me out of your hair."

There was a long silence. Then Sam said, "Greg Donovan gave me the damn etching," and he hung up.

Chief Hunter replaced the receiver and double-tapped his desk. "Now I can talk to the judge," he said, smiling.

"Do you have enough to get a warrant?" I asked.

He glanced at his watch. "It's late. I'm sorry to have kept you here so long."

I got the message and didn't ask anything else. According to the big round clock mounted over Cathy's desk, it was two minutes to nine.

What a waste, I thought, as I drove home. A waste of Ashley's talent. A waste of Greg's well-established business. I was glad to know the origin of those scrimmed and etched objects, but I didn't feel any sense of closure. The most pressing questions remained unanswered— who killed Frankie, and why?

CHAPTER THIRTY-SEVEN

I parked in back of Ty's SUV, turned off my headlights, and leaned over the steering wheel, resting my head on the cold leather, worn to a nub.

I sat back and looked at my little house, my home, through fog and drizzle. I felt the familiar rush of gratitude at being able to come home to a place I loved. I got out and stretched, then saw that Ty was standing at the door watching me.

"Hey," he said. "Come on in out of the rain."

"Hey, yourself," I said, walking toward him. "It's not raining that much. It feels good. Fresh."

"Sounds like you had quite a day," he said, holding the door for me, allowing me to pass by.

"You have no idea. Pretty much, I'm reeling."

He opened his arms, and I stepped into his embrace. I stood there listening to his heart beating, my face buried in the flannel of his shirt, enveloped by his love.

"Hungry?" he asked.

"Yes," I said. "I want soup."

"Do you have any?"

"No."

"Am I going out to the store?"

I leaned back and gazed into his eyes, then touched his cheek, my blues fading away.

"Thanks, but no. I think Zoë will have some—and I want to bring her up to date. That's the wrong way to put it. I don't want to, but I know she'd want me to. Oh, Ty, it's all so tragic and sordid and sad."

He raised my chin with his finger and kissed me, then kissed me again, then stepped back to look deep into my eyes. "Drink or tea?"

"A Lemon Drop, please. If ever there was a dark night in which I needed some silver light, tonight's the night."

"I'll make a shaker-full. Zoë will probably want one, too."

"Did you eat?" I asked, following him into the kitchen. "I was supposed to grill you a steak."

"I'm fine. I ate everything in your refrigerator."

I smiled. "Good."

I sat in Zoë's kitchen, stirring steaming chicken noodle soup, waiting for it to cool off. Ty sat next to me.

"How does this relate to Frankie?" Zoë asked after I explained what the police had learned about the fraud.

"I don't know. Maybe it doesn't."

She nodded and played with the stem of her martini glass. "My birthday's coming up," she said. "I don't feel much like a party."

"I don't blame you. We'll have one anyway, though—I insist on celebrating the day you were born."

Zoë reached her hand across the table to touch my arm.

"Frankie wanted to bring the cake," I said.

"What a sweet kid he turned out to be, you know?" Zoë said, staring down into her drink.

"Yeah," I said, and then we sat in melancholy silence until my soup was gone.

Chief Hunter showed up just before eleven the next morning and pulled me out of the tag sale.

"We got the warrant for Donovan's house, gallery, and car," he said, "to look for the etching plate, forged designs, scrimmed objects, business records, and scrimming machines and tools. I need your help to ID the items."

I grabbed my tote bag, told Cara I was leaving, and was out the door at a trot.

The police tackled Greg's car first. It was parked in the Rocky Point police station lot.

"Did you keep him here all night?" I asked Chief Hunter, astounded at the thought.

"Yes."

I waited for him to explain, but he didn't. The single word hung in the air like a threat. I glanced at him, but he wasn't looking in my direction. He was watching Griff.

Using tools I thought were illegal to possess, Griff opened the car in about five seconds flat. Chief Hunter turned to me and must have seen something in my expression, because he said, "According to the warrant, we don't need either his permission or his key."

Officers Griffin and Meade crawled inside the car and peered under it and poked through the upholstery with a probe. In the white glare of the bright late-summer sun, the silver metallic paint shimmered. The glove compartment contained only the owner's manual and a small ice scraper. Detective Brownley ran a sensor over the inside door panels. Chief Hunter examined the inside of the trunk. In addition to the spare tire and jack, there was a set of flares, a wool blanket heaped off to one side, and a half-full bag of kitty litter, emergency supplies for winter—the flares to get attention, the blanket for warmth, and the kitty litter for traction in snow. He tapped the sides and lifted the carpet. They found nothing related to art or fraud in, under, or on the car.

Chief Hunter issued hushed instructions to his team, telling me to ride with him. When we arrived at Greg Donovan's beachfront Colonial, the chief entered first, flipped on the overhead lights, put on plastic gloves, and warned me not to touch anything.

Greg's house was decorated in a traditional Americana style with rag rugs, maple furniture, speckled pottery, and folk art. To my eye, it looked stilted, not homey, as if a decorator had styled it for a magazine, not for real people who actually lived there.

"I want us to do a quick once-over," Chief Hunter stated. "I expect the objects we're looking for will be at the gallery, so consider this a preliminary sweep and notate any areas you think require more attention later."

I watched as the police examined the contents of drawers, cabinets, closets, custom-built shelving in the cellar, and trunks stored in the attic. To no one's surprise, they didn't find anything suspicious anywhere.

Our little convoy drove to Sea View Gallery.

Suzanne Jardin greeted us. She had straight chestnut-colored hair that hung almost to her waist. Her eyes were brown. She wore a red dress and knee-high black boots.

"Hi, Josie," she said as I approached the desk with Chief Hunter. Her eyes opened wide as I introduced them. She glanced at him, then looked back at me. "Greg called around eight to ask me to open up, but he didn't say why. Do you know what's going on?" she asked me.

"No, not really," I said.

Chief Hunter explained the search warrant and asked if Suzanne had any information that might help us locate the items listed.

Her mouth opened, but no sound came out. She cleared her throat. "Me? No. I just work here. Part-time. I mean, the scrimming machine is in the workroom at the back. There are tools there, too. I guess the financial records are on the computer. I don't know."

Chief Hunter looked toward the rear. "What's back there?" he asked.

"The office, a little storage room, and the workroom. Across from the workroom is the kitchen and the bathroom."

"Where do you do framing?" I asked.

"In the basement," she said.

Officer Meade began a methodical search of the office. Officer Griffin began searching in the storage room, and I accompanied Chief Hunter into the workroom.

The scrimming machine attached with vises to the worktable appeared similar to the ones I'd seen at Lenny's. Scrimmed objects sat in neat stacks nearby. An architectural file cabinet contained scores of prints, silkscreens, and etchings, none an Ashley Morse original or repro.

Narrow stairs near the kitchen led to an unfinished basement room. Uncovered sixty-watt bulbs dangled from electric-tape-wrapped wires.

Settling cracks covered the concrete walls and floor like spiderwebs. The furnace and water heater stood in a corner. It was eerie. Two doors, one open, one closed, were on the left. The open door led to a fluorescent-lighted framing room. It was bright and cheerful. The Sheetrocked walls were painted lemon yellow. A huge worktable sat in the center. Work lights clamped to all four sides provided ample illumination. Officer Griffin finished searching the storage room and joined us downstairs just as we were looking through the racks of mats and samples of wood that covered one long wall. A storage cabinet contained cutting and measuring tools, wood, pieces of glass, and sheets of Plexiglas. The table was clear. Nothing was in process or waiting to be framed.

Chief Hunter asked Griff to run up and ask Suzanne if she had the key to the locked door. She didn't, and Griff reported that she said she'd never seen the door open and knew nothing about it. He'd searched through the desk but hadn't found any keys.

They used a crowbar to gain access.

A full-sized printing press was positioned against the back wall. A copper plate sat on a table across the room.

"Look," I said, pointing to it. "It's *The Herring Net*."

"Can you tell if it's a fake?" Chief Hunter asked.

"Probably," I said, "but not here, not without tools and equipment."

Griff tugged on a tan metal cabinet's handle. "This one's locked," he said.

"Open it," Chief Hunter instructed.

Griff wedged the crowbar into the space between the two doors and snapped them apart. A laptop sat on a shelf. Next to it sat a digital camera and cell phone.

"Sweet," Chief Hunter said, holding up the phone so we could see it. Laminated tape affixed to the back of the unit read: SAM. "Can you believe it? He labeled it."

"In a kind of creepy way, that's really organized," I said.

"You gotta love it," he remarked.

The evidence was damning. I couldn't believe that Greg could have been so devious—or so stupid.

———

Back in the Rocky Point police observation room, I watched Greg for several seconds before I sat down. Even through the two-way mirror, I could see the red rimming his eyes and the worry lines wrinkling his forehead. A young man in a brown suit sat nearby, a yellow-lined pad in front of him. *His lawyer,* I thought. He looked tired, too. The video camera was on. Chief Hunter sat at the head of the table. Chief Hunter pushed a legal-looking document encased in a blue cover across the table.

"Mr. Davis," he said to the young man, "we've just executed this warrant." To Greg he added, "We've searched your car, gallery, and home."

Greg glanced at the document but didn't pick it up. Mr. Davis did. He scowled as he read it.

"What were you looking for?" Greg asked.

"Evidence of fraud."

"Fraud," Greg said. "That's a good one. Did you find anything?"

"Yes. Yes, Mr. Donovan, we did. Here's an inventory."

He slid another document toward him. Greg kept his eyes on the chief as he reached for the paper. He scanned the listing, then slid it toward his lawyer and looked up again. "Why didn't you just ask? Sure I have bookmarks, teeth, etchings, and a printing press. I own a gallery. I market artists' and artisans' wares, lots of them reproductions. So what?"

"Did you notice the laptop and cell phone on the list?" Chief Hunter asked.

"Please," the lawyer said, raising his hand to stop the questioning. He placed his hand on Greg's arm and whispered something in his ear.

Greg replied in a hushed tone, then nodded and looked back at the chief. "Mitch here says to tell you the truth. I want you to know that's all I've done—everything I've told you is the truth. Did I notice the laptop and cell phone on the list? Sure. I keep some private records on the laptop and lock it up so my staff can't access it." He shrugged. "I use disposable phones to help me keep business relationships separate and straight. What's the point? You don't like how I do business?"

Chief Hunter looked at him as if he thought he might be joking. "Let's start with the Homer etchings."

Greg seemed completely at ease. "What about them?"

"They're fakes."

"They are? Then I've been snookered. They were consigned to me by Ashley Morse."

Chief Hunter nodded sagely as if he'd expected that reaction. Maybe he had. I hadn't. I was astonished to see Greg keep his cool.

"I don't know," Chief Hunter said. "They'll be proven to be counterfeit—and we found them in your place, not hers."

"Have you looked in hers?"

"Can you give me a reason to?"

The lawyer raised his hand again, stopping Greg from answering. They whispered back and forth; then Mitch Davis said, "Mr. Donovan is eager to answer, but I'm hesitant to allow him to say things that, while true, implicate others."

"He's your client, Mr. Davis, but from where I sit, a little coopera- tion wouldn't be a bad thing along about now," Chief Hunter said, shrugging. "Plus, if he's telling the truth, it's a no-brainer—and if it can't be proven, we can't act on it. What's the downside?"

Mr. Davis whispered to Greg again, tapping his finger on his note- pad, making a strong point. Greg listened and nodded, then looked across the table at Chief Hunter. "I can prove that Ashley consigned the objects to me as antiques. I've got her signature on consignment forms." He took his cell phone from his pocket. "Shall I call my gal- lery? I can tell Suzanne where to find the paperwork. She can fax the docs to you."

"You mean these?" Chief Hunter asked, sliding a manila file to- ward him. "We found these forms in your office."

Greg's eyes darkened. "Of course," he said. "I forgot you went through everything." He opened the file and thumbed through the papers. "Yes, these are the forms I meant. As you can see here, Ashley Morse signed a consignment agreement for each object or lot." He held up a sheet of paper. "The etched plate is listed here. See? It's de- scribed as a Homer original. The form authorizes me to sell it or to print etchings and sell them."

"I'll be asking her about these forms."

Greg shrugged again. "Please do."

Maybe he isn't stupid after all, I thought. He might just have crafted a foolproof plan to lay the entire blame on Ashley.

Chief Hunter left Greg and came to see me.

"What do you think?" he asked me. "Why would she sign those forms? It puts her in the crosshairs."

"Because she has absolutely no business head and Greg was paying her good money. Probably she didn't even read what she signed. She did the same thing when you asked her to sign that she understood her rights. She didn't even glance at it." I shrugged. "My dad made me promise never to sign something I haven't read. Most people never met my dad." I paused. "Probably Greg simply told her to sign it, and she did."

"Smart man, your dad," Chief Hunter said.

I smiled and nodded. "What do you do now?"

"Call Judge Halpern about another warrant."

I glanced at Greg. "What do you do about him?"

"Get the details of how his operation ran, clarify the whereabouts of the other 'originals,'" he said, punctuating the air with finger-quotes, "and determine who else, if anyone, was involved."

"You don't need me for any of that. May I go back to work?" I asked.

"No."

"How come?"

"'Cause Judge Halpern's going to say yes."

CHAPTER THIRTY-EIGHT

W e had a deal," Ashley said from just inside her front door. Her cheeks were flushed.

"We still do—if you told the truth," Chief Hunter replied. "If not, by the terms of your plea bargain, the agreement's null and void."

She looked down at the warrant Chief Hunter had handed her. "I can't believe this. What are you looking for?"

"Mr. Donovan showed us the forms you signed, consigning goods to him. There's no mention of repros. We're looking for counterfeit objects and designs—including the Myrick tooth that's missing from the Whitestones' collection."

"Are you saying that you think I sold Greg fakes *and* stole the Myrick tooth?" she asked, growing pale.

"We're investigating that possibility, yes."

She began breathing fast, her fingers gripping her smock. "If he sold my objects as real—that's his business. I had nothing to do with the selling. Nothing."

"Do you recall signing the consignment documents?" Chief Hunter asked.

"I don't know—I sign lots of things for him."

"This one explicitly states that the objects you consigned were authentic antiques."

Ashley didn't respond. She stood immobile, her chest heaving. Her eyes moved to my face as if she were seeing me for the first time.

"What are you doing here?" she asked.

"She's helping us out," Chief Hunter said.

She turned to him. "If you're trying to humiliate me, you're succeeding."

"That's not our intention. Please step back so we can enter."

She crossed her arms and pursed her lips but did as he instructed.

"Officer Meade, will you please stay with Ms. Morse?"

Ashley sidled to her worktable, then stood in icy silence, as rigid as a post, her teeth pressing into her bottom lip and her hands clenched into tight fists by her thighs.

I stood beside Chief Hunter in the center of the living room, then followed him as he walked from room to room. The options where her designs and objects could be secreted were limited. Open shelving built into the worktable provided space for works in progress and spare materials, and a bookcase in the bedroom housed partially scrimmed teeth, but there were no storage or filing cabinets anywhere. In fact, the house was austere. There were no photographs, knickknacks, or personal touches. It looked and felt more like a utilitarian efficiency unit in a boardinghouse, the kind rented by the week to transients, rather than a young woman's home.

In the bathroom, everything—the floor, walls, fixtures, and ceiling—was white. She used only a clear liner as her shower curtain.

The small galley kitchen was equally minimalist. There were standard-issue discount-store sets of dinner dishes, flatware, and glasses. She had a five-piece set of aluminum pots and pans, a toaster, and a Mr. Coffee machine. The refrigerator contained half a head of iceberg lettuce, an unopened jar of yellow mustard and another of grape jelly, and three English muffins.

In the bedroom, a chipped pine dresser stood against an inside wall. There was no mirror or chair. Nothing hung on the walls. A double bed rested on a metal frame—there was no adornment. The bed was unmade. There were no decorative pillows. The dresser was haphazardly stuffed with underwear, socks, T-shirts, and jeans. One dress, a short-sleeved, to-the-knee black sheath, hung in the closet.

I watched as Chief Hunter peered in back of the worktable and under the love seat. He removed drawers, tapped walls, wiggled fireplace bricks, removed the toilet tank cover, examined ice trays for foreign objects and soup cans for false bottoms, and sought out secret cupboards and cubbyholes hidden in the wood flooring and closets.

He walked the rooms slowly one last time, perusing every inch of space, then said, "That's it."

"Are you satisfied?" she asked through clenched teeth.

"I'm going through your car."

"No."

"Read the warrant," he said. "Do you want to give me the key?"

She shook her head slowly, as if she were trying to shake off the drowsy residue of interrupted sleep. He didn't ask again. She stood at the doorway and watched as we approached her vehicle. It wasn't locked. He did a quick once-over of the inside, then popped the trunk. Wedged into the space were a large blue plastic storage box and a cardboard tube, the kind used to ship posters.

Chief Hunter opened the tube. Inside was a rolled-up print of *The Herring Net*.

"Is this the same as the one you're appraising for Mrs. White-stone?" he asked me.

"It looks like it. I can't tell for sure without comparing them and testing the paper and ink."

He nodded, eased it back into the tube, and then bagged it, tube and all, in a jumbo evidence bag. I glanced at Ashley. She was gripping the doorjamb as if she might collapse without its support.

He opened the storage box and extracted an archival file folder. In the folder were eight sheets of onionskin paper, separated from one another by slip sheets. Six showed traced drawings of typical Myrick design elements—a compass, a waving banner, a fishtail border, sails. One showed the design on the missing Myrick tooth, telltale highlight line and all. Looking at it, I was struck by how clever she had been to combine an exact copy of Myrick's rendering of the *Susan* with several other known Myrick elements. The overall design was evocative of his work, but because it wasn't an exact copy of any extant tooth, an appraiser might find it credible that it was a previously un-discovered example, not a fake. The last sheet showed a similar compilation of elements, this one featuring the ship *Ann* to create the illustration that had been, apparently, scrimmed onto the tooth currently under review in Hawaii.

"I was asked to help a museum in Honolulu appraise a tooth at-tributed to Myrick," I whispered, explaining my role. "That's the design. I'll bet you dollars to doughnuts that Ashley scrimmed the teeth and handed them off to Greg, who handed them off to Sam, and it's he who arranged for their sale."

"You said that Mr. Yamamoto got the tooth from a Boston art gallery. Would Mr. Holt have contacts at a place like that?"

"I doubt it. My guess is that Greg orchestrated it all. Like calling Maddie about the Homer etching. No way does Sam read *Antiques Insights* magazine—the idea had to come from someone else. Sam said that a guy he knew took the photos. You should ask your tech guys to check the camera we found at Greg's gallery. I bet the photos are in Greg's camera."

He nodded, made a note, and then asked me to e-mail him Mr. Yamamoto's contact information. He transferred the items to his SUV and walked toward Ashley.

"You see what we're taking," he said. "I'll write out a receipt."

"You have no right . . . I created repros, that's all."

"Do you have any information that will help us locate the missing tooth, Ms. Morse?"

"No," she said.

"I want to remind you again of the plea bargain arrangement you signed off on. Your active assistance is required." He stared at her for several seconds. "If I find out you're withholding information, you'll be charged with fraud and grand larceny. *And* obstruction."

She raised her chin defiantly. She looked both indignant and apprehensive, the very picture of a damsel in distress.

My first thought as we headed back was how disappointed Wes was going to be that I didn't get any photos for him.

My second thought was of Frankie. There he'd been, living his life, doing his work, staying on the right side of the law, while all around him people were skirting the line or crossing it full on.

My third thought was of Ashley. How could she have done such a thing? I recalled something she'd said to Maddie the day they met at Sea View. She'd said that she considered herself a storyteller as much as a scrimshander, and since her designs memorialized a moment in time, she felt an enormous obligation to communicate the truth. I'd loved that view of art. Her betrayal was profound—she was a traitor to her calling.

I turned to look at the ocean. Past the dunes and the wispy tall grass blowing in the light breeze, frothy whitecaps dotted the midnight blue water. I spotted tiny twinkling lights far out to sea. A ship was on the move.

My fourth thought was to wonder about the missing Myrick tooth. Facts came to me.

Ashley created repros.

Greg committed fraud. Maybe she knew his intention all along, maybe not.

The only object stolen from the Whitestones' lighthouse was the Myrick tooth.

The police had just finished searching Ashley's house and car, and the tooth hadn't been found. It hadn't been found in Greg's possession either. Of course, in the days that followed the theft, either one of them could have stashed it anywhere—it could have been buried in the backyard, shipped to a friend in a distant state, or secreted in a safe deposit box or mini storage unit.

I couldn't imagine that either Ashley or Greg would have disposed of it. An artist with an ego the size of Ashley's would never destroy work she'd slaved over and loved, and an opportunist like Greg would have been loath to miss the chance to double dip by reselling it. Yet as I thought of it, I began to wonder if I was right—wouldn't it have been smarter for them to cut their losses and destroy the fake tooth? *No.* Destroying this one counterfeit tooth wouldn't keep the police from discovering other fakes. In order to totally eliminate the risk of exposure, they would have had to track down every object they'd sold, an impossible task in a business where resales were common and frequently anonymous. Pandora's box had been opened, and there was no turning back. But some mythology experts believed that at the bottom of Pandora's box lay hope—had Greg optimistically expected the to-do to blow over?

I looked at Chief Hunter. As if he could feel my eyes on him, he glanced in my direction, met my eyes for a moment, and smiled.

"A penny for your thoughts," he said.

I looked back out over the ocean. "I'm feeling sad."

"Why?"

"Mostly, 'cause of Frankie." I sighed. "Also, not like it matters compared to Frankie, but I hate thinking how an artist like Ashley has wasted her talent by creating bogus objects. And Greg—his business seemed to suit him so perfectly." I sighed again, then shook my head a little to dispel my gloom. "It's awful—and it's awful in a lot of different ways. For them, for the people they cheated, for all the honest artists and dealers trying to make a go of it." I sighed again. "I understand how people become cynics."

"Why aren't you?" he asked.

The distant lights I'd seen far out to sea only a minute earlier were gone. The ship had passed, or we'd passed it.

"My dad, I guess. He once told me that the most common reason people become cynical is that they're surprised by an unexpected turn of events, a lie, or a betrayal. If you expect the best but prepare for the worst, the only surprises you'll ever experience are good ones."

"Yeah," he said, and from his sardonic tone and the tension that tightened his jaw, I wondered what example had come into his mind. "Easy to say. Hard to do."

"Not so hard, not really," I said. "At this point in my career, having worked with feuding heirs, divorcing couples, lying dealers, and scheming collectors, I've seen enough to never be shocked by people's ability to rationalize doing the wrong thing."

"How about in your personal life?" he asked.

"Ditto." I shrugged. "I don't get surprised, but still . . . it makes me sad."

CHAPTER THIRTY-NINE

I 'm back!" I announced as I walked into the front office. I greeted everyone, asked how things were going but didn't really listen to their answers, then climbed the stairs to my private office. I knew I should go to the tag sale to relieve someone, but I didn't. Instead, I sat by my window, watching the xanthous and flame-red leaves on my old maple shimmy in the soft breeze, thinking about Frankie and the missing tooth and Frankie's two thousand dollars and blackmail and Lenny Wilton and Harlow's.

I scanned my desk and saw a printout of catalogue copy ready for proofing, a financial report ready for analysis, and a proposal to expand our database management contract ready for review. I didn't even try to work. Instead, I thought some more, methodically reviewing facts and sources.

Suddenly, I gasped. I hadn't asked Eric about Frankie's two thousand dollars. Surely he would know if Frankie had withdrawn the money for an innocent purpose.

I dashed downstairs, ran across the warehouse, my footsteps echoing on the concrete, yanked open the tag sale door, and stood, seeking him out. More than a dozen customers were poking through our inventory. Three others were in line to pay. Eric stood near the front.

I caught his eye and gestured that he should join me. He hurried in my direction, his brow furrowed.

"Is something wrong?" he asked.

"No, no. It's just that I have a question," I said. I kept my tone low. I took a step back and gestured that he should follow me. "Frankie took two thousand dollars cash out of his bank on the Friday before he died. Do you know what he did with it?"

He looked at me and swallowed, a troubled look clouding his eyes. He took a deep breath as if he were bracing himself to confess a sin.

"Maybe." He looked down. When he met my eyes, he looked worried. "There's a chance he used the money to buy a motorcycle. A guy around the corner from where I live was selling one at a great price. I thought it would be fun, but Grace said she'd worry every minute I was on it, so I decided not to get it. Frankie offered to buy it without her knowing anything about it, so I could ride it. He was just joking, you know? I told him no. I didn't want to lie to Grace, and I didn't want her to be scared." He swallowed. "Do you think he bought it anyway?"

"I don't know. Did it cost two thousand dollars?"

"Twenty-three hundred. Maybe Frankie talked him down."

"Can you check with the seller for me?" I asked.

"Sure."

"Can you do it now?"

I waited while he called. When he hung up, he said, "The motorcycle hasn't sold. He never spoke to Frankie."

Another dead end.

Cara announced that Wes was on the line. I ran upstairs to my office to take the call.

"Listen, I've got news," he said. He lowered his voice. "We've got to meet."

"I can't, Wes. I have too much to do. I've been out all day."

"I know. You've been helping the police." Wes's voice dropped to a whisper. "They arrested Greg for fraud and grand larceny and some other charges relating to conspiracy."

"I'm not surprised," I said.

"Yeah. He'll be out on bail within hours, probably."

"So?" I asked. "That's not a surprise either."

"Do you remember how the phone records showed that Frankie called Greg at eight thirty on the day he died?" he asked. "And Greg denied it? Well, guess what? Greg was telling the truth. He didn't speak to Frankie because Frankie didn't call. Curt did. When Curt got to the lighthouse at eight thirty to help Frankie with the door, he called Greg to see if he had any work for him that day. He called from the lighthouse phone. The police *assumed* it was Frankie who called because it came from the lighthouse and they knew he was on-site—but it wasn't. It was Curt."

"Is Curt involved in the fraud somehow?"

"No. It looks as if he has nothing to do with anything. The police have been pecking away at him since yesterday. You know how Curt said he didn't return Frankie's noon call? That was true, too— he didn't need to. Frankie left him a message telling him to come back to the Whitestones' at three thirty. The phone log shows the call. Frankie thought you were smart to clean the gutters before it rained, so he called Curt to ask him to come back and do the same at the lighthouse and at the two cottages. When Curt got there, he recognized Frankie's Jeep, but not your car. He thought it was probably the Whitestones' and wasn't any too keen on meeting them. But Frankie had told him to be there, so he soldiered on. He rang the bell, and when there was no answer, he gave the door a little jiggle to see if it was locked. It was, and he figured that if the Whitestones had shown up, Frankie was otherwise occupied, and if not, they could clean the gutters in the morning, so he just blew out of there."

"The timing's right—but why wouldn't he have told the police that? What's the big secret?"

"He didn't want to admit being anywhere near the murder scene that day. He said he knew he wasn't the sharpest knife in the drawer, but neither was he the dullest. He said you hear all the time how innocent guys get convicted of crimes they didn't commit, and he damn sure wasn't going to be one of them."

"What about the drive-by at my house?"

"What drive-by?" Wes asked.

He jotted notes as I filled him in on the mysterious car that had spooked me Thursday evening.

"I'll get back to you," he said.

"Do you have any more news about the fraud case? Specifically, do you know if the police discovered if Lenny Wilton is involved in any way? He tried to sell a tooth to Harlow's and has consistently refused to say who he was acting for."

"Chief Hunter went to see him, told him that Greg had been arrested, and got him to admit whom he'd been acting for . . . are you ready? Greg. Lenny was doing Greg a favor, which he explained he'd been glad to do since Greg had given him his first break."

"So when Lenny couldn't sell the tooth, he gave it back to Greg, right? And Greg, having at that point met the Whitestones, sold it to them."

"Right," Wes agreed. "Which leaves the murder. You have any new ideas?"

"No," I said. "Do you?"

"Nope," he said, sounding frustrated. "I don't think the police do either. I do have a little good news, though. I sent in a first draft of my article about the investigation to date to *Metropolitan*. Mr. Austin loved it."

"Oh, Wes, that's wonderful!" I said, and I realized that I wasn't just glad to have confounded Bertie, I was also genuinely thrilled for Wes.

Zoë called.

"Ellis just left," she said. "I gotta tell you, Josie, I think he's pretty special."

"I have a very good feeling about him," I said. *Ellis,* I thought, finding the sound of his first name odd.

"Yeah. I'm liking him a lot, but I'm also concerned . . . do you think I'm attracted to him for real or is it just 'cause of Frankie and I'm an emotional wreck and he's offering a strong arm and a shoulder to cry on?"

"He quotes Alexander Pope and hangs Norman Rockwell illustrations in his office. If you ask me, that's pretty solid evidence that he's a good guy, so . . . I think it's real."

"Yeah, that's what I think, too. I'd like to invite him to my birthday party."

I smiled. "Shall I call him or do you want to?"

"Would you mind?"

"Not a bit."

We promised to talk later, and I decided to call him right away. I reached him on his cell phone.

"I'm having a barbecue a week from Saturday for Zoë's birthday," I said. "I hope you can join us."

He accepted, sounding really pleased at the invitation. As I hung up, I thought how funny life was—in the midst of loss, gain.

CHAPTER FORTY

After Frankie's funeral on Monday, Chief Hunter, Ty, and I went back to Zoë's. The kids were upstairs playing, and occasional shouts and shrieks and giggles reached us as we sat in the kitchen sipping tea.

"Do you think it's going to rain?" Zoë asked, her hands cupping her mug for warmth. "For a warm September, it sure got cold quickly."

"Naw," Ty said. "The clouds are breaking up. But you're right about the chill. If you ask me, it's cold enough for a fire. I'll make one if you want."

"Thanks," she said, nodding.

As we made our way into the living room, I asked Chief Hunter, "Has either Ashley or Greg filled in any blanks?"

"I've explained to Zoë that I can't discuss the details of an ongoing investigation, but I can say that both of their attorneys are instructing their clients to stay mute."

Zoë sat on the couch, staring into the fire, her tension evident in the set of her jaw. Chief Hunter sat next to her, gently rubbing her arm. I sat on the floor near the hearth, glad for the fire's warmth.

"I thought the eulogies were beautiful," she said. "I was really touched by what Ellen said about how much Frankie added to the singles group. Maddie wrote me the nicest note, too, saying how much they valued Frankie, and how sorry they were that they couldn't attend the funeral."

Ty added a log, and within seconds sap popped, sending orange embers shooting into the screen. Another burst of sap sent sparks arcing up the chimney. I swallowed a sudden rush of tears as I remembered where the wood came from—Frankie had chopped up a limb from an old maple last spring after a storm felled it. Pepper-red flames teased the bark, then caught, flaring up and spreading the length of the log.

Ashley had a fire going the day Frankie died.

I looked toward Chief Hunter, still sitting on the sofa comforting Zoë. He met my eyes and saw stunned urgency.

"What is it?" he asked.

Could it be? I asked myself. It seemed impossible, yet I knew the answer. *Yes.*

I stood up. "We need to go." I looked into Chief Hunter's eyes. "You and me."

I turned to Ty, then Zoë. "I'm sorry. We'll be back."

Ashley wasn't home, and I hoped we weren't too late.

I rode with Chief Hunter. Officer Meade followed in a patrol car. The chief used a tool I'd never seen, a kind of spinning wrench-looking thing, to open Ashley's front door.

He and Officer Meade removed the firewood from Ashley's built-in cubbyhole one piece at a time, placing the logs on a plastic drop cloth she'd spread over the floor.

When the pile was half empty, I saw a sliver of blue. My pulse spiked. "Look," I said, pointing.

"Yeah," Chief Hunter said.

Thirty seconds later, enough wood had been removed to show the tub's placement. He took some photos, then shook his head ruefully. "I can't believe I looked for false bottoms in drawers but missed the woodpile. Jesus H. Christ. Sometimes I think I'm getting too old for this work."

They continued removing wood one piece at a time. On the floor, the stack of splintered logs and shredded bits of kindling grew higher. When the tub was completely visible, sitting on a two-log-deep layer of wood, he took additional photos; then, using only the tips of his gloved fingers, he moved it to the floor and thumbed open the plastic latch. I held my breath. He raised the lid. Inside was a chamois-covered object. He flipped the chamois aside with one finger, revealing a scrimmed tooth.

"Is this the missing tooth?" he asked me.

Using the loupe and small flashlight I keep hooked to my belt, I squatted to examine the coloration and fracture lines.

"This appears to be the tooth that was stolen from the lighthouse," I said. "Without further analysis, I can't positively ID it."

I stood up as Chief Hunter slipped the tooth into a large plastic evidence bag and sealed it up. As he dropped the chamois into another bag, I gasped and pointed to a cordovan-colored stain in the middle and a frayed area near the bottom.

"That looks like dried blood. And look at the bottom—it's torn. Frankie was clutching a sliver of leather when he died." I looked at him. "Chamois is leather."

He held my gaze for a long three-count. "At the time, you said you saw something wispy in his grasp. I'm not going to ask how you know that the something wispy you saw was in fact leather," Chief Hunter said dryly.

I looked down and felt myself blush.

"Take a photo of it for him if you want," he offered.

I looked up. "Thanks."

I used my cell phone camera to snap photos of the tooth, the chamois, the plastic box, and the cubbyhole, then froze at the sound of a car engine. I looked at Chief Hunter. He gestured that he wanted me to move toward the middle of the room, then turned to face the door. Officer Meade stood next to him, and from the tilt of her head, I could tell that she was listening, too.

The door opened. Ashley stepped inside, taking in the scene in one sweeping glance. Her eyes paused at the wood strewn across the drop cloth, then swung to the nearly empty cubbyhole, the opened plastic tub, and the bagged tooth and chamois. She backed away from us one slow step at a time until she ran into her worktable. She reached in back of her, finding the table's edge with her hands, one on each side, holding herself up.

"Are these yours?" Chief Hunter asked, holding the two evidence bags.

She gasped for air, hyperventilating, then began to tremble. It was horrifying to watch. She spun around, as if she couldn't bear us seeing her disintegration.

"We found the tooth, probably the missing Myrick, in your wood-pile," Chief Hunter told her back. "Want to explain how it got there?"

She bellowed, a guttural sound of despair, then twirled to face us, her arm arched high above her head. I saw a flash of silver as she catapulted herself up and over the love seat, flying toward Chief Hunter.

"She has a knife," I yelled, instinctively stepping back and stumbling into the coffee table. I tumbled, then scrambled to my knees.

Chief Hunter grabbed Ashley's arm while she was still midair, twisting it hard, and the knife, an échoppe, clattered to the ground. Ashley screamed and clutched her arm to her chest as she landed in a heap at his feet.

"You broke my arm!" she screeched.

I scampered up, panting, staring, horrified. Officer Meade had drawn her weapon and held it steadily, pointing it at Ashley's midsection.

"You attacked me!" Ashley yelled, then moaned while rolling side to side as if she were in mortal agony.

"Stay still," Chief Hunter told her, his calm, cold tone contrasting with her hysterical ranting. To Officer Meade, he added, "Call an ambulance."

Ashley lunged for the échoppe. He kicked it aside and held her in place by pushing against her shoulders and thighs. She kept screaming and thrashing about, until finally she wore herself out and her yelling faded into pitiful and unintelligible mewling. I looked away, shaken at seeing such raw emotion. It was half frightening and half nauseating, and even after Ashley had been strapped to a gurney and wheeled away, her wordless shrieks echoed in my ears.

Officer Meade accompanied Ashley to the hospital, and Chief Hunter transferred the evidence bags to his vehicle, sealed her cottage with police tape, and said, "Ready?"

As we drove, I e-mailed the photos to Wes, saying only that we'd found the missing tooth in Ashley's cottage and that I'd explain everything later. When he got a gander at those photos, he'd be doing a happy dance for sure. Not me. I still felt sick, as if I'd been punched in the gut and hadn't fully recovered from the blow.

Chief Hunter drove straight to my house. He rolled to a stop in front of the hedge.

"Thank you, Josie," he said.

"She grabbed a knife and swung it at you," I said, still quavery, "just like she must have done with the rolling pin at Frankie. She tried to kill you."

"If you see Zoë, please tell her I'll call her as soon as I can with an update." He paused. "I'd appreciate it if you let me fill her in. There are still a lot of loose ends."

"Like why Ashley killed Frankie."

"Like loose ends."

"Like blackmail."

"Thanks again," he said, and then he was gone.

I stood on my porch watching Chief Hunter until he disappeared around a curve in the road, and then I stood awhile longer. Ty was still at Zoë's.

I turned on my home computer. I needed to update the stolen object reports I'd filed about the missing Whitestone tooth, and I needed to call Mr. Yamamoto with the bad news about the supposed Myrick he was appraising in Hawaii. Instead, I sat looking out my window over the thick privacy hedge, past the stone wall, trying to catch my breath, trying to compose myself, seeing nothing, taking in only the colors and the shapes, an abstract tapestry of life.

I felt as if I were on a ship without my sea legs, woozy, as if my emotional upset were affecting my balance. I wished I had a talisman or knew an enchanted phrase that would allow me to magically alter myself from fretful to serene, but I didn't. All I could do was breathe and wait and hope this discombobulating distress would pass. It didn't, but neither did it worsen, and finally, after several minutes, I turned back to my computer, ready to do what needed to be done.

I went to each stolen antiques site and wrote that the missing object had probably been found, and asked that any possible sightings still be reported since there might be additional fakes in the marketplace. After I'd finished, I called Mr. Yamamoto and got his voice mail. I left a message explaining why I thought his tooth was probably a fake, then sent his contact information to Chief Hunter.

Wes called just as I was ready to call Ty and ask him to come home.

"So how did it go down?" he asked. "Tell me everything."

"Not now, Wes."

"Why not?" he whined.

"I can't. Not today."

"When?"

"Did you get the photos?" I asked.

"Yeah. Thanks. They're awesome."

"You're welcome," I said, and at his request I helped him draft captions, a mental task that helped calm my turbulent emotions.

"Can we talk tomorrow? I need the info, Josie. I really do."

"I'll see."

"Josie!"

"I'm hanging up now, Wes. I'm sorry." I knew I'd disappointed him, and I knew he wasn't being completely unreasonable. He was a reporter on deadline, and we had a deal. Still, an "I'll see" was the best I could offer at the moment. I needed time to distill everything I'd witnessed, to find context, to assimilate the horror of what had transpired. I needed time, and I needed Ty.

CHAPTER FORTY-ONE

y sat beside me on my sofa, holding my hand, as I recounted what I'd seen and heard.

"It's so sordid, Ty," I said. "Frankie died for no reason. None."

He leaned forward and kissed the top of my head.

"The only lesson I can take away," I continued, "is not to overlook the obvious. It took me days to recognize the significance of Ashley's having a fire on a warm day. It's like the time I came into work to find that Gretchen had hung wind chimes on the inside of the front door. I asked her why, and she looked at me as if she thought it was a trick question. Finally, she said, 'Because they sound good.' Frankie's death should have more significance than teaching me a lesson I shouldn't need to relearn."

"Sometimes there's no lesson at all, Josie. There's just the sad reality of loss."

I pressed my face into his chest, and he wrapped his arms around me, and we sat there, curled together, for a long, long time.

"Chief Hunter is here," I said later, as I glanced out the window toward Zoë's and saw his SUV.

"Good," Ty said.

"Why good?" I asked.

Ty shrugged. "It's his job to tell Zoë what happened. Knowing is an important part of healing."

She called soon after and asked us to join them, and Ty and I went right away.

She and Chief Hunter were sitting in the kitchen. In the distance, I heard the chortling of animated characters. *The kids are watching a movie,* I thought.

"Thank you for coming with no notice," Zoë said, her eyes red and moist. "Ellis has filled me in. I have some questions for him, but I know myself—no matter what the answers are, I figured I'd be needing your shoulders."

"Of course," I said, touching her arm.

She turned to Chief Hunter. "I've been trying to picture what happened, to understand, and I can't. I mean . . . I get it that as soon as Ashley learned that Josie had been hired to conduct an appraisal, she called Greg, worried that Josie would discover the Myrick tooth was a fake. I can see that Greg would have told her to get the tooth out of there immediately."

"And the corresponding receipt," I interjected.

"Right. What I don't get is how Frankie could have interrupted her. Didn't she know he was in the lighthouse?" she asked. "His car was there."

"Some of what I can tell you is fact, some is still under investigation, and some is speculation," Chief Hunter said. "This falls into the latter category—logic-based speculation. Probably she did, in fact, recognize Frankie's car. When she entered, she called to him. If he was upstairs but outside, checking on whether the gutters on the widow's walk needed cleaning, for instance, he wouldn't have heard her. When he didn't reply, she probably assumed that he was doing outdoor work in the back. She wouldn't have worried about getting caught unawares, because she figured she'd hear him if and when he came inside. Except that he didn't come in from the backyard like she expected, he came down the steps. If that's what happened, Frankie might have caught her dead to rights with the Myrick tooth in her hands."

"I still don't get how that led to murder. Why wouldn't she have lied and said she was dusting it or something?" Zoë asked.

"Maybe she did. Or it's possible that she'd already packed the tooth up and he caught her slipping it into her tote bag or something. Whatever happened—whether he ended up accusing her of stealing the tooth or she just went nuts because she was afraid he was going to—she flipped out."

Like today, I thought.

"Based on what I witnessed today," Chief Hunter continued, "if Frankie told her he was calling the cops or the Whitestones, there's no question in my mind that Ms. Morse would have lost it. She would have charged him and knocked his cell phone out of his hand. My guess is that he ran to the nearest landline, which is in the kitchen. If she realized that she'd just made a bad situation worse, she would have dashed after him and tried to reason with him, to convince him that she only wanted to dust the tooth, like you said, Zoë, or to study it back at her place, or to simply hold the master's work in her hands, but Frankie wasn't buying it. When he reached for the lighthouse phone, Ashley wrenched open the drawer looking for a weapon and found one—the rolling pin. She wrapped it in a handy dish towel, maybe for a better grip, or maybe because she had the wherewithal to worry about fingerprints. And she attacked."

I closed my eyes for a moment, the horrendous images of blood and death that had haunted me from the moment I'd found Frankie's body flooding my consciousness again.

"How could Ashley have overpowered him?" Zoë asked, sounding sick. "He was as strong as an ox!"

"She was in the throes of panic-induced strength. You know how every once in a while you hear about a small woman lifting a two-ton car off her child or her husband? I think what comes over her is similar. Today, when she attacked she flew. I'm not exaggerating—she literally launched herself and went airborne." He shrugged. "Plus, she's taller than Frankie was, she weighs more than he did—and don't forget, she used a weapon."

Tears ran unchecked down Zoë's cheeks. "Go on," she murmured. "What do you think happened next?"

"They struggled, and somehow Frankie got hold of a sliver of chamois—probably she had a piece in her hand or tucked into her belt. I'm guessing it was old and already frayed. At this point she was truly crazed. She swung and she connected. And then she was covered in blood and Frankie was dead. She dropped the rolling pin and towel. She might have been horrified at what she'd done." He shrugged again. "Who knows what she was feeling? It's enough to know what she did . . . what she must have done. She opened the window, hoping to confuse the time-of-death calculation. She ran back to the display case to shift the other artifacts around so there wasn't an obvious empty space. She scooped up Frankie's cell phone, maybe with the chamois so she wouldn't leave any fingerprints, and stuffed it in his pocket. Then she bolted. Back at her cottage, she made a fire and burned her bloody clothes. Probably she showered, then scoured the tub with bleach, hoping to eliminate all traces of Frankie's blood. She hid the tooth in her woodpile, as good a hiding place as any, and better than most." Chief Hunter nodded in my direction. "That's when we got there. After the fire was out, she cleaned the fireplace, throwing away the ashes, maybe scrubbing the masonry with bleach, too. The next day, after the initial shock wore off, she realized that in her rush to get out of the lighthouse, she forgot to get the receipt for the tooth. She had to destroy it before Josie saw it. From what I understand from Josie, she probably thought that if she could destroy the receipt, there was a better than even chance Mr. Whitestone wouldn't even notice the tooth was missing."

"Isn't that a little far-fetched?" Zoë asked, glancing from Chief Hunter to me.

"Some collectors are like that," I said. "They love the acquisition process, the thrill of the hunt, and don't pay much attention to the objects themselves."

"Besides, if either of the Whitestones did notice it, so what?" Chief Hunter continued. "They would ask Mr. Donovan for a replacement receipt and he would say no can do, that he hadn't kept a copy of the paperwork or a photograph of the tooth. It would be embarrassing but not criminal. He'd look like a doofus is all. It didn't come to that, though, because of Josie. Ms. Morse was going through Mr. White-stone's papers in the ground-floor study when she called down from upstairs. Ms. Morse was listening to her iPod. She must have been completely shocked to realize that not only had Josie begun the ap-praisal, she'd already reached the top floor. She knew what that meant—she was too late. She might even have toyed with the idea of killing Josie to buy herself time to complete her search, but when Josie told her that I would be back momentarily, she decided it was too risky. She figured that her best hope of escaping punishment was to do nothing."

I reached for Ty's hand. He clasped mine tightly.

"Greg Donovan has put the murder totally on Ms. Morse, and the ADA believes him. Having seen her swing a knife, I believe him, too," Chief Hunter stated.

"Did she sell the fakes to Sam herself?"

"We don't think so. We think Mr. Donovan took care of that part. Josie had an idea that we believe has merit, right, Josie?"

"Not that it really matters," I said, "but yes. Based on the high quality of the cufflinks Sam is selling, I think they're Lenny Wilton originals. Lenny probably scrimmed them when he first invented his scrimming machine—before he created the Leon line. Sam bought a boatload of them way back when and hasn't sold them all yet."

Zoë nodded. "Will Greg go to jail?" she asked.

"Yes," Chief Hunter said. "The only question is for how long. Probably he'll take a deal. There are about a dozen counts of grand larceny pending, plus some additional charges related to racketeering and fraud that the ADA is still considering. For sure he won't just walk."

"Will Ashley?"

"No. The evidence is strong. She'll probably plead out, too."

"I hope she burns in hell," Zoë said.

"She will," Chief Hunter said. "But first, she'll spend most of the rest of her life in prison."

Her tears still flowing, Zoë said, "Good."

CHAPTER FORTY-TWO

es called the next morning with scores of questions. I stood by my window, looking out toward the ocean, watching the fire-bright leaves dance in the gentle wind, and answered them all.

"I have an answer for you about that car driving by the other night," he said at the end. "It was Curt. He was out for a drive and decided to hit you up for work first thing in the morning. The cruise-by was to confirm that he had the address right."

"Some things are just what they seem to be," I remarked.

"Yeah. So can you sum Ashley up for me? What's her fatal flaw? Was it that she wasn't as talented as she thought she was?"

I shook my head. "No," I said. "It's more complex."

Overestimating her talent hadn't led Ashley to kill. Underestimating the importance of other factors was her undoing. She was both arrogant and supercilious. She was competent but uninspired, like a musician who never misses a note but whose playing lacks soul. She also disdained business and communication skills, believing her work should speak for itself. Her downfall was due to the "old ego meego," as a friend of mine named Nancylee once labeled it. When Ashley realized that success required more than technical expertise, she spiraled down into the underbelly of ambition. Her fatal flaw was a deadly combination of ignorance, hubris, and greed.

"Ashley didn't overstate her talent, Wes," I replied. "It's darker than that." I described my thinking. "Chief Hunter made a good point, I think, when he said, 'Who knows what she was feeling? It's enough to know what she did.'"

"Good one, Josie! I can use that."

He ended the call moments later with a chirpy "See ya!" and for the first time in days, I was able to work.

On my way home that afternoon, I heard Wes discussing breaking news on the local radio station. Ashley had signed off on a deal. She agreed to plead guilty to second degree murder, conspiracy to defraud, and grand larceny. Her sentence was twenty-five to life. It didn't seem long enough to me, but no sentence would.

Once inside my house, I ran upstairs. I wanted to take a shower. I left my clothes in a heap and hurried under the steaming water. The nightmare was finally over, and I wanted to wash away the stink.

CHAPTER FORTY-THREE

T he next Monday, Guy called to ask how the appraisal was coming.

"We're writing it up as we speak," I said. "You'll have it in a few days."

"Any other finds?"

"Not really. But no major misses, either."

"I don't like the sound of that," Guy said. "How many minor misses were there?"

"Several," I said, knowing Guy preferred direct talk. "Building a collection of the caliber you intend requires specialized knowledge that you don't have."

"Like what?" he asked, bristling.

"Like knowing that Nantucket baskets are still manufactured. Like knowing that if a Myrick tooth is offered for only twenty-four thousand dollars, there's probably something wrong with it."

"I get your point. I knew the price Greg was asking was a steal, by the way. In fact, I thought *Greg* was ignorant. Pretty ironic, huh? *I* was the ignorant one."

"It happens. You knew enough to know that the price was low, and that's huge. One thing to think about is that when you're offered an unrealistically low price by a theoretically reputable dealer . . . well, that alone is enough of a red flag that you should probably delve deeper."

"That's completely logical. All I can say is that I'm glad you're in my corner, Josie, and that you're a helluva teacher."

"Wow," I said, grinning. "That's one of the nicest compliments I've gotten in a long time. Thanks!"

We chatted awhile longer; then he said, "We're going to use an agency to hire a new caretaker and housekeeper."

I told him I thought that approach made sense and asked him to give my regards to Maddie. After we hung up, I got to thinking that Guy wasn't the only person interested in learning more about collecting antiques. Maybe, I thought, I should start a series of Prescott-branded workshops. We could call it "Prescott's Antiques & Collectibles: How to Build a Great x Collection." *I'll start with vintage clothing,* I decided, an always popular collectible. Prescott's Antiques & Collectibles: How to Build a Great Vintage Clothing Collection. I nodded. I liked it.

I grabbed a pad of paper and began making notes.

CHAPTER FORTY-FOUR

I snuck out early from the next tag sale to prepare Zoë's birthday dinner. When I arrived home around three, steaks, baking potatoes, and salad vegetables in hand, I found the house empty and a note on the counter.

"We're at Zoë's," Ty had written. "It's chocolate chip cookies war."

I put the perishables away and ran next door, interrupting a polite but heated discussion Zoë was having with Ty about butter and chocolate. Zoë insisted that better butter led to better chocolate chip cookies. Ty maintained that what mattered most was the quality of the chocolate. Chief Hunter, who'd asked me to call him Ellis, had volunteered to oversee a blind taste test, the winner to be selected by a committee comprised of Jake, Emma, and me. They were deep in trash-talking one another's recipes when the doorbell rang.

"I'll get it," I said, chuckling at the thought of dueling cookies.

"Winterelli residence?" a tired-looking man with a fringe of white hair asked.

He wore a gray uniform. A white and silver Morris Electronics truck blocked the driveway, its blinkers on. Another man, younger than the man on the porch by a generation, but still older than me, stood by the open back doors watching us.

"Are you Ms. Winterelli?" the man on the porch asked.

"No. One sec," I said. I called, and Zoë appeared in the doorway. "A delivery," I explained, opening the door wider.

"Really? I'm not expecting anything."

The older man handed her a stylus, angled his electronic clipboard toward her, and told her to sign at line eight.

"What is it?" she asked.

He glanced at the display. "A Pro-Tech D63 with surround sound."

"A flat-screen TV?" she asked. "I didn't order a TV."

He looked again at the display, touched the screen twice, read a remark, then called, "Billy! Is there an envelope attached to that Pro-Tech?"

Billy's torso disappeared into the truck. When he reappeared, he waved a clear plastic envelope, the kind shipping departments use to attach packing slips to boxes. "Yeah."

Zoë looked at me, a question in her eyes, and I shrugged.

"Bring it up."

Billy handed the envelope to Zoë. Inside was an orange greeting card envelope. "Zoë Winterelli" was written on the outside.

"That's Frankie's handwriting," Zoë whispered, staring at the writing as if she were looking at a ghost.

I watched over her shoulder as she eased her finger under the flap and wiggled the card out. The outside showed a vase filled with chrysanthemums and autumn leaves. Under the vase were the words "For You." She opened the card, and a white slip of paper fluttered to the ground. "Happy Birthday" was printed near the top. Frankie had written:

Dear Aunt Zoë,
Thanks for everything.
You're the best aunt a guy could have.
Happy Birthday.
Love, Frankie
P.S. I'll put the receipt in here in case you need it.

She pressed the card to her chest. "Oh, my God!" Zoë whispered. "What did he do?"

I couldn't imagine the feelings that must be rocketing through her head. She'd just received a message from the grave. I bent over and picked up the receipt.

"I need you to sign," the man on the porch said.

She scrawled her name with the stylus, then stood back as the two men wheeled and hoisted the components of her new surround-sound TV system into her living room. One of the boxes barely fit through the door. She decided to have them install it in the den.

Hearing the commotion, Jake and Emma came running in, followed by Ellis and Ty.

At the sight of the biggest box, Jake jumped up and down. "Open it! Open it! Let's open it!"

Emma stood to the side, as subdued as her mother.

Ellis cocked his head, asking a question without speaking. Zoë handed him the card. He read it. "Where's the receipt?" he asked.

"I have it," I said, handing it over.

"Another mystery solved," he said.

I nodded. The receipt was for $1,998.99; the two thousand dollars Frankie had withdrawn was now accounted for.

"Isn't this just the nicest thing you've ever heard of?" Zoë asked, still misty-eyed.

"Yes," I said and hugged her.

"I'll oversee the TV setup," Ellis said, "while you guys bake."

"And while I cook," I said. "Steaks are beckoning."

"May I come with you?" Emma asked.

"Don't you want to help bake the cookies?" I asked.

"I'm a judge," she said. "It wouldn't be fair if I helped."

"That's a very good point," I said.

"Do you want to watch me set up the TV?" Ellis asked.

She shook her head and reached for my hand. "I want to go with Josie."

"I do!" Jake shouted joyfully. "I do!"

"Done," Ellis said.

Emma and I left through the front, crossing the little patch of lawn to reach my house.

"Look," she said, pointing to a crimson maple leaf on the ground.

"It's beautiful," I said. "Let's pick it up and press it."

"Okay," she said. "Will we use a cookbook? That's what Mommy does, because she says she never opens them anyway."

I laughed.

She laughed, too, and together we walked into my house, ready to cook.

CHAPTER FORTY-FIVE

Our booth at the Harvest Festival was in a prime location—abutting the village green, across from the bandstand where the festival organizers would be auctioning off food grown or produced by local farmers and vendors and seasonal decorations made by area craftspeople. I'd spied bushels of crisp, tart apples, wedges of cheddar cheese so rich and flavorful it would give any Vermont cheese maker a run for his money, and tubs of thick, aromatic dark and amber maple syrup. There were countless gourds, rattan and wire cornucopias, boxwood and dried-leaf wreaths, and clusters of gold and brown Indian corn. It was a perfect autumn day, sweater weather, sparkling bright with fluffy clouds floating in a bright blue sky. Fallen leaves in opalescent hues crunched underfoot.

Sasha, Gretchen, and I, along with six part-timers and temporary workers, had our hands full. I wished I could have had Fred, Eric, and Cara with me, too, but it was a Saturday, tag sale day, and running two full-out events in two separate locations, we were stretched thin.

Zoë sat on a bar stool in a corner of the booth, her hands flying as she folded paper into origami figures. She wore a rhinestone tiara. Sasha and I sat on matching stools at the other end of the booth painting faces. Our signage indicated that 100 percent of the day's proceeds would go to the literacy charity the festival was sponsoring, and we were packed.

"I saw you at Frankie's funeral," a woman I didn't recognize said as she led a boy of about three up for his turn. "I'm Christine Leblanc." She was in her twenties, with strawberry blond hair cut in a soft bob.

She had a smattering of freckles on her nose. "I knew Frankie from church. I liked him a lot."

I stood up to greet her. "I'm so glad you introduced yourself. Frankie was special."

"Is that his aunt?"

I nodded. "Yes."

"Please tell her how much I enjoyed knowing him."

"I will," I said, then asked Christine's son what he had in mind for his face painting. He wanted to be Spider-Man, and I smiled, relieved. He'd be my fifth Spider-Man of the day, and I had it down.

Later, Ty joined the face-painting line, and when it was his turn, he handed me a twenty-dollar bill and said, "Make me a superhero."

I slipped his money through the slot in the money jug. "Too late! You're already a superhero. You're *my* superhero."

He reached his hand out and stroked my cheek. "I'm going home to make a batch of my award-winning chocolate chip cookies."

I laughed and glanced at Zoë. "Don't tell her. Every time she thinks about losing to you, she gnashes her teeth and grumbles something about a fix being in."

He smiled and said he'd see me at home. I watched him weave his way through the crowd, thinking as I always did that he was the answer to a prayer and a dream come true.

"You look like you're a million miles away," Ellis said, coming up from behind and startling me.

"Oh, hi!" I laughed. "I was just thinking sweet thoughts about Ty."

He turned to look at Zoë. "I understand," he said smiling.

"Are you glad you moved to Rocky Point?"

"Hell, yes. Cities are great, but I'm thinking that Norman Rockwell had it right."

I watched Zoë's eyes light up when she spotted him.

"Josie!" Sasha called. "This little girl wants to be a tiger."

"Excellent! That's my specialty," I said, laughing as I waved goodbye to Ellis. "Come on up, sweetie! You're going to be ferocious!"

After we broke down the booth, loaded the van, and unloaded everything onto the loading dock back at Prescott's; after I thanked everyone for their above-and-beyond efforts and secured the building for the night; and after I got home and showered, Ty handed me a cookie.

"Sweets for the sweet," he said.

"Yum," I said.

"I'm taking you out tonight."

"You are? How come?" I asked.

"'Cause we've been working hard and not playing enough. It's time to go dancing." He reached out his hand, and I took it. He pulled me upright and toward him.

"Can I wear my new green lizard cowboy boots and my black skirt with the flirty flounce?"

"I wouldn't know a flirty flounce from a feather, but I sure as shootin' like the sound of it."

I fed him the last bite of cookie. "Just you wait. I'm going to dazzle you with my new side-wrapped V-neck silky top."

"You don't need to wear a side-wrapped top to dazzle me," he said. "You dazzle me no matter what you wear."

I hugged him hard, then hugged him again, then hurried upstairs to change.

ACKNOWLEDGMENTS

Special thanks go to Leslie Hindman, who, with her team at Leslie Hindman Auctioneers, continues to appraise antiques for me to write about. Please note that any errors are mine alone.

As a member of the New York chapter of Mystery Writers of America board of directors and the chair of the Wolfe Pack's literary awards, I've been fortunate to meet and work alongside dozens of talented writers and dedicated readers. Thank you all for your support. For my pals in the Wolfe Pack and fans of Rex Stout's Nero Wolfe stories everywhere, I've added my usual allotment of Wolfean trivia to this book.

Thank you to Jo-Ann Maude, Katie Longhurst, Christine de los Reyes, and Carol Novak. Thank you also to Dan and Linda Chessman, Marci and James Gleason, John and Mona Gleason, Linda and Ren Plastina, Rona and Ken Foster, Sandy Baggelaar, and Liz Weiner. Special thanks also go to George Stanko, who helped me understand the legalities of getting search warrants.

Independent booksellers have been invaluable in helping me introduce Josie to their customers—thank you all. I want to acknowledge my special friends at these independent bookshops: Partners & Crime, Front Street Books, The Poisoned Pen, The Well Red Coyote, Clues Unlimited, Mostly Books, Mysteries to Die For, Book'em Mysteries, Mystery Bookstore, Legends, Book Carnival, Mysterious Galaxy, San Francisco Mystery Bookstore, "M" is for Mystery, Murder by the Book stores in Houston, Denver, and Portland, Schuler Books, The Regulator, McIntyre's, Quail Ridge Books, Book Cove, Remember the Alibi Mystery Bookstore, Centuries & Sleuths Bookstore, Fox Tale Books, Kate's Mystery Books, Mystery Lovers Bookshop, The

Mystery Company, The Mysterious Bookshop, Partners in Crime, Booked for Murder, Aunt Agatha's, Foul Play, Windows a Bookshop, Murder by the Beach, Books & Books, Moore Books, The Bookstore in the Grove, Uncle Edgar's Mystery Bookstore, Seattle Mystery Bookstore, Park Road Books, and Once Upon a Crime.

Manhattan's Black Orchid Bookstore is still sorely missed; I remain grateful to Bonnie Claeson and Joe Guglielmelli for helping launch Josie.

Many chain bookstores have been incredibly supportive as well—thank you to those many booksellers who've gone out of their way to become familiar with Josie. Special thanks go to my friend Dianne Defonce at the Border's in Fairfield, Connecticut.

Thanks also to Nili L. Olay and Gene C. Gill of the Jane Austen Society of North America, Linda Landigran of *Alfred Hitchcock Mystery Magazine,* Barbara Floyd of *The Country Register,* Aldon James of the National Arts Club, Wilda W. Willliams of *Library Journal.* Many thanks also to Molly Weston and Jen Forbus.

Special thanks to my librarian friends David S. Ferriero, Doris Ann Norris, Sally Fellows, Mary Russell, Denise Van Zanten, Mary Callahan Boone, Cynde Bloom Lahey, Cyndi Rademacher, Eleanor Ratterman, Jane Murphy, Jennifer Vido, Judith Abner, Karen Kiley, Lesa Holstine, Monique Flasch, Susie Schachte, Virginia Sanchez, Maxine Bleiweis, Cindy Clark, Linda Avellar, Heidi Fowler, Georgia Owens, Eva Perry, Mary J. Etter, Paul Schroeder, Tracy J. Wright, Kristi Calhoun Belesca, Paulette Sullivan, Frances Mendelsohn, Deborah Hirsch, and Heather Caines.

Thank you to my literary agent emerita, Denise Marcil, and my fab new literary agent, Cristina Concepcion of Don Congdon Associates, Inc. Special thanks go to Michael Congdon and Katie Kotchman as well.

My editor, St. Martin's Minotaur executive editor Hope Dellon, continues to provide wise and discerning feedback about the manuscript, helping Rocky Point become the kind of community readers want to visit over and over again. Special thanks also go to Laura Bourgeois, assistant editor, for her insightful comments. I'm indebted to them, and to the entire St. Martin's Minotaur team. Thank you also to those I work with most often, Andy Martin, Hector DeJean, and Talia Ross, as well as those behind the scenes, including my production editor, Julie Gutin; copy editor, India Cooper; and cover designer, David Baldeosingh Rotstein.